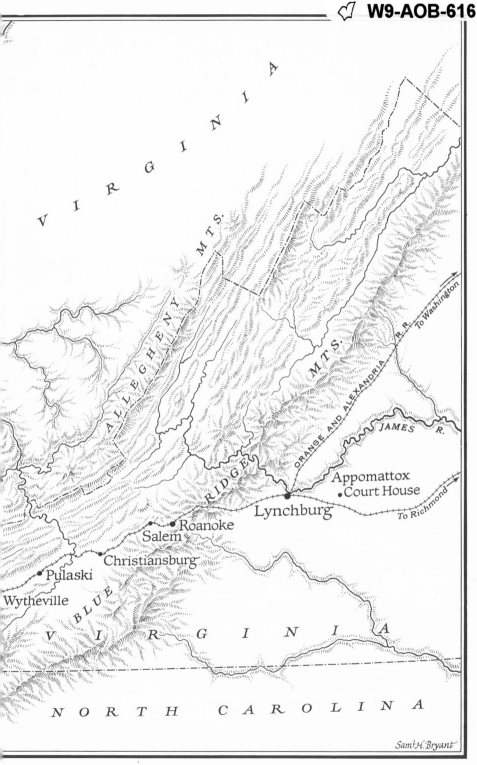

VIRGINIA

ALLEGHENY MTS.

BLUE RIDGE MTS.

ORANGE AND ALEXANDRIA R.R.

To Washington

JAMES R.

Appomattox
Court House

Lynchburg

To Richmond

Roanoke
Salem
Christiansburg
Pulaski
Wytheville

BLUE

VIRGINIA

NORTH CAROLINA

Sam.ᵗ H. Bryant

# Books by F. van Wyck Mason

Valley Forge, 1777
Proud New Flags
Rivers of Glory
Golden Admiral
Cutlass Empire
Blue Hurricane
Silver Leopard
Our Valiant Few
The Young Titan
The Colonel North Stories
Manila Galleon
Brimstone Club
Roads to Liberty
Trumpets Sound No More

*Edited by F. van Wyck Mason*

Fighting Americans
American Men at Arms

# Trumpets Sound
# No More

# Trumpets Sound No More

## F. van Wyck Mason

LITTLE, BROWN AND COMPANY · BOSTON · TORONTO
1975

SECOND PRINTING
T08/75


*Library of Congress Cataloging in Publication Data*

Mason, Francis van Wyck, 1901-
   Trumpets sound no more.

   I.  Title.
PZ3.M3855Tt    [PS3525.A7943]    813'.5'2    75-12702
ISBN 0-316-54931-2

Designed by D. Christine Benders

*Published simultaneously in Canada
by Little, Brown & Company (Canada) Limited*

PRINTED IN THE UNITED STATES OF AMERICA

This book is affectionately dedicated to
W. John and Helen Carswell
who so often have proved as the shade of a rock in a weary land.

# Author's Note

IN THIS WORK I have attempted to describe, in part, the fearful privations, problems and dangers prevailing in certain sections of the South after the Civil War, or as some prefer, the War Between the States. Finally it had ended with the surrender at Appomattox Court House of General Robert E. Lee to General U. S. Grant and, shortly afterwards, the capitulation of General Joseph E. Johnston to General William Tecumseh Sherman at Durham, North Carolina.

Despite four terrible years of sacrifice, death and destruction, for many Southerners the worst was yet to come. Their country was bankrupt; there was no civil government and no law except that imposed by the victors at often widely separated points. As a result, lawlessness became rampant in all save the few towns and cities well garrisoned by Federal troops. Disbanded Confederate regulars, generously paroled by their former enemies, and hundreds of thousands of hungry, homeless and directionless former slaves roamed the countryside. Bands of ex-Confederate partisans or irregulars, gangs of bushwhackers and other savage outlaws committed heinous crimes — generally with impunity.

Businesses were in chaos and since most banks had failed no credit was obtainable even against the soundest of securities.

For a long while no real newspapers, no regular mail or telegraphic services were available over wide sections of the prostrate South.

Worst of all was the loss of so many irreplaceable lives and, as an added burden, the return of all-too-many permanently crippled veterans. Many Confederates, rich, middling well-off, or downright poor, returned often to find their homes reduced to blackened ruins. Frequently their families, or those of them who had survived, had become dispersed to God only knew where.

Nevertheless, a handful of large estate owners, doctors, civil engineers, lawyers and bankers made valiant attempts to carry on as before. A great majority of these returned veterans and their families made out despite a "sea of troubles" and doggedly set about trying to restore, often vainly, the society they had once known.

I have labored to present an accurate vignette of this period, 1865–1866 in Western Virginia — *not* West Virginia — by using fictional characters bearing family names indigenous to that region. The Tilts, the

Author's Note

Renfrows and residents of Wytheville are examples of this approach. All actual events, troop designations and historic figures here presented are as authentic as an unbiased and painstaking research can render them.

Among those institutions to which I am indebted for invaluable assistance are: the Alderman Library of the University of Virginia, the Library of the Boston Athenaeum, the Archives Division of the Virginia State Library, the Preston Library of the Virginia Military Institute, the Harvard College Library and that of Washington and Lee University.

Also, I gratefully acknowledge the admirable patience and able assistance cheerfully given by my secretaries, Mary Howe and Carol-Ann Basden, and by Jeanne Hand Mason, who also helped to edit this book.

"Hampton Head"
Southampton, Bermuda

# Contents

## Part I  Z Company

## Part II  Moluntha  Garrison

Contents

# Part III Wavering Hopes

# Part IV The Expedition

# Trumpets Sound
# No More

# Part One

# Z Company

# 1

# Two Letters

107 Bridge Street
Providence
Rhode Island

2nd April, 1864

My Darling Louisa:

How profoundly anxious I have been over having received never a word with regard to either of two letters I have addressed to you over the past two years. I suppose this is not to be wondered at since nowadays mails are so irregular and no doubt much of it has been lost or destroyed through raids and campaigns. Nevertheless, I still refuse to abandon hope of receiving word from my beloved "Almost Sister."

What fond memories do we not share of those wonderful, peaceful summers at Saratoga Springs? As I remember, it was in '58 that we first encountered one another and became such intimate friends!

Ah me, if *only* it were possible to turn back the clock to those joyous occasions when our elders "took the waters" at the Spa and our respective dads got a bit "tiddly" on occasion; when they reveled, gamed recklessly, and bet so heavily on the horse races. As near as I can recall, whether one won or lost made not a whit of difference.

Will you ever forget that famous day when your dad's Chapultepec beat Pa's Constellation to the wire by only a nose? How carefree and merry all we innocents were!

In one of my lost letters I mentioned that Marcus and I have been blessed with two children: they are called Hepzibah and Antonius, after Marcus's grandsire. Praise the Lord, both my little darlings are sturdy and as merry as grigs.

When last we heard from Marc's Father he had become a colonel in the U.S. Corps of Railroad Engineers but where he is serving now God alone knows.

Not long ago Marc received his commission as a major in the 5th Rhode

Island Volunteer Artillery. According to the little that we have heard, my husband has served with considerable ability and distinction. Since I have had no direct word from him in weeks, all I know is that he is campaigning somewhere in Virginia. God send it is not in the Western part of your State! On the other hand, if he *is*, Marc might be of assistance to you at Moluntha Garrison, for which he still entertains so many fond memories of his stay among you.

We women spend much time at hospitals attending the wounded, arrange "sociables" for the benefit of those poor fellows' families and then go home to roll bandages. We suffer serious shortages of so many articles we used to deem necessities but now know for luxuries.

Enough of me and my problems. Dearest Louisa, your situation must be *far more serious and tragical!*

I pray your reliable and handsome Rodney remains safe and well. Somewhere, I heard that of his brothers, Otho died leading a charge at Antietam and that young Albert perished of disease somewhere out West; also, Marc wrote he'd heard that Bushrod got wounded in the Battle of the Wilderness. Let us pray most of these sad reports will prove false!

How I wish I might be there to help you, dearest "Almost Sister." I can readily imagine that in these times life must be dreadfully uncomfortable, lonely and dull in so remote a spot as Moluntha Garrison.

How has President Lincoln's Emancipation Proclamation affected matters at Moluntha?

I sometimes wonder whether Faith is enough. Nevertheless I remain confident that the Lord in His infinite wisdom knows what is best for humanity.

Rather than trust to the mails I dispatch this letter by Captain Herbert Scott, an infantry officer who has been posted to the Knoxville area which, as I recall, lies not too distant from your home. I have given him plenty of money to hire a reliable native Tennessean with Union sympathies to deliver this missive personally into your hands.

With a heartful of love to you and Rodney and to the rest of your family,

> Your forever
> devoted Friend,
> Eliza W. Peabody
> (Still "Freckle-face" to you!)

> Moluntha Garrison
> Wise County
> Virginia
> 30th September 1864

Darling Eliza,

Such an *indescribably delightful* surprise to receive a letter from you after all this time. It sets my mind at rest for, most terribly, have I missed hearing from my "Almost Sister." Your last letter arrived over a *year* ago!

Every time I recall those glorious, happy times we had back in '58, '59 and '60 at Saratoga Springs I cry a little — in private of course.

What romantic fantasies didn't we girls indulge in in those days! What dreams we had of courtly romances and later of married bliss! Now they have vanished amid the heartless blasts of War.

I dispatch this note in the care of a seriously wounded Federal officer who is being exchanged. I was lucky to come across him, since no longer are healthy officers or men to be exchanged between the Armies. Bushrod explains this is so because the North can afford to replace captured troops whilst we cannot.

I was most grieved to learn about your Father-in-law's serious wound and the death of your brother Abner at Antietam. But enough. All of us nowadays are so overwhelmed by condolences that they serve only to depress and not to comfort the most of us.

Being "expectant" within a few weeks (I calculate) and with no physician of any description available, I would that Rodney could be here to lend me strength and comfort during my confinement. But knowing that our Country needs his services more than I, I will rely on Grandma Ruthelma and certain black "wise-women" to help me during my travail. They say that some Negro women, although otherwise ignorant, are quite knowledgeable about such matters. Alas, there are no medical supplies to be had at any price.

Living at Moluntha we now have only my brother-in-law Bushrod, but poor Bush was crippled by a partially smashed ankle he suffered during that ghastly Battle of the Wilderness; he gets around only with difficulty.

Also present is Grandma Ruthelma, who is austere but loving in her rough way. Loretta is here, too. She is, as you no doubt recall, Rodney's twin. Having lost her "intended" through disease, she remains listless and her heart seems as if it had been frozen within her.

All our personal, bed and table linens suitable for medical use went long ago to make dressings and pledgets for our wounded Heroes. Finding goods to make garments for my expected baby calls for considerable ingenuity. Grandma and Loretta have unraveled an old soft sweater and are knitting a coat and some bootees, whilst I am sewing and cutting diapers out of nearly worn-out calico petticoats.

Nowadays we subsist largely on corn pone, yams and turnips; for meat we must rely on game shot or trapped by Hannibal, our faithful Negro hunter. He fetches in rabbits, raccoons, 'possums, a bear or two and even a deer if he is lucky. With help of an old mule which is all we have left of our once-splendid livestock he tends a vegetable garden which during spring and summer is a great help.

Dear Heavens, 'Liza, will this horrible war *never* cease? Along with our fighting men, so many women and young children are hungry and suffering and all too-often perish needlessly.

I pray your Marcus remains safe and will return to you as the same fine, upstanding gentleman I met in what seems like an eternity ago.

With regard to your query concerning the Emancipation Proclamation, you must have forgotten that it long has been the custom of the Tilt family to free slaves as quickly and quietly as possible without antagonizing their neighbors; therefore some have remained loyal to the family and help out in their humble way. Only foolish young ones run away toward so-called "freedom" and an unknown fate.

Pray God this hideous conflict will end swiftly — *no matter how!*

Please, dearest 'Liza, let me hear from you *at the first possible instant.* Only to you can I confide how terrified I am over the prospect of bearing my first baby unattended by a physician.

Beyond measure I crave compassion and understanding such as no male, no matter how devoted and well-intentioned, can impart at such a time.

Your ever-devoted
"Almost Sister"
Louisa Merryman Tilt
(Once your Pretty Kitten)

# 2

---◆◆◆◆---

# Last Bivouac

O N A PLEASANT MORNING early in April of 1865, a red-shouldered
hawk wheeling lazily above the newly verdant rolling terrain of
Appomattox County, Virginia, at first might have wondered why such a
large number of rusty-black turkey buzzards should be planing and
wheeling above these fields and pastures until he noted dozens of dead
or dying horses scattered about them.

Until now this countryside had been a lovely, peaceful area across
which several little creeks and brooks meandered before emptying into
the still unimportant Appomattox River. In all directions fields were
beginning to green, fruit trees were budding and bright with blossoms.
Sizable areas of woodland created a gigantic bucolic patchwork pattern
surrounding a hamlet consisting of only a few small frame dwellings,
barns, corncribs and other outbuildings clustering haphazardly around
that simple court house for which this settlement had taken its name.

The only structure of distinction was a two-storied, porticoed house of
red brick belonging to one Wilmer Maclean who had moved west to get
away from the fighting after his land had been overrun and a lot of men
had died upon it during the first Battle of Bull Run — or Manassas as
Southerners called it for, whenever possible, the Confederate authorities
named an action after the nearest village or town while Union forces
usually identified the same engagement after the nearest outstanding
natural phenomenon. Hence it was "the Battle of Sharpsburg" to South-

erners and "Antietam" to Northerners; "Pittsburgh Landing" was called "Shiloh Creek" in Union dispatches.

The harrier floating on all-but-motionless pinions could have viewed trampled and wheel-marked fields cluttered by slowly moving columns or immobile clusters of men clad in ragged gray or butternut-brown uniforms or even civilian garments.

Twisting blue-gray pillars of smoke raised by hundreds of smoldering campfires obscured many bivouacs of the Army of Northern Virginia, now concentrating in an irregular oval formation on wide fields almost completely hemmed in by low, wooded hills.

Six days earlier the Southern Army's retreat from blazing Richmond and that complex of fortifications protecting Petersburg had commenced, but had been so relentlessly pursued by Blue cavalry that most Confederate supply trains had been captured or cut off. Artillery limbers and caissons had been parked hit-or-miss, not in orderly rows as in the past; only a few command tents had been erected.

A few miles southward could be seen the right-of-way and silvery rails marking the route of the Virginia & Tennessee Railroad from Bull's Gap, Abingdon, and Lynchburg. Here and there its course had been blocked by the broken and charred wrecks of rolling stock and burnt bridges. Also, many sections of rails were missing, expertly ripped up by Sheridan's, Crook's and Custer's swift and far-ranging cavalry.

The hawk also could have sighted numerous strategically disposed elements of blue-clad Federals gathering upon those heights ringing Appomattox.

Many units of the Federal Army, mostly artillery and cavalry, still were in movement trending generally toward the north and west, intent on seizing still more high ground — dominating positions hastily selected and held only by the hopelessly disorganized and outnumbered remnants of the Army of Northern Virginia.

Had the bird circled lower it would have spied, close by Appomattox Court House, several open fields separating immobile outposts and skirmish lines. The Army of the Potomac and the Army of Northern Virginia were with grudging respect once more confronting one another.

Around midday a pair of officers wearing remarkably clean gray uniforms rode out of the Confederate lines and at a smart trot set off toward Wilmer Maclean's red brick house, on the veranda of which stood waiting a lone Union officer.

A short distance away, perhaps a dozen high-ranking Federal officers, who already had come up under a white flag, sat mostly lean and long-ungroomed mounts. The few who had dismounted and had been smoking seegars swung back into their saddles on noting the unhurried approach of a pair of Confederate officers under a white flag.

One, sitting very erect and staring straight ahead, wore a short, well-trimmed gray beard and bore the insignia of a full general, C.S.A. His companion was a bespectacled, black-haired individual distinguished by a short but very pointed goatee.

Blue-clad Colonel Babcock, who'd been waiting on the veranda, stepped down from Maclean's porch and smartly saluted when the gray-bearded General and Colonel Marshall rode up accompanied by a sergeant who smartly dipped a white cloth lashed to his guidon's staff.

As General Robert E. Lee approached, the Union party waiting near the Maclean house stiffened in their saddles, and when General Ord removed a broad-brimmed black slouch hat as a mark of respect, his fellows successively followed the example — some with evident reluctance.

Amid a silence so intense the chirping of robins and the barking of a squirrel could be distinctly heard, the Commanding General of the Armies of the Confederate States of America dismounted and unhurriedly passed the reins of Traveller — that tall, gray charger which had carried him through so many campaigns — to the sergeant displaying the white flag. Colonel Marshall did the same.

In the vicinity of the Court House the unnatural hush persisted but somewhere, a long distance off, sounded artillery and infantry fire. Probably such units were unaware that a truce, negotiated the day before, still was in effect.

Hardly had the two figures in gray followed Colonel Babcock into the Maclean house than a small group of weatherbeaten and liberally bewhiskered general officers headed by the chunky, dingy, almost insignificant figure of Lieutenant General Ulysses S. Grant rode up to dismount and slap dust from their uniforms.

Colonel Babcock reappeared, descended the porch steps, and spoke briefly to Grant, who nodded, then beckoned his officers to follow him indoors. Among these were Generals Meade, Sheridan, Ord and Rawlins, Grant's chief-of-staff. Among those who crossed the porch was Colonel Ely Parker, a full-blooded Iroquois Indian and War Chief of the Six Nations. Parker was so dark-complexioned many Southerners mistook him for a Negro and cursed fervently.

By the edge of a grove of flowering apple trees whose delicate scent had become lost amid the reek of filthy, sweat-soaked garments, uncleaned leather and ungroomed horses, waited Colonel Rodney Ajax Tilt, commanding Lee's escort. He sat loose in the saddle of Resaca, that tall, golden-bay stallion he'd named after a charger which his father, Major Rushmore Tilt, had ridden during the war with Mexico.

Mechanically, Rodney Tilt chewed on a stem of sweet grass and looked about so intently that, years later, he could recall almost every detail of this scene. Beside him sat Captain Peter Holt, a ruggedly hand-some and yellow-haired young captain whose wide and good-natured mouth was contradicted by too-old-looking eyes of pale blue. His right arm was supported in a dirty white sling.

Tilt, reasoning this meeting in Maclean's house would not prove brief, ordered his escort to dismount and allow their gaunt animals to graze. They hadn't been really fed in over a week — no corn or oats or hay. The troopers also eased girths, then, in order that air might pass freely over sore backs, lifted malodorous saddle blankets.

Absently, Captain Peter Orville Holt again scratched at a mane of straw-colored hair; with warmth, lice were becoming active again. Yawn-ing, he turned to his commanding officer. "My God, Rod, how much longer do we have to wait for all those gen'rals to decide what's to be done with us?"

Tilt passed a grimy hand over jet eyes hollowed through hunger and prolonged sleeplessness, "Only God knows. I'm almost too tired to care." Right now he felt ready to sell his immortal soul for a few hours' sleep unbroken by the summons of bugles, drums, the roar of artillery or the spiteful rattle of small arms.

In another orchard directly behind Lee's escort, semi-dazed detach-ments of infantry stood in disorderly ranks. Some men lay stretched flat on the ground sound asleep but mostly they stared at the Maclean house, dully wondering what might be taking place inside. It seemed to many in both armies as if they all interminably were holding their breath.

A few Confederates still were wearing *képis* — forage caps of French design — but most preferred a wide-brimmed felt or straw hat. Dressed in a wide variety of uniforms and parts of civilian clothing, they stood under bayonets fixed to grounded rifle muskets and had slewed their cartridge boxes ready in front. One never could be sure that some dirty Yankee trick might not be impending.

Only a few had retained knapsacks, haversacks or even a blanket roll, but all had clung to canteens. The Federal pursuit had proved so relent-less some soldiers carried no weapon beyond a Bowie knife or possibly a revolver jammed into the belt. Many had abandoned their issue rifles, become useless because of emptied cartridge boxes.

From the direction of Appomattox Station sounded chopping, hammer-ing noises and the ring of iron on iron, testifying that those damned, tire-less Union engineers must be already repairing the Virginia & Tennessee Railroad.

A short distance to Tilt's left a horse emitted a gusty sigh before its knees buckled. The animal crumpled to the ground and lay just as dead from hunger and exhaustion as if struck down by a bullet.

Colonel Tilt glanced over his shoulder at a short, swarthy and extra-long-armed corporal who always made his mark on the payroll opposite the name "Rimfire Hamrick." "How many of our men had reported to the bivouac when we rode out this morning?"

"Nor more than a baker's dozen or so, suh, but they was plenty o' stragglers hopin' for a handout." Rimfire batted little, red-rimmed, steel-gray eyes. "Co'se, suh, we hadn't nuthin' to give 'em, so, mostly, they just moseyed on."

A rising undertone of voices ended the unnatural quiet around the Maclean house when a group of more or less resplendent blue-clad officers descended from the porch to line both sides of a rutted driveway leading to the front steps.

Tilt immediately ordered his escort to mount and form before General Lee appeared, holding himself rigidly erect despite his fifty-eight years. He paused deliberately to pull on spotless white buckskin gauntlets. Colonel Marshall then appeared and halted a stride short of his superior while the sergeant, still carrying his white flag, led forward both chargers.

Cheering, which had commenced on Lee's appearance, faltered and then died away when the dark-bearded, short and solid-looking figure of General Ulysses S. Grant clumped down the porch steps.

The Union Commander-in-Chief, Rodney noticed, was wearing an almost shapeless black slouch hat encircled by gold cords tipped by the conventional acorns — otherwise he was clad in the rumpled uniform of an ordinary private soldier. Only those gold cords around his hat and three silver stars on each of his gold-edged shoulder straps indicated Grant's exalted rank.

By contrast to Lee the Union commander wasn't wearing a sword; for some reason he seldom carried one, even when in the field. But somehow, as a West Pointer, he now regretted that his ceremonial weapon had become misplaced during the pursuit.

Both commanding officers halted, facing one another. Grant then gravely lifted his hat, at the same time offering his hand, which Lee took and shook briefly before stalking stiffly over to Traveller. Muffled sounds of satisfaction arose from Confederate onlookers on noticing how deftly "Marse Robert" managed his sword while mounting. So he'd *not* been given the humiliation of parting with that beautiful weapon presented him so long ago by the grateful State of Virginia!

Who ever would have imagined rascally Yankees capable of such courtesy?

To the end of their days not a single one of the Confederates present would forget the bearing of their revered commander-in-chief while he rode toward them. His features were expressionless, silvery head held high, but his gaze was fixed straight ahead. A few bright streaks, however, shone on Lee's cheeks, traced silvery courses downward till they disappeared in his grizzled beard.

Normally, ear-splitting Rebel yells and prolonged cheers would have greeted "Marse Robert's" presence, but now only a stunned, miserable silence prevailed until someone called in a breaking voice, "Gen'ral, suh, are we-all truly surrendered?"

General Lee appeared not to have heard, but dark-haired Colonel Marshall shouted in a clear, parade-ground voice: "Yes. I regret to report we have been forced to submit to overwhelmingly superior forces. This Army has been surrendered, but *only* on honorable and unexpectedly generous terms."

Marshall then dropped his reins and, cupping gauntleted hands, shouted, "Men, you will be pleased to learn that all of us are to be paroled and *not* imprisoned! Under the terms, you all will be furnished with essential supplies as soon as possible. In the meantime you must return to your bivouacs and wait, causing no trouble whatsoever."

When General Lee reentered the Southern lines, haggard, ragged soldiers either saluted or stood to attention till he had ridden by or, sobbing unashamedly, crowded forward to kiss or touch any part of Robert E. Lee's person, or even to touch Traveller.

Icy rivulets commenced to trace the length of Rodney's spine with realization that, after almost four years of mingled triumphs and defeats, of seemingly endless marches in scorching heat or frigid weather, and the gradual waning of high hopes an end had come to it all. Or had it really?

Following a long-established custom for important occasions Rodney pulled out a scratched silver case watch and noted the hour to be exactly half-past four on this afternoon of April the 9th, 1865.

Barely was he aware that Northern and Southern couriers had started galloping off in various directions to spread the epoch-making news that the once-invincible Army of Northern Virginia had fought its last battle.

Using stiff fingers Rodney Tilt gathered the reins of Resaca, who although twice seriously wounded, during the past three years had carried him safely through campaigns, raids, retreats and trifling skirmishes which could kill a man just as dead as some great, crashing battle.

A shaggy, bearded North Carolinian, weeping, flung away his musket, choking, "Blow yer horn, Gabriel! I'm ready to meet you!"

Another, features hidden between grimy hands, moaned, "My God, why should I have been spared to see this? Better I'd perished before Petersburg."

"Escort dismissed! Eleventh Virginia men will follow me!" Black-mustached Colonel Tilt then moved off at a slow walk, followed by Captain Peter Holt and a mere handful of troopers across a wide hayfield on which hundreds of soldiers were sitting with heads bowed on arms, lying collapsed as dead men, or just aimlessly wandering about. Here and there a group would collect to kneel in prayer and raise mournful hymns but the great majority only cursed and blasphemed their fate at the top of their lungs.

Repeatedly cries arose: "Are we really *surrendered* or is this only another armistice?" "Maybe." "Then to hell with that, this war ain't over yet. I aim to head south and join Joe Johnston's army. Anybody feeling like-minded can join me."

Many declared they felt the same way.

Tilt rode past hundreds of muskets planted butt-upward, supported by bayonets driven up to their sockets into rich brown soil. To the imaginative and educated, such suggested a crop of evil weeds sown by Cadmus himself.

Dully, Peter Holt watched an infantry officer suddenly draw his sword, break its blade across his knee, then dash its parts onto the ground and, sobbing, stamp on them. "Any Goddam Yank wants these is welcome to 'em."

Men seeking to locate a rally point kept calling out their unit's number or name — for so furious had been the pursuit that very few troops had been able to maintain even a semblance of organization.

Most of all they wanted to learn what Grant's surrender terms had been. Colonel Marshall had described them as "generous," but just what did that adjective mean to starving, rag-clad veterans, many barefoot or with dusty toes sticking out of cracked and broken boots. Men far from home looked especially anxious.

Home? Rodney Tilt pondered on what might have happened at Moluntha Garrison. Had the old place been burned down or merely ransacked? Despite three Union cavalry raids along the Clinch and Holston valleys he'd heard about, it still seemed possible that the property, quite remote from the railroad, might have been spared serious damage.

If *only* there remained hope of finding Louisa alive and well — but he'd learned through a chance-met neighbor that his wife had died in childbirth last winter. Who else might be inhabiting Moluntha always provided the place still stood?

Through long-established custom, cavalry and horse artillery units set up their picket lines apart from the infantry, so Tilt experienced little trouble in locating the 11th's bivouac amid the pink-and-white blossoms of an apple orchard hemmed in by towering white oaks.

At present the bivouac and regimental command post consisted of only a dozen or so shelter halves — many of Union issue — pitched every whichway in the vicinity of a weatherbeaten canvas forage wagon cover marked "C.S.A." Under this lay Private Ed Peebles, who'd taken a minié ball through his side during that last and hopeless rearguard stand at High Bridge two days earlier.

Conspicuous because of his clean uniform, Tilt found Farrier Sergeant Philemon Knox using the last of his horse liniment on a scrawny, dull-eyed animal standing with head hanging low, hitched to a picket line that sagged between flowering apple trees.

Significantly, no droppings marked the line — none of the animals having been fed grain in over a week. Watered at a nearby runlet, they'd already cropped every blade of green within reach; some even had begun to gnaw buds, young leaves, and even the bark off nearby trees.

When his men saw their colonel riding in with long, strong, bronze-hued features fixed and tense, Major Philip Ramseur got to his feet and saluted gravely. The South Carolinian had combed a thin goatee, which, like his long hair, showed blue-black in the afternoon sun. Ramseur advanced, sensitive well-boned features working. "Please tell me, Rod, have we indeed been surrendered?"

Tilt only jerked a nod while swinging out of his saddle.

On dismounting, Captain Holt swayed and would have fallen and further damaged his wounded arm, but Corporal Rimfire Hamrick leaped to steady him. "Easy, suh, easy does it."

Not until Jasper, looking mighty melancholy and with pink lower lip outthrust, had secured Resaca's reins and started for the picket line did Tilt address Ramseur: "Sorry, sir, tomorrow morning is the earliest we can hope to learn detailed terms of the surrender."

A bowlegged trooper saluted. "Beggin' yer pardon, Colonel, ain't there no rations or forage comin' to us? Most of us ain't swallered a real mess of vittles since Farmville."

"Afraid not. Seems that the Yankees have cut the railroad at several points and captured supply trains coming east from Lynchburg. There'll be nothing for us to eat tonight. Just tighten your belts another hole."

The trooper sighed wearily, "Cain't, suh. Ain't no holes left."

From a nearby campfire someone shouted, "Cheer up, you-all. Just heard the Feds will send us all the supplies they can spare before sundown."

"Hell! Damned if I believe Yanks would ever be that generous."

Straight dark brows knitted, Tilt stalked over to that wagon cover sheltering the wounded youth named Peebles. One look sufficed; ever-cheerful Ed Peebles who, for time out-of-mind had sung and played his banjo to celebrate a triumph or to raise spirits shaken by defeat, never again would make music.

That he'd played his last tune really didn't matter much, Peebles muttered. He'd lost his precious instrument at Farmville when an avalanche of Blue cavalry had closed in on the headquarters supply train so swiftly that the Confederate commander-in-chief's orderly, some staff officers and Rodney Tilt, commanding H.Q. guard detail, barely had opportunity to snatch their best uniforms and equipment from baggage wagons — which explained why only General Lee and a very few other officers had been able to turn out this memorable day, wearing clean, pressed uniforms.

Private Peebles's pinched, tallow-hued features tried to form a smile as he lay, looking incredibly collapsed, on a pallet contrived of branch tips covered by filthy horse blankets. In his small brown eyes had commenced to show a luminescence often compared to the final flare of a guttering candle.

Rodney, followed by Ramseur and Holt, crawled under the fly to crouch on their heels above the dying youth. The South Carolinian, intense black eyes filling, reached into a side pocket to pull out a small silver flask. "A touch of French brandy for you, son. Perhaps 'twill ease your pain."

The officers had to bend over the boy's lavender-hued lips to catch what he was saying. "Thank you kindly, suh, but reckon Ah've sung my last ditty."

"Nonsense," Tilt lied. "You're not done yet, Peebles. Far from it."

" 'Fraid ye're wrong. Ah'm feelin' mortal cold — weary —"

Holt, lowering his tangled yellow mane, queried gently, "Anybody I can write to for you?"

"Thanks, suh, but where Ah comes from in the Geo'gia hills, ain't nobody much lettered. Oh, jist one little thing. Ah'd like fo' Phil Knox to ride my gray. His own critter's near done for an' he knows more about hossflesh 'n anybody. He'll take fine care of Nellie."

"That will be done," Rodney promised. "My word on it."

Peebles drew a shuddering, shallow breath, looked up into Tilt's angular bronzed features, then whispered, "Reckon, suh, Ah'm the lucky one after all."

"Lucky?" Ramseur was startled into asking. "What can you mean by that?"

"Ah won't have to lay down my arms befo' no damn' Blue-bellies."

Gently, Rodney Tilt's dirty fingers closed over Peebles's. "You're right. That's a humiliation us survivors won't be spared. Isn't there anything we can do for you?"

"Yessuh. 'Fore you plants me for good would you tuck a little piece of our battle colors in my breast pocket?"

"Of course," Tilt choked. Ramseur and Holt turned aside, shoulders quivering.

"Thank you, suh —" Peebles sighed deeply, then died.

Once the three officers together had recited the Lord's Prayer, Tilt backed out from under the canvas and instructed First Sergeant Duncan to select a detail to lug Peebles's slight body over to the nearest collecting point for the dead, now expanding all too rapidly.

The detail waited with lowered gaze while Rodney Tilt made his way over to the regimental colors drooping on its staff and used a penknife to hack a patch from its bullet-torn and tattered silk fabric.

He was tucking the bit of cloth into Peebles's breast pocket when the *crack!* of a pistol shot sounded very close by. Catching up weapons, Tilt's men peered through eye-stinging woodsmoke raised by campfires to watch a figure sway amid swirl of gunsmoke before crumpling onto the ground.

"My Gawd!" cried an awed voice. "Cap'n Held's done slew hisself."

# 3

---❖---

*Exeunt Omnes*

NOT UNTIL the return of those troopers who'd carried Private Edward
Peebles's slight body to lie under flowering apple trees among
more and more stiff and angular forms did Rodney Tilt become aware
that Jasper, the loose-jointed, blue-black body servant who'd been with
him from the start, was nowhere to be seen.

First Sergeant Duncan, a lantern-jawed Tennessean, drawled, "Reckon,
suh, he's off foragin' somewheres — same as usual."

Trooper Shaun Connors shook his head. "Naw, I bet right now, like
the rest of the niggers, he's hightailing for the Fed lines."

Sergeant Duncan glared. "By now you ought know better'n that, you
goddam Roman Catholic harp. When Jasper gits back I reckon men
and mounts might eat; never have seen a cleverer bummer."

Corporal Hamrick grunted, "Hope ye're right and that black bugger
comes back soon 'cause mah belly's bin telegraphin' up to learn iffen mah
throat's bin cut."

While the sun disappeared below a lemon-hued horizon officers and
men checked arms and equipment. Because so many mounts had collapsed or died, remnants of the 11th Virginia were able to salvage a few
usable saddles and bridles, some spare horseshoes and other cavalry
equipment, but, without exception, such forage sacks and nosebags as
they brought in collapsed flat on the ground.

Sergeant Knox raised his balding, sandy-red head from dressing a bruised pastern to indicate a ribby black horse near the end of the 11th's brief picket line.

"Colonel, suh, my critter ain't gonna go nowheres from here, so I'll welcome riding Ed Peebles's hoss — she's quarter-bred and plenty strong and fast over short distances."

"You needn't worry on that score," Tilt reassured. "Peebles left you Nellie."

Everybody stopped what they were doing when, in the near distance, sounded shouts and a dull rumbling of wheels and the creaking of ungreased axles.

"Hallelujah!" someone shouted. "Damn' if them Blue-bellied bastards really ain't sendin' in supplies. Hallelujah! We'll sup tonight."

"Aw, stow that gab. They can't be bringing us much so quick."

Tilt turned to Major Ramseur. "Take Sergeant Duncan and a pair of extra-handy bummers along and draw the most you can. As a major, you may rate preference over enlisted men."

Ramseur's detail hadn't even set out when a pair of shoeless infantrymen slouched by, cursing bitterly.

"Save yer hosses, boys," one growled. "Ain't no use goin'. What few rations the Yanks fetched in have already been gobbled."

Holt shrugged his good shoulder. "Sorry, it appears we're going to have to go supperless again."

The fifteen-odd troopers remaining in the 11th Virginia Cavalry's encampment swore, then resignedly squatted on their heels to boil a few handfuls of parched corn or stretched out, exhausted and dispirited, beside the campfire.

A succession of crackles sounded in the nearby underbrush; an owl hooted softly three times. Hamrick, knees showing through nearly wornout yellow-striped breeches, sprang up, yelling, "Praise Gawd! That'll be Jasper!"

Presently the lanky, sharp-featured Negro rode into the circle of firelight astride a furry gray mule and leading another long-eared creature which hadn't been with him when he'd departed.

"Evenin', genmuns. Done come acrost a few eatments and found this heah mule strayin' about in need of a home." What immediately attracted everyone's attention was the fact that, draped across the mule's withers, dangled a pair of bulging leather saddlebags of U.S. issue: furthermore, the second mule was carrying a pair of U.S. canvas grain sacks with a small truss of hay balanced between them.

Jasper slid off his animal, shuffled up to Colonel Tilt, and managed a vague salute.

"Cunnel, suh, you knows rations in these pahts am powerfully hard to come by, but Ah got lucky an' found 'nough to give us all a bait of food." He sighed, then scratched at his fuzzy head. " 'Tain't much, suh, mebbe only a few mouthfuls apiece. Yonder's a sheaf of cured hay and some moldy corncobs fo' the hosses."

With ill-concealed pride the Negro then emptied both saddlebags near the fire. They yielded a couple of dozen hardtack biscuits, a side of bacon, half a ham and some sweet potatoes.

He passed the grain bags to Sergeant Knox, whereupon the farrier sergeant grinned in the depth of a full, brown beard. "That's as fine a piece of bummering as ever I heard tell of, Jasper. Reckon if our animals get even a trifle of grain into 'em they might keep going long enough to carry us away, once this mess is over."

Only discipline, long-instilled, prevented starving men from fighting over this meager supply of food. Lean, unshaven jaws working, they watched Sergeant Duncan use his Bowie knife to slice the bacon with impartial precision, then equally distribute hardtack and yams.

Through tacit agreement all three officers refused to accept more food than the privates.

The night, which seemed to predict a fall of rain, should have been quiet, but there sounded too many incoherent cries from delirious and wounded men, moans and groans from others suffering cramps caused by near-starvation.

Also there were continual crashing noises caused by stragglers blundering about in the dark and calling out in attempt to locate their units.

Persistent racking coughs in the nearest bivouac kept yellow-haired Peter Holt awake despite grinding fatigue and a dull, unrelenting pain in that half-healed saber slash taken across his upper right arm at Cedar Creek. It had reopened during a gallant but futile brush with Sheridan's blue-coated cavalry near Farmville.

All day his wound had kept throbbing and visibly was swelling. Since the rags covering his hurt had grown so foul-smelling Peter reckoned that, come daylight, he'd better do something about it even though doctors, medicines, and hospital supplies in this beaten Army had become almost nonexistent. Still, he hesitated. So many men were in far worse condition than himself.

Like countless others that dreary night he wondered what he'd find when, as, and if he ever reached home — Richlands, the family estate near Tazewell, lying in a county by the same name near the extreme end of southwest Virginia.

All too well he'd learned from various sources that no less than three Federal cavalry raids led by Generals Crook, Burbridge and Stoneman had created havoc along the Holston River, by which ran the Virginia &

Tennessee — a railroad strategically vital to the Confederacy since it transported the only important supplies of lead and salt south of the Mason and Dixon Line.

Would he, upon return, find nothing of Richlands beyond stark black chimneys, tumbled ruins, and weed-choked fields, empty slave cabins and outbuildings, and heaps of charred rubble which once had housed human beings?

Since Grandfather Richard Holt had built his spacious, gracious home not very distant from the railroad's right-of-way, didn't it stand to reason that Richlands *must* have suffered only God knew how much damage?

How farsighted Rod's ancestor, Colonel Ajax Tilt, the Revolutionary War veteran, had been to take up his soldier's land grant and build Moluntha Garrison far from the Holston River and the railroad which now paralleled it after piercing the Cumberlands at Bulls Gap.

Returning from accompanying Colonel John Donelson and his pioneers on their perilous winter journey from Watauga Forks in northwestern North Carolina to Frenchman's Lick, Tennessee, back in 1779, Rod's great-grandfather had remembered a pleasant, mountainous valley, and had staked out his veteran's grant beyond Moccasin Ridge above Abingdon, high and well-removed from traffic following roads and traces along the Holston River Valley. He'd also been proved farsighted through acquiring several sizable adjoining tracts of land and had built a home of limestone blocks on a plateau almost completely hemmed in by steep but not very high mountains.

Eventually, Old Ajax had come to own nearly two thousand acres of soil on which flourished that same bluegrass such as had made Kentucky-bred horses famous.

Moluntha, therefore, should not have suffered too badly unless irregulars or bushwhackers had passed that way.

Like so many wearing gray, Captain Holt for many weeks had failed to receive direct word from Richlands.

His three older brothers he knew had either been killed in action, were missing, or like all-too-many others, had died of disease in the field. If Richlands had been burned, what would have become of Mother and his two young sisters? Most likely they'd have sought refuge with relatives; but with which ones? Poignantly, he dreaded his return.

All along, he'd found Philip Ramseur, the South Carolinian aristocrat, something of a puzzle for, despite courtly manners, elegant speech, and obedience to an archaic code of chivalry, this fire-eating Union-hater wasn't above cutting down surrendered Yankees.

A few feet away, Colonel Rodney Tilt lay huddled under his saddle blanket and slept like the dead until a violent rainstorm aroused him.

Exhausted though he was, Rodney couldn't go back to sleep, so lifted his head to glance at his sleeping companions, shapeless outlines in the dark. What fate lay in store for most of them?

As for himself, well, at least he might contemplate the future with some hope. Colonel Ajax Tilt had constructed Moluntha Garrison of heavy, bulletproof limestone blocks and in his time the house could only be entered through a single door. Windows on this stronghold's ground floor were little wider than musket loopholes, so Moluntha Garrison's interior always had been somewhat somber even on sunny days.

Of course, back in Ajax's time there'd been plenty of vengeful Indian bands roaming the mountains, hungry and desperate through having been deprived of their famous, game-rich Great Hunting Grounds.

Invariably, Colonel Ajax Tilt's garrison house had beaten off attacks, although at times its defenders might have numbered but a handful of men and half-grown boys. By this time most Cherokees, Shawnees and other red men had perished through liquor and white men's diseases. What redskins remained among the high Alleghenies after the rest had been forced to emigrate westward consisted of only a few handfuls — mostly half-breeds — far too weak to discourage Ajax's son, Brian, and Laura-Lee Downey, his pretty, vivacious bride from Richmond, from widening upstairs windows and adding graceful but sturdy wings to the old pioneer's original severe structure.

What kept Rodney sleepless was information he'd gleaned from a straggler who belonged to a company largely recruited in the vicinity of Wytheville and Saltville. This soldier claimed to have labored awhile in one of the Tilt family lead mines. Careful questioning revealed that, last winter, a sizable foraging party of General Stoneman's Federal Cavalry had captured and plundered Moluntha.

It was said the Federals had looted relatively few valuables but had driven off every head of livestock they could find, including the famous Moluntha thoroughbred breeding stock.

"What happened to the barns, stables, slave quarters and other outbuildings?"

"Dunno, Cunnel, except I heard somewheres that one of yer brothers — the one what got crippled — and his wife and children and a old lady still was livin' there. Reckon they'll make out somehow, iffen bushwhackers, guerrillas and their like leave 'em alone."

The straggler had sighed. "Such outlaws are doin' turrible things to people who cain't nohow defend themselves. Yes, suh, thieving, burnin', rape, torture and murder is the order of the day with such."

Rodney's anguish increased. "What sort of creatures are these outlaws?"

"Mostly deserters from both sides, escaped, unparoled prisoners of war, and downright criminals. Worst of it is, them devils sometimes dress like

Feds but next day they'll wear parts of our side's uniform. They strike, then vanish among the mountings."

Rodney had given the fellow the last of his hardtack and wished him luck in reaching home.

And what of Marc and Eliza Peabody? He knew no more concerning the Peabodys than what Eliza had written 'way back last year. Fervently, he hoped Marc had survived — what a rare, fine friendship they'd enjoyed till this cursed War had begun, and now was lost.

What the straggler reported aroused fresh pangs of concern about the fate of Moluntha Garrison; also it renewed poignant grief over the loss of Louisa and their baby. How would it be, on his return, to find no loving, ever-cheerful and capable wife to welcome him? Lord, how he dreaded the prospect.

How well had Bushrod recovered from his wound? In Louisa's final letter before her confinement, she'd said Bushrod had improved sufficiently to ride a mule or a very gentle horse for short intervals.

Grandma Ruthelma, he'd deduced, really must be running the establishment. Of old pioneer stock, that tough and capable little lady knew how to make do, how to plan, give orders, and then see them carried out.

Poor Loretta, it seemed, was only gradually emerging from that bog of despondency into which she'd sunk following the death of David Petty, her fiancé.

Well, if anything remained of Moluntha he'd start putting things to rights, provided he could persuade certain members of Z Company to settle there, or at least linger until postwar confusion had somewhat subsided.

Louisa, oh my darling Louisa! All I've suffered these past years would have been worthwhile if only you were still living. Only your memory determines me to restore our property the best I can. Oh, Louisa, Louisa, my darling Louisa. How can I keep on, lacking your love and confidence?

Finally, he fell asleep.

# 4

## Major Marcus Eames Peabody, U. S. V.

AT DAYBREAK chilling rain increased with no promise of letting up, rendering the 11th Virginia's exhausted, dispirited and hungry troopers more wretched than ever, especially once firewood got wet and increasingly hard to find.

Here and there bugles did sound reveille, but few units of the Gray Army paid heed. Nothing seemed more important than to find shelter while waiting to learn just what General Grant's terms of surrender included.

Unyielding observance of discipline caused the hollow-eyed and shivering remnants of the 11th Virginia Cavalry to be among those few units which fell in to answer roll call.

Once lantern-jawed First Sergeant Duncan had issued the order, the men slouched into a single rank and stood staring dully at the muddied ground. Drops kept dripping from improvised ponchos and weathered Army slouch hats or nondescript civilian headgear.

Forage caps copied from French *képis* at the start of the war had long since lost favor; this type of headgear afforded its wearer precious little protection from sun, wind or rain unlike a broad-brimmed hat of felt or close-woven straw.

Major Ramseur alone was wearing an India "gum" or rubber blanket captured at Yellow Tavern although by now this precious garment had become so cracked and torn it admitted almost as much moisture as it deflected.

Acting on the supposition that a rations detail headed by a full colonel possibly might secure more favorable consideration than one led by some raggedy-ass noncom, Rodney Tilt and Major Ramseur selected four troopers mounted on fairly strong horses and, joined by Jasper and his mules, sought a trampled country road over which Rodney calculated supplies most likely would be delivered from Appomattox Station — always provided the Blue-bellies kept their promise.

To his no great surprise other veteran officers had been equally astute and were following this same rutted road leading south toward the railroad.

Gradually the rain lessened, then ceased. The sun barely had lifted above the hills when from the direction of the Virginia & Tennessee appeared a line of white-covered supply wagons, guarded by a large force of hard-faced Union cavalry.

A few yards in advance of the supply train was riding a square-shouldered, narrow-waisted officer whose chestnut-hued hair and flowing sideburns gave off coppery hues in the early sunlight.

Calmly the Federal, a major by the gold oak leaves embroidered on his shoulder straps, ordered deployment of his supply train; so many wagons into this field, so many into that. Once carts had creaked to a standstill, their guards were hard-put to control swarms of gaunt and ragged Confederates who started to rush forward like a pack of winter wolves closing in on snow-foundered moose.

All at once Tilt blinked. Was there something vaguely familiar about that wide-shouldered Union officer? He urged Resaca through the melee.

"Follow close behind me," he directed, as he and Ramseur caused their mounts to rear and so force a passage through the cursing, milling throng with his troopers and Jasper's mules in his wake.

On approaching the supply wagons around which Union cavalry who, cursing, were attempting to clear an area into which supplies might be off-loaded in orderly fashion, a red-faced Federal commissary sergeant bellowed, "Here y'ar, Johnnies. Come and git it! If the quality of these victuals ain't to yer taste don't blame Uncle Sam. These are yer own rations we captured at Lynchburg!"

To help maintain order the Federal Major spurred forward until under the brim of a weathered black slouch hat could be seen penetrating, wide-spread and very bright blue eyes. He and Rodney Tilt goggled for a long instant, then simultaneously they urged their mounts through the throng toward one another.

Despite Marcus Eames Peabody's unfamiliar dark-red burnsides or muttonchop whiskers Rodney Ajax Tilt experienced no difficulty in recognizing the man with whom he'd been so intimate before this war had begun.

"Rod! Can it really be you?"

"Marc Peabody, by God!"

Yankee guards, and Confederates waiting to draw rations, gaped at the astonishing sight of officers, one in blue and the other in gray, grip hands, then lean far out of their saddles to pound shoulder blades like long-lost brothers.

Few onlookers in the vicinity of Appomattox Court House were aware that similar encounters were taking place, for a good many Union officers had approached the Confederate lines in search of prewar friends; especially members of that small but elite fraternity who once had attended West Point.

Seldom was any display of bitterness or vainglory in evidence.

At length Major Marc Peabody of the 5th Rhode Island Volunteer Artillery ceased grinning and asked, "Where are you camping, Rodney?"

Tilt pointed: "What's left of the 11th Virginia Cavalry are bivouacked in an apple orchard under that stand of tall white oaks. Why d'you ask?"

"Want to increase your supplies at the first possible moment." His expression softened. "Besides, there are other matters we need to talk about."

An unpleasant incident occurred when Peabody pulled off a gauntlet and, having greeted Peter Holt as a boyhood acquaintance, offered his hand to Philip Ramseur, which the South Carolinian ignored. Defiantly he raised his goateed chin and looked aside. "I will shake hands with no damned Yankee. There are no real gentlemen among them."

Although gone scarlet and tight-lipped, Marcus Peabody chose to ignore the South Carolinian's insult.

Rodney was ready to knock Ramseur off his horse when Holt hastily intervened, "Major Peabody, sir, can't you, right now, spare us just a little horse fodder? Many of our finest animals are dying of sheer starvation."

"Sorry, Captain, my orders are explicit: men are to be fed first. Possibly tomorrow I can send or bring in some fodder but, under present circumstances, I have no choice. Men must be first to eat."

At first Tilt found it difficult to identify this hard-faced officer with the rusty-red burnsides, in that stained and dusty dark-blue jacket, as the same youth whose father, back in 1858, had been invited south to design and improve machinery for the Ajax lead mines.

How often had he and young Marc raced horses against one another; had camped out while hunting quail, turkeys and deer and the odd bear. Yes, for nearly three years Marcus's father and Emily, his mother, had lived in a rented home near Wytheville while Mr. Enos Peabody superintended seating and operation of his improved machinery. One shaft belonged to Peter Holt's father.

During that peaceful period lasting friendships had developed between the Peabodys, the Holts, the Tilts and other families prominent in Wise, Washington and Smythe counties.

The Northerner gathering reins ordered his escort to fall in. He then turned to Tilt saying, "Spread the word: more supplies will be issued tomorrow morning. General Griffin is humane; he'll do everything possible to furnish food for your people and animals." In a lowered tone he added, "I'll come to your bivouac — 11th Virginia Cavalry, isn't it?"

"Yes. You'll be welcome anytime."

In moving on, Peabody cast a frosty, almost contemptuous glance at Ramseur, still glowering in the turbulent background.

During their return to the bivouac Tilt's detail more than once were forced to protect their scant supplies through use of the flats of their sabers.

Captain Peter Holt, having gone to have his ever-angrier-looking wound dressed by an overworked medical orderly, returned to the encampment to find Rodney and Ramseur crouched under that same fly beneath which young Peebles had died.

First Sergeant Knox, followed by Jasper, dark and loose-jointed, tramped up and saluted wearily. "Suh, ain't there *nothin'* to feed the hosses? The last of them rations Jasper fetched in last night has been et up."

"Sorry, Knox. So far the Feds haven't had time to send in forage for the animals."

Next morning after Peter Holt had washed as best he might he sought Rodney, and found him burnishing his tunic's buttons — a task which Jasper normally would have attended to.

"Sit you down, Peter. I still can't get over having bumped into Marc Peabody like that."

"Such things do happen, I reckon, but what would Peabody be doing in this neck of the woods?"

"He's said he's a temporary aide to General Griffin. His family lives in Providence. Glad he showed up, though. Someone told me he saw Peabody get badly hit at Gettysburg so I guess that's why Marc's been transferred from line duty to staff work. Speaking of wounds, how's your arm?"

Holt attempted to look cheerful. "A sawbones's mate cleaned considerable gurry out of the slash, then poured horse liniment into it. It stung like fury so I reckon it ought to heal well and quickly. Think Marc really will come to look us up 'cause I'd like to admire again the way he brought down that monstrous gobbler on the wing at least forty yards off. Remember?"

Tilt nodded. "Of course. That was a memorable shot."

"Aye. Marc's afraid of nothing; his word is good. He'll show up."

Holt inclined his head toward Ramseur's who, lips pursed in concentration, with needle and thread was replacing a button missing from his tunic's front.

Around five in the afternoon a squad of tough-looking Union cavalry led by Major Marcus Peabody appeared, after picking a devious route between campfires and around heaps of abandoned equipment. Confederates only stared dully at their former enemies except for a few veteran officers who remembered their training and stood up to offer this auburn-haired Yankee Major perfunctory salutes. Neither side said anything.

The difference between the thin but otherwise well-conditioned Federal mounts and those drooping bags of bones tied to Tilt's picket line was poignant.

On arriving at the 11th Virginia's bivouac, Peabody ordered his men to dismount and lead forward a pair of well-loaded horses.

A thick-bearded Union supply sergeant indicated the pack animals and drawled, not unkindly, "Here y'are, Johnnies. We all wish it could be more, but this is the best we can do."

"Thanks, Billy," drawled First Sergeant Duncan, crouching to inspect the rations. "Right now, we-uns are hungry 'nough to eat crabs off'n a dead nigger's ass."

Major Peabody settled onto a log between Tilt and Holt, knuckled red-rimmed eyes. "Sorry we couldn't bring in more than this. As it was, I had to do a lot of thimblerigging to draw even this amount."

He smiled. "Too bad we can't make this a purely social visit, Rod, but I've a duty to perform." He delved into a dispatch case and brought out a sheaf of papers. "Please examine these parole forms very carefully: they may prove of vital importance to you and to your men."

Bright-blue eyes level, he gave Tilt a quantity of the printed forms and, in a crisp New England accent, announced: "Here are the detailed surrender terms and parole forms. On signing these parole forms, all officers and men of the Army of Northern Virginia will be free from Federal interference so long as they observe the parole terms.

"Only commissioned officers will be allowed to retain their mounts, sidearms, swords, pistols and personal baggage. Other weapons and all Confederate Government property must be turned in at a capitulation ceremony scheduled for tomorrow morning."

While Tilt scanned the forms Marcus Peabody, in some embarrassment, stroked flowing, dark-red sideburns. "Everybody who can read and write must complete and sign his parole form at once. For men who are illiterate, you officers will have to explain the terms to them, then countersign each man's mark.

"Your command must be impressed that these paroles — passports if you like — are priceless and that the Federal Government will guarantee that every man's life and liberty will be protected so long as he remains unarmed till he reaches home.

"Once the railroads have been repaired, free transportation will be granted by Union authorities to men as near to their homes as is possible."

Peabody got to his feet: "Listen well, all of you! Go straight home, obey local laws, and swear never again to take up arms against the United States. Do this, and you have nothing to fear."

Holt queried, "What about men who sneak away unparoled?"

"If taken not bearing properly executed parole papers, a man is liable to immediate imprisonment." Peabody's voice took on an edge: "But if captured *bearing arms* against the United States, said man will either be shot or hanged as an outlaw."

When Tilt led Peabody and Holt over to the fly, Ramseur remained sitting in the rain, glowering into the campfire while quite unnecessarily cleaning his handsome revolver made by Robert Adams of London. With it he was a crack shot.

Once they had settled onto empty ammunition boxes, the broad-shouldered Federal offered a pint of bourbon far smoother tasting than either Southerner had tasted in many a moon.

Tilt sighed while the liquor "spread out," then looked his old friend in the eye. "Tell us more concerning the surrender ceremony you mentioned a while back, Marc."

Peabody's broad and red-brown features contracted. "On my honor, Rod. General Grant and most of our generals wish to dispense with a formal surrender ceremony of any description. But, unfortunately, certain vindictive and radical politicians in Washington have insisted that the defeated forces be made to march to a certain designated point where they will stack arms, surrender regimental flags and all government equipment in the presence of a limited number of Union troops and members of the Capitulation Commission. You will then be free to depart to your homes."

"Which means —" Ramseur demanded —"despite all you've said, we still will be forced to suffer public humiliation."

Marc Peabody replied sharply, "It may make you feel better, Major, to know that in no way will surrendering troops be made to suffer humiliation. There will be no formal handing over of swords or sidearms by your officers; there will be no bands playing victory tunes, no taunts. Not even salutes are to be fired by our artillery.

"Our troops have orders to stand well back, remain in ranks, and stay quiet — after all, haven't we all suffered and died alike?"

"True enough," Holt admitted, easing his bad arm in its sling.

The auburn-haired Northerner produced a few cigars and a tobacco pouch and passed them around before continuing. "General John Griffin, on whose staff I'm serving for the time being, is sensitive and humane.

"For example, this morning he issued orders that, since so many of your animals are perishing of hunger and we cannot quickly furnish forage, artillery and cavalry units will be allowed to surrender first on fields lying to the north of the Court House. You will be informed exactly where."

He recirculated his bottle. Outside, Peabody's escort were offering plugs of chewing tobacco and even sugar and coffee in exchange for Confederate buttons, belt buckles and the like.

Peabody was saying, "After all you've been through I can only guess what it must mean for you to surrender." He stared at muddied knee boots. "Were the situation reversed, I'm damned if I know how I'd conduct myself."

Absently, Tilt's grimy fingers twisted at his ragged and drooping black mustache. "Seems most of us feel dazed, just as if some big shell had just burst nearby."

Major Peabody nodded, then added uncomfortably, "At our headquarters rumors have come in that certain of your troops intend to bury or burn their regimental battle flags and smash their gun carriage spokes. As a friend, I earnestly advise against such practices which would produce a most unfortunate effect on the present not unfriendly attitude of our troops and, most important, on the Federal Government."

"I can understand such resentment." Rodney Tilt's gaze sought the 11th's bullet-pierced and faded Stars and Bars drooping and dripping between two stands of stacked muskets. By heart he knew the names of battles inscribed on it: Second Manassas, Fair Oaks, Sharpsburg, Cedar Creek, Gettysburg, Yellow Tavern and Fredericks — the balance of that particular battle's name had become frayed away, along with some others.

In lowered tones Rodney said to Peabody, "We are honorable officers and soldiers, so when the time comes, we shall surrender our colors with sorrowful pride."

"Your General Rosser has already instructed that early tomorrow morning all cavalry must report on time." Hurriedly, Peabody continued, "As no doubt you already have heard, under the terms of surrender any enlisted man claiming to own his own mount, be it horse or mule, will be allowed to keep said animal in order that when he arrives at his home he will have something to pull a plow and so make a crop for himself and his dependents."

Holt inquired, while wrinkling his nose over the smell of his wound, "What about our infantry? They're in terrible shape — many go barefoot and all are weak as rabbits."

"Tomorrow they will march to appointed areas and there lay down their arms." Peabody again circulated the nearly emptied flask. "Let us hope that before then plenty of rations and other supplies will have arrived. It's possible since the railroad between Lynchburg and Appomattox Station runs nearby. Our commissary wagons are in readiness to receive them."

Major Peabody then ordered a red-faced sergeant to fall in as escort. The Northerner was preparing to leave when Rodney queried: "Marc, won't you tell me something of what you've done since you quit Harvard in such a tearing hurry back in '61? I've just been soldiering: Fredericksburg, Antietam, Gettysburg, the Wilderness and so on. I'll give you the details another time. What about you?"

"I stayed in college long enough to finish that term," Peabody replied, "then went home to Providence where my Dad was raising and equipping a regiment. The volunteers wanted to elect him colonel but he refused, knowing that he'd only very limited field experience during that fool war with Mexico. Besides, he suffers from recurrent rheumatism, so refused field duty."

"And instead?"

"He went to Washington to work in the office of the Chief of the Corps of Military Engineers. Last I heard Dad was about to be made a brigadier-general."

"Where is he now?"

"Still on duty in Washington, I expect."

A puff of eye-stinging smoke curled under the fly, set them to coughing. "You married?" choked Tilt.

"Yes. I married Eliza Whipple just before I rode off 'way back in '62. Now we have two children to bless our union, as the preachers say. What about you?" The Northerner's clear, dark-blue gaze sought Rodney's small jet eyes — inherited perhaps from his great-grandmother, the Shawnee Chief Moluntha's niece.

Holt broke in: "Sad to say, Rod's wife Louisa died last winter '64 in childbirth at Moluntha."

Quietly Tilt queried, "I presume your Father's affairs are prospering?"

"Aye, after a fashion. Mining engineers can just about write their own ticket. Now that the war's about over I expect he'll go back to designing machinery just as he did when he brought us to Wytheville. Mother and the rest of our family remain moderately well-fixed and with *no* Army contracts to thank!"

Peabody pulled on his gauntlets and smiled within the frame of flowing red sideburns. "Before I go, Rodney, I want you and Peter to remember that, when the dust settles at last on this war, if either of you should need backing financially or politically, or both, I stand ready and eager to help you the best of my ability. By the way, Dad has been forced to remain on

rather intimate terms with that cockeyed bastard, General Ben Butler."
Quickly he amplified, "Dad's no friend of 'Silver Spoon,' but through
Butler's vast political power he can get pretty much what he wants. I
mean what I've just said."

From a worn dispatch case he pulled out a notebook and of all things
used a sharpened bullet to scribble his home address. "Now I must leave
— I'm already overdue at headquarters — but before I go, tell me what
you two intend doing right after the — er, surrender?"

"We'll head straight for home. Must find what, if anything, remains of
our homes and property."

# 5

## Last Roll Call

Toward morning as the rain let up orders were circulated among the campfires that, no later than ten of the morning, all officers and men serving in Brigadier "Rooney" Lee's cavalry brigade should rendezvous at Colonel Tilt's bivouac, riding or leading their mounts and fetching along any Confederate Government property and weapons of all descriptions.

The scope of the disaster which had befallen the once-magnificent Army of Northern Virginia became inescapable when emaciated and disheveled officers and men commenced to straggle in at the appointed time. All were required to give their name, rank and unit, which Major Ramseur, lips flat and colorless, wrote down on a form provided by Union officers.

Dear God! Indescribable anguish numbed Rodney Ajax Tilt's being on realizing that only seventy ragged and gaunt troopers now represented a brigade which more than once had numbered better than half-a-thousand sabers!

Once the men had formed a double rank Tilt pressed Resaca forward before, speaking slowly and distinctly, he called out: "By now I expect you all have signed or have made your mark, duly witnessed, on your parole papers. Guard these with your life! Inside of half an hour we will move out. In the meantime I wish you to do whatever's possible to improve your appearance and that of your mounts."

Not much could be done; far too many buttons were missing, too many brass C.S.A. hat ornaments, belt buckles were dull or had been traded as souvenirs for food and tobacco; quarter-straps revealed crude mending, and once-shining curb chains, bits and crown pieces remained tarnished for want of cleaning materials.

"Break ranks, come near, and listen well," Tilt directed. "During the ceremony I expect every one of you to bear himself like the honorable, courageous and undaunted soldier he is.

"For your information I am to report that General Lee and several of his Corps Commanders already have departed elsewhere. Therefore I will now read to you our beloved Commander-in-Chief's farewell message:

> Headquarters, Army of Northern Virginia, April 10th, 1865. After four years of arduous service, marked by unsurpassed courage and fortitude, the Army of Northern Virginia has been compelled to yield to overwhelming numbers and resources. I need not tell the survivors of so many hard-fought battles, who have remained steadfast to the last, that I have consented to this result from no distrust of them but, feeling that valor and devotion could accomplish nothing that could compensate for the loss that would attend the continuation of the contest so I have determined to avoid the useless sacrifice of those whose past services have endeared them to their countrymen.
>
> By the terms of the agreement, officers and men can return to their homes and remain there until exchanged.
>
> You will take with you the satisfaction that proceeds from the consciousness of duty faithfully performed; and I earnestly pray that a merciful God will extend to you His blessing and protection.
>
> With an increasing admiration of your constancy and devotion to your country and a grateful remembrance of your kind and generous consideration of myself, I bid you an affectionate farewell.
>
> R. E. Lee,
> General

Tilt added, "I also have heard that, in order to spare our feelings, Generals Grant, Meade and Sheridan will not attend the surrender ceremony."

"Why do they say until properly exchanged," someone asked.

"Because Johnston's still fighting and peace hasn't been declared," Tilt explained.

Wearily, the Virginian then straightened in his saddle. "I presume that most of you have been wondering what comes next."

Some shrugged or looked at the ground. Someone said: "Ah just runned away to jine the army so Ah don't know where to find any kin. Ain't heard nothin' from 'em in the longest time."

Another stated: "Likely my folks have just headed west along with a lot of others so Ah'm aimin' to go join Joe Johnston. Like Cunnel jist said, he's still fightin'."

Sharply Ramseur reminded the last speaker: "Many will wish to do the same thing, myself included."

"But don't forget," Tilt continued: "We all are on parole now and can't fight more."

First Sergeant Duncan sang out, "What about you, Colonel, suh?"

"Captain Holt and I live not too far from here. Therefore we intend to make our way in the direction of Wytheville, which lies near the westernmost tip of this State. Our families own land near there and possibly we will find some of our property left."

He looked about. "Once the surrender ceremonies are completed, any well-mounted soldiers wishing to accompany Captain Holt and myself can give their names to Sergeant Duncan and assemble here."

Feeling grimmer than he had since learning of Louisa's death, Rodney drew a very deep breath, then rasped: "Form up! Draw sabers! Sergeant Duncan, advance the colors. Present arms!"

Blades rasped free of dented scabbards and brass hilts were pressed hard against bearded lips. Some commenced to sob but stopped when Captain Holt, managing his wounded arm, ordered: "Form fours! Fall in behind the Colonel! Remember to hold your heads high and look only straight ahead. We have been defeated, sure enough, but for God's sake don't let those damn' Yankees for an instant imagine they've *whipped us!*"

Remnants of the Army of Northern Virginia's field artillery now commenced to roll by wheels rumbling, equipment clattering, and turned onto a rutted dirt road running eastward.

The waiting cavalry noted that only four guns remained in Haskell's North Carolina Battery, three to Poindexter's South Carolina, and only five Napoleons represented Captain Donnel Smith's famous 10th Virginia Battery.

In every case each unit's battle flag fluttered before limbers drawn by gaunt horses seemingly not strong enough to pull off a man's hat. Not much time passed before the last battery had rolled by.

Significantly, there was plenty of room for these guns on the trampled new green grass. While waiting, the cavalrymen allowed mounts to nibble voraciously at tufts of succulent spring grasses.

At length a haggard Confederate captain rode up to Colonel Tilt and, after saluting, instructed, "Sir, fall in your force and follow the last battery — 'tis Colonel Boston's Fifth Virginia Artillery, I think."

"Very well, sir." Colonel Rodney Tilt glanced over his shoulder at the column behind and bit his lip. Some men were wearing faded and threadbare gray or captured blue jackets, others were in butternut brown, but quite a few were clad partly in dingy civilian garments.

While a few officers bestrode gaunt but clean-limbed products of Kentucky, Tennessee and Virginia breeding farms, most men were riding mules or ungainly, heavy-footed farm horses. A few were mounted on "tackies," ugly little mountain-bred horses which didn't appear worth a dented dime but had proved beyond price during a hard campaign when forage became scarce and distances seemed endless.

Struggling for self-restraint, Peter Holt brooded over this caricature of bygone days; companies often were represented by only a dozen or even fewer troopers, but color guards tried to sit erect under their regimental standards. Major Ramseur, with jaw set tight, rode just behind Rodney Tilt, apparently noticing nothing. Glaring, the South Carolinian appeared to be in a sort of trance, as if all this was but a vivid, evil dream. Holt, who'd cleaned his grease-spotted jacket after a fashion and had scoured its remaining brass buttons with sand, sat ramrod-straight, did his best to copy Rodney's bearing.

Never before, or ever again would that sleepy hamlet named Appomattox Court House witness the presence of so many thousands of men, nor could its inhabitants yet foresee that their settlement's name would forever be preserved in the annals of history.

In dense, dark-blue ranks, Federal infantry stood under fixed bayonets, but drawn up well back from the road. The victors remained almost completely silent when Confederate cavalry entered that same cornfield upon which surrendered artillery had been parked any whichway and then abandoned save for dying horses and men too weak or too seriously wounded to move on.

Carbines, sabers and muskets had been piled like giant jackstraws beside the disorderly array of caissons and gun carriages — excepting for certain neat stacks employed to support faded regimental colors which, forlorn-looking, drooped from their staffs, level to the ground.

Struggling to keep long, high-cheekboned features impassive, Rodney Tilt oddly enough was reminded of Grandma Laura-Lee's once saying: "Never forget, Roddy, when matters seem to get as bad as they possibly can, they sometimes grow worse."

"Yes, Grandma, but what does a fellow do at such a time?"

"One can commit murder, or smile and remain courteous. There's no law against acting courteously, but committing murder isn't the best solution for a bad fix. There are laws against it; Bible says so."

Rodney therefore forced a fixed and mirthless smile.

Gathered on a grassy hillock stood knots of blue or gray-clad horsemen composing the Surrender Commission. Among officers wearing gray, Peter easily identified Generals Longstreet, Pendleton and John Brown Gordon.

To the right of the Confederate group their opposite numbers, wearing black slouch hats and dusty blue, impassively sat their chargers. Peter reckoned yonder tall, thin officer wearing a major general's stars and a dark goatee likely must be General John Griffin, because Marcus Peabody was sitting his horse beside him.

Another Union Commissioner must be General Wesley Merritt, reportedly the best cavalry leader on the Union side. Too often his ability made life a misery for such famous *beaux sabreurs* as "Beauty" Stuart, Rosser, Lomax, Mosby and Jubal Early.

It came time for the 11th Virginia to turn off that dirt road on which they'd been waiting and to ride out onto a pasture indicated by a Confederate captain. The dismal little column then moved right oblique toward a spot where other cavalry units already had stacked sabers, carbines, cartridge boxes and enlisted men's revolvers.

Once Tilt had halted the abbreviated column he wheeled Resaca about and shouted: "Eleventh Virginia! Prepare to dismount! Dis-mount! Horse holders, forward!"

How bitterly absurd it seemed to issue such orders to this handful of weatherbeaten, ragtag and bobtail troopers.

"Stack arms!" Barely in time Rodney recalled Grandma Laura-Lee's dictum and steadied himself when dismounted troopers, many of them lacking footgear of any description, tramped forward lugging saddles and other gear, any whichway. Distinctly, he heard Philip Ramseur behind him hiss, "By God Almighty, we'll make these damned Yankees pay dear for this."

First Sergeant Duncan yelled: "Stack carbines and sabers. Unsling cartridge boxes and hang revolvers, bayonets and sabers onto the stacks."

Despite himself. Rodney's voice broke momentarily when he called, "Sergeant Duncan! Advance the standard, support it level with the ground between two of the tallest stacks."

A stifled groan arose when the First Sergeant limped forward, favoring a foot wounded a year ago in that savage cavalry battle near Yellow Tavern, Virginia. Tears streaming down lined, bacon-hued cheeks, Duncan obeyed, hung the flag on its staff so it hung drooping toward the ground between stacks. He then saluted the 11th's battle flag of which less than half remained, thanks to bullet holes, weathering and the fact that, recently, men surreptitiously had hacked off pieces of fabric to be cherished till their dying day. Duncan then about-faced and limped back to his horse.

Accompanied by Ramseur and Holt, Colonel Rodney Tilt rode up to the surrender officials and saluted smartly with his sword. "Gentlemen, I have the honor to report the 11th Virginia Cavalry, as required, has placed at your disposal our colors, arms and all other Government equipment."

To steady himself Tilt kept his gaze on Marcus Peabody's imperturbable ruddy features framed in auburn sideburns.

"Thank you, sir," called an aide to General Gordon. "You are dismissed.

It might be wise to remind your men that, until properly exchanged, they must observe the terms of their paroles to the letter until peace is declared."

Symbolically, perhaps, the road from the surrender grounds wound south.

# 6

## Z Company

ALTHOUGH a good many men on fairly well-conditioned horses scattered, alone or in small groups, the moment they'd reached that fateful road leading southward through Appomattox Court House, a majority, mostly veterans of long service, gathered around officers they trusted and tramped slowly back to their bivouacs for consultation.

Among these groups were Rodney Ajax Tilt and Peter Holt, followed by a dozen-odd hard-shelled enlisted men who'd served in K Company, 11th Virginia Cavalry, a long time. With them rode hatchet-faced Philip Ramseur, although he'd been in command of a different squadron of the 11th which, during the retreat from Richmond, had completely disintegrated through death, wounds or desertion.

Many mounts were limping from wounds or a lack of shoes; others had become so reduced in strength by hunger that their riders hurriedly dismounted and took to leading their beasts, heads hanging low, at the end of reins or halter shanks.

Once the bivouac in the debris-littered and nearly deserted apple grove had been regained, Tilt's men were surprised to find Jasper waiting. Grinning whitely, he pointed to the mules he'd stolen the night before and a pair of horses too sickly to appear on the field of surrender had been groomed after a fashion.

Holt dismounted awkwardly, nursing his arm, and asked wearily, "What are your intentions, Rod?"

"Yes. I'd also like to know," Ramseur said. The South Carolinian's darkly handsome and aquiline features contracted. "You see, I've heard that beyond doubt my family home and plantation buildings near Charleston have been burned down or otherwise ruined and all our slaves have fled. So I've no inducement to return there and lament like Marius among the ruins of Carthage." He vented a mirthless laugh. "Since I will *never* consent to live under a Yankee Government, I reckon I'll seek my fortune somewhere abroad. Most probably I'll head for Mexico."

"Why Mexico?" Tilt asked. "From what I hear, all is bloody turmoil down there, what with only a few thousand French bayonets keeping Emperor Maximilian on his throne. Seems that a regular Mexican Army commanded by Creoles — Mexican-born Spaniards — are also backing the Emperor, and the clergy plus some ambitious *mestizos* leading peons which must number into the thousands; they control most of the country's wealth."

Someone called from the background, "Aye, but 'tis reported that that half-breed General Juarez is gathering strength every day so Maximilian and the French are about to find their hands full, especially since our war's pretty near over. The Federal Government is likely to invoke the Monroe Doctrine and mass a lot of veteran divisions along the Border."

Ramseur held up a hand. "Therefore Maximilian is going to need plenty of experienced officers and men like us to keep him going. Since his treasury is full, why won't he be willing to pay poor ruined devils like us whatever we ask?"

Tilt said: "Probably he would pay experienced troops and proven officers and generals plenty — *if* they can get to him and manage to keep what they earn."

"Even so, Colonel, can you think of a more likely prospect? There's more of silver, gold and other riches to be won down there than anywhere else nearby. Mexico's always been richer than rich even before Cortez landed and —" he added in a rising voice "— best of all, such wealth is concentrated in comparatively few hands, so it should be more readily come by."

He looked about at the drooping figures huddled about the campfire. "Think on what I've said, men. Right now I feel inclined to improve our lot, below the Rio Grande."

"Such decisions can and must wait," Tilt spoke sharply. "Right now our main concern is to stay alive and to reach our homes."

Quite a few stray men came slouching in to listen. All of them, from fuzzy-cheeked youngsters to grizzled veterans, appeared anxious and confused.

The Master of Moluntha Garrison stepped into an open space. "I want only men from K Company to form a circle around me."

Once the evil-smelling fellows closed in, Rodney looked each one full in the face for a long moment before saying, "You all know it's no longer lawful for me or any other Confederate officer to issue orders. However, under present circumstances, I believe it lies in our common interest that we carry on as before. All of us long ago learned that disorganized bands don't amount to a hill of beans, no matter how numerous they are.

"Any man who enrolls in the force I have in mind must swear to carry out orders just as in the past. I intend to form a private company, like some fraternal order, subject to discipline.

"Since 'Z' is the final letter of the alphabet and we are the last of the former 11th Virginia —" he smiled faintly —"I think from now on I will designate this irregular unit simply as 'Z Company.'"

"Sounds all right to me, provided everyone of us keeps his word," said Corporal Hamrick.

Ramseur and others looked puzzled when the young colonel continued, "Since we will draw no pay we will share and share alike in whatever turns up by way of shelter, supplies, and fodder. In the strict observance of discipline lies our best hope of salvation. Already I have been told that the railroad route through the Holston Valley is being overrun by freshly disbanded troops and common rascals in uniform and — keep this well in mind — we'll probably encounter Reb-hating Yankee patrols. Therefore I feel our best hope is to keep away from the Virginia & Tennessee's right-of-way and travel generally westward, paralleling the railroad at a distance and as high among the foothills as proves practicable."

As if to underline Tilt's remarks, a locomotive whistle moaned in the distance; also the faint chuffing of locomotives could be heard moving along the newly reconstructed railroad.

Feeling anxious as seldom before, the Master of Moluntha Garrison continued, "Is anyone present at all familiar with the back-country roads, the trails and traces of these parts?"

A black-bearded private wearing a checkered shirt and a single gallus to support wornout breeches stepped forward: "Ah does, suh. Done trapped and hunted these parts, man and boy, long 'fore this cussed wah broke out."

"Your name?"

"Maxwell, suh. Johnny Maxwell."

"Want to take your chances with us?"

"I'd sure admire to suh, as far as Christiansburg, at least. Mebbe Ah still got me a cabin, a woman, a passel of sprats and a patch of good farmland nearby." He patted the shoulder of a gaunt gray tacky. "Reckon Jessie'll last to git me there."

A man joined the group, growling, "Jeezis. Goin' about 'thout no arms like this sho' do make a man feel nekkid!"

Corporal Hamrick nodded. "Know how you feel. When I stacked my carbine on that goddam surrender field I pats her down gently and says to her, quietlike, 'Rest easy, Kitty, many's the Blue-belly you've made to bite dust!' "

Sharply, Tilt broke in. "Enough of such talk! Sergeant Duncan, take down the name or mark of men wishing to enlist in Z Company, provided they first swear to honor their parole and obey orders, no matter what happens."

The First Sergeant pulled out a worn and greasy yellow daybook. "Anyone thinks himself able to keep up with us as far as Wytheville take one pace forward!"

Biting his lips as usual — writing always had been a chore — Duncan scribbled on the new muster roll first his own name and then those of Farrier Sergeant Knox, Corporals Rimfire Hamrick, Shaun Connors, and Andy Scoggins; Privates Joe Kinnard and Klass van Korputt, all of whom had served in the old K Company.

Toes peered through some boots when they stepped forward. Van Korputt was going entirely barefoot but had brass spurs strapped over calloused brown heels. Altogether eight privates gave their names.

Knox inclined his head toward Jasper. "What about him, suh? Cain't enroll a nigger."

Tilt's mouth curved momentarily beneath sweeping black mustachios. "Enroll him as 'Jasper Jett Tilt!' "

"Yessuh. What rank?"

"Um. Well, as a supernumerary private."

The blue-black Negro demanded uneasily, "Suh, what am a soopernoomery private?"

Holt laughed. "It only means you've been enrolled as an indispensable forager for Z Company."

Once about a dozen troopers out of the 11th's other companies had been enrolled — and some acceptable appearing men from other units — the rest wandered away. Z Company's muster roll now included twenty-eight names.

Tilt announced, "We will now examine animals and equipment and find out how fit we are to travel any distance."

Horse furniture turned out to be mostly in poor condition but some of it was sound, having recently been captured from the Federals. However, a tally of weapons revealed the shocking fact that, for protection, Z Company had only the three officers' revolvers and swords.

At length Tilt instructed First Sergeant Duncan, "Fall in the men for a showdown inspection. No one must conceal an illegal weapon because, if any are found, a Union patrol could or possibly would shoot or hang the offender and endanger the rest of us."

During inspection Tilt took Major Ramseur to one side. "Am I mistaken or did you not fail to sign the muster roll for Z Company?"

The South Carolinian tugged at his tangled black goatee. "That's right, Colonel. I haven't yet done so because I remain uncertain about my future. I occupy a difficult position since I've taken a solemn vow never to live under the Stars and Stripes."

"Every man is entitled to his opinion," Rod stated evenly. "Possibly your solution is a valid one. But who can be certain that, granted time and reason, hatreds and hurts won't heal and the United States won't become a great, fast-growing nation once more?"

The South Carolinian frowned, joining slim, black brows. "Maybe like a good many others I'll head for Canada, just as some of my Tory forebear did after the Revolution, and perhaps make a fresh start there. Not that I'll linger — I abominate cold weather."

Under a captured blue watch cloak Ramseur shrugged. "I've been told there's gold to be won down in Mexico or Paraguay, in the Argentine or perhaps Brazil. Seems there's always some dictator eager to hire reliable, well-trained mercenaries at a high price. I've already talked with some officers who'll jump at such a chance of winning quick riches."

"Who wouldn't?" Peter Holt queried.

Surprisingly, Philip Ramseur's hand closed over Rodney's. "Whatever conditions prevail on your property, you're bound to need cash — probably a lot of it — and in a hurry."

Tilt studied his companion's anxious expression: "Everything depends on what I find at Moluntha Garrison."

Ramseur invited, "Think again, since you've no wife or children to consider. Believe me or no, I've met many Spanish-speaking Americans who say they know how small fortunes can be earned by experienced veterans with ability, courage, and not too many scruples."

"Provided one lives to enjoy them," Tilt pointed out. "It's common knowledge they have many dangerous diseases in those parts: yellow jack, malaria, black vomit, smallpox, typhoid — even leprosy." Steadily, Tilt considered the other. "Think again about your present situation, Major. You can reach Canada easier by traveling west and then north rather than by struggling through the South, torn as it is by despair and lawlessness to some port along the Gulf."

Gradually Philip Ramseur's tense expression relaxed. He pursed his lips. "You've made some telling points, Colonel, so, if you're willing, please enroll me in Z Company. I promise to obey orders and do my best to prove useful."

"Good," Tilt said, then added uncomfortably, "However, there's one drawback we must face. While we will keep our officer's rank by name, such rank will carry no *legal* authority over the members of Z Company."

The South Carolinian's jet eyes slitted. "Is this necessary?"

"Yes, but only through our common need to survive. Remember, Major, since yesterday all Confederate commissions have become worthless."

"How does Captain Holt feel about this?"

"The same as I. He's young, but practical. Incidentally, Peter is my first cousin. After the Revolution his family came out to the frontier at about the same time as mine. They own a deal of land and property of considerable value. So, in the foreseeable future neither of us is about to depart for foreign parts. Virginia and Wythe County remain *our* country."

Ramseur nodded. "Fair enough, so let us hope that a band of all of twenty-odd casual soldiers led by a so-called colonel, a major and a captain can accomplish something." He pulled out a well-gnawed plug of tobacco, bit off a minute portion and fell to chewing before wryly saying, "Sounds sort of like some South American army, plenty of officers and noncoms but damn few privates. Come to think on it, Z Company is something like a troop serving in a foreign army as mercenaries."

Holt suddenly rasped, "Goddam it, no, sir! We'll not be anything like mercenaries, jayhawkers or bushwhackers. I consider us more like vigilantes, enforcing law and order in the absence of regularly constituted authority."

Sergeant Knox grunted, "That makes real sense to me, sir."

Murmurs of approval arose from all sides.

"So be it." Tilt, having gained this much, beckoned the rawboned fellow named Maxwell. "A while back, didn't you say you know this countryside?"

"Yessuh."

"What was your unit?"

Said he, standing straight in a torn and badly repaired butternut-dyed jacket, "I served with the Third Tennessee Volunteer Horse Battery. Like I said, I bin trappin' and huntin' this neck of the woods since I was a tad; 'specially toward the westward along the Moccasin and Copper Ridges."

Peter decided this wiry mountaineer looked like a throwback to those wild Scots Highlanders who, a couple of generations ago, had elected to settle among the wild fastnesses of the Cumberlands, the Blue Ridge, the Alleghenies and lesser ranges.

Although the black-bearded private probably had not yet celebrated his thirtieth birthday, his strong but not unattractive features were lined and suggested intelligence.

Further questioning revealed that Johnny Maxwell, standing near six feet tall, had been born and reared near Bristol on the Virginia-Tennessee border. His wide shoulders were thin and his gangling torso tapered too long; hairy and slightly bowed legs barely were concealed by the remains of homespun civilian pants. His hair was even blacker than Rodney's since it lacked that certain dark-blue hue inherited from Moluntha's niece.

Ramseur inquired sharply: "You've never been a bushwhacker or a deserter?"

Maxwell flushed, snapping indignantly, "No suh! I hate such vermin!"

"Let Sergeant Knox take a look at your mount. It will have to measure up if you're to go along with us."

The lanky mountaineer led forward a stunted brown-and-white spotted gelding whose ribs stood out like barrel staves; otherwise the animal appeared to be in fair condition.

"He really strong?" demanded the farrier sergeant.

"Yep. Me and Harry here have traveled a hell's mint o' miles 'mongst these mountains." Maxwell exposed stained yellow teeth in an uncertain grin as he turned toward Tilt. "What gen'ral direction air you aimin' to take, suh?"

"Toward Lynchburg to begin with, then Salem, Christiansburg, Pulaski, Wytheville and if we have to, maybe Abingdon. Never forget this. We must avoid approaching towns or even large settlements. The Holston Valley and the railroad must already be swarming with surrendered Confederates and Federal troops. By bypassing Lynchburg high among the hills we lessen the chance of getting shot at by Yankee patrols who haven't yet heard about the surrender."

Whooping and cheers in the distance suggested the arrival of Union wagons fetching in food and fodder — this time probably rich Northern rations.

Tilt reacted immediately. "Major Ramseur! Take four of our best-mounted troopers, Jasper's mules, and bring back as many supplies as you can grab. Tomorrow we will pull out at daybreak, before the bulk of our troops get moving."

Despite grinding fatigue, First Sergeant Philemon Knox didn't fall asleep straight away. What were the odds against this wretched company, almost unarmed, ill-fed, and with no unit loyalty left to hold them together as far as Christiansburg, let alone Wytheville or Abingdon? He foresaw desertions, quarrels, and the collapse of nearly irreplaceable mounts, as well as attacks or ambushes from Yankees or bushwhackers.

Why return to the mountainous terrain with its meager, hardscrabble soil and his little holding in Wyoming County? It was a good thing he'd remained single, had no ties whatsoever. More than likely his lonely trapper's cabin long since had caved in or been burned down by one side or the other.

What to do? In his breast pocket reposed about $1,500 of Confederate notes, but they were worth no more than the paper on which they'd been printed.

At first Philemon figured maybe he could rebuild and, knowing the woods as he did, once more earn his living as a trapper. He foresaw, however, that as things were there would be plenty of tough mountain men in competition.

Maybe it would be smarter for an old coot nearing forty to set himself up as a blacksmith and farrier near some small town which looked as if it might grow. Yep. That, Knox decided, was what he'd do. Couldn't miss; everywhere horses were a prime necessity — men simply couldn't do without them. Besides, during this war he'd learned a lot about dosing and operating on sick or wounded animals. Time and again he'd proved himself more knowledgeable than most farriers he'd encountered.

Sergeant Knox shifted once under a musty and sodden saddle blanket. Too bad he'd had no opportunity to examine more closely newly enlisted troopers' mounts. Several of these animals — if they soon weren't fed on grain — looked ready to collapse once they were put to such steep grades and rocky heights as lay ahead.

Nor had Jasper fallen asleep — he was that overjoyed over the Cunnel's having bestowed on him his own family name when Z Company's muster roll had been drawn up. "Jasper Jett Tilt" sounded downright elegant; made an ignorant freed man like him feel he really amounted to something.

Fervently, Jasper prayed Massa Rod wasn't about to grant others of his race the use of a name so well-known and respected throughout Western Virginia. Yep, when and if Z Company reached Moluntha he would settle there, after picking out some strong and willing young wench for a wife.

How lucky he'd been, although at first he hadn't realized it. Ever since old Ajax Tilt had taken up property and built his home in Wise County the Tilts, along with quite a few other influential families, never really had favored slavery. True, to avoid being branded by neighbors as "Abolitionists" or "Nigger Lovers," such people always had had to keep a few slaves in bondage — easy-living house servants for the most part.

Years ago, Brian Tilt, old Colonel Ajax's son and heir, had set this precedent at Moluntha by emancipating his black chattels as soon as they'd proved themselves loyal, hard working and reasonably intelligent.

Necessarily, a limited number of field hands were required on the Tilt estates, but a majority of these were occupied with the care of fine horses or laboring in the family's lead mines down in the Holston Valley. Since these mountainous regions didn't lend themselves to crops of labor-consuming rice, corn or cotton, the Tilts had devoted much time and a lot of money toward the development of lead mines once the Virginia & Tennessee Railroad had come as far as Abingdon.

Rodney's great-grandsire, Ajax, back in post-Revolutionary times, shrewdly had observed that a free black man, granted a plot of land spacious enough on which to build a cabin and grow a small crop for himself, was more likely to prove faithful, and would work harder, than any chained wretch driven by whips and suffering other abuses.

It soon became family policy, whenever possible, to purchase Ashanti and Senegalese. Members of these African tribes generally "had a way" with livestock, especially with thoroughbred horses such as Brian had begun to breed. Over the years animals bred and trained at Moluntha Garrison came to command top prices.

Another thing. Thanks to Great-Grandma Lucy Poinsett, Negroes "keeping company" were ordered not merely not to "jump de broomstick" but to get properly married by some dusky preacher before setting up housekeeping — especially if the wench was pregnant. Moluntha therefore enjoyed a minimum of runaways and never had suffered fear of slave insurrections.

Over the years Moluntha's blue-green pastures and paddocks steadily grew until they extended far down the narrow valley almost completely hemmed in by mountains.

Until the War broke out increasing herds of purebred mares, frisky colts and pedigreed stallions disported themselves. The Tilts also reared half- or standardbreds because Army remount buyers favored them. Would Moluntha ever see such animals again?

Too bad, mused Jasper Jett Tilt, Massa Rushmore, Brian's son and Massa Rodney's Papa, for all he'd retained traditional interest in the breeding farm, had allowed himself to become increasingly occupied with the business of mining lead.

Nosuh, Mistuh Brian never should have sent his Massa Rodney 'way out East to study at Harvard College where, he'd heard, students became infected by some mighty queer ideas.

Rimfire Hamrick's sleep likewise proved fitful. Tomorrow likely would prove a day to remember; God alone knew what might happen during and after the surrender of the Army of Northern Virginia.

Rimfire had tried his hand, generally without much success, at trapping, horsebreaking, farming and occasionally, when matters got really tough, working in mines.

What should he do when Z Company's march came to an end? Right now, Rimfire reckoned, unless something went very, very wrong, he'd stick with Colonel Tilt tighter than a poor relation.

# 7

# Assassination!

J UST BEFORE DAYBREAK of April 19th and causing only a minimal amount of noise, Z Company saddled up in the gloom, adjusted girths, halters and bridles more by sense of touch than anything else, then slung canteens and other gear, including nearly empty haversacks and limp forage bags.

By whispered count the party now numbered twenty-eight officers and men, the original roster having been increased by a pair of hard-looking but steady-eyed troopers late of Wade Hampton's South Carolina Legion. Since the new men were reasonably well-mounted according to Sergeant Knox, Z Company's commander was persuaded to offer no objection.

While leading up his animal almost every trooper suffered humiliation over no longer being able to sling a carbine or to strap a saber beneath his left knee. It came as something of a relief, however, that now there was no need to buckle on a heavy cartridge box or to sling a shoulder-cutting bandolier which, at the end of a long march, dragged like a hundredweight of lead.

Dawn had commenced faintly to tint an apparently cloudless sky with faint salmon hues when Colonel Rodney Tilt passed word to remain dismounted and, in single file, follow him and that dark-bearded mountaineer known as Johnny Maxwell. This proved easy since for ready identification the guide had pinned a spoiled parole form between his shoulder blades.

He led Z Company along a cautious route, avoiding as far as possible

smoldering campfires about which lay huddled figures sleeping or coma-
tose through exhaustion. No pickets challenged, nor did anyone bother to
demand a password. Who these unknown cavalrymen might be, or what
lay behind this furtive departure no longer interested the surrendered
army.

Among the orchards sick horses coughed continually, and here and
there some wounded man moaned or cried out in delirium. Everywhere
among the tree trunks showed the stark outlines of hundreds of muskets
standing butt-up like some evil crop and only supported by bayonets
plunged deep into the earth.

Other muskets had been rendered useless through broken stocks, bayonets had been bent, and there were plenty of empty scabbards lying
about. Here and there loomed the outlines of gun carriages and caissons.
The wheels of some had been smashed by embittered cannoneers lest
their pieces prove of ready use to the victors.

The trampled earth further was littered by bloodied bandages, broken
haversacks, worn-out shoes and bits of ragged clothing. Dead horses and
heaps of human excrement already were attracting clouds of flies.

Judging by a peculiar, sickish-sweet odor hanging in dense patches of
underbush it was inescapable that many dead men must have remained
unburied.

That rough country road Maxwell had selected led upward into foothills rising to the northwest of Lynchburg.

Occasionally Z Company encountered small, disorderly parties of infantry who, also wise in the ways of war, were getting underway early,
probably in the hope of discovering supplies of some sort.

Only when such random parties became less numerous did Tilt issue
the order to mount up. Rodney, with Maxwell at his side, felt immeasurably relieved. Once more he was leading troops, even a bedraggled lot
such as this.

It would have helped matters considerably if sometime during the night
someone hadn't stolen his dispatch case containing his only map of Western Virginia. Briefly he patted Resaca's bony neck, then passed a hand
over the grip of Pa's Mexican War sword once more secured under his
knee. Somehow, this lent him a sense of reassurance. Next he drew his
Navy Colt model 1851 six-shooter from the holster dragging at his side,
and twirled its cylinder to make sure it was fully charged.

It proved a bitter thing to realize that, under the terms of surrender,
only sidearms belonging to commissioned officers had been retained; three
swords and as many revolvers remained with which to defend his "command" during his projected march of around two hundred and forty miles
across rough and mountainous terrain replete with countless narrow
defiles well-suited for ambush by Union troops or outlaws.

When at length Maxwell reined in to study a fork in the road they'd been following, Tilt ordered the troopers to dismount, ease girths, and allow their animals to graze or to drink at some nearby runlet.

Holt asked Rodney, reins looped over his elbow, "How do the horses seem to be doing?"

"Sergeant Knox knows better than I."

"I already have asked him. He reports most animals are in from fair to middling condition but they all must be rested whenever possible."

Rodney pushed his broad-brimmed felt hat back onto his head while Maxwell eased bright red suspenders he'd donned in place of that dirty gallus which hitherto had sustained yellow-striped gray breeches. "How soon do we meet really hard going?"

"Suh, most rises along this hyar trace don't amount to much, so the goin' won't git steep and rocky till sometime tomorrow."

"When?"

"Depends on how fast we c'n travel, suh."

"Which branch of this fork do we follow?"

"Right one, suh."

Z Company remounted and followed Maxwell's faded and sweaty checkered shirt up a gentle slope into sun-dappled fresh green woods which soon eclipsed all view of those tragic fields and orchards around Appomattox.

In single file the company moved across flower-decked patches of grass. It was discouraging to see that many horses were limping and all but a few animals carried heads low to the ground. Although sagging in their saddles, the troopers nonetheless observed the prescribed distance of "four feet from head to croup" when the brief column commenced to move upward.

After a while Rodney signaled another halt, during which he announced: "Everyone wearing footgear will go barefoot on dismounting, so long as this road remains fairly smooth and easy. We must save shoe leather for the sharp and rocky stretches we'll soon meet. The weak horses will have to be led."

He then set an example by pulling off perfectly sound boots and slinging them over Resaca's saddle tree.

Major Ramseur and some others grumbled under their breath but complied. Most were pleased to realize how good this fresh morning air felt on sweating, dirty and evil-smelling feet. Presently Z Company resumed the march on foot through peaceful forests in which unseen birds whistled and sang. The ugliness of war might have been hundreds of miles distant.

Tirelessly, bushy-bearded Sergeant Philemon Knox ranged back and forth examining wounds and saddle sores; whenever possible he tightened loose horseshoes, all the while profanely lamenting that no grain of any description had as yet become available. "Ain't nothin' like a bait of oats or corn or barley to refresh animal's vigor. Even plenty of hay or grass can't do the trick."

Toward noon Rodney Tilt surveyed the unit straggling behind and ordered an hour's halt. All horses were to be unsaddled and their backs and legs rubbed down.

While consuming meager remains of Union rations, the men found time and sufficient interest to survey the ever-lovely valley below, along a considerable stretch of which ran the Virginia & Tennessee Railroad. Its shiny rails gleamed hardly more than a mile distant but they were carrying, in close succession, trains crammed to capacity with blue-uniformed troops.

Heretofore it had appeared that the Yankees were solely occupied with repairing bridges, culverts and replacing rails on sidings between Danville, Lynchburg, Christiansburg, Salem, Appomattox and points farther east.

Johnny Maxwell, chewing thoughtfully on a stalk of sweet grass, drawled, "Cunnel, suh, reckon time's about come for me to put to you a serious question."

"Well?"

"How much real rough climbing d'you figger most of these crowbaits can take?"

Tilt sighed, tugged drooping sable mustaches. "Not much, Johnny, unless first we come across decent forage and find a place where we can rest safely for a couple of days."

"Well, suh, I recalls a little trace runnin' higher than this which is rough but ought to prove a heap freer of Blue-belly patrols."

When, early next morning, the thirty-odd men comprising Z Company reined in for a rest atop a tall knob overlooking Lynchburg Junction, even the dullest trooper could tell that alarming news of some sort must have arrived during the night. Had fighting been resumed? This seemed quite likely since, down in the sprawling little railroad town below, bugles were blaring incessantly and drums were rattling.

"Assemble on the double."

The haggard men on the hilltop looked at one another and wondered what could have occurred to start not only soldiers but civilians, men, women and children to scurry about like ants from a disturbed hill. Everyone could see Federals running to form companies, battalions and regiments under their colors.

Groups of surrendered Confederates also were plainly to be recognized hovering uncertainly around the outskirts of Lynchburg. Some had begun to walk quickly, then run, toward the edges of the town.

Presently the unmistakable sharp crackle of rifle fire commenced, delivered not in regular volleys but in scattered, spasmodic bursts.

"My God!" snarled Ramseur, glaring about. "Those treacherous Yankee bastards are shooting at surrendered troops!"

This was so beyond doubt. Men in Confederate uniform were scattering, running for their lives. Every now and then some gray or brown figure would collapse and lie still, or crawl along like a crippled animal.

Snarled Peter Holt, "God damn them! I've seen Blue-bellies act mighty mean sometimes, but I've yet to see regular troops shoot down unarmed men! What *can* have happened?"

No one ventured an opinion.

The minute several strong units of Federal cavalry started to fan out and head for the surrounding hills Tilt snapped at Maxwell, "How soon can we get off this road?"

"Suh, should be a trail turnin' off right soon."

"Where does it lead?"

"Nowhere but nor'west, suh, and it's mighty rocky and steep."

Someone in Z Company yelled, "Hey you! Halt right where you are!"

Most of the company had not noticed the appearance from the direction of Lynchburg of a roughly dressed farmer; he was out of breath and riding a lathered, lop-eared mule.

Tilt called sharply, "Yes. Speak up, man! What's going on?"

"Be you surrendered Rebs?"

"Yes. Ex-regulars."

"Be that the case, mister, you-all had better hightail outta these parts the fastest you kin."

Ramseur demanded grimly, "What's happened?"

From between stained, gapped teeth the civilian squirted tobacco juice onto a bush of budding azaleas. "Telegram just came in sayin' some Rebel sympathizer done murdered President Lincoln last night."

The men crowded in, incredulous. Sergeant Duncan demanded, "But why would anybody do such a thing?"

"Dunno," the farmer wheezed, "but all us Rebs are now going to catch partic'lar hell."

"You're *sure* President Lincoln has been murdered?" snapped Rodney Tilt.

"Yep. My cousin Fred, he's the V & T's head railroad telegrapher, got a message that Abraham Lincoln died this very mornin'. He tol' me so *directly*. A Fed operator was on hand and he checked back. Lincoln sure enough was murdered!"

"Murdered!" burst out a gaunt trooper. "By God, whatever the President may have done, that was a downright cowardly thing to do!"

Someone growled, "Aw, t'hell with that damned nigger-lover. He got no more'n he deserved."

"Naw," Sergeant Knox rasped. "Death in war is honorable, but cold-blooded killing is a heap different."

Tilt led his horse over to the civilian. "Hear any details?"

"Fred said the killer was a actor — name of Booth. He shot Mr. Lincoln from behind whilst he was at a theeater."

He looked about. "The Feds are ragin' mad so you fellers, like me, had better make yourselves scarce in a hurry. Me, I'm off to my huntin' camp till matters cool down."

"We'll take your advice, friend," Tilt snapped. "Such a piece of villainy is bound to cost the South dear."

"Aye, mister," agreed the countryman, rheumy gaze roving over this motley group. "For a while t'won't be safe for no known Southern sympathizer, let alone anybody wearin' Confed uniform, to get taken up. Though most Yankee officers are seekin' to hinder their men, some Blue-bellies have gone crazy-mad and are takin' pot-shot at anyone in gray or butternut, even if they kin show parole papers."

A slow, monotonous tolling of church bells began to clang down in the town. Everywhere, Union flags were being pulled down to half-mast.

The civilian accepted a chew of tobacco, then, bristly jaws beginning to work, advised, "Was I with you fellers I'd ride nawth fastest I could and never draw rein near till I was high 'mongst the mountains."

The farmer flapped a brown, work-warped hand. "Wal, so long, friends; good luck to ye and, by the bye, aside from Yankee patrols, ye'd better keep a sharp lookout for bushwhackers. They're everywhere and meaner than skin-sheddin' rattlesnakes."

Hurriedly Z Company adjusted gear, remounted and, for the first time since leaving Appomattox, kicked their mounts to a slow, heavy-footed trot.

Before long Johnny Maxwell, continually bending under low branches and parting laurel and rhododendron tangles, led onto a trail climbing steeply from the road.

Now and then a turkey or a ruffed grouse would burst into thunderous flight and rocket out of sight. No one paid them the least attention.

Soon the party slowed to a walk, when men astride feebler mounts had to get off and lead their beasts along by their reins.

The higher the party toiled, the more they could see of the tender late springtime countryside. Generally it consisted of steep but gently rounded green hills and low mountains: occasionally, a narrow red-brown road curved briefly around their bases, then disappeared.

Only widely scattered strata of blue-gray woodsmoke indicated that at

least a few dwellings remained inhabited, but buzzards in unusual numbers circled endlessly, indicating where tragedy had struck among these
lovely foothills.

Now and then Z Company came across a clearing in which stood the
remains of a pitiful little log cabin and its barn, but nowhere were domestic animals or fowls of any kind to be seen. This land must long since have
been abandoned.

Following a pause at a sparkling spring, Tilt, with mounting anxiety
concerning Moluntha gnawing ratlike in his mind, was about to order the
march resumed when Maxwell returned at a trot from scouting the trail
ahead.

Looking anxious, he dismounted, led Tilt to one side, and informed in
hurried undertones, "Suh, jest now Ah noticed a place where fairly fresh
hoofprints have turned onto this here trail and are following it. I'd say
they cain't be too far ahead."

Tilt ordered sharply, "Assemble the men, Sergeant! Mr. Maxwell here,
says horsemen are riding this trail ahead of us."

Peter Holt winced when his bad arm got brushed by a horse's head.
"How far ahead are they?"

"No tellin', suh. Maybe 'twas this mornin', maybe 'twas yesterday
evenin'; ground's that shaded and damp there's no sure tellin'."

Ramseur's face lighted and he unbuttoned his holster's flap. "How
many d'you reckon they number?"

Opined the mountaineer, "Hard to be sure, suh, but I'd say they number mebbe a dozen or so. Maybe they're only some of our side headin'
homewards — which would help if we run into trouble."

Ramseur pointed out, "It just as easily could be some Blue-belly patrol."

Joining furry brows, Sergeant Knox asked, "How did them hoofprints
look? Were shoes sharp or worn-lookin'?"

"Mostly they looked new. Read only one barefoot mount amongst the
lot — which means more 'n likely it's a Yankee patrol ahead."

An infuriating sense of helplessness seized Peter Holt on realizing that
the sum of Z Company's weapons consisted only of the officers' sidearms.

Tilt now addressed his men as a whole. "Want to turn back or keep on
till we find out what's what?"

No one wished to turn back.

Presently this rocky track approached a place where riders were forced
to circle close around the base of a great brown rock towering sheer into
the air.

The officers cocked revolvers, then passed their swords to noncommis-
sioned officers. Tilt, revolver ready, cautiously urged Resaca around the
obstruction to discover at the bend's far end a single, slightly built and

wild-haired figure wearing a dirty, blue-and-white checkered shirt, home-spun jeans, and a Confederate cap with a broken visor. This apparition was, or seemed to be, unarmed. It stiffened then, quick as a weasel, dove out of sight amid a tangle of laurels.

"Scoggins! Hamrick! After him! Don't let him get away!"

At this point information of any description was as pearls and fine gold.

The men soon reappeared, hauling along what appeared to be a squalling, biting, and kicking youth, whose long, light-brown mop of hair was flying like a wind-torn gonfalon. "You let me be, you devils."

The instant the captive spoke it became obvious that here was no youth, but a female. Not until she was dragged before Rodney Tilt did the prisoner seem to recognize his rank and stop struggling. Nevertheless, her gracefully oval, sunburned and thorn-raked features remained frozen into sullen immobility. She fixed her gaze on the ground between poorly patched boots.

"Take it easy, ma'am," Holt soothed when the girl bowed her head and clasped grubby hands as if in prayer.

"For the love of our Heavenly Father don't harm me. I'm just a friend-less lost fugitive attempting to stay alive."

Holt laughed pleasantly as Private Tyler, one of Wade Hampton's men who'd enlisted in Z Company back in Appomattox, stepped aside sucking a scratched knuckle. "Leave her be, Hamrick. A single wildcat can't do much damage to a band of heroes like us."

After carefully scanning their surroundings once more the officers returned revolvers to holsters, but Tilt, having decided this was wise, told the noncoms to retain the swords they'd been lent.

"Miss," Tilt said, "so long as you give your real name and a true account of how you came to be here and promise to furnish any information we ought to know, you'll suffer no harm."

The girl shuffled stockingless feet in homemade shoes sizes too large, then raised large, black-rimmed hazel eyes which never wavered from Rodney Tilt's craggy features.

"Sir," said she, "from your sleeve braid I judge you must be a Confederate colonel?"

"Yes. I am, or was until recently. I am Rodney Tilt."

The forlorn creature flushed, "Thank you, sir. As for me, my name is Margaret Denning Forsythe — called 'Meg' for short."

Breeding and intelligence were apparent in the quality of this young female's voice. Tilt surprised himself by adding, "At your service, ma'am."

Ramseur broke in. "Take care, Colonel. This female, for all her fine speech, may very well be serving as bait for an ambush."

"Miss," Tilt asked carefully, "suppose you explain straightaway what you're doing here and if you really are alone."

"If this is a trap," warned Ramseur, staring at the captive as if attacked by persistent doubts, "you'll be the first to die."

Although the disheveled girl's expression remained unchanged, her chin went up as she cried almost defiantly, "I am not given to lying, sir. I *am* quite alone. My family are — or were, Union sympathizers. My father, Ulrich Forsythe, was a major in the Union Army Corps of Railroad Engineers. He was killed by a sharpshooter during the siege of Nashville."

Holt asked quietly, "Where was your home?"

"We were living near Nashville when the war began."

"Nashville!" Ramseur burst out. "Nashville was full of Southern sympathizers. Yet you say your people were Unionists?"

"First off, Major, although my people lived and worked in Tennessee for a while, my father came from Philadelphia and my mother from Maine. Further, like many families among Blue Ridge, the Alleghenies and other ranges, many folks they deemed it sinful to hold fellow human beings in bondage."

"To each his own beliefs." Tilt spoke sharply. Then, in kindlier tones, "Why are you traveling alone?"

Meg Forsythe again raised her small, firmly rounded and dimpled chin. "Sir, two days ago, after my family took refuge with cousins in a small house near Fincastle some wild-looking horsemen, mostly wearing gray, on learning we were pro-Union, used that as a pretext to kill my two young brothers and carry off my mother and sister." For the first time the slight, almost skinny figure's scratched features quivered. "God alone knows what's become of them."

"How come you alone got away, Sissy?" demanded Rimfire Hamrick.

"When those Rebel horsemen closed in, I was off searching for a strayed heifer."

Tilt bent forward, compassion mingled with concern. "Miss Forsythe, can you be sure those horsemen were Confederate soldiers?"

"To tell the truth, sir, I'm not absolutely sure," admitted the girl, mechanically hitching up baggy homespun pants. "Lately, so many of your regular troops have been so badly equipped and dressed 'tis hard to tell. However, most of those villains *were* wearing gray or butternut-brown clothing." Her lips quivered. "All the same, I doubt they really belonged to your Army."

Rodney dismounted, pulled off his hat, and treated the forlorn apparition to a brief head bow. "For that we thank you, miss."

Ramseur also got off his horse and acted almost respectful. "How many did those raiders number?"

"There seemed to be a lot of them, but since I was hiding I couldn't tell much."

"Give a guess," Holt directed. "Ten, twenty, or more?"

Meg Forsythe looked about helplessly. "I'd hazard there were at least twenty or twenty-five, but there was so much confusion I can't come closer."

"They were well-armed and mounted?"

"Yes, sir."

Tilt asked, "How long ago was your home attacked?"

"Two days ago, sir."

Damn! If this country — his country — was swarming with rampaging, nondescript soldiers, how would Moluntha have fared?

The girl swayed and caught at a branch to steady herself.

Members of Z Company continued to exchange glances.

Unexpectedly, Ramseur queried, "Is there anything we can do for you, straight-off — er, miss?"

"Yes, sir. I am truly famished. I've drunk water till I'm fit to burst, but it doesn't help. If you'll only give me a piece of hardtack, a slice of meat, or even a few beans, the good Lord will bless your kindness."

"Right now we could use His blessing," Peter said, smiling. "We'll see what we can manage."

Using a worn knife, Private Tyler, that enigmatic Texan who spoke — which was seldom — with a faint foreign accent, opened a precious tin of U.S. Army corned beef while First Sergeant Duncan expertly shattered a hardtack biscuit upon a rock, then set its pieces to soften in a smoke-blackened billycan.

"There ye are, miss," the sergeant said after a bit. "Eat and don't be fearful. We don't look like much but all of us are regulars."

Mouths working and watering, gaunt troopers left off adjusting gear to watch Meg Forsythe crouch and, in pathetic eagerness, devour the uninviting mess.

Tilt slapped a horsefly from Resaca's neck, then, squatting onto his heels beside the girl, quietly asked, "Please tell me something, Miss Forsythe. Why is your speech so — er, very different from dialects used among these mountains? You talk like a lady!"

"I might pose you the same question, sir. Dirty or not, you talk and act like a gentleman — all political convictions aside."

"Thank you, ma'am. We'll go into that later, but first please satisfy my question."

Employing the back of a slender and thorn-raked hand, Meg wiped her mouth. "Sir, my mother, Faith Abbott, as I've already stated, came from Bangor, Maine, which is 'way up in New England. Before she married my father, although our family is well-connected Mamma taught school for a while, so she brought us children up to use good grammar and speak uncommon pure English around home.

"Please don't misunderstand, gentlemen, even when we were forced to take refuge in the mountains Mother never criticized local speech or customs. I —" Abruptly she fell silent when in the direction of the valley an increasing number of whistles began to wail and locomotive bells to clang.

What prompted members of Z Company to eye each other was the fact that this lot of trains had started moving westward, not in the customary easterly direction but toward Christiansburg, Saltville, Wytheville, Abingdon and Knoxville.

In a hurry and without command the men tightened girths and got on their horses.

Tilt said, "Since the Federals seem to be moving westward, Miss Forsythe, we must be on our way. Question is, what's to be done about you? We can't abandon you alone with guerrillas and outlaws everywhere."

Meg suddenly darted over and flung arms about Tilt's yellow-striped leg. Convulsively, she pressed a cheek against his dusty knee boot. "Oh, Colonel, take me with you. I promise I'll not prove a burden. I'll earn my salt."

"No doubt you mean what you say, miss, but what could you do?"

"I'll sew for all of you, and I can doctor wounds after a fashion. They say I cook extra well — frontier style — if there's anything to cook."

"All to the good," Holt nodded gravely. "Any other accomplishments?"

A faint smile curved Meg's wide, sunburned lips, "I can sing sweetly and better than most can play a zither or a dulcimer."

Tilt couldn't help laughing. "I'll take your word on those last accomplishments and hope you'll soon find opportunity to prove your skill over a cookfire." He cast a look about. "Whose horse is strong enough to carry double?"

Farrier Sergeant Knox raised a hand. "Reckon suh, a lightweight like her could ride behind me. I've got me a spare cinch and a blanket so's I kin rig a pillion of sorts."

"Very well."

Searchingly, Major Ramseur considered the girl, one swarthy brow cocked. "Before we start on our way, suppose Miss Forsythe tells us how long ago she heard other mounted men traveling in this vicinity? That is most important since we've become aware that at least one party can't be far ahead of us."

While raking aside locks of greasy, light-brown hair from faintly almond-shaped and dark-rimmed hazel eyes, the girl considered, aware that, for all his grim expression, this cavalier retained a certain courtly manner.

"About an hour or so ago I *did* hear what sounded like some horsemen following this same trail."

While easing his hurt arm, Holt inquired, "How many would you say?"

"Maybe six or eight at the most. From my hiding place I could only tell one thing —" Her gaze shifted. "They — they were wearing blue uniforms."

Blue! Z Company straightened in their saddles, studied their surroundings with fresh intensity.

"How long ago was this?"

"As I've said, about an hour or so ago, sir. I've no watch so I've no choice but to guess at the time."

Gathering Resaca's reins Tilt said, "We won't wait to rig a pillion. Miss! Climb up behind the sergeant right away."

Someone in the background sang out, "Hope that critter's spine don't split you wider'n Nature intended."

"Whoever said that is a low dog," rasped Peter Tyler, the eagle-nosed, dark-complexioned and generally silent trooper who so unobtrusively had signed Z Company's roster that last evening at Appomattox.

Crisply, Rodney Tilt ordered, "Sergeant Duncan, you and Maxwell take two well-mounted men and ride point two hundred yards in advance."

The heterogeneous company, riding in single file, hadn't followed the trail above an hour before, perhaps half a mile ahead, sounded the familiar staccato rattle of carbine and pistol shots, accompanied by shrill, yelping shouts resembling Rebel yells.

Rodney Tilt whipped out his revolver and used it to gesture forward his men, then drew and passed his sword to Sergeant Duncan.

Ramseur, after cocking his English revolver — an Adams self-cocking five-shot 54 bore — lent his blade to Corporal Hamrick. Peter Holt, who couldn't effectively manage a weapon, gave his sword to tough Corporal Connors and his big Navy Colt revolver to Sergeant Knox.

The rest drew carving and skinning knives which thanks to repeated honings glittered in the fresh spring sunlight.

The tatterdemalion troopers then took up a smart but wary trot. To Z Company's unspoken astonishment, sounds of conflict above had ceased abruptly.

"Close up!" shouted Tilt. "If there's more shouting, ride like hell and yell *loud!* As if some big outfit was coming up!"

He spurred Resaca. Stung, the stallion bounded forward so fast Tilt had no time to avoid many low-sweeping boughs. Purely by chance the trail at this point widened sufficiently to allow three troopers to ride abreast.

Startled shouts went up when Z Company burst out of the woods and galloped onto a forest meadow where about a dozen bearded men wearing gray or butternut were busy. Some scrambled onto mounts and in frantic haste, galloped out of sight along the mountain trace. A few riderless, white-eyed animals went blundering about, stirrups flapping, without purpose. Dismounted men ran after them, at the same time fumbling with their weapons.

Ramseur, without taking obvious aim, fired his Adams at a hatless fellow in a ragged gray tunic, who at once threw up arms and collapsed, to lie limp and motionless. Following his second shot another man toppled and, screaming, rolled and writhed on the hay grass until he also died.

Tilt shot a man neatly between the shoulder blades as did Sergeant Knox who, despite the handicap of Meg's spasmodic clutchings, leveled Peter Holt's Colt and killed yet another fugitive. Others of Z Company used their officers' sabers expertly to cut down a pair of ragged fugitives sprinting across the meadow.

Duncan experienced a savage satisfaction at once more feeling his blade crunch into flesh and bones, but Peter Tyler cut down his fugitive with absolute dispassion: this was merely another job to be done, just as it had been done many times before.

Then Tilt and his men noticed six blue-clad figures sprawled in awkward positions about a small fire over which they'd evidently been heating rations.

Horsemen still were crashing headlong away through the woods but a pair of handsome bay mounts bearing Federal trappings and tethered to saplings neighed fright, plunged and circled, equipment flapping and rattling.

What had occurred became unmistakably apparent to even the dullest member of Z Company. Bushwhackers, mostly wearing parts of Confederate uniform, must have surprised and slaughtered members of a small Union patrol.

Only one Federal, a spindly, pimple-speckled youth remained able to speak — but with difficulty. Too much bright blood was escaping his beardless mouth.

Tilt bent low and raised the Federal's head in hopes of slowing the hemorrhage.

"Who attacked you?"

"A passel of goddam unsurrendered Rebs —" He coughed, literally spraying sweet-smelling grass with scarlet.

"Sure they weren't guerrillas?"

"Dunno. They was led by . . . big, yellow-whiskered feller they called 'Red Grainger.'" Ugly bubbling noises punctuated his speech. "They fought mean — saw 'em slice Shaw Sprague's throat even while he was kneelin', beggin' to be spared." Dazedly, he stared into space.

Sickened, Meg watched his eyeballs roll back.

"Hope all damn Confeds roast in hell for —" The young trooper half sat up and vomited torrents of gore. Then his spare body collapsed onto the scarlet-spattered grass.

In the distance, more faintly now, sounded noises made by fleeing riders. Gripping his still-smoking revolver, Ramseur and two well-mounted men attempted a pursuit although Tilt knew it would prove fruitless — steep ravines and wild honeysuckle tangles were too many.

For a moment the Colonel remained exhausted and embittered. After Appomattox he'd cherished an illusion he'd witnessed the last of such carnage. Trotting, he made a survey of the meadow and the murdered Federals, and their surroundings before returning to his men, now dismounted and cursing loudly.

He faced Peter Holt. "The enemy won't return. Have the men round up stray horses; others will collect food, arms, ammunition and other useful equipment, but remain ready for instant action."

Peter, brow wrinkled, queried, " 'Arms,' you said?"

"Yes. All of you are to arm yourselves from the fallen. Parole or no parole, we can't risk getting murdered like these poor devils. Bushwhackers will jump anyone weaker than themselves — especially an unarmed company like ours."

Off to one side, Meg bent over a bulging haversack while slowly recovering from shock. She thought she'd steeled herself against horror and death — but now she was white and shaking, felt all melted inside.

Holt pointed to the dead youth, "Didn't I hear that dying Yank mention 'Red Grainger' as commanding the outlaws?"

Major Ramseur jerked a nod. "Sounded like that. 'Twould prove a real pleasure to ambush such brutes and stretch their dirty necks."

A few pleasurable facts became evident. Z Company had come into the possession of five strong cavalry horses completely equipped and carrying full grain sacks, and to the party's armament had been added six Chicopee sabers, as many Colt revolvers and, infinitely more valuable, three repeating Spencer carbines, which many Confederates claimed bitterly, if inaccurately could "start shootin' on Monday and never quit till Thursday." Also, there was plenty of precious ammunition.

Once the blood-stained corpses in blue were arranged in a row with glazed eyes fixedly regarding a cloudless sky, the slain outlaws were stripped of weapons and left to lie where they'd died.

Quickly, Margaret Forsythe, swallowing hard on nothing, knelt to gently close the fallen Federals' eyes while murmuring a prayer. To her surprise Peter Tyler assisted by crossing the corpses' arms and decently arranging their clothing.

Meg approached Tilt, who at the moment was examining the Spencer carbines. "What is it?"

"Please, sir, these clothes and boots I'm wearing are so worn I'm scarcely decent." Her gaze sought the body of the young trooper who'd just died. "I'm about to wash in the creek. Could — could I perhaps — er, put on some of his garments?"

"Of course, Miss Forsythe. Help yourself to his horse and anything else of his you need — they're no longer of use to him."

Tilt beckoned Peter Tyler. "The lady's about to wash in yonder creek. Whilst the rest of us dig a grave, pull off this young Yankee's boots, coat, breeches and shirt. If his jacket's too badly stained, pick out another."

To Meg he said, "Once you've finished washing, just holler and Tyler will fetch over the clothing and leave it handy." He smiled into the girl's dirty, scratched features. "Oh, one thing more, select only what fits comfortably, no matter how poor it looks. We're in for a long, hard ride; 'twould do you no good to get chafed and suffer more than you already have."

Holt, on completing a tally of captured equipment, reported, "Jasper's already feeding our critters captured grain. God, suh, you should watch them poor brutes wolf it down!"

Z Company's troopers roused and grinned when at length Margaret Forsythe aroused a small commotion by emerging from the underbrush wearing a checkered red-and-black shirt, a dark-blue shell jacket and paler-hued, yellow-striped breeches of the same color descending to brass-spurred half-length boots, sound, but obviously sizes too large.

Now that her heavy light-brown hair had been braided and stuffed under the remains of her Confederate forage cap — she didn't think it wise entirely to masquerade as a Yankee trooper — she put Rodney Tilt in mind of certain fresh-faced cadets from Virginia Military Institute he'd noticed during the Battle of Newmarket where too many lads had fought and died like grown men.

The girl drew herself up to attention before First Sergeant Duncan who, chuckling, fingered a bristly jaw. "I'm reporting for duty."

"Kin you ride well? Kin you really care for a hoss?"

"Better than most boys, Sergeant. I — I, well, I once owned and cared for a horse of my own."

Tilt sighed. He felt so almighty weary of everything. "Sergeant Knox, assign her that little, short-coupled dark-bay. I reckon he can manage her weight."

Tyler approached, offered a battered tin cup of hot coffee.

"Tell us again," Holt invited, "where you lived — before the war, I mean."

"As I've told you — when the war broke out we were living near Nashville. After a bit, Father, who was a civil railroad engineer and a Union sympathizer, made over his property to my mother." Meg's wide mouth tightened. "That done, he kissed us goodbye and told the neighbors he was off to enlist."

Ramseur, puffing on a short seegar, commented, "I presume the rascal said nothing about which side he was about to join?"

"Rascal!" Meg burst out, eyes glittering. "You, Major, are not the gentleman I mistook you for. You have only fought for your convictions; my father died for his! This war has cost my family as dear as any of yours. Now we're dispersed, bereaved, penniless and defenseless!"

Ramseur, flushing, raised a placating hand. "Your pardon, Miss Forsythe. I spoke through the bitterness of defeat. Please forgive me."

Meg flushed. "I'll think about it. If your sort haven't yet comprehended the depths of sorrow and suffering your beliefs have caused up North, you soon will learn!"

Holt hurriedly intervened. "Under their constitutions, both our countries entitle every man freely to voice his opinion."

"Excepting slaves. Once our neighbors and former friends in Nashville learned that my father was serving the Union and not the Rebel cause, they made our lives a misery. Three times my mother was forced to move us farther east and ever higher into the mountains, where live many more Union-minded folk than any of you Rebels have any notion!"

# 8

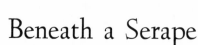

# Beneath a Serape

IN VIEW OF their mounts' continued weak condition and the state of Z
Company, Rodney Tilt decided it would be wise to recuperate in this
vicinity for a day or two, although he yearned to reach or get news of
Moluntha as soon as possible — God alone knew what tragedy even a
few hours' delay might precipitate. But how to ascertain the state of
affairs at home?

With suddenness of an explosion came an inspiration; who would be
likely to bother a solitary Negro, such as Jasper, ostensibly fleeing northward, especially if he'd no possessions worth taking? Jasper was a fine
woodsman and fairly familiar with the countryside ahead. His appearance
at Moluntha might lend survivors, if any, reason to hold out till his master
arrived with reinforcement.

Considerable persuasion was required since Jasper now considered himself a full member of Z Company and, more important, the Colonel's personal servant and bodyguard. In the end a formal order sufficed.

"Us is gonna go mighty hongry from now on," Hamrick observed. "That
nigger sho' knows how to find food where there ain't none."

"Just tell them at home to hang on and that I'm on my way. Move as
fast as possible," Tilt directed, then, for the first time in his life, shook
hands with a black man. "You've never yet failed me, Jasper. I know you
won't now."

Tears filled the lanky Negro's eyes. "Marse Rodney, you bin mighty good to me — freein' me so long ago. Ah ain't none too sure 'bout this country, but Ah'll sholy do mah best."

Armed with only an old carving knife which once had graced the Tilts' gleaming dinner table, Jasper climbed aboard his mule and disappeared without a backward glance.

Considerable activity ensued once Jasper had departed. Taut picket lines soon were rigged between trees; then horses were groomed, fed, watered, and doctored by Sergeant Knox. Shelters were improvised from branches which then were roofed by malodorous saddle blankets. Beneath these, bough beds were improvised to accommodate the company's twenty-seven remaining members.

Meanwhile, Rimfire Hamrick helped Meg and Tyler to build a sizable stone fireplace, then equipped it with lug-poles fashioned of green sticks.

Since two of the captured Federal horses had carried entrenching tools strapped to their saddles, these were employed to dig a common shallow grave for the fallen Federals. A spot in the meadow was chosen where the soil appeared deep and not too stony. Quietly, the bloodied, blue-clad corpses were arranged in it.

Once six improvised crosses had been planted above the mound's raw earth, Rodney Tilt ordered the company to fall in without loss of time, ominous, purple-gray rain clouds had commenced to roll over surrounding mountaintops.

Sergeant Duncan offered a bulging feed bag. "Sir, here are all the letters, papers, valuables, cash and greenbacks found on the dead men."

"Thank you. If ever we find time, their units will be informed of their loss and all personal property will be returned. Their money we'll keep — some greenbacks in our situation may prove vital as food."

He cupped hands and called to First Sergeant Duncan, "Fall in the company for funeral services."

Tilt looked about uncomfortably. "Hats off! Wish I were on more familiar terms with the Prayer Book. Can anyone recite the burial service?"

Margaret Forsythe, the lone figure in ill-fitting blue, stepped forward. "If you please, Colonel, my mother was a clergyman's daughter. I know the Church of England's burial service word for word."

"Thank you, miss, but please be as brisk as you can. It's about to pour any minute and there's still much to be done."

While Meg's clear voice prayed for the fallen, all stood with heads bent. Over the years they'd attended all too many similar occasions.

Once work was resumed, Meg crouched onto her heels, eyes smarting amid wavering smoke to cook a "slumgullion" consisting of bacon, corned beef, crumbled hardtack, budding ferns, and a number of fat, pale-brown roots Rimfire Hamrick had unearthed. "Yessum, these are right good an' healthy. Dunno what they're called, but the old-time Creeks and Cherokees used to feed on 'em a lot."

When cold rain commenced to slant down through the treetops, the three officers squatted to examine captured documents under that same tattered wagon cover beneath which Private Peebles had drawn his last breath.

Among the most industrious and intelligent of the enlisted men, Tilt noted, was that recruit who, at the Appomattox bivouac, had given his name as "Peter Tyler" and his former unit as "Beach's 3rd Texas Volunteer Cavalry."

Diffidently, this dark-faced young fellow had asked to enroll in Z Company. "I'm a regular, sir, and used to obeying orders," he'd stated simply. "Besides, I'm a sharpshooter, can ride anything on four legs, and I've done plenty of campaigning."

Instead of the usual issue blanket this individual carried, strapped onto his cantle, a length of brown-and-black striped woolen cloth, light, warm, and all-but-waterproof. Men who came from the Southwest said such was called a "serape."

Meg and a few others also noted that, on occasion, there were in Tyler's otherwise ordinary Texas manner of speech, barely detectable and unfamiliar inflections.

Gradually the girl also came to realize that when the sun shone brightly this hawk-nosed volunteer's long and wavy-black hair sometimes showed elusive, red-brown tints. Also she noted that Peter Tyler's slightly slanted eyes weren't truly jet-black like an Indian's, but rather of a very dark blue-black, while his gaze seldom rested long on any object but shifted ceaselessly about like that of a true frontiersman.

Peter Tyler didn't stand tall, five-foot-seven at the most, yet his body was so perfectly proportioned he lent the impression of being considerably larger.

Without demur Tilt and the other officers had agreed to enroll this remarkable fellow, especially since he had been leading a pitifully thin but otherwise strong-appearing bay mare.

Encamped, with a generous ration of nourishing, hot food in their bellies, Z Company gradually relaxed and began to recover a measure of self-respect. No longer was this a nondescript, defeated and unarmed gang of men wandering apprehensively among the mountains.

When with the onset of darkness icy rain increased in volume, Corporal Shaun Connors, with water dripping from the brim of his battered felt hat, bent under the cooking shelter's canvas and, wiping moisture from drooping walrus mustaches, informed gruffly, "Sissy, whilst you was fixin' that damn fine supper, Tyler, me, and some others have rigged you a private shelter of sorts 'mongst them maples yonder. There's a pile of boughs in it and if they don't make much of a bed, at least they ought to keep you free of puddles."

Meg's eyes stung from more than woodsmoke; then, suddenly she began to sob, "Thank you all very much."

Clumsily the corporal patted her shoulder, "No call to take on, ma'am. We ain't done much, really."

"I'm sorry, but it — it's s-so long since anyone's sh-shown me kindness. Why?"

Grunted Connors, backing out into the pelting rain, "Right from the start you put me in mind of my wife."

"I'll take that as a great compliment." Using the heel of a hand, Meg hurriedly wiped away her tears.

"Katie's been dead over two years. Bunch of jayhawkers came to our cabin, raped, then slew her. Come along. Here's a purty clean blanket."

With water trickling under her ill-fitting uniform and aware that her hair was stringier than a wornout mop, Meg followed the corporal. Once they reached the shelter with its pallet of bough tips arranged shingle-fashion, Connors turned and quietly passed her a big-bladed knife.

"Ye'd best borry this Bowie, Sissy. Never kin tell who might get idees; remember we're all cavalrymen so, no matter what our rank, we're supposed to be extra randy, and we ain't been sociable-close to a female in a damn long time; 'specially a tolerable pretty young 'un like you."

"Very well, I'll do as you say," said Meg, accepting the broad-bladed weapon. She found it surprisingly heavy in a sheath of cleverly woven leather. "Thank you, Corporal. Good night."

Shivering violently, Margaret Denning Forsythe crept inside the shelter, there to roll up in a foul-smelling saddle blanket. She felt sure she'd drop off to sleep at once, she felt so bone-weary, so drained physically, mentally and emotionally but, to her surprise, she remained fully awake.

If only she'd been granted time to wash her father's cut-off "long johns" of pure Scottish wool, which drawers she'd worn for days on end. Despite all precautions they'd become disgustingly soiled and so evil-smelling she positively hated herself.

As if to make bad matters worse it soon became evident that the dead youth's uniform was alive with "gray backs," or lice — which, stimulated by her body's warmth, commenced to bite with a vengeance. Could this sorry creature she'd become be that same gently reared girl who once would have squeaked at the very sight of a cockroach?

Rain continued to drum relentlessly, causing the improvised tent to leak icy trickles that couldn't be avoided no matter how she twisted and turned. Lord! Had she ever been so cold, so utterly miserable in body and spirit?

In fetid darkness she bit her lips; Father, she knew, had died in battle — his effects had been returned, so there could be no doubt about that. She next recalled how drunken, shouting bushwhackers had unconcernedly cut the throats of her screaming younger brothers John and James as if they'd been but a pair of shoats; fervently, she wished she could forget that scene in particular. But what could have become of Mother, and Sister Agnes who, though a spinster, had remained young-looking and pretty?

Following a lifetime habit, Meg clasped grimy hands and through chattering teeth commenced to repeat the Twenty-Third Psalm.

Next, what was about to happen to herself? True, these shaggy and sullen Confederates had treated her with rough respect, especially the officers and a soldier calling himself Peter Tyler.

This curious company's commander seemed a fine man, apparently capable of reacting instantly and surely to a variety of problems. Obviously, Colonel Tilt had been campaigning a long time; his powerfully-cast yet sensitive features showed lines which were obliterating what once must have been a genial expression.

By now she'd learned quite a bit about him; he'd been a widower for some time, having lost his wife in childbirth. He also had lost an uncle and two brothers, killed in battle. Also she'd ascertained that he'd a badly crippled brother living with his wife at a place called Moluntha Garrison, lying somewhere among the mountains of Western Virginia.

The other officers she hadn't yet considered, except that Captain Peter Holt's wounded arm badly needed attention. He seemed a pleasant but not overly intelligent young fellow.

As for raven-haired Major Philip Ramseur, despite his fire-eating attitude she found him, inexplicably, somewhat attractive.

A button on a jacket she was using for a pillow dug so hard into her cheek she roused in time to realize that someone was reaching under her shelter and had grasped one of her muddied boots.

She roused instantly, calloused fingers clamped hard upon Corporal Connor's Bowie. She gasped, "Scat! Get out of here instantly or I — I'll —" she started to say "kill you" but choked instead. Already, she had seen too much of death — often in hideous guises.

Over the patter of rain a soft voice urged, "For God's sake, Miss Forsythe, don't cry out or take alarm. I swear I mean you no harm. Although a common private, Peter Tyler is a gentleman who under no circumstances would offend a decent female."

"Stay out! What do you want?"

The voice somehow carried conviction. "With me I have brought a Mexican serape which is warm, and because of natural oils in its wool it sheds much water. The night is so very cold and this rain promises to continue, so please, señorita," the soft voice pleaded in increasingly accented tones, "I find myself miserably chilled. Under this serape we could keep one another quite comfortable — others are doing so only a few feet away. You have only to call out and they'll be here at once."

"But they aren't of different sexes. I'd rather freeze!"

"Before God, Miss Forsythe, you have my most solemn oath as a gentleman I will not again trouble you like this or attempt the least familiarity. This is simply a matter of practicality. I will leave before anyone else awakes."

Only because she was so near complete exhaustion and was shaking violently did Meg hesitate before saying wearily, "Maybe I'm a big fool to trust a complete stranger like you but I — I can't think straight right now." She broke off, her teeth chattered so. "So I — I will accept your word and you had better keep it! I have here a very sharp knife ready and I won't hesitate to use it."

"You will find no call to, señorita." Again, Tyler's mellow undertones somehow brought conviction. "The word of a Cinquegrana y Gonzales is sacred as Holy Writ."

" 'Gonzales'? They've told me you enrolled as Peter Tyler!"

" 'Tyler' was, and is, my mother's name," explained the intruder as he crawled in out of the downpour and started to unroll his striped brown-and-black serape. "You must know, because of your trust in me, that my father is General Francisco de Cinquegrana y Gonzales. At this moment I believe he is leading a revolutionary army in the Republic of Mexico against reactionaries and French invaders supporting the so-called Emperor Maximilian."

"I still don't understand why you do not bear your father's name."

A mirthless laugh escaped Tyler who, smelling like a wet setter, expertly folded the serape back in halves, then placed her own horse blanket at its foot ready to be pulled up.

"Please to lie on the inside." He ignored that faint gleam in her hand as, bewilderedly, she obeyed.

Once he had extended himself beside her with back turned, Tyler said, "I am about to disclose what no one else in North America knows."

"Can't it wait till later?"

"No. You must now know and understand me a little, one hopes. My sainted mother came from a noble English family much distinguished in your country's Foreign Service. Her name — she has been dead a long time — was Harriet Tyler. When her father, Sir Edmund, was posted as First Secretary to his Ministry in Mexico City my mother, still quite a young girl, fell desperately, madly, in love with my father." He stirred, pulled the horse blanket higher. "Due to religious differences a marriage between my parents remained an impossibility — even after I was born."

"Then — then — you are a — a —?"

"*Por favor*," he gritted, "do not mention that word! I was brought up in Texas by my mother's sister with financial help from my father. Therefore, Church and the law notwithstanding I consider myself to be legitimate and bound to respect a Spanish *hidalgo*'s code of honor."

Yawning, Meg mumbled, "I can't understand your motive in disclosing such a secret to an unknown girl. Tomorrow I may understand, but now I *must* get some sleep."

Gradually, she extended her aching body along the serape's inner fold, at the same time gripping Connors's knife; slowly her hold on it relaxed.

"Soon we will begin to get warm. You permit?"

Gradually, perhaps too expertly, he worked an arm under and about her shoulders, then tugged the serape tight about them and pulled the horse blanket still higher. It was astounding how rapidly the heat of their united bodies went to work. The last thing she remembered was Tyler saying, "*Por Dios*. We smell so bad let us pray no bear mistakes us for dead ones!"

# 9

# Tortuous Trails

A PERSISTENT MISTY DRIZZLE fell all day long, and at such an altitude among Clinch Mountains felt positively glacial. All the same, these gaunt scarecrows comprising Z Company kept reasonably warm through collecting firewood, repairing and cleaning tack, rubbing down and otherwise attending to the horses. Finally, deep little ditches surrounding their improvised quarters were dug to drain off rainwater.

At night Peter Tyler took shelter with various men; nothing was said or thought about that first miserable night. During heavy downpours men clumsily replaced missing brass buttons with ones cut from the tunics of dead Yankees, impartially interspacing "C.S.A." with "U.S.A."

All cartridge boxes, carbines, revolvers and sabers underwent minute inspection by Major Ramseur and First Sergeant Duncan.

Eventually every member of the twenty-six officers and troopers now composing Z Company found himself fairly well equipped and armed with a lethal weapon of some description.

Wearing Connors's broad-bladed Bowie strapped about her waist, Meg thoroughly checked her garments for lice, then boiled her underwear, rain or no rain. Laundry completed, she cleaned a currycomb, then used it to separate the worst tangles from strands of waist-long and rather coarse light-brown hair which she then plaited in crude fashion, much like a show horse's tail.

Trying to ignore painful throbbing in his ever-swelling arm, Peter Holt watched the girl draw her knife, then beckon Peter Tyler and, assuming a grimly determined expression, order him to hack her braid off at collar's length. Although he protested strenuously awhile, he ended by obliging.

Men grinned when they noticed the brown-featured young fellow surreptitiously tuck the severed strands into his saddlebag.

Most men, Philip Ramseur in particular, with mounting resentment, already noted how the young Texan, as he described himself, kept his eyes on Meg. But he remained pointedly respectful in speech and manner while assisting her with chores whenever possible.

Over a supper of stewed 'possum, Rodney observed that, for all this torrential downpour was a damned nuisance, it also might serve to dampen the first fierce heat of Union outrage over President Lincoln's assassination. He swallowed the last of his coffee and while thoughtfully fingering his mustaches predicted, "Let's hope his murderer will be caught swiftly and hanged higher than Haman. I've the notion that, because of this wretch's act, we Southerners are going to be made to pay a dear price."

Toward the end of Z Company's second night of encampment the rain at long last let up, mists evaporated, and the sky cleared sufficiently to permit a waning moon to reveal details of dark, still-dripping forests crowning a succession of steep, but not very lofty, mountains composing the Clinch Range.

Long before sunup Z Company had broken camp and, saddles creaking and curb chains jingling, in single file resumed their march behind Johnny Maxwell. The unerring manner in which the mountaineer almost invariably selected the correct fork in any track inspired confidence.

Tails jerking, striped little chipmunks sauced the passersby and birds sang so melodiously it seemed incredible that in the valley below, inescapable evidences of destruction and abandoned farmlands marked the verges of the Virginia & Tennessee's right-of-way between Lynchburg and Danville.

How grand it felt once more to ride stronger, well-groomed mounts and to be fairly well-armed; self-respect mounting, everyone's spirits improved, for all Z Company, at best, remained a distinctly tatterdemalion outfit. If only a fellow knew what he could expect when, as, and if he reached home, his spirits would have risen higher still.

Although some horses still limped and had to be led unmounted, Sergeant Knox had reshod and doctored the fitter beasts to the best of his considerable ability.

On encountering any steep rise Rodney Tilt invariably ordered all hands to get off and lead. Even on level ground, the company was ordered to dismount every half hour, to ease girths and briefly lift saddle blankets that air might circulate over sore, spotted and bony backs; progress therefore remained painfully slow, nothing like the space-eating speed with which these men had ridden behind such leaders as Jeb Stuart, Jubal Early, John Morgan, Mosby and their like.

But why hurry? Many had no foreseeable future beyond aimless wandering about, until death settled their problems once and for all.

When the pointed white church steeples of Salem became visible far below Tilt, now more familiar with this terrain than Maxwell, attempted to identify various landmarks and took over as chief guide, leading toward the approaches of a still-distant bypass called Ajax's Gap which should lead across the North Holston River over Moccasin Ridge toward Copper Ridge and, God willing, to Moluntha Garrison.

Even under misty conditions it proved fairly easy for Tilt to keep directions fairly straight for, down in the Clinch Valley, occasional faint whistlings and the bells of locomotives helped a lot. Union engineers obviously had restored those same rails, culverts and bridges they'd ripped up so efficiently only a few weeks earlier.

At this point Major Philip Ramseur, especially when Meg was present, appeared to shake off his depression, actually smiled on occasion and complained less about the total lack of liquor, decent food and amorous pursuits.

Meg Forsythe, now clad in a clean, red-and-white checked shirt, blue shell jacket and yellow-striped breeches supported by shortened suspenders, brought up the rear commanded by Peter Holt who, daily, was growing weaker because his wound was turning a gangrenous green.

Alas, Z Company now counted but twenty-one souls including Margaret Forsythe for, only the day before, some troopers from Georgia or Alabama had ridden off into the hills, ostensibly to scout for forage, but had failed to report back. Perhaps, now that their horses were in better condition, they figured on riding south to join Joe Johnston's reportedly still unsurrendered forces, or had they been cut down in some swift and silent ambush?

Smoke rising in various directions argued that Z Company was far from being genuinely isolated.

# 10

## News from Wytheville

S PIRITS ROSE a few days later when, while crossing a spur of the
Brumley Range, Hamrick circled out along both flanks and discovered, amid a clump of redbuds growing behind an abandoned cabin, a
log corncrib still containing a fair supply of undamaged oats. Who might
have deserted such precious fodder or why, was anybody's guess.

Colonel Rodney Tilt, freshly shaved and with sweeping dark mustaches
trimmed after a fashion, felt infinitely relieved on sighting in the distance
a group of four rounded, blue-green hills of nearly equal height surrounding a hamlet and crossroads; Wytheville, Virginia, must lie not far
ahead.

Half an hour later he reined in above the town just below the skyline,
then on foot advanced to study a miscellaneous collection of freight and
passenger cars occupying a small marshaling yard on the outskirts of the
sprawling and once-thriving town of Wytheville.

Smoke arose above one house chimney in three of those dwellings
that remained standing.

He wasn't astonished to note no fumes whatsoever drifting out of the
Ajax lead mine's lone and lofty brick smokestack. Of the red brick office
building, storage sheds, foundries and labor barracks only charred ruins
remained.

Down yonder a bell-funneled, smoke-spouting locomotive was starting
to haul a train of passenger cars laden with blue-clad troops out of the
town in a westerly direction.

Rod's lips tightened. How often had he, Peter, Marc Peabody and other local gallants ridden into Wytheville to visit friends or kin, or perhaps to attend some revival meeting, a political rally, or to participate in someone's wedding? Sometimes during such festivities some young buck would tilt: this meant galloping with a leveled lance in an attempt to tear free a brass ring suspended from a limb and thereby earn the right to name some lovely lass to be crowned with flowers as "Queen of Love and Beauty." Would another "tournament" ever take place? Not in a long time, by the way things were going.

Had Tilt possessed a telescope or field glasses, he might have discovered details of particular significance to a major shareholder in the Ajax mine like himself — but of course he didn't.

To ease a cramp forming in one buttock he remounted and draped a booted and spurred leg across Resaca's withers while recalling the one and only time Marc Peabody had got so royally drunk on champagne punch he'd insisted on conducting the Italian orchestra at Laura Jackson's debutante cotillion after flattening its conductor.

And what manner of homecoming would Marcus Eames Peabody receive once he returned to Providence? At least Marc probably would find his home intact, his family and his family's business thriving. Or would he? The Enos Peabody branch of that distinguished family, unlike many Yankee nabobs, almost without exception had set duty to Country above the worship of the great God Mammon ever since the successful Siege of the mighty fortress of Louisburg way back in 1745 without the aid of any British troops whatsoever. The Colonists then first had discovered that in union lay strength.

A great many Northern families must feel like the Enos Peabodys, otherwise why should Federal casualty lists have proved so appallingly high throughout the War? Knowledgeable men estimated that the North had lost three men killed for every dead Southerner.

After supper Tilt assembled the company amid drifting cooking smoke and told them that intelligence concerning the true state of affairs in this region was absolutely essential. Riding blindfolded about the countryside like this was to invite all manner of dangers. Would someone familiar with Wytheville, but not well-known in town, volunteer to ride down and quietly collect such significant news as might be available? He'd do so himself were he not too well-known.

A dish-faced, scrawny, and otherwise insignificant-looking trooper named Andy Scoggins lifted a grimy paw and allowed that he'd once toiled in the Ajax mine, so knew the place tolerably well.

"No chance of anybody's recognizing you?" Tilt queried. "That wouldn't do at all — at all."

"Naw, suh, I only worked there a few weeks and that wuz befo' the war."

"Very well," Tilt said briskly. "Leave your carbine behind, ride a mule, and early tomorrow go into town like the homeward-bound paroled veteran you are. Ask as few questions as you can, but listen hard and try to learn what the enemy — er, the Federals, intend to do. But, no matter what, rejoin us here before dark and make certain you're not noticed or being followed."

Anxiety racked Z Company's commander's thoughts. Suppose some strong Blue patrol — there must be plenty scouring these mountains for deserters and bushwhackers — suddenly closed in and, contrary to parole terms, found his force bearing arms?

The sun was about to set when a crackle of underbrush and the clip-clop of Scoggins's lop-eared mule sounded below, setting everyone on the alert. Still employing a rope hackamore, a ragged blanket and a surcingle in place of a saddle, the emissary appeared, grinning through gapped teeth.

"Yep," he told the officers. "I sure fooled them Blue-bellies complete. They let me wander wherever I listed, even about the freight yards."

"How badly hurt is the town?" Holt asked.

"Pretty bad off. Nigh half the houses are burned down or wrecked and all have been plundered."

"If you never once got stopped," Sergeant Duncan observed, "they must be 'way off guard."

"No they ain't. I seen tough-lookin' provost patrols halt quite a few of our surrendered officers, mostly well-mounted men, and demand to see their papers. If they couldn't show any they got arrested on the spot, then hauled off to a stockade they've throwed up along the west side of town."

Ramseur, scowling, asked, "Was this stockade crowded?"

"Yep, suh, them provosts are a suspicious lot. They 'llowed there was room for plenty more Rebs and they was lookin' for customers ever since Mr. Lincoln wuz slain."

Everyone looked apprehensive, especially when Scoggins added uneasily, "Colonel, suh, I bin told that in the olden times a messenger bearin' bad tidin's got kilt for his pains. Better ready that Colt, suh, 'cause I've got ill news about yer mine."

Rodney Tilt's deep-set dark eyes narrowed and his slash of a mouth tightened. "This is 1865, so don't hesitate to speak up. In what shape is our mine?"

Nervously, the trooper squirted tobacco juice at a clump of blossoming laurels. "Suh, I didn't dast try to get a real good look down the main shaft, but above ground all the works sho' are wrecked and burned like Satan and all his crew had done it. General Stoneman's raiders must ha' had some miners along; nobody else would know just how to wreck minin' machinery so complete."

Peter Holt drew a deep breath. "Then the Ajax really *is* ruined?" Holt's family also had had an interest in the operation.

"Dunno, suh, I ain't no real miner — only worked above ground, thank God; but I overheered knowledgeable men sayin' that, sure as Scripture, 'twill take one hell of a long time and a mint o' cash to get that there shaft fit to work again."

Unexpectedly, Peter Tyler asked, "What would you say about how the ordinary folks are feeling about the surrender at Appomattox?"

Scoggins shifted uneasily. "Well, friend Tyler, all I kin say truthful-like is that most people down yonder are pleased the war's over, no matter what."

"Damn such spiritless swine!" rasped Ramseur. "Our Cause is *not* lost! We've still plenty of men in the field — Johnston's for example, and more across the Mississippi!"

Scoggins managed to appear more miserable than ever as he mumbled, "Beggin' yer pardon, suh, but all over Wytheville I saw broadsides posted sayin' that, a few days ago, Uncle Joe Johnston surrendered his army to that nigger-stealin' bastard Sherman; almost everybody's 'bout ready to holler 'quits.' Some even wuz talkin' 'bout joinin' the old Union and startin' over, even if they ain't likely to forgit and forgive what's happened these past years."

Stiffening, Ramseur growled, "I don't believe it! Only a cowardly pack of spiritless Western Virginians would talk like that!"

For the first time since Z Company set out, furious color surged into Rodney Tilt's high-boned features. Fists clenched, he confronted the South Carolinian. "Major! I demand an immediate apology for that remark. Western Virginians may not talk so loud as some of you Tidewater fire-eaters, but we have fought as long and maybe harder than any troops in the Army of Northern Virginia!"

The South Carolinian attempted a placating smile. "I spoke in haste, sir, and in anger." When he offered his hand Tilt took it with evident hesitation. "The fighting may be over but our Cause is *not* lost! Far from it! Please forgive me."

Tilt then turned abruptly to Scoggins. "Aside from the mine, how badly damaged is the rest of Wytheville?"

Margaret Forsythe, standing unnoticed on the edge of the group, strained to hear the reply.

"Like I said, suh, most houses is empty and pretty well smashed up; most civilians refugeed and ain't yet come back since the place is fair crawlin' with Blue-bellies of all arms. Every nigger in the County 'ceptin' fo' the old, the ailin' and very young uns is clearin' out or fightin' to board any train headin' east."

Holt wearily commented, "Which means there'll be no labor to be had for God knows how long. What's to be done?"

Rodney fingered his jutting blue-black chin. "Something will be done — it'll have to be." Again he wondered where Marcus Peabody might be found at this moment. Yankee or not — in him seemed to lie his only hope for immediate assistance should worse come to worst. Through Marc's family connections, which included the despicable but politically omnipotent General "Silver Spoon" Ben Butler, something might be accomplished.

During their brief conversation at the bivouac, Marc had stated that his father, after having suffered a crippling wound at Gettysburg, was in Washington on duty with the War Department.

Following a pause Tilt inquired, "Hear anything about Federal patrols being sent toward Brumley's Gap?"

"Yep. A good many troops headed that-a-way. Some wuz supposed to scout even beyond Ajax's Gap."

At this Holt roused momentarily. "Any troops heading for Russell County?"

"Yep, some rode in that direction." He screwed up red-rimmed little eyes. "Say, Cap'n, didn't I hear you say once yer Paw's place is named 'Richlands'?"

The yellow-haired captain nodded. "Yes. What about it?"

"I heerd tell Yankee cavalry burned the hull place lock, stock and barrel, flatter'n Maw's flapjacks, then traveled on toward Ajax's Gap in Moccasin Ridge."

# 11

## Ambush

As if to atone for the generally wretched weather prevailing after the surrender, the last weeks of April burst into unusually warm and tender glory. Patches of dogwoods, laurels, redbuds and wild azaleas brightened dark hills and mountainsides with delicate, eye-catching color.

Deer and their leggy, spotted fawns, not having been hard-hunted in nearly four years, proved provocatively unwary but, in obedience to strict orders, no member of Z Company dared fire on them — for all that weathered and bearded mouths watered over the thought of venison as relief from the monotony of a scanty and nearly tasteless diet of army rations, occasionally relieved by snared rabbits, fledgling birds, or clubbed porcupines.

In all directions birds warbled or chirped and great bevies of bob-white quail whirred off over mountain meadows. Sweet, warm odors from freshly leaved trees gradually became perceptible to nostrils too long inured to such subtle fragrances.

Just below the rest of an especially steep rise on the northern side of Moccasin Ridge, Rodney Tilt reined in and raised a hard brown hand, whereupon his followers at once dismounted without command to commence the familiar routine of rubbing bony legs, easing girths and raising saddle cloths. Meanwhile their ribby mounts cropped eagerly at any greenery within reach.

Margaret Forsythe decided, while slipping a hand beneath her belt to massage a sore and aching bottom, that now the appearance of Z Company, for all its still unkempt appearance, offered a definite improvement over the band she'd first encountered nearly a fortnight ago on that lonely mountain trace. Gaunt features had filled out visibly and showed healthier hues — all save Peter Holt. Why, just yesterday, Rimfire Hamrick had declared himself ready and able to lick his weight in wildcats.

Remains of uniforms had been washed and, whenever opportunity offered, Margaret Forsythe had strained eyesight by firelight, replacing buttons and mending a variety of rips and tears. She even stitched rough, varicolored patches over spots where cloth worn thin at last had given way.

Although the mounts appeared noticeably stronger, not one would have won a booby prize at even the roughest sort of a county fair. However, their coats no longer were stark or manes snarled, nor were their eyes dull; so much time had been devoted to currying and grooming, a majority of sores and wounds had healed, thanks to the skill and devotion of Farrier Sergeant Knox.

Mounts worn-out beyond hope of redemption had been abandoned only because this meant more food and care would be available for the remaining animals.

Edged weapons of all sorts had been scoured and then sharpened on flint outcroppings. Ammunition and firearms — all had been cleaned and oiled to admiration.

Unobtrusively, Peter Tyler saw to it that Avalon, as Meg had christened her small, dark-bay mare, along with his own "claybank" gelding, received liberal shares of such meager fodder as Z Company managed to come across.

Leading Resaca by reins looped over an arm, Rodney Tilt joined Philip Ramseur who, with Tyler, enjoyed the keenest eyesight in the company, now shrunk to sixteen members.

Gripped by apprehensions, Tilt, firm long jaws shaven clean again, watched Maxwell, wide-brimmed Union black slouch hat flopping, advance before offering a clumsy salute. The Colonel returned it, then invited, "Well, Maxwell, what is it?"

"Please, suh, Ah'd like to ax somethin' of you."

A quality in the veteran's tone drew Tilt's attention. "What is it?"

"Suh, by yer leave I'd like you to discharge me so's Ah kin quit this track and foller a trail I done recon'ized a while back. Heads south toward Bristol and mah own neck o' the woods."

Sharply Ramseur broke in, "Why, of all times, should you quit us now that we're scarce three days' ride short of Moluntha?"

Using a patched boot toe the lanky mountaineer scraped rusty pine needles on the ground. "Well, suh, till I j'ined up back in '62 I dwelt and trapped for many a year only a long hoot an' a holler to the no'th of

Bristol. Ain't going wait longer to find iffen I've a home or any family left."

Peter Holt said quickly, "No one can blame you for that—"

"You'll never get there alone," objected the South Carolinian. "Besides, your quitting will weaken us at a critical time."

Maxwell surveyed the Major with an unfamiliar gleam in his small black eyes. "Remember suh, when we-uns signed up for this company back in Appomattox 'twas understood any of us could drop out freely when he felt so minded, provided he give notice, which some ain't done. I've done my full duty with this company."

"And much more than some." Smiling, despite sharply rising anxiety, Tilt offered his hand. "Maxwell, you have the undoubted right and per-haps an obligation to ride southward. Too bad there's no proper way we can thank you for those perils your guiding has spared us." His grip grew firmer. "Never forget, John Maxwell, a warm welcome awaits you, or any of your close kin, at Moluntha Garrison. Stay as long as you please and I hope you'll take up a holding on my property, free of cost."

Peter Holt thought, but did not say, providing Moluntha is still standing.

Grinning like a well-fed fox, Maxwell rode down the line clapping this or that man on his shoulder or shaking hands. He got the surprise of his life when Meg kicked forward her mount till she got close enough to bend over and brush lips across his cheek. "Hope you don't mind, Mr. Max-well. God send you find your home whole and your dear ones safe."

Maxwell's eyes suddenly filled. "Why, why, thank 'e kindly, miss. Reckon the Good Lawd just might listen to *your* hopes for me.

"So long, boys! The best of luck to one and all!"

The mountaineer reined aside his rangy buckskin, with carbine held ready and balanced across the pommel.

"So long." "Take care o' yerself!" "See you sometime, sure 'nough!"

All present knew how often Maxwell had spared Z Company miles of useless or dangerous travel, how tirelessly he'd scouted this beautiful but often forbidding countryside with a skill approximated only by Peter Tyler and Rimfire Hamrick.

Before starting to descend this steep trail leading downward and paralleling a brook gurgling and splashing toward a little river below, Tilt watched a few trout dart away before turning in his saddle and softly calling, "Hamrick, what about that ford?"

"Everything 'pears all right around this crossin', suh. Seems shallow 'thout too many boulders."

"Good, but all the same I'll lead a point a quarter-mile ahead. Tyler and Hamrick, come along. You, too." He motioned forward the Forsythe girl, who with shortened hair and wearing yellow-striped blue breeches resembled more than ever a stripling youth, of which there were far too many in both armies — especially the Southern.

"Yours is a good animal, Meg, so you could get back fast to alert the main body should we find anything amiss. Major Ramseur will be in command with Sergeant Duncan as his second. Captain Holt and Sergeant Knox will bring up the rear."

Tilt couldn't help smiling to himself. How pretentious to issue such grandiose orders to a handful of shabbily garbed and ill-accoutered riders.

Gaze probing heavy underbrush shrouding the far bank, Tilt led the point downward, slipping and starting a miniature cascade of pebbles rolling down to the crossing's ripples.

At this point Tilt calculated the ford measured only about fifty or seventy yards across. Nevertheless everyone unslung carbines, maintained an extra-sharp lookout; fords like this were well-known to be favored spots for ambushes.

Tilt now noticed that this track rose very steeply beyond the water. Nothing untoward was seen or heard so, dripping, the point splashed out of the water and then their mounts started bucking and scrambling upward, again sending a volley of small stones to rattling downward.

On casting a final backward look, Tilt noticed that Philip Ramseur, his hat set at its usual jaunty angle, was sitting straight as if on parade while leading his followers to the water's edge where he must delay until the point opened its lead. A sharp dip in this trail then concealed all vision of the shimmering, boulder-strewn ford.

To Major Philip Ramseur it was pleasing again to feel on his own, at least momentarily. While he and Rodney Tilt were by no means antagonistic, they'd exchanged only necessary communications and courtesies since the South Carolinian's disparaging comments concerning Western Virginians.

Ramseur delayed a full fifteen minutes before ordering an advance, after the point had become lost to sight. Through force of habit he loosened the lanyard securing his long-barreled revolver and drew it from its holster, at the same time calling, "Men! Ready your arms."

Once the party entered the water it became strung out because cold water commenced to curl about the animals' legs and a few riders had allowed their mounts to halt long enough to gulp a few mouthfuls.

At once Ramseur noticed, shouted angrily, "Keep closed up, dammit! Duncan, keep 'em closed up!"

The abbreviated line's leader was only thirty feet short of the far bank when, with the suddenness of a conjurer's trick, a stocky, red-faced Federal officer, the brass buttons on his blue tunic winking in the sun, stepped out of a clump of the underbrush.

Leveling a carbine he yelled, "Halt, you damn' Rebels! Halt where you are! Drop those weapons into the water!"

Sight of that hated blue uniform, yellow-striped breeches and all, started a flaming whirlwind abruptly to spin and roar about Philip Ramseur's brain. He then made the mistake of his life. Although wearing full Confederate uniform, he took instant aim and shot the Union officer dead.

Sergeant Philemon Knox, riding just behind Peter Holt and therefore last in column, always had been blessed with quick reactions. So the instant he glimpsed that brass-ornamented black slouch hat and soldiers in blue rising magically amid underbrush he wrenched about his rangy "claybank" gelding and recrossed those few yards of water separating him from the trail he just had quitted.

Hunched low over his mount's neck, Knox, although usually a gentle man, raked sharp-roweled spurs along his animal's sides even as the report of Major Ramseur's shot commenced to echo along this steep and narrow valley. Next, he heard furious shouts and irregular but heavy carbine fire, so paid attention only toward retreating in a big hurry.

Even while the familiar, rank-smelling smoke of his revolver eddied about him, Ramseur simply could not believe what he'd done; only stared as if mesmerized at about thirty blue cavalrymen who came running and shouting out of the underbrush and starting to fire. He saw the officer he'd killed jerk spasmodically forward until his hat fell off, then drift away downstream; his carbine splashed into the current, raising a diamantine shower of spray. The Federal's body then tumbled after it, limp as any rag doll.

Once a volley of shots crackled, the South Carolinian's black charger reared convulsively up, up until it fell heavily over backward into the shallows and pinned its rider's leg beneath it. Ramseur's head struck a rock when he fell, so he only half-heard his followers open fire.

Captain Peter Holt no longer had cause to worry over his gangrenous arm; a minié ball had struck him directly between his bright blue eyes.

Some ex-Confederates, ignoring the deadly whistling of lead, raised a wavering Rebel yell, drew sabers and spurred forward, while those carrying firearms fired a few ineffective shots before a volley from the far bank killed Sergeant Duncan and emptied three other saddles.

Two horses screamed, then collapsed. Bodies, streaking the water with scarlet, started tumbling downstream under the current's powerful propulsion.

Corporal Connors flung away his saber, then raised hands, screeching, "For Mary's sake, don't kill us all!"

A short-bodied and hatchet-faced officer, a lieutenant by his shoulder straps of yellow velvet, bellowed, "Drop yer weapons and come this way, slow. Clasp hands over yer heads, else ye'll get blown to bits!"

Icy-cold water in a measure restored Philip Ramseur to consciousness but, spasmodically, he still was clinging to his revolver when blaspheming blue-clad troopers splashed over the shallows toward him. They wrenched away his weapon, then dragged him ashore, spurred and booted legs trailing.

Only two members of Z Company remained mounted. Rigid with fear, they rode toward the bank where cursing, furious Federals stood waiting, carbines ready.

Features quivering and scarlet beneath his scrubby yellow beard, a big-framed officer, whose men addressed him as "Lieutenant Basden," ordered both riders dragged from their saddles and the men on foot to be seized immediately.

"Tie these bastards up and tie 'em *tight!*" He drew a deep breath before looking about. "I call on all you men to bear witness that every one of these sons of bitches is wearing Confed uniform and that they have fired upon uniformed troops of the United States Army. Secure loose horses."

He then beckoned a couple of leathery-faced corporals. "Wade out and drag Captain Chamberlain's body ashore."

Once the corpse of the officer Ramseur had shot lay, dripping and inert, on the beach's trampled yellow sand, Lieutenant Basden shouted, "Sergeant Fogarty. Fetch me that officer who murdered the Captain, but don't shoot the son of a bitch. I want him alive."

Features gone a ghastly yellow-white beneath his black hair and goatee, the South Carolinian made an effort to straighten up, but a punch in the belly caused him to double over again.

Once the five prisoners had been lined up, shaking and white-eyed, within a ring of grim-faced captors, Lieutenant Basden remembered something.

"Sergeant Beecher! Take two squads and ride like hell after that point we let pass. Bring 'em back dead or alive!"

Apparently no one seemed to have noticed Sergeant Knox's abrupt retreat.

Colonel Tilt guessed what had happened the instant carbines started to crackle at the ford.

"Ride like hell," he ordered. "If the Feds start to catch up, scatter — meet later — somewhere along this trail."

Tilt then dug spurs into Resaca as never before. Low branches quickly knocked off the fugitives' hats, including Meg's gray cap, mercilessly whipped faces, and momentarily half-blinded them. The horses made poor time, slipping as they did on loose or moss-covered rocks or stumbling over roots and leaping wind-felled trees.

Tilt and the Forsythe girl bent low over their mounts' extended necks and soon outdistanced Tyler and Hamrick, but they still could hear shouting and the clatter of hoofs growing steadily louder.

First Rimfire Hamrick then, moments later, Peter Tyler veered off the trail into promising openings, creating what sounded to them like an almighty racket.

Although separated, the fugitives, as experienced campaigners, pulled up the moment they reached a possibly safe distance. Dismounting, they led their winded horses deep into wild tangles of honeysuckle vines and underbrush where they waited, carbines cocked, breathless. Their luck proved good. A column of Federals pounded right on by.

Purposely, Rodney shouted orders now and then while following the trail with Meg only a couple of lengths behind him. So long as he kept on creating a racket he reckoned the Blue-bellies might follow him and leave Tyler and Hamrick to win clear.

At length the Master of Moluntha yelled over his shoulder, "Meg! Turn off — that thin spot. Ride in — stay quiet till you're certain all Feds have turned back before you return to trail!"

Face crisscrossed crimson by lashing branches and cropped hair fluttering, Meg, utterly breathless, turned into the woods. For a while she could hear Tilt still panting orders to imaginary followers.

At long last, when she recognized no sounds of pursuit she collapsed, shuddering and weeping uncontrollably. To make matters worse the "Curse of Eve" chose that moment to manifest itself.

Corporal Andy Scoggins simply couldn't credit what was happening. Here he stood, dripping, hands bound tight behind him, ringed in by hard, hate-filled and mostly bearded faces. From a corner of his eye he glimpsed Major Ramseur's wet, gray-clad figure sway while the Feds tied him up. The South Carolinian kept babbling incoherently, blinking and shaking his head as if trying to clear it; blood and water continued to trickle inside his greasy collar of yellow velvet.

As for the other three prisoners, they remained slouched and passive in attitudes of hopeless resignation.

A brass device of crossed sabers decorating the front of Lieutenant Basden's slouch hat winked like an angry eye when, still trembling with outrage, he strode up to Ramseur. "Tell me, Major — I judge by the braid on your uniform you must be one — can you offer any legal excuse why you parole breakers shouldn't be hanged here and now?"

The South Carolinian managed a defiant look. "Sir, we are but a party of surrendered troops traveling homeward."

"— Under parole?"

"Yes, sir. Granted at Appomattox. Look inside my jacket and you'll find my parole."

"No point. I've read such plenty of times, so I know just what it says. Can you deny that you took oath not to take up arms against Federal troops until properly exchanged?"

Ramseur straightened. "You ambushed us!"

"True, but all the same you've broken your given word. You and your men were armed and, without being fired upon, attacked Federal troops on duty. Isn't that so?"

Ramseur could only glare.

Corporal Scoggins, eyes rolling, whimpered, "Please, suh, we only carried them arms to defend ourselves 'gainst outlaws."

"Perhaps, but weren't we wearing regulation Federal uniforms and acting under orders? Did we look like outlaws?"

"N-no, suh. But it all came so sudden —" he commenced to blubber. "Please, suh, I've a wife and two little children. W'thout me they — they'll starve. For God's sake don't hang us. We didn't go for to —" A blow on the jaw silenced Scoggins.

"Shut up! You ought to have thought about them before breaking your parole terms."

Once more Philip Ramseur attempted dignity, tried to stand to attention. "Sir, all this is my fault. Execute me if you must, but for God's sake don't kill my men. As gentlemen, as one officer to another, I implore —"

Snarled the Union lieutenant, "You may be an officer, because the Rebs have been hard up lately, but where I come from you don't rate as a gentleman. Gentlemen are honor-bound to honor their word! As matters stand, you rate no higher than a bushwhacker or an ordinary outlaw!"

Long and bony features gone gray but with tufted chin lifting, Ramseur said steadily, "Nevertheless, sir, I *am* a gentleman. Shoot me if you must, but for God's sake don't hang me like a common felon."

A trooper in the background looked at his captain's body sprawled on the sandy beach and watched dark blood still oozing through a red-ringed hole in the center of the dead man's tunic, then growled, "Shut your goddam dirty mouth, Reb! Quit whining and try to meet your God like a brave man."

Lieutenant Basden snapped, "Shut up everybody. We'll now get on with this execution. Hawkins, Martin, Williams, McBride and Bellows, cast loose your tether ropes. You, Peters, shinny up yonder oak and pick a sound, strong branch. Does anybody present know how to tie a proper hangman's noose?"

"I can," volunteered a bony-faced trooper. "Seen such tied plenty of times down to Andersonville."

Once the prisoners had been relieved of their parole papers Lieutenant Basden barked, "Lift these bastards onto horseback and lead 'em below the nooses, then, on my signal, pull the animals out from under 'em!"

All was over with almost incredible rapidity. Five gray or brown-clad figures swayed with heads cocked unnaturally to the right and with boot toes pointing downwards. Urine from some bodies dripped slowly to the ground.

Sergeant Fogarty wanted to know, "Shall we bury the Captain here or do we fetch his body back to camp?"

"Tie his body across his saddle, you fool. Captain Chamberlain deserves and will get a Christian burial. As for those brutes, for all I care they can swing till their necks rot through."

Basden then calmed somewhat and pulled out a pencil. "Sergeant, hand me all their parole forms."

On a flat rock the lieutenant smoothed the paroles and scrutinized them before endorsing each with his name, rank and regimental number. Then he printed on each: "Thus to all Rebel parole-breakers."

Once Basden had finished writing he snapped, "I want these buttoned tight onto the corpses. Maybe they'll serve as warning that parole terms are to be observed!"

# Part Two

# Moluntha Garrison

# 12

---◆---

# A Baying of Hounds

To Major Bushrod Grady Tilt, C.S.A. (retired), it appeared that this drizzling rain and mist which for two days had been obscuring the dark forests, sharp, high hills, and low mountains almost enclosing Moluntha Garrison's rich acreage, seemed ready to let up.

He and three women, huddled under shawls to shield themselves against the persistent chill pervading Moluntha Garrison, sat around a scarred but delicate card table made of fruitwoods set as close as possible to a small fireplace ornamented by a mantelpiece of handsomely carved English walnut that once had heated Brian Tilt's pine-paneled cardroom.

Near the table's center stood a single coal-oil lamp whose flame, through a badly cracked chimney, gave off sufficient light only to emphasize shadows, although its wick painstakingly had been trimmed by Ruthelma Donelson Tilt, mother to Bushrod, Rodney, Otho, Albert, and Loretta, and grandmother to Bushrod's own little son, Oliver.

Rodney's twin sister, Loretta, reached out to turn down the lamp since it contained the last kerosene remaining in Moluntha. Caroline, Bushrod's wife, seemed lost in thought.

As always, one place, fully set, remained unoccupied at the card table. At Grandma Ruthelma's insistence this was kept so in anticipation of Rodney's return. Before her death in childbirth last winter Louisa Merryman Tilt had exacted a solemn promise that this should be done.

A once-lovely boot-scarred and battered paneled door giving into the butler's empty pantry had been left slightly ajar, not only to simplify communication with the kitchen but also to admit a trifle of heat from that direction.

Tableware presented a bizarre mixture of ugly but sturdy native-fired crockery and items of delicate French and English china which, somehow, had survived destruction through a brief occupation by a Federal scouting party. General Stoneman's men had proved rapacious but otherwise fairly well-behaved. Of course when they'd arrived not a single item of silver or plate was to be seen, all of it having been buried many months before.

Frowning, Bushrod knitted heavy brown brows while settling back in his big George II armchair. He was thinking back to last year when, on Christmas Day, a half-troop of Blue cavalry suddenly had surrounded Moluntha and had lingered for two days, thawing out, refreshing their horses, and also efficiently ransacking not only the main house but also its outbuildings.

Although offering no intentional insults or physical violence whatsoever, the Yankees nonetheless had loaded into captured phaetons, carts and buggies all they could carry off of such useful items as leather harness, fodder, blankets, and warm clothing of any description.

When they departed they'd also herded along with them every head of livestock Hannibal and Benjy hadn't been able to drive to safe hiding. Too bad a layer of new-fallen snow had betrayed the route to all but a few of these hideaways.

Unfortunately, on the last day of their stay, the Yankees had discovered Brian Tilt's secret wine cellar with the result that considerable wanton destruction had ensued. Windows and mirrors had been smashed and priceless furniture which couldn't be carried off had either been ruined or mutilated.

Possibly such restraint as had been employed by the raiders was due to the fact that their commanding officer's hometown lay in eastern Kentucky and, when slightly drunk, he once had admitted having several close relatives wearing gray.

Bushrod locked teeth but winced while shifting on a hassock an ankle struck by a stray minié ball during that bloody struggle of the Wilderness. It still caused much pain but by now he'd come to appreciate how fortunate he'd been on having this wound treated by a competent surgeon; such being all too scarce in the Army of Northern Virginia. This "sawbones," as the troops termed all doctors, had refused to amputate, saying, "In my opinion, Major, your foot is not in such bad shape as it might appear. With care it should heal eventually but you'll never do much running about or jumping again. However, you probably will be able to ride a gentle horse, which is a damned sight better than stumping about on crutches or wearing a peg leg like so many other poor wretches."

Although a year younger than Rodney, round-faced Bushrod appeared older, thanks to a long, light-brown beard, bushy side-whiskers, and lines traced across his features by almost continual pain.

Sighing, the cripple reached for a steaming tin pot of burnt-acorn coffee. The best that could be said for such a miserable, bitter brew was that it was hot and clean, though tasteless, since sugar and even molasses for months had been utterly unobtainable and Stoneman's raiders had led away the family's only milk cow.

His wife, Caroline, blond hair carelessly braided, held out a chipped Sèvres cup lacking its saucer, then blew on its contents, saying in the musical accent of her native New Orleans, "Now that this dratted war seems to be about over, wonder how long 'twill be before we taste real coffee and sugar?"

"God only knows and He won't tell," sighed Bushrod, again easing his wounded foot. "Tomorrow's Sunday. Is it my turn to put flowers on Louisa's and the baby's graves?"

"Yes," said his wife. "But I'll do it for you since your foot's got sore again."

Another patter of rain tapped at the cardroom's windowpanes, all of which had been spared by the raiders for some inexplicable reason, although out of sheer deviltry they'd shattered so many panes in the dining room, in the withdrawing room, and in most of the upstairs bedrooms that snow and rain often created puddles on once-gleaming French parquet floors which had been the pride and joy of Laura-Lee Downey, that lovely but firm-willed belle whom Rodney's grandfather, Brian, had married and carried off from Richmond to dwell in the "wilderness" as her aristocratic, if slightly inbred, family usually described the western part of their State.

Even at seventy-two, sparrow-thin Grandma Ruthelma still sat straight as any arrow and never touched shoulders to her chair's back. Her figure, clad in rusty-black bombazine and a heavy shawl, remained amazingly supple. Her small and piercing jet eyes yet shone as bright and clear as water in a mountain spring, and only a few gray strands were visible amid straight, blue-black hair which, parted in the middle as usual, was drawn severely back into a bun knotted above the nape of a wrinkled brown neck.

The matriarch's unusually high and prominent cheekbones plus certain faint coppery tints in her complexion lent credence to a persistent rumor that, at some time, Indian blood had entered her lineage. Although even nowadays anyone who admitted having Indian blood in their veins was considered only a few cuts superior to those with a touch of the tarbrush in their pedigree, Ruthelma Donelson Tilt was fiercely proud that her great-grand-dame had been niece to Moluntha, that Shawnee half-chief who, during the bitter winter of 1779, had attacked, then had helped to guide, Colonel John Donelson's settlers from Watauga Forks all the way out to Frenchman's Lick on the Cumberland near middle Tennessee.

While pushing aside a cracked earthenware plate the old lady remarked, "Bushrod, reckon we ought to offer thanks to the Almighty for this spell of stormy weather."

Caroline arched a graceful brown eyebrow. "Why so?"

"Should serve to keep stragglers, bushwhackers and such murdering trash from ranging about too much."

Gravely, Bushrod stroked his well-trimmed and curly light-brown beard. "True, ma'am, but this time of year the countryside will dry out real quick. I dread watching roads, traces and trails become easy going again."

From the kitchen occasionally came the harmonious, low-pitched voices of Lydia and Hannibal her husband, that freed blue-black farmer, hunter and handyman who, right from the beginning of the war, had stuck by the Tilt family. Regularly, even during the bitterest weather, he'd fetched in badly needed provisions of some sort.

Hannibal and Lydia's son, Benjy, a gangling sixteen-year-old and his slightly younger sister Pookie kept up endless shrill chatter in a kitchen stripped bare of cooking utensils save for an odd assortment of battered pots, pans and skillets.

Benjy was saying, "Ah kin so sight a gun near as Paw. Just give me the chanct."

Hannibal grunted, "Hush yo' fuss, boy. Got no powder to waste on no such foolishment. We'll wait till they's live targets to shoot at, then we'll see."

Pookie giggled. "Fust time Benjy fired a musket it kicked him halfway 'crost the lower paddock."

Loretta Tilt's ruler-straight mouth curved a trifle, for all that she seldom had smiled since that dreadful day when the news arrived that David Petty, her intended, had been mortally wounded at Gettysburg during Pickett's charge.

Pushing back his chair, Bushrod heaved himself erect. "If half of what they say about lawlessness in these parts is true I reckon Benjy maybe *had* better be taught to handle a firearm. I'll let him have a charge or two of powder; time may come and maybe sooner than we think when every firearm in Moluntha will count even if a report only helps to scare off would-be raiders." Quietly he added, "If only Rodney would turn up, how different things would be."

Mentally, Bushrod made a tally of effective defenders should Moluntha suffer attack. He and Hannibal were the only really dependable shots, excluding Mother, who, descended from a long line of pioneers, probably knew a deal more about handling firearms than most men. Yes, Benjy just might prove useful.

He had trained Loretta and Louisa to load, shoulder, take aim, and fire, but their marksmanship had remained deplorable. What a pity that his wife, Caroline, should abhor firearms of any description. Nevertheless, she continued bravely to bear this primitive existence so much at a variance with the social and physical comforts and pleasures of her native New Orleans.

Long since, Bushrod had determined that, in the event of attack, he'd concentrate on defending old Ajax Tilt's original stone garrison house and let the outbuildings go — unless he was considerably reinforced.

A series of thin wails from above caused Caroline to light a candle and hurry upstairs.

Brushing a sable strand from her cheek, Grandma Ruthelma queried, "Bush, if the weather clears, what are the orders?"

"Normal routine. You and the other ladies will take turns on Copper Hill lookout — don't want surprises at this late date. We men will work close by; must replace the home paddock's posts and rails those damn' Yanks burned for fuel.

"Next, we'll start building more fences and breeding horses fast as possible. Horses mean ready money and we'll need a lot if I'm to get the lead mine running again. Remember, if I sound three blasts on my fox hunter's horn, drop whatever you're doing and run to your stations."

The black-haired old lady commented, "As you say, after all this rain let's hope swollen brooks and creeks will keep trouble away for a time." She fell silent when, all at once, Hannibal's coon hounds, Flip and Brandy, set up a furious baying in their run near the kitchen end of the house. "Now what can be ailing those critters?"

"Likely 'tis only a 'coon or maybe a bear," said Bushrod.

Moluntha's grand-niece shook her head. "They don't bay like that except at human beings."

Hannibal excitedly came running in from the kitchen carrying an ancient rifle-musket.

"Misto Bushrod," he panted, "better get yo' carbine ready and tell the ladies to stand by with their weepons."

Above the howling, Bushrod, while grabbing his Sharp's carbine from the mantelpiece, yelled, "Those dogs have scented something wrong."

"Yessuh. They's sho' 'nuff peoples outside."

Without instruction Grandma Tilt took up her dead son Otho's double-barreled English piece and stuffed cartridges into a bag she kept handy, before hurrying to her post at a narrow window giving onto the front driveway. Loretta carried a revolver to another window.

Benjy, eyes white with excitement, appeared lugging a powder horn and an ancient flintlock converted to cap-and-ball. It was taller than himself.

Bushrod snapped, "Don't anybody shoot till I say so unless you've seen a stranger so close you can't miss. Caroline! Pass ammunition!" But everyone knew what to do, having often rehearsed such a contingency.

All at once the hounds quit baying and snarling, began to raise happy yelps. Bushrod glanced over to Hannibal, guarding the opposite wall.

"What's up?"

"Dunno, suh. Mus' be somebody they reco'nize out yonder."

Bushrod cupped hands, then yelled through the narrow window before him. "Who's out there? Speak up or we shoot!"

Out of the dimness sounded a trample of hoofs. Then a familiar voice sang out, "Laws, suh, doan shoot! 'Tis only me, Jasper!"

Since somebody appeared to be on the mule behind Jasper, Bushrod called, "Who's that with you?"

"A Confed officer Ah done found on mah way home."

"He armed?"

"Nossuh. Says he ain't no fightin' soljer."

"Tell him to dismount and follow you up to this door and hold his hands high in the air."

Jasper dismounted. "Laws, Mistah Bushrod, Ah's sho' glad to get home. Hey, Hannibal! Hush them dawgs, will ye?"

Once the racket had subsided, Bushrod called, "Where's Mister Rodney?"

"Dunno 'zactly where he is now, suh, but he say he come home right soon."

"When?"

"Dunno, suh. Soon."

"He all right?"

"Yessuh. Last I saw of him."

"Thank God for that. Jasper, just you put that mule away, then go 'round to the kitchen. I'll call you when I'm ready."

Bushrod opened the front door just a crack — one couldn't be too cautious these days — and demanded, "You, out there! Who are you? Are you really unarmed?"

A rich, almost melodious voice replied, "Yes, sir. On my honor, I am Lieutenant Samuel Shepherd, C.S.A., unarmed and quite alone now that my dusky friend, guide and philosopher has departed."

Slowly the stranger advanced, hands held on a level with his shoulders. Bushrod made out a chunky white-haired individual whose waist seemed uncommonly well-filled for a Confederate. He was wearing spectacles; quite thick ones.

"Step inside. Make no quick movements."

Watched by distaff members of the family the officer naming himself "Shepherd" entered warily. The door's lock promptly clicked behind him, then, to everyone's astonishment, the stranger jerked a series of small bows toward each of the women. "Your servant, ladies."

"Stand easy, sir. I need to speak to Jasper." So saying, Bushrod disappeared toward excited gabble in the kitchen, where Hannibal and his family were making Jasper feel he really was home again.

"Jasper, what are you doing here without my brother? Where is he?"

Jasper backed away a step from Bushrod's savage expression. "Laws, suh, he done order me to mek tracks for home fastest Ah could. Yassuh. He mus' be three-fo' days behind. He say he comin' home fastest he kin."

"Thank God. Now tell me what's happened recently."

Beginning with the formation of Z Company, the loose-jointed black obliged. Infinite relief flooded Bushrod. "So he's got some good men with him? How many?"

"Dunno, suh. Some troopers just kept droppin' off now and then 'thout no 'by-yer-leaves.' Last Ah recalls they wuz 'bout fifteen or so."

"Was his company moving fast or slow?"

"Dretful slow, suh. Most hosses was still so poorly."

Following rapid calculations, Bushrod reckoned Jasper must have arrived at least several days before Z Company could be expected to appear — always provided it didn't meet with hindrance of some description; their traveling only partially armed suggested unpleasant possibilities.

Once he'd ascertained other important facts concerning Rodney, Bushrod limped into the living room to find the white-haired officer surrounded by womenfolk. All save Grandma Ruthelma were talking fast and often not even waiting for answers from this fellow in a rumpled and threadbare gray uniform. On its collar of sweat-stained white velvet he was wearing an unfamiliar device.

"This insignia is that of the Paymaster's Department," he explained, blinking even in the disordered living room's dim light.

His complexion despite obvious and prolonged exposure to the elements remained a ridiculous shade of pink-white, and the stubble on his jaws and his curly hair was so completely colorless Bushrod at first took this intruder to be an albino. But he wasn't for beneath long and curving white lashes the stranger's eyes showed a clear, light blue, and his rather fleshy lips were reddish. His hands were long-fingered yet somehow strong-looking, not effeminate.

Shepherd stated he'd been serving with the Paymaster's Department over three years.

Once Bushrod had relayed Jasper's tidings Loretta, then Caroline, started to weep softly. "Thank God! Thank God Rodney's been spared."

Grandma demanded sharply, "Did Jasper say Rodney isn't wounded?"

"Not recently, although he did suffer a light saber cut at Yellow Tavern about a year ago."

Loretta voiced what lay at the back of everyone's mind. "How soon does Jasper think it'll take Rod to reach us?"

"Provided nothing interferes, reckon he should show up the day after tomorrow or thereabouts."

# 13

————◀◉▶————

# Samuel Shepherd, C.S.A.

ONCE A SUPPER of wild turkey, yams and hominy grits had been consumed Bushrod lit his pipe. When it was well aglow he settled back to satisfy curiosity hitherto restrained in interests of good manners.

Occupying a straight chair with a seat of split hickory the guest, without seeming to, divided his attention between Bushrod and Loretta; she of all people seemed covertly captivated by this white-haired officer of about thirty.

In soft yet clearly enunciated tones, Shepherd explained he'd originated in New Orleans where his family, over several generations, had been engaged in shipping and the export-import trade, which business was named the Eastern Star Company.

"When the war began I tried to enlist," he explained quietly, "but for two reasons no one would enroll me in a fighting unit."

Grandma Ruthelma demanded, "The first reason, please?"

"I'm so shortsighted I can barely see across the room without these." Shepherd pointed to his thick glasses. "So I enlisted in a noncombatant service — that of the Paymaster's Department — since I've always been handy with figures that's where I remained till Richmond fell and I had to — er, retreat with the rest. Before long I got lost and strayed the countryside till Jasper found me."

"And the other?" Bushrod demanded while Caroline's knitting needles clicked monotonously on breeches she was making for little Oliver.

Slowly Samuel Shepherd's glance circled expectant faces and he stood, very straight, to all of five feet, six inches. "As I've said, I come from New Orleans. My mother was Lucy Caldwell. She came from a family prominent in Baton Rouge."

"And your father, young sir?" relentlessly demanded Grandma.

"My father is — or was — Joseph Mordecai Shepherd — a Jew. He was Daniel, son of Ezekiel, son of Abraham —" He broke off. "Since we of the Sephardic sect have no family names my great-grandfather adopted the name of 'Shepherd' when he fled Spain with other Hebrews. His family emigrated direct to New Orleans and have remained there ever since."

"A Jew!" Loretta blinked. "But you don't look the least bit like one!"

The paymaster-lieutenant bowed gravely in her direction.

"I am but half-Jewish. My mother was as blond as — as you." He glanced over to Caroline. "Obviously, I have taken after my mother physically — which I'll admit is unusual, since as a rule Semitic characteristics predominate."

"Are you a practicing Jew?" Bushrod inquired.

"No, sir. Nor am I a Christian. During this war I have become what most people term an 'agnostic' because I've come to feel that no formal religion can explain beyond question the universe or our origins, anymore than an ant can comprehend calculus. To me and many others of all faiths the Golden Rule best represents all religions."

Surprisingly, Grandma Ruthelma nodded. "Many Indian tribes agree with you on there being a Great Spirit or Supreme Being. Of course, like whites, red men differ in their beliefs and forms of worship."

Silence fell during which the distant scream of a panther on a hill behind Moluntha sounded faint as a pinprick let in on the horizon.

When Hannibal shuffled in to drop sticks on the fire, Loretta arose, poured acorn coffee, then circulated it, saying, "Isn't Mr. Judah Benjamin, our present Secretary of War, one of you?"

"Yes, ma'am."

A slow sigh escaped Bushrod. All this was beyond him except the fact that this shortsighted fellow probably couldn't hit the broad side of a barn with a firearm. He indicated a chair while fighting down a prejudice that this fellow, half-Hebrew, was another sort of mulatto. "Sit down."

Eyeglasses glinting, Sam Shepherd obeyed, then, pulled out a slim silver seegar case, politely inquired whether any of the ladies objected.

"Lord, no," sighed Grandma. "Seems years since I've scented even a poor one."

Once his slender black seegar had commenced to give off fragrant fumes Lieutenant Shepherd inquired diffidently. "Shall I be permitted to lodge here — temporarily at least?"

"Of course," Bushrod told him. "There's no other shelter within many miles' ride. You can sleep in the west bedroom if you can stand a deal of wind and the cold; most of its windows are shattered."

"Thank you, sir. In return I shall attempt to make myself useful in any fashion you wish during my stay. Sorry, I can shoot only at very close range." He seemed to gather confidence. "Also, should your accounts need attention, I'm confident I can set them in order quite promptly."

Loretta said, "You talk like an educated man. Are you?"

From behind the thick lenses set in steel-rimmed frames, Shepherd's pale-blue eyes came to rest on her. "With all modesty, ma'am, I speak Spanish, Portuguese, some French and a little German — not to mention Ladino. You see, I was attending the University of Edinburgh when the war commenced and I hurried home to offer my services."

"Ladino?" Loretta queried softly. "I've never heard of such a language."

The stranger's pale head inclined. "Nor, ma'am, have many others."

"Why not?" Caroline demanded. "You said you come from New Orleans and so do I. Down there one can hear spoken almost every tongue in the world. But — sir —" she struggled to employ the honorific term, "— Ladino's entirely new to me."

Delicately, Shepherd flicked his seegar's ash into the fireplace. " 'Tis small wonder, ma'am, for 'tis not a written language *per se*. Spanish is used as a basis, but Ladino includes other Iberic tongues, Hebraic and Moorish words and constructions, so —" he parted slim, expressive hands —" 'tis only sung on certain special occasions."

Brown beard outthrust, Bushrod demanded, "You say you served in the Paymaster's Department in Richmond? How did that happen and for how long?"

"For nearly three years, Major, through the kind offices of Mr. Judah P. Benjamin when he was Secretary of the Treasury. You, sir, of course are aware that Mr. Benjamin has held many posts in Mr. Jefferson Davis's Cabinet. In fact he remains the only original member of it."

"Ever do any fighting at all, er, Mr. Shepherd?"

"No, sir. Although I held a captain's commission in the Home Guard, I was never under fire until the Government was abandoning the capital. Then with the rest of the Treasury officials, I was armed and ordered to flee. We had to fire a few shots but I doubt whether I hit anyone. Eventually I became separated — involuntarily, I might add — from my company during the flight from Richmond."

" 'Retreat' you mean!" corrected Bushrod.

Shepherd took the correction calmly. "It started as a retreat, sir, but when the enemy closed in so fast and so hard it became a case of every man for himself." He leaned forward on his chair and lifted a heavy belt as if to ease his stomach. Caroline noticed this.

"Continue," directed Grandma Ruthelma, eyes narrowing. "With what troops did you retreat?"

"Please, ma'am," explained the paymaster, "there were few organized units left when we fled — er, retreated westward. I was only one of a mob seeking to avoid capture. Noncombatant though I was, I couldn't be certain some Yankee wouldn't put a bullet through me simply because I was wearing gray."

He blinked behind his thick lenses. "Since that fate seemed a shameful waste of a good mind and a fine education, if I do say so, I joined a party of stragglers heading for the mountains."

"Did you surrender at Appomattox?" Loretta demanded evenly.

"No, ma'am. The party I was with must have been traveling north of that place. When we got news of the surrender we separated at once. I'd been lost and wandering for some time before your servant, Jasper, chanced across me, wet and starving."

Bushrod grunted, "Then you've no parole papers?"

"No, Major, but I wish to obtain some at the earliest possible moment. I have no desire to hang as an unparoled Confederate."

Briefly, he rubbed expressive hands, held them toward the remains of the fire. "Sir, ladies, would you mind calling me 'Sam Shepherd'? I'm bored with 'Lieutenant Shepherd' — and all that so lowly a rank implies."

Bushrod said, "Surely, since as you say, you were under Mr. Benjamin's influence during three years' service you should have been offered promotion?"

"Yes, sir, I was, but I refused all offers."

"Why?"

"Because traders and shippers like us, who see something of the outside world, foresaw that the South, much as we love it, never could hope to overcome the North's vast industrial resources and superior manpower. As a lowly officer, I might, once peace was restored, more easily resume peaceful pursuits."

"You have, er — connections abroad?" Loretta suggested, gathering skirts more tightly about her legs — the chill was increasing.

"Before the War the Eastern Star Company had several agencies in Europe, but the bulk of our business was done with Mexico and certain republics lying farther south."

After once more easing his crippled foot Bushrod asked, "What sort of business? Any specialties — such as arms, for example?"

He in the rumpled gray nodded his silver-hued head. "I suppose we did, but having been mostly educated abroad I knew very little concerning the nature of our trading."

"Your company still keeps its connections abroad?" suggested Grandma Ruthelma.

"I presume so, ma'am, although I've no notion of what fate has befallen the Eastern Star Company under Union occupation. Last I heard we had transferred our flags to those of neutral countries, although the Federals insisted the Eastern Star maintain United States registry on a certain number of our vessels.

"God knows what's become of them. Mails for the last months, as we all are aware, have become most unreliable while telegraphic communications with New Orleans since General Sherman's march have been impossible."

To Bushrod it proved something of a treat to converse with a traveled, well-educated and apparently well-informed individual. Nevertheless, he still found it difficult to credit that Samuel Shepherd, being half-Jewish, was wholly to be trusted.

# 14

## Onslaught

To everyone's surprise ex-Lieutenant Samuel Shepherd's accomplishments proved to be as useful as they were varied. He'd a knack for fixing almost everything mechanical, from a broken window latch to the handsome grandfather's clock which still stood on the staircase's landing. Everyone, from little Oliver up, felt reassured and cheered to hear the clock's mellow chimes again sounding the hours. Better yet, the former paymaster replaced the lock on a Sharp's carbine abandoned by Stoneman's men. Alas, only a handful of cartridges could be found to fit it.

The weather having turned gloriously warm, Sam Shepherd removed whole panes of glass from the salon and utilized these to render three bedrooms completely weathertight.

Lydia became darkly radiant when one of her hens appeared from a nest hidden in the underbrush leading a brood of eight bright-eyed, downy, black-and-yellow chicks.

Jasper set about plowing a small vegetable garden after convincing his mule, very unwillingly, to submit to a harness contrived of odd pieces of strap and rope. Without fuss Grandma Ruthelma delved into a chest, concealed under worn-out clothes in her closet, and produced little bags of seed: grain, oats, corn, pumpkin, carrots, turnip, spinach and the like.

Bushrod and Loretta hoed along with Lydia, Benjy and even Pookie, while Hannibal saw to the seeding, just as he had before the world had become turned upside down.

All seemed serene save that every now and then shots were heard —

sometimes quite a few at the same time — but happily in the far distance.

Caroline did the housekeeping with little Oliver's misguided "assistance."

The unspoken thought in everybody's mind was, when would Rodney and his men appear? Adding to the urgency of this question was the sight of smoke — not the color of forest fires — arising in various directions; some not too far away. In fact, it soon became inescapable that in ever-increasing numbers men were roaming these mountains.

Who they were, and what they wanted, raised such doubts in Bushrod's mind that he posted more frequent watches — four hours on duty and four off in the Copper Ridge and Gazebo lookouts even if this meant curtailment of regular duties and repairs. Loretta, Caroline and Grandma insisted on taking their turn and thus shortened the duty period from four hours to three.

Two days passed before lantern-jawed Sergeant Knox rode in after raising a few warning yells — he'd no desire to get plugged at this late date — leading what Bushrod and Jasper immediately recognized to be a thoroughbred black mare heavy in foal. Knox, stroking the mare's head, swore he'd found her grazing near an abandoned house — whose, he'd no idea.

There were somber expressions in Moluntha Garrison when the big, yellow-bearded sergeant described his escape from that ambush which had decimated Z Company. Once he'd satisfied himself the Federals really had departed, he explained, he'd waited till he could cut down the dangling corpses, but of course there'd been no opportunity to bury them; he'd been thankful to escape with his life.

"What happened to the point?" Bushrod queried sharply. "Did they all get away?"

The Sergeant hesitated. "Well, suh, after the skirmish at the ford I didn't hear no more shots, even though I lingered pretty close to the crossin' a good while; nobody seemed to have seen me skiddadle back so quick as I did."

Commented Loretta, "Then you believe Rodney and the other three men got away safe?"

"Yes, ma'am. There was the colonel, two men named Tyler and Hamrick, and a young gal named Forsythe, Meg Forsythe."

Caroline's hazel eyes widened, "A girl?"

"Yes, ma'am." Knox then described the finding of her and the story she'd given.

There was no describing Bushrod's mounting anxiety. If, as seemed likely, Sergeant Knox's account proved accurate, Z Company no longer could be counted upon to defend Moluntha in case of need. On the brighter side, Rodney and presumably his companions had safely escaped the ambush.

By the third day after Jasper and Lieutenant Shepherd had appeared and there still came no word from Rodney, Bushrod and the rest of the family grew increasingly depressed especially since, on several occasions, bursts of not-too-distant small arms fire rattled and echoed amid the Big Stone Range lying to the north and west of Moluntha; therefore everything was done to render the old garrison house even more defendable.

It was Sergeant Knox's suggestion that all four-legged livestock should be driven into the battered and windowless salon.

"Should the enemy number more than a few, they can take the stables and burn the outbuildings without half trying," Bushrod stated. "We'll concentrate on trying to defend the house."

"What raiders generally want is food and livestock," Knox agreed. Accordingly at dusk, both heifers, Bush's old horse, Knox's mount and the pregnant mare along with Jasper's mule were herded indoors. Penned in one corner were Moluntha's surviving swine — a sow and her farrow of brown-and-black piglets. Last year's dry cornstalks and a few armfuls of rushes were all that could be found to protect the salon's once-gleaming parquet flooring.

Hannibal, Jasper and Knox, taciturn as ever, fetched in an astonishing assortment of edibles; nevertheless this barely sufficed to fill a dozen-odd mouths even on short rations.

What was to be done?

Bushrod figured that as soon as Rodney returned they'd no choice but to dig up the family's silver and try to barter it for bare necessities.

The attack came at midday, a most unusual hour, so caught the household dispersed, attending to various duties.

If Hannibal hadn't been out ranging the mountainside behind Moluntha where he'd noticed a number of fresh deer traces, the results would have been tragic. On sighting an armed stranger sneaking on foot toward the old garrison house, the hunter had fired immediately and killed a rough-clad fellow.

As it was, at the report of his shotgun, persons indoors rushed to their posts. Jasper and Benjy quit plowing and Hannibal made for the house at top speed. Jasper hated to leave his mule behind yet Hannibal's warning yells decided him.

As it was, attackers appeared out of the woods on horseback or on foot and from various directions converged on Moluntha. Most were wearing rough civilian clothes or parts of Confederate uniform — only here and there did a flash of blue appear.

The leader, a broad-shouldered fellow wearing a Confederate officer's uniform, pulled up on a long-legged light bay in the shelter of the barn, all the while shouting for his men to rally there.

When Benjy attempted to dodge in from the smokehouse across a clear space toward the garrison house's back door a rifle cracked. The boy staggered, convulsively threw up his arms, then crumpled when another bullet crashed into his fuzzy head. He lay sprawled in the open, skinny brown-and-black form squirming a little as creatures often do when shot through the brain.

Some little time elapsed before the last of the assailants, about twenty in number, could collect in the lee of the barn — a respite which granted the defenders precious moments to get ready.

Bushrod posted his people chiefly along the north wall facing the barn, but ordered Jasper and Shepherd to guard the locked and barred front entrance. No telling what these strangers might do; Bushrod thought there was something unusual about these raiders; they appeared to observe a loose sort of discipline quite unlike typical bushwhackers.

The big leader, wearing a short red beard, stuck his head around a corner of the barn and sang out, "Surrender! Else we'll charge and grant no quarter!"

Bushrod shouted, "Leave us be! We've women and a child in here!"

"Go to hell!" yelled Sergeant Knox, drawing a bead with his Spencer on that corner where the red-bearded man had showed himself.

"Charge!" shouted the leader. "Devil take the hindmost!"

Whooping attackers appeared running around both ends of the barn. Some coolly dropped onto one knee before taking aim but the majority sprinted toward the house from which gunsmoke gushed through ground-floor windows. No less than seven men dropped, dead, or so seriously wounded they couldn't advance any further, but, shouting obscenities, the rest pressed on. A few cautious raiders took shelter behind a horse trough but their fire only pockmarked Moluntha's sturdy walls, creating irregular pale stars in the light-brown paintwork.

To the end of her days Loretta Tilt, coughing hard, would never forget this choking smoke billowing about the living room, the deafening reports, yells, shouts and occasional screams of anguish. Once, when firing a revolver through a dining room window she, to her shocked surprise, watched the wild-looking fellow she'd aimed at drop his gun and fall onto his knees as if in prayer, before collapsing sideways to lie motionless in the bright sunlight.

Bushrod, along with Grandma Ruthelma, kept on shooting and only paused to call for ammunition from Caroline, who was running about lugging a pair of willow wythe baskets heavy with brass cartridges.

Bullets whistled about her head so she bent low while hurrying over to Loretta who, smoking revolver in hand, was crying, "Can't shoot anymore. Thing's jammed!"

Knox shouted, "I'll come in a minute."

Resounding blows battering at doors and Lydia's eerie screaming from the kitchen all added to the tumult.

Fortunately Ajax Tilt, in his wisdom, had followed the frontier precaution of felling all large trees growing within a radius of forty yards from his garrison house. True, in later times, dogwoods, small ornamental shrubs and fruit trees had been planted closer in, but their trunks offered little or no protection to an attacker.

Once he'd shot the fellow who'd killed Benjy, Bushrod reloaded in time to drop another attacker who now seemed ready to run away.

Hannibal, wise in arts of hunting, waited until two gray-clad attackers crossed each other's path before shooting just as he would at a rising bevy of quail, so his charge of buckshot simultaneously dropped a pair of assailants.

"Hi-yah!" shrilled Grandma Ruthelma. "Got me another! Carrie! Fetch some cartridges, I —"

The old lady got no further. A bullet, penetrating one of the narrow windows, struck Chief Moluntha's great-grand-niece in the lower throat. Its impact knocked her off her feet, and left her lying senseless, dying. For the moment no one realized what had happened except Sam Shepherd, blindly firing a revolver to her left.

Then Bushrod through whirling smoke glimpsed his Mother's collapsed figure but only roared, "They're wavering! Keep on shooting!"

Knox and Jasper's marksmanship continued to be deadly; Hannibal also was firing and reloading as fast as he could. Loretta, now at the far end of the line, was clutching a big Colt revolver with both hands. She was taking her time, only shooting when a good target presented itself.

By their method of attack and semblance of organization, Bushrod long since had decided Moluntha was being assailed by partisans — bodies of irregular troops such as had followed leaders like Mosby, Morgan and others of their like so long as matters went well. When they didn't, these undisciplined individuals would simply pull out to reassemble at some predetermined rendezvous or ride away in search of some more fortunate leader. There was little distinction between them and out-and-out bushwhackers save that partisans generally served under officers bearing a Confederate commission and they would not accept proven criminals or Yankee deserters among their number.

Of all things, a bugle sounded, whereupon the assailants turned and pelted at top speed for the nearest cover, leaving behind seven dead men and three so badly hit they only were able to lurch and hobble after their retreating companions.

On Bushrod's orders these last weren't to be shot at — they'd not be coming this way again and scant ammunition must be conserved. Thank God for this respite!

He found Shepherd, Loretta and Caroline bent over Grandma Ruthelma's slender and blood-drenched black-clad form. The girl from New Orleans kept crying wildly, "She's gone — Grandma's dead. Oh-h — oh-h —"

"Let her rest in peace —" choked Bushrod, then, tears silvering his cheeks, he directed, "All of you get back to your posts. They've been badly stung but they'll be back before long, figuring since we've put up such a fight there must be plenty of valuables in here."

In silence Loretta dashed upstairs to return with a patchwork quilt which served to cover Ruthelma Donelson Tilt's black-clad figure but could not conceal the gradual spread of bright tendrils of blood creeping across a parquetry floor littered by empty cartridge cases and other debris.

Grimly, Sergeant Knox, Shepherd and the other defenders resumed their posts when Bushrod, leaving Sergeant Knox in command, limped upstairs where little Ollie's terrified outcries finally had died out through sheer exhaustion.

From his bedroom window Rodney's brother obtained a more comprehensive view of their present situation.

On the greening grass of a lawn usually kept short by grazing sheep lay ten bodies, some in oddly contorted positions — that of Benjy and nine attackers — the wounded had disappeared among the outbuildings where the red-bearded leader could be heard saying, "Didn't think they were so damn' many in there."

Mounted men, maybe ten in number, could be seen dodging from one shelter to the next toward the red-painted barn where, apparently, a conference of sorts was taking place.

Jasper's mule had been caught and was being led into the woods.

Loretta, still not fully feeling the impact of her Mother's death, helped Caroline reload. Both had powder-blackened faces.

Presently, Bushrod called down from upstairs, "Looks like they're going to try and draw us out by firing the outbuildings."

His prediction proved all too accurate. Men could be seen kindling a fire behind the smokehouse; then, pretty soon, they appeared brandishing flaming sticks. Some disappeared toward the chicken house, others ran to various places among the Quarter's cabins.

"Oh, Maw," moaned Pookie, "doan let 'em burn down our cabin. Mah bestest apron's in there and mah yaller hair ribbon."

"Please, Boss," Hannibal called upstairs. "Lemme pick off a couple. Ah kin, easy and sure, suh."

"No. Too short of ammunition. They'll find that out soon enough."

Sam Shepherd, maintaining spurious calm, watched as flames and smoke commenced to climb from the smokehouse, the hen house, the servants' cabins and even empty corncribs. Next, the handsome but empty thoroughbreds' stable beyond the hay barn took fire, but the barn itself was spared for the present; probably because it offered protection and a convenient rallying point.

Steadily, the roaring crackle of the conflagration increased until a huge whirling pillar of smoke, sparks, and flaming embers climbed high into a sky of flawless blue.

# 15

## Warrior's Return

THE SUN'S WARMTH added to the raising of Colonel Rodney Tilt's spirits. Every furlong covered now brought him that much nearer Moluntha Garrison and the Big Stone Mountains looming blue-green beyond.

Once they'd crossed Moccasin Ridge, they entered a rough and lonely farm road leading northward. Here the countryside grew wilder. They encountered only a few ruined dwellings standing forlorn amid stump-lots covered with weeds, briars and, occasionally, pathetic stalks of self-sown grain; poignant reminders of days gone by.

Margaret Forsythe was commencing to feel more herself, less numbed by the past and feeling that the future offered some sort of security, at least as long as she remained among these men she'd come to admire and trust. Even under the worst of conditions they'd always treated her with consideration and respect.

Most of all she admired Rodney Tilt, now that he was beginning to thaw somewhat into the amusing, capable and always cheerful man he must have been before the war and the tragic news he'd received from Moluntha last winter. What he could have been like before that she could only surmise from occasional flashes of wit, gallantry and love of sports.

What had his wife been like? One of his own sort, of course, although from Maryland. What fools people were to risk marriage lacking bonds of good breeding, similar religions, and many common interests. Privately, she dreaded for him the moment when for the first time he'd stand before Louisa's grave and that of their child. How many countless thousands, North and South, must be facing similar ordeals?

By now she'd learned not to try to foresee beyond the immediate future. What sort of a reception could she, clad in Yankee blue, expect? How she hated the uncomfortable necessity of wearing harsh-on-the-skin male attire — no matter its hue — but from what she'd overheard it wasn't likely she could dress decently for some time to come.

The little party was riding as usual: Colonel Tilt followed by herself, then Hamrick, then Peter Tyler who, since that first night under the serape, had never mentioned the event. Invariably he treated her with courtesy, to the point of deference. What an enigmatic character, by turns morose or almost bursting with cheerfulness. It seemed as if Peter Tyler must be wrestling with a series of profound inner problems — then, on solving them, he'd brighten up.

Naturally, she'd made no mention of his confession to anyone. Odd — there was an innate superior quality about this Texan which prompted conjectures on what he really intended. That his father was a Mexican general in the field suggested innumerable possibilities.

This rock-studded dirt road wound through steep foothills tenderly green and teeming with wildlife. Bluejays sauced the riders, a flicker drumming on a hollow log seemed to beat a tattoo of welcome to spring. Squirrels barked and raced among treetops, patches of laurel and dogwood blossoms relieved somber hues in the woods all about. Nevertheless, all four riders balanced short and dully gleaming carbines across their pommels — that ford two days earlier also had *seemed* peaceful. All the same, the riders slouched comfortably in their saddles.

Rodney Tilt even had slung a leg over Resaca's once more arched and gleaming neck. Meg kicked her feet free of box stirrups in order to ease cramped muscles and ankles chafed and blistered by socks and shoes sizes too big.

As for Tyler, the Texan amused himself by neatly braiding that part of his mount's mane within easy reach. Only Rimfire Hamrick remained unrelaxed; he kept looking up and down each sun-dappled glade as they passed.

Thank God, mused Rodney, I'll learn the truth about Moluntha the moment we top yonder hill. Usually, on reaching the crest, he would have sent a series of fox hunter's view-halloos across pastures up to the house to warn servants to be ready when he arrived, but today just before the familiar vista opened up, he noticed the passage of a light-gray cloud which dimmed the sunlight. Instantly he unslung his leg, then arm-signaled his companions to look alive and close up.

Hamrick, too, had noticed that shadow in the sky. To Tyler's questioning look he muttered, "Somethin's burnin' ahead; likely 'tis only a brush fire set by someone clearin' land." Yet instinctively he knew that couldn't be the true origin of yonder smoke, its color was wrong. Just then an irregular crackle of musketry broke out in the distance.

Spurs urged the little party to the top of that rise overlooking many of those broad acres about which Meg had heard so much. Across the meadow, leaping spirals of smoke were soaring above a cluster of buildings dominated by a solid-looking light-brown structure with white-painted wings. Instantly she identified the place as the home Old Ajax Tilt had built nearly a century earlier.

"Oh my God!" Tilt gasped when he saw the puffs of smoke bursting through narrow, ground-floor windows. Gray-white blossoms also were spurting from between burning outbuildings and among ornamental trees and shrubbery.

"Yell!" Tilt snapped. "Everybody yell like hell! Make 'em believe we're the point for a larger force."

Grimly he remembered that once upon a time this would have been no lie. To attract attention, he fired his Colt. Knox and Tyler followed suit but ·Meg couldn't, her only weapon being a Spencer repeating carbine so heavy she could scarcely raise it to her shoulder.

Hoofs drumming, necks extended, the horses quickly crossed the pasture and took to the driveway leading upward.

That what appeared to be nothing other than gunsmoke was issuing from Moluntha Garrison Tilt appreciated at once. The house thus far at least was not ablaze. He also felt relieved to see that only the wooden end of the capacious horse-breeding stables was smoldering; all other outlying buildings save the cow and hay barn had been set on fire.

That those shots fired by Tilt's party had attracted attention was obvious from the way various raiders quit what they were up to and started toward the woods. Some, however, mounted up and closed in around a commanding, red-bearded figure wearing Confederate gray and with a black ostrich plume jauntily tucked into a pinned-back fold in his tan slouch hat in a style rendered popular by the famous Jeb Stuart.

"Them there look and act like partisans — irregulars, not guerrillas!" Hamrick yelled. "They're wuss!"

The leader was standing in his stirrups, apparently bawling a series of commands unheeded by the greater part of his followers, who merely vanished among woods behind the estate.

"You! Stop there!" the leader yelled at a man setting foot to stirrup. "They're only a handful. We can take 'em, easy!"

"Cap'n Grainger, ye're mistook," retorted the other, settling into his saddle. "Yonder's only the point for a lot of cavalry. I've seen plenty of such."

"Look again, you fool!" Grainger shouted. "Can't you see they're wearing gray?"

"Don't mean nothin'!" shouted the fellow, while wheeling his mount. "Be them reg'lar Secesh troops, they'll hang raiders caught red-handed, like us, quick as any Blue-bellies. Me, I'm clearin' out while the goin's good!"

As a result, by the time Tilt and his followers urged panting horses up the driveway, only eight or ten fellows wearing slovenly gray or brown uniforms lingered to confront them. Noting this, Rodney Tilt, as he pounded up toward his home, emptied his revolver at that knot of men wavering about that commanding figure with a full red beard, and experienced savage satisfaction at seeing a raider sag on his horse, which then galloped off dragging its rider along by a foot caught in the stirrup.

Long since aware that shooting from horseback seldom accomplished much, Tyler and Hamrick dismounted before opening fire with their Sharps. As a result two more partisans were hit and fled, howling.

Margaret Forsythe, pale under her tan, followed their example even when bullets commenced to hiss past her head; she clenched teeth, aimed her carbine as she'd been taught, fired, and nearly got knocked over backward by the weapon's vicious recoil.

Meantime Moluntha's defenders, aware of a change in the situation, increased their rate of fire, which caused three raiders to reel in their saddles, then gallop for the woods. Shaken by such unexpected resistance, the irregulars broke and fled in various directions; some loose horses followed them but others uncertainly lingered near the barn.

Alone, Rodney Tilt spurred headlong toward the big red-haired leader, a captain by the loops of tarnished and frayed silver braid above cuffs on his uniform. Cursing himself that he'd so thoughtlessly emptied his revolver, the Master of Moluntha wrenched out his sword, thankful that his opponent likewise appeared to have expended the last of his ammunition. He also was alone, his followers having scattered.

Whatever his faults the partisan leader was no coward. He drew a heavy-bladed saber and, bending well forward, raced to meet Tilt so fast his black ostrich plume streamed straight out behind.

Rodney fixed attention on his target, the center of a double row of brass buttons on that gray jacket. Unexpectedly savage pleasure seized him. Weeks had passed since he'd found use for Grandpa's ornamental but sturdy sword.

Extended low over Resaca's neck, he concentrated his weight behind the point and swiftly closed the interval separating him from his enemy, mounted on a tall and powerful-looking light-bay.

As if by tacit consent both sides ceased firing, although the crackling of flames drowned out all sound of drumming hoofs.

Somehow, this reminded Tyler of a duel between Homeric champions such as Hector and Achilles. Once Tilt closed in, Captain Grainger leaned farther forward, point aimed at Tilt's chest but the latter at the last instant twisted sideways and diverted the other's thrust at the cost of partially missing his own target.

Grainger's saber only ripped Tilt's sleeve while Rodney had to settle for a glancing blow that created a long tear along the side of his enemy's jacket.

Immediately they'd passed one another, both men wheeled their horses and began to slash and cut instead of thrusting, which suited Tilt since, through years of instructing recruits, he'd become expert at this business.

The partisan aimed a tremendous cut which Tilt parried but felt his sword arm jarred up to its elbow. Nevertheless, he turned Resaca almost within the animal's own length and delivered a savage cut that the other barely diverted to a ringing clash of steel. Grainger recovered quickly and aimed a slash at his enemy's head which Tilt avoided by ducking under it. In the brilliant sunshine both weapons glittered like miniature metallic windmills.

At the next interchange, through sheer power Tilt's blade broke through Grainger's parry, then sank deep into the juncture of his neck and left shoulder.

Instantly blood spurted from a severed artery. The partisan, sword dangling from its knot at his wrist, swayed in his saddle and convulsively used both hands to clasp his neck while his horse carried him over level green turf in the direction of Moluntha Garrison.

Tilt, spurring in his wake, with grim satisfaction watched bright arterial blood continue to spurt from between Grainger's fingers in such powerful jets there was no need to drive his point into that sweat-marked gray back.

The partisan fell heavily. His plumed hat was trampled into shapelessness beneath Resaca's hoofs. No one immediately came out of Moluntha but Bushrod hailed, "Welcome home, Rod! Aren't there any more men?"

"No."

"Isn't that a *Yankee* with you?"

Rodney, breathing heavily and shaking from anxiety and overexertion, trotted past fallen figures scattered about the grass.

"Hi, there, Bush! This Yankee's no soldier — only a girl. For God's sake turn everybody out to fight fires."

"Sure there're no more raiders around, sir?" Shepherd yelled through the cardroom's window.

Too shaken to perceive that a stranger had spoken, Rodney yelled back, "Reckon so, but we'd better make sure."

A swift reconnaissance of the vicinity revealed that only dead raiders remained around Moluntha while distant crashing noises in the woods argued that the partisans had no intention of lingering where they'd lost their leader and approximately half of their force — or more, if one counted wounded men who, bleeding and cursing, wobbled in their saddles as they fled.

No time now for reunion greetings, introductions, or for anything else save fighting soaring, crackling flames, which so far had destroyed four of six former slave cabins and were spreading to other outbuildings.

Entirely typical of him was the speed with which Rodney organized a bucket brigade from a generous mountain spring which, for generations, had supplied Moluntha Garrison with water as icy as it was pure. The women, smoke-streaked and disheveled, joined in passing slopping wooden buckets as fast as Jasper and Hannibal could fill them.

Unerringly Rodney concentrated on saving the wooden end — roughly a third of Moluntha's stables designed to accommodate racing thoroughbreds and mares heavy with foal. Fortunately this section refused to burn readily, thanks to its slate roof and a long, wet spring.

None present ever forgot those coughing shapes, male and female, eerily appearing then disappearing amid whirling clouds of eye-stinging smoke. Sometimes they stumbled over sprawled corpses.

The fire already was being brought under control when a hard, late-spring shower abruptly rolled down from the mountains and effectively extinguished most embers glowing among blackened timbers and clouds of mingling steam and smoke.

By dusk everyone at Moluntha was singed, hungry and thoroughly exhausted — mentally as much as physically. Only little Oliver again was making his feelings known in no uncertain fashion.

To men who'd served in the field over many months or years Moluntha Garrison presented a not-too-appalling scene; they'd smelled burned plaster and charred wood before, had been quartered in partially burned or otherwise wrecked and gutted structures in far worse conditions.

By sundown the livestock had been led out of the salon and back to their customary shelter. Meanwhile Sergeant Knox, Corporal Tyler and others succeeded in rounding up five stray partisan mounts, Jasper's mule and that pregnant mare Knox had come across. The enlisted men made themselves comfortable in the hay barn as veteran campaigners usually do.

Together, Rodney and Bushrod had led the family and Sam Shepherd indoors where Lydia's and Pookie's wails over Benjy persisted until Loretta with unaccustomed harshness bade Lydia to hush up and start preparing a cauldron of stew made of anything she could come across.

To his astonishment Rodney came upon Margaret Forsythe's slim, blue-clad figure sheltering in the kitchen woodshed. Her hands, pock-marked by burns and blisters, were clutching the reins of Avalon, as she'd named her dainty little mare.

Dazedly, Meg peered upward, met Rodney's intent glance, and for the first time read a quality in his gaze she'd never previously noticed.

"Why aren't you inside?"

"I wasn't sure I'd be welcome wearing this uniform."

"Nonsense. Jasper, put this horse in the barn with the others." To the girl he said in a voice hoarse and thickened by smoke fumes, "Please come indoors and meet my family. I regret, ma'am, I can't offer you a warmer —" he smiled thinly —"let's say a more suitable welcome to Moluntha Garrison."

# 16

# Dust to Dust

AT FIRST LIGHT the remaining souls present in Moluntha Garrison reluctantly roused to face still another day fraught with dreadful uncertainty.

Following a scant breakfast, the bodies of fallen partisans were collected, and searched for anything of value. However, only a little over a hundred dollars in Federal greenbacks was discovered, not to mention quantities of sodden and utterly valueless Confederate bills. Nevertheless, dead men's mounts, weapons and ammunition were priceless at this time.

Among the burial detail headed by Lieutenant Shepherd, only he felt queasy while delving into the pockets of a scrawny young fellow wearing butternut brown. During his service in Richmond the paymaster had seen and ministered to plenty of wounded, had attended all too many military funerals, very impressive and orderly to start with, but becoming less formal and more hurried once the Union Armies relentlessly closed in upon the Capital.

Yes, he'd certainly heard more than enough concerning death and destruction, but never before had he beheld so many grisly sights at close range. Now, more than ever, he marveled over the quiet courage, constancy and endurance displayed by so many Southern women of all classes.

Finally the rain ceased but continued to drip drearily from eaves and branches.

Of Rodney, Bushrod asked harshly, "What shall we do about the carcasses of these murdering swine? Such don't deserve decent burial and they'd start smelling soon!"

"I don't care a thin damn what's done with them, except for the officer. He fought well."

Because he'd been commissioned, Captain Grainger's body, in observance of some chivalric if archaic code, was wrapped in a wornout horse blanket then laid in a shallow grave hastily dug near an abandoned sawpit. A crude cross fashioned of laths and bearing the dead man's name then was planted upon it. Probably hay grass and wild flowers soon would flourish — especially well here.

From Moluntha came sounds of hammering. When Rodney raised a brow his brother explained in a low voice, "Jasper, Hannibal and Sergeant Knox are knocking together a coffin for Mother. The ladies are preparing her remains for burial." He shot his older brother a worried glance, "We'll manage, but who can we find to conduct the burial service? There's no preacher nearer than Gladesville and he's very old."

"That's a pity," commented Rodney. "However, I happen to know that Miss Forsythe is a minister's granddaughter and can conduct the Anglican service. I've heard her do so." He gave a brief description of the service Meg had performed over the fallen Federals. "It's one of their uniforms she has on; her own clothes were in rags."

Numbly, Bushrod muttered, "Very well, if you think it's fitting. If only she weren't wearing Federal blue! The very sight of it sickens us all."

Rodney nodded, said quietly, "For the moment that can't be helped. But does it really matter what Miss Forsythe wears? She's a true Christian and," he added pointedly, "a lady. She's truly eager to resume female garb as soon as possible."

"What about these dead bandits?"

"Hold on. Is the old sawpit beyond the pigsty still empty?"

Bushrod nodded, sunken eyes still red from weeping. "It is, and I reckon 'twill just about accommodate that carrion out yonder."

Before long damp bodies, often stiffened into grotesque positions, were dragged by the mule to their final resting place and there arranged in a double row at the sawpit's bottom.

Piled like that, the cadavers presented a hideous sight — their long tangled hair was matted with mud and their dirty uniforms often were agape. Fortunately rain had washed most of the gore from those waxhued faces.

Hannibal and Jasper, once they'd dug a last resting place for Ruthelma Donelson Tilt, next sought what once had been the slaves' willow-shaded cemetery, situated not far from the Tilt family's stone-walled burying ground. When they spaded for a second time the hole then dug was considerably smaller, Benjy having not yet attained full growth.

When Rodney, stony-faced, took the Forsythe girl aside and invited her to conduct the burial service for his mother, the girl's slight figure stiffened and her large hazel eyes brimmed over before she could murmur, "Although I-I'm not qualified, I-I would feel deeply honored to b- b-be of help, b-but I can't. Not d-dressed like this. C-can't something more appropriate be found?"

"Not in the hurry we're in. Loretta says the Yankees cleaned us out pretty thoroughly last winter. They took even women's things."

The most suitable garment to be found in a hurry proved to be a black velvet cloak Caroline had worn years ago to church in New Orleans. For a head covering there was only a small black-chip bonnet belonging to the deceased.

Meg knew she must cut a grotesque figure in cavalry boots and with stretches of blue-and-yellow breeches showing every time the wind blew open her cloak.

Somewhere Caroline discovered a strip of black material which the brothers cut in two and knotted about one another's left arms.

Shortly after noon the family gathered amid wreckage in the salon and there, muffling sobs, listened to Meg recite the Episcopalian funeral service over a rough pine coffin supported on a pair of well-used sawhorses. Upon the casket reposed a pathetic little bunch of hastily gathered wild flowers.

Grandmother Ruthelma's weight was so slight only four pallbearers were required so, when the service ended, Lieutenant Shepherd, Sergeant Knox, and Corporals Hamrick and Tyler effortlessly lifted the casket onto their shoulders and waited to follow Margaret Forsythe and the family out-of-doors.

Although miserably conscious of her extraordinary attire, the young woman steadily led the way to the family's private cemetery. Everyone else, with bared heads, fell in behind. Only when he saw the raw red earth heaped around the grave did Rodney's swimming gaze briefly traverse the little cemetery to seek the last resting place of his wife and child.

How many new graves there were! The older headstones had become spotted by yellow-gray lichens, like that of Colonel Ajax Tilt, U.S.A., b. 1743, d. 1810. On the marble also was engraved, "He loved his family only less than his Country." Close beside this stone stood that of his wife, Lucy Poinsett Tilt of Dinwiddle, Virginia, who had departed this life in 1821.

Then there was the gray granite headstone of Brian Tilt, Captain, U.S.A., b. 1803 — d. 1856. Coupled with it was that of his wife, Laura-Lee

Dabney of Richmond, Virginia. Fortunately she had died early in 1861, before hostilities had broken out. The last marble headstone was that of Rushmore Tilt, Major, C.S.A., b. 1836, d. 1862, who'd fallen at the First Battle of Manassas — or "Bull Run" as the Yankees termed that engagement. Scattered among these stone markers were the headstones of various children who had died.

Recent graves, significantly, were marked only by wooden slabs. On one had been painted, neatly enough, Otho Tilt, Lt., C.S.A., b. 1839, killed at Sharpsburg, 1862.

A sharp spasm shook Rodney Ajax Tilt when he read inscriptions on the two newest slabs: Louisa Merryman Tilt, b. 1842, d. 1864. Close alongside stood a very small marker which read "Infant Tilt, d. 1864." These lay closest to the grave dug for Moluntha's great-grand-niece, Ruthelma Donelson Tilt.

Once the pallbearers tramped up, the ladies, all of whom had managed to find headgear of some description, joined the men in bending heads.

Summoning a supreme effort, Margaret Forsythe steadied her voice and recited, without ever looking at the Bible in her hands: "Man born of woman hath but a short time to live and is full of misery. He cometh up, is cut down like a flower; he fleeth as he were a shadow and never continueth in one stay —"

Then, while the casket was being lowered, her voice grew husky: "Earth to earth, ashes to ashes and dust to dust."

The chief mourners, once the ceremonial handful of dirt had been sifted onto the coffin, briefly clung to one another. For the first time in his adult life, Rodney broke into tears, while with quivering arms he embraced Loretta and Bushrod.

Loretta, the calmest, said, "I reckon Mother died as she would have wished, swiftly and without fear. Let us pray that the red gods, as well as our own, will grant her eternal peace."

A few minutes later the ceremony was repeated before the entire company when young Benjy was laid to rest.

# 17.

## Lament in the Moonlight

Two NIGHTS after the relief of Moluntha Garrison Rodney Ajax Tilt lay, fingers laced under head, on the ticking of a mattress that covered the same wide and handsomely carved mahogany four-poster on which, eons ago it seemed, he'd bedded Louisa as his bride.

Aching not only from head to foot but also in mind and heart, the night being chilly he rested, fully clothed save for boots, beneath a pair of rough army blankets, staring at the ceiling's waterstained and fly-specked plaster. He attempted to think ahead and decide which repairs were most urgently needed.

The home paddock already had been fenced in rough-and-ready fashion by employing sometimes charred but still useful planks and timbers from burned outbuildings and the ruined end of the stables. Broken windows in the main house also had been boarded over until that happy day when glass again might become obtainable.

Every female, white or black, pitched in to scrub and clean the living room and the downstairs and to patch up essential items of furniture.

The overseer's cottage, having been not too badly damaged, next would be fixed up both as a temporary office and as quarters for Paymaster Lieutenant Shepherd who at present was occupying a mattress set on the living room floor.

He'd spent several days with Bushrod collecting and roughly sorting a wild hodgepodge of records and other documents presumably pertaining to Moluntha's management. To make any sort of order or sense out of this mass of often faded and damaged papers would require days, if not weeks.

That a glorious bright full moon was beautifying the lovely valley in which he'd grown up, lived and loved, quite escaped Rodney's notice.

Hot and weary eyes wide open, he felt faintly reassured to hear the pacing of a sentry walking his post by regularly circling the mansion; no use running risks at this late date.

Long since he'd divided officers and men into squads, all well-armed now and charged with duties best fitted to their abilities. Some devoted themselves to caring for the livestock; others applied their efforts toward patching together outbuildings such as the least damaged slave cabin, the spring and smokehouses and even a corncrib although, as Loretta pointed out, there seemed little possibility of its proving useful in the near future. Some aided Jasper and Hannibal in plowing an extensive truck garden behind the house. Even Pookie helped to plant seeds in neat little drills.

Reliable shots such as Rimfire Hamrick and Peter Tyler, following Hannibal's advice, ranged hills and meadows near a saline spring, and sometimes Jasper's mule brought in the limp carcass of a deer, more occasionally that of an elk, animals which, frightened off by the fighting around Moluntha, now were returning to accustomed haunts. Game of all description proved plentiful and not very wary; after all, it had been a long while since they'd been hunted hard.

Nevertheless Rod foresaw that this source of supplies could not last more than a few weeks at most — not when so many mouths needed to be filled. Very soon, somehow, somewhere, a basic stock of supplies would have to be found: flour, salt, bacon, molasses and cornmeal and such. Also, a lot of hardware, nails, hinges and harness were essential.

From the little he could ascertain through talking with white stragglers and homeless Negroes wandering aimlessly among the mountains, occasionally appearing in hopes of a handout, it would appear that properties and hamlets lying to the north and east of Moluntha seemed largely to have escaped occupation or other depredation.

Through the window floated the sweet, liquid notes of a night-singing mockingbird. How Louisa had loved to listen to such melodic trills and calls.

Tomorrow, Rodney decided, he'd take the wagon and, with a couple of reliable men, reconnoiter along a country road leading in the general direction of Grady and of former U.S. Congressman Lewis Renfrow's property. Lew, because he'd been born with a withered arm, had been kept out of the fighting and, by maintaining a vociferous neutrality, had managed to continue farming and boiling salt from a small saline spring, of which there were quite a few in this region.

Carefully, Renfrow had seen to it that no wandering Yankee or Rebel ever left "Edgewood" hungry or otherwise worse off than when he'd arrived. While gradually relaxing, the Master of Moluntha felt confident Lew might extend credit for a while. After all, hadn't their families shared identical social standards and even intermarried on occasion?

It was fine that Hannibal had been able to conceal a stout farm wagon's front wheels so well that Stoneman's raiders had been forced to leave the vehicle behind. Rodney wondered just what would happen should Lew be forced to demand at least some cash; always there arrived a time when friendship between gentlemen must be suspended and sordid business matters considered.

Come morning, he'd rise at dawn and see about fixing the wagon and contriving harness of some sort. Wasn't it lucky Philemon Knox and Peter Tyler both were skilled and inventive about such problems?

He lowered his arms and was about to drift off but roused, revolver in hand, on hearing his bedroom's door opening stealthily.

"Rod, 'tis only I, Loretta," a voice whispered, and a shadowy outline materialized.

"What can you want at this hour?"

"It isn't really late, Rod, only nine o'clock. But I just can't get to sleep so I'm going to walk in the moonlight where it's so clear and peaceful. Besides, I want to be near Mother awhile. I know you'll understand, as only a twin can, why I must. I'll be all right and won't be gone long."

Too exhausted to argue, Rodney vented a long-drawn sigh. "I understand, Sis. If I weren't so damned pooped I'd go along; best tell the sentry below where you're going and warn him to keep the hounds quiet. The men need their rest. G'night."

Not in a long time had such fragrant peacefulness, such serene beauty, prevailed about Moluntha Garrison. Of course during the past few years there must have been other such nights, but what with Bushrod's crippled return, Louisa's death, and all that happened since, Loretta couldn't recall many.

Perhaps, she thought while skirting Hannibal's lightless cabin and setting foot to the path leading to the burying ground on its knoll, tonight might preface a return of that comfortable peace she and Rushmore's other children for so long had taken for granted?

Somewhere far across the valley a wolf howled mournfully at the moon; then, disturbingly close by, a great horned owl raised eerie ululations. The next sound came from beyond a row of hickorys and sumacs fringing the cemetery.

Loretta halted; was she imagining or was someone actually singing up there? Cautiously, she advanced until, from the edge of the woods, she could obtain a clear view of galaxies of stars gleaming above the burying ground on its hillock.

Someone *was* singing something, not loudly but well, and with a touching, plaintive quality of tone. Curious to learn the origin of this dolorous melody, Loretta carefully parted branches and tiptoed among bushes at the cover's extreme limit, and to her utter astonishment recognized the chunky, silver-headed figure of Lieutenant Samuel Shepherd standing just outside the cemetery wall with head thrown back so far the moon clearly illuminated his rather rotund face.

While he sang, or rather chanted, the paymaster rhythmically was striking his chest, first with one clenched hand and then with the other. She strained to identify the language he was using but failed.

When from the direction of the house one of Hannibal's hounds commenced to answer the distant wolf's howling, Shepherd abruptly fell silent. Then, unerringly and in no great hurry, he descended the path to where Loretta, hair dew-drenched and with heart hammering, crouched among a clump of sumacs.

Pleasantly, the paymaster lieutenant invited in his rich, English-inflected voice, "Pray come out into the moonlight, Mistress Tilt."

"P-please, sir, forgive me appearing to eavesdrop like this — won't you kindly continue your chanting? It was most moving."

While smiling wryly, the paymaster turned toward the baying hounds, then pointed at Moluntha. "Thank you, no, ma'am. I've never been able to stand competition in the arts. Shall we ascend to the cemetery? I assume you, like I, have come to visit it and lament the departed."

By the moonlight his long and colorless hair glistened like a casque of polished silver and for the moment, clad all in gray, he suggested a ghost but, to her own great surprise, Loretta without hesitation accepted the arm he offered with Old World courtliness.

"Please say you forgive me," Loretta murmured once they neared the burying ground's ivy-draped stone wall. "I can't imagine what possessed me to eavesdrop."

Said he quietly, "You have every right, ma'am, to be near the dead you knew and loved, whilst I am but an intruder. I came only to show respect."

"But, but you scarcely knew my mother."

"True, yet old Mrs. Tilt was gracious for all —" bitterness briefly entered his tone —"I'm half-Jewish."

"I still can't understand."

"Then let me say that I came here not only to lament her but also the brave men interred here. Also I chanted prayers for the repose of all mankind who have suffered and died needlessly for any reason — or lack of it," he added softly.

She plucked a tuft of dewy sweet grass. "What was it you were singing, sir? Your music sounded most moving and plaintive."

"An old Sephardic lament taught me by Joseph, my Father. We were unusually close, perhaps because he was expelled from his congregation for marrying outside the Faith."

She peered intently into his rounded features, felt inexplicably moved at the sensitivity of his expression. "But what language did you use?" she persisted. "I could make nothing of it."

"I sang in Ladino," he explained, pretending to study the rows of headstones.

"I have never heard Ladino, spoken *or* sung, but then, I am scarcely a well-educated female."

After hitching up a bulge about his middle, Shepherd spread expressive hands. "To repeat what I've previously explained, Ladino is a language spoken but not written. It was used among Sephardic Hebrews in Spain and Portugal as a private means of communication during cruel persecution by the Holy Office of the Inquisition."

He motioned Loretta to seat herself on the wall then, settling beside her, said seriously, "Ladino, basically, is antique Spanish, but also it includes many Portuguese, Moorish and Hebrew words and constructions. Yes. It was kept secret even after our arrival, generations ago, in Charleston, Savannah, New Orleans and a few other places in the South."

"But why didn't your ancestors go North? Weren't there far greater opportunities up there?"

"True, but most Yankees are a very shrewd lot and at that time many of them were dangerously bigoted. My Father was cantor for his congregation until he was expelled, as I have already explained, for marrying a Christian. However, as a scholar, he taught me the language and songs. Nowadays only a few of us even suspect its existence."

"Is the music complicated?"

"No. They are only simple airs. Most are laments such as I've just sung, because our history has been sad ever since the dawn of time. But also we have gay, lively dance tunes, and of course love songs."

Methodically, Loretta smoothed a worn and wrinkled dark skirt. "Someday I — I think I might like to hear some of those — the last."

"Yes, Mistress Tilt, someday, perhaps. Who can foresee?"

Shepherd got to his feet, then stood in thought, chin cupped under a hand. "Mistress Tilt, this is delightful, but don't you think we had better direct our thoughts more toward the present?"

Vigorously Loretta shook her dark head. "I *hate* the present! Won't there ever again be peace and order among men? Kindness and love?"

"Not for a considerable while; at least not in North America, I fear." He stared fixedly over the valley, resplendent by moonlight. "True peace will be a long time coming. Too much deep hatred has been aroused to vanish easily. Therefore I fear your family, you and I, all of us, must face up to realities and decide what immediate and practical steps can be taken to preserve Moluntha and ourselves from the bitter winds of defeat."

Inexplicably, Loretta was seized by an impression that she and this enigmatic young man sitting there in the moonlight by a graveyard for the moment were occupying a peaceful islet set in a stormy universe tormented by sorrow, and suffering soon to be further afflicted by ruthless ambition and greed.

Finally she arose, saying, "Mr. Shepherd, I must return to the house — alone of course. Be sure to alert the sentry in plenty of time when you come back." She offered a slim but rough hand, and looked straight into his pale eyes. "Thank you, Mr. Shepherd. I — I believe I understand your motives in coming here tonight, so I will pray that whatever Power you worship will reward you. Goodnight, sir, and may God bless you."

Once the young woman's outline disappeared along the path to Moluntha, Samuel Shepherd remained motionless and reluctantly allowed this moment's euphoric quality to dissipate.

At long last he sought an apple orchard originally set out by Ajax Tilt not far below the cemetery. Long since it had been abandoned in favor of a more productive and convenient location.

The moonlight shone so strongly Shepherd experienced little difficulty in locating a pile of old stones in the midst of which he'd discovered what seemed to be a satisfactory hiding place. He was unbuttoning his jacket when he thought he heard what sounded like a faint crackling of twigs somewhere among the trees below. They ceased, but he remained motionless until he concluded the noise could only have been caused by a foraging deer. Reassured, he undid his jacket's cold brass buttons, then pulled it off. He shivered. It really was cold up here.

With stiffening fingers Shepherd untied the wide leather belt he invariably wore laced about his middle and laid it across a flat stone all the while hoping there might be no rattlesnakes lurking in this rocky pile — there were plenty in the vicinity. Next, with almost loving care, he arranged a sizable collection of gold coins in rows according to size and value.

Among the pieces were solid-looking red-gold English sovereigns, thick, beautifully designed Mexican twenty-peso pieces, a fair number of Napoleons, and a few very rare American double-eagles.

Long ago he'd reckoned that, on today's market, these should bring $5,000 at the least, probably more if he could wait and locate the right buyer, once political conditions settled down. Through force of habit he then leafed through his supply of United States Treasury notes. Good! These came to exactly $1,776, which purely by coincidence, was the year of the Declaration of Independence. Some notes were of large denomination, but through foresight he'd included a good many small and thus easily exchangeable bills, even some "shinplasters." These lesser notes, worth ten, twenty-five or fifty cents, he carefully folded lengthwise and replaced in his money belt. The coins he dumped into a leather pucker-bag, then knotted its drawstring with great care.

Larger bills he folded tightly and rolled into a strip of well-oiled silk, and for the time being replaced in his money belt.

Next, the paymaster gently raised a moss-covered triangular-shaped rock he'd located not long ago. It lay among ferns and was barely visible above ground level. Kneeling, he thrust the heavy bag of coins into a small crevice below the stone, then gradually eased the stone back into position.

Once more he thought he detected a faint rustling noise from among nearby trees. They ceased at once, since Peter Tyler was an expert stalker, which might also explain why Loretta hadn't suspected she was being followed on the way up from Moluntha.

Tyler's experience had warned him to halt, but at such a distance he couldn't overhear what Rodney's twin and Shepherd were talking about.

Once Loretta Tilt had departed, the Texan lingered where he lay until the ex-paymaster lieutenant entered the woods, so nearby that Tyler didn't dare risk coming closer. He remained completely motionless until Shepherd appeared, wiping his hands and took the path leading to Moluntha.

# 18

## Margaret Forsythe

MARGARET FORSYTHE lay wakeful in what originally had served as Moluntha's sewing room. She rested on, or rather occupied, a plain iron bedstead once used by the late Otho Tilt. It had been equipped with a hard, flat pillow and a lumpy canvas sack filled with corn husks and dried moss. Judging by a faint odor, mice at some time must have nested in it.

Wearily, she hoped she'd conducted the funeral service adequately. Since, being a female, she could not study for the ministry or be ordained, the ceremony therefore had been of no real religious significance and should be repeated at some later date.

Through half-closed lids she viewed with acute disgust hanging from a peg that uniform she'd been forced to wear all this time. True, its breeches and jacket were as clean as repeated washings could render them; nevertheless, they remained uncomfortable and unattractive male attire. She wondered why neither Loretta nor Caroline had offered her female garb of any description, for all they otherwise remained polite enough — even helpful at times.

By now she had come to accept this attitude as a result of the shock over old Mrs. Tilt's sudden violent death and the vicious, bloody turmoil of the partisan attack plus Rodney's often moody and withdrawn manner.

In Loretta she sensed an instinctive hostility toward herself perhaps attributable to the fact that she always was wearing the hated Union blue. Hopefully, the Colonel's sister's attitude would soften. In some ways she resembled her twin, being supremely self-controlled yet possessing a certain inner warmth which occasionally broke through her hard crust of imperturbability.

For a while she twisted and turned on the miserable bed, trying to achieve some degree of comfort. She listened to the tramping of the sentry below, heard him challenge what sounded like a hail from Loretta. Judging by the moon's position, the Northern girl guessed the hour must be nearing eleven o'clock but of course she'd no means of making sure.

She shivered, then pulled higher about her a yellowed old cotton nightgown she'd found hanging in the sewing room closet. At this altitude, even in late spring, nights were far from balmy. Sunny South? Bah!

Concerning Bushrod, Meg thus far had formed no opinion beyond the fact that this cripple was a long way from being anywhere near as capable and decisive as his older brother. Poor Bushrod! What with all these unusual exertions his wounded foot must be causing him agonies; one could tell that from the way his limping steadily became more pronounced — that and the way he'd bite his lips from time to time to stifle groans.

Already she'd deduced that, aside from farming and horse breeding, Caroline's husband understood next to nothing concerning business affairs or legal matters.

Lieutenant Shepherd, very tactfully to be sure, had intimated as much during a casual conversation following the funerals. "I've been attempting to help him, but with poor results," he stated. "The records are a shambles."

Still wakeful, Meg continued her summation of the Tilts. She'd better make no false assumptions, since for the time being she was altogether dependent on this family and their good opinion. Nevertheless, she'd never allow herself to be "put-upon"; weren't the Forsythes every bit as well-born as the Tilts?

It was only toward Caroline she experienced a degree of affinity. Why? All at once she understood. Like herself, Caroline, who'd been born Caroline Menier, did not belong by blood ties to the Tilt clan, for all she was Bushrod's wife and little Oliver's mother. So in differing degrees she and Caroline shared a common disadvantage; both were foreigners in Moluntha Garrison.

Aside from her loveliness the girl from New Orleans was more than just pretty and far from the mental lightweight her sometimes flighty mannerisms suggested.

Meg worked aside a nubbin of corncob stubbornly digging into her thigh while deciding whether she should appeal to Caroline for garments befitting her sex.

What could have become of Mother and her sister, or rather what could not have happened to them? She bit the lining of her mouth — a childish trick she'd never got over. Considering the casual way with which those bushwhackers had butchered her small brothers she doubted if they still lived, but if they had managed to survive, where were they?

Appropriately enough, an owl commenced to hoot lugubriously in a nearby tree. More comforting was the sound of a soft whinny from that rough paddock in which most of Moluntha's livestock had been penned, under guard. Perhaps the call came from Avalon? What a hot-blooded yet generally docile creature was her small, well-conformed black mare.

To be sure she'd no legal right to Avalon, yet she considered the animal her one and only asset. Moonlight, streaming through broken window-panes, illumined a faint smile. Meg guessed she now was nearly as devoid of worldly possessions as she'd been when she'd entered the world. But what if the mare was worth real money? All along, Sergeant Knox had maintained Avalon must be at least three-quarter or even clean-bred. Unfortunately, since no papers existed to support the farrier's opinion, any foal she might drop would have only its sire's pedigree, if one existed to be counted upon.

What to do? *What to do*, without a penny to her name and in an unfriendly land. Another handicap lay in that, through some quirk of genetics, both sides of her family had few members.

As near as Meg knew, Azael Forsythe, her Father's older brother, was her sole close relative. A confirmed bachelor, he practiced law in Falmouth Foreside near Portland, Maine. She'd met him only once when she and her mother had passed through that city on a visit to her now deceased grandparents who'd lived in Bangor, Maine, and that lone encounter had taken place some years before the war had begun, so she couldn't even be sure whether Uncle Azael was still alive. Of course, without a cent to her name, the cost of a trip all the way to Portland was beyond consideration.

Curiously enough, the only person in the world now alive who seemed genuinely interested in her was that curious *soi-disant* Texan calling himself "Peter Tyler." She tried but failed to recall Peter's father's full name. All she could remember was the "Gonzales" part of it, and "Gonzales" south of the Border, men said, was as common a name as "Smith" to the north of it. Gonzales?

For some time she'd sensed Peter might be falling in love with her, despite the fact that the Texan never once had attempted familiarities, either vocal or physical. All the same she felt somewhat wary. Peter Tyler was given on rare occasions to sudden fits of blazing temper which had got him into serious fights with tactless members of what once had been Z Company.

Then, too, she'd noticed that Peter could be an artful thief, but excused him on the grounds that army life must lead to such lapses, and also he never seemed to steal for his own benefit, but always for her or to help some distressed companion.

More embarrassing was the way he or his gaze followed her whenever possible, but whatever Tyler said or did one fact remained inescapable — he was not of the common sort and was brimming with ambition to accomplish great things. However, he remained practical and seemed aware that under present conditions his colorful planning for the future might prove highly risky.

At last Meg commenced to feel drowsy while deciding that tomorrow she really must speak to Caroline about some female garments, no matter what state these might be in. An accomplished seamstress thanks to Mother's insistence, she probably could mend and alter such hand-me-downs to suit her after a fashion.

She was about to drift off when, in that inexplicable suddenness with which some memories recur, she recalled Uncle Azael's address as 83 Lowell Street, Falmouth Foreside, Near Portland, Maine.

Of course old Mr. Forsythe might have died or have moved away from that address, but it could do no harm to write describing her situation so that possibly she might secure a measure of assistance; Uncle Azael, Mother had implied, on rare occasions was considered to be fairly well-off.

Would the fact that she now probably was his only living relative, so far as she knew, induce that tight-fisted old codger to take an interest in his niece? Well and good, but where would she find the necessary stamp money? When one wrote to Uncle Azael one invariably enclosed return postage — Mother always had done so.

If she approached Mr. Shepherd tactfully enough perhaps she might obtain a tiny loan since the ex-paymaster once briefly had exposed a small roll of "shin plasters." Although her impulse was to write the very first thing tomorrow, two considerations militated against so precipitate a procedure. Wouldn't it be wiser to wait until the situation at Moluntha Garrison became clarified and Western Virginia had started to work out and establish some form of civil government capable of restoring public services to something like normal?

Once the day's chores had been completed, Margaret Forsythe found occasion to accompany Oliver and his mother for a stroll down to that somewhat isolated gazebo on Copper Point which long had served as a lookout station, since it afforded an excellent view of the valley and surrounding ridges and mountains. The Federals also had used it for that purpose, but for a wonder hadn't damaged it.

"I sense you wish to chat," Caroline remarked, stooping to pick wild daisies. "Am I correct?"

"Yes, Mrs. Tilt."

"Please drop formality with me, my dear," Caroline invited pleasantly, then used an apron to remove dusty sweat from smooth, pink-and-white cheeks. "There have been too many 'Mrs. Tilts' around here. My friends, and I hope to include you among them, call me 'Carrie.' I'll call you 'Meg,' just like Rodney and the rest of your company. Now, what's on your mind?"

The Northern girl slapped dust from her uniform's work-stained jacket and yellow-striped blue breeches.

"First off, I'm sick and tired of wearing men's clothes which, as you can guess, not only are uncomfortable for a woman but serve to keep reminding me and your people of tragedies which had best be forgotten as quickly as possible." She stepped closer and with a wistful look added, "I, well, I was wondering, Mrs. er, I mean Carrie, if there aren't *any* female things left in the house — no matter how old or worn?"

The other inclined her yellow-blond head. "There must be. Yes! Come to think on it I remember that, soon after Louisa died, we put an old trunk up in the attic filled with her things, along with some of Grandma Ruthelma's old clothes and a few of mine." Impulsively, she placed a hand on Meg's wrist. "I don't blame you a bit for feeling miserable wearing a man's clothing."

"He who wore these wasn't yet a man — only a youth murdered by outlaws." She saw again with painful clarity that gangling, blood-stained figure sprawled on clean spring grass.

"War's so horrible. My late brother-in-law, Otho, wasn't yet twenty." Caroline picked a few more flowers. "Tomorrow, my dear, we'll climb up to the garret and see what we can discover. I'm sure Rod and Bush will approve, Rod especially because — although he doesn't say much — Loretta and I both can tell he's full of admiration for you and respect for your courage. Never forget one thing, Meg. I've always believed that true respect always should precede expressions of — well, tenderer sentiments and —" She got no further because Oliver tripped over a root and was gathering breath to howl his curly little head off.

# 19

---◼◆◼---

# Practical Considerations

B<small>Y THE EVENING</small> of the third day after Ruthelma Donelson Tilt and Benjy had been laid to rest, Rodney followed Sam Shepherd and Margaret Forsythe in joining a group of men surrounding Sergeant Knox. He was saying, "Reckon that bay mare I found along the trail is gettin' ready to foal anytime now; we'd best put her in the loose stall. Tonight, I'll rig a pallet of sorts and sleep alongside. Let's hope the sire was clean-bred."

On noticing Meg he strode over, touched a frayed straw hat. "Been meanin' to look you up all day, Miss Meg, on account of Avalon. Your mare is coming in — well, in heat." If he expected the Northern girl to blush he was disappointed. Since the war had begun she'd seen enough of farm life not to be affected by the act of creation — human or animal.

"What do you think ought to be done, Philemon, considering Avalon has no papers?"

"Well, as possible sires there's the colonel's Resaca and Major Bushrod's Molino. Both have thoroughbred papers and were foaled on this property. Of the two I reckon Resaca would prove better. Molino —" he broke off, grinning through his sparse, sandy-red beard. "Did you know his registered name is 'Molino del Rey'?"

"Why so?"

" 'Twas another one of them Mexican War battles Major Rushmore fit in. Well, as I was sayin', Resaca's younger by two full years and for all his wounds and campaignin' he's in much better shape. Any foal he'd sire might start the famous Tilt strain off to a fine fresh beginning."

Sam Shepherd, who'd appeared unobtrusively, remarked, "That stallion's seen a lot of hard times. Let's hope he's still potent. A blooded colt these days is a valuable piece of property. With Avalon's get, you'll have some valuable collateral."

"Guess that's true. Philemon, will you er — make the necessary arrangements at the right moment? I'll help if necessary."

" 'Twon't be. You forget most of us are cavalrymen."

Rodney came up and, chuckling, agreed Resaca might be in for a treat. "Knox, how are the other mounts coming along?"

"About well as they ever will be."

"Good. Now come along and pick out some cold-bred critters not likely to object too much over hauling a wagon or a plow."

He looked about the weary, unkempt group, said pleasantly, "All right, men, you've put in a long, hard day's work and must be hungry. Dismiss!"

Odd how, even now, military terms persisted!

In an open space before the barn men set about cooking over open fires. They wouldn't be doing so much longer, since rebuilding of a large outdoor kitchen which in the past had been used by field hands was nearing restoration.

Just where certain individuals had obtained civilian clothing remained a mystery to the Tilts, yet every day fewer items of uniform, jackets in particular, were in evidence.

Following a meager supper, Rodney and Loretta led Bushrod, hobbling ever more painfully, out to the gazebo. There, Rodney and Bushrod sank onto a wickerwork settee and lit pipes while Loretta arranged her skirts about a rattan armchair which, miraculously, had escaped destruction.

Rodney drew a deep breath and commenced in a lowered voice. "Since I intend this conversation to concern only the immediate family I've not invited anyone not blood kin to attend."

Frowning, Loretta shoved a loose strand of dark hair back into place. "What a pity Mother, Father, Albert, and Otho can't be present."

Bushrod sighed, remarked, "I've been wondering why you didn't ask Caroline along."

"She's only a Tilt by marriage," Loretta reminded. "This meeting concerns our own family property. What are we to do in the immediate future to preserve Moluntha Garrison and our mining interests?"

Thoughtfully, Rodney tugged at sable mustaches he'd trimmed and shortened considerably since arriving home. "I'll admit the immediate future looks dark but not necessarily hopeless, provided we use our heads. Now then, let's cast up a rough account of our situation.

"First, on the credit side, we own this estate and more than two thousand acres of prime farmland and stands of valuable timber. Second, a two-thirds interest in the King Salt Works at Saltville. Third, we have full ownership of the Ajax Lead Mine near Wytheville."

"True, but from all I can learn," Bushrod interjected bitterly, "the mine at present can't produce so much as a single pig of lead. They say Yankee wreckers did a very thorough job."

Impatiently, Rod shook his head and then peered at his brother through the starlight. "We'll go into that later. What we need to talk about is, where in Hell can we find sufficient cash for food, help, and essential building materials? Right now, we're penniless except for those few Union bills we found on the damned partisans."

Bushrod stared out over the valley. "Well, we've still got the family silver you and I hid but I've no idea how much it might be worth."

Rodney said impatiently, "Probably a fair amount if sold to advantage, but to find a proper purchaser will take a lot of time, which is another commodity we're short of."

Too well Loretta could recall the day, nearly two years back, when Rodney had ridden in, unannounced, during one of his rare leaves of absence. He'd produced a copy of the Jonesborough *Daily Telegraph* picked up along the way. At a glance Bushrod, newly invalided home, had guessed that whatever news was contained in that single, ten-by-twelve-inch sheet of newsprint must be far from encouraging. All he'd said was, "All right, Rod, let's have it."

Once all the family had collected in the living room, Rodney had spread the newspaper flat on the marred Chippendale table and had read aloud that, on July 4th of 1863, the Southern Cause had suffered two calamitous defeats. He'd continued:

" 'At Vicksburg General Pemberton, after a gallant defense, has been forced to surrender to Major General U. S. Grant about 31,000 veteran troops, 172 cannon and over 60,000 muskets; thus the full length of the Mississippi is lost to the Union, save for minor strongholds which soon must yield to superior Federal forces.' "

Rodney had looked up, saying, "On this same Fourth of July, ended a great and bloody three-day battle fought at Gettysburg up in Pennsylvania which, I regret to say, ended in defeat for the Army of Northern Virginia. It cost the South so many of its finest and irreplaceable veteran troops I fear there no longer remains any real hope of again invading the North or even of capturing Washington."

Characteristically, Grandma Ruthelma had summed up the import of such information. "From now on, we-all will have no choice but to fight on the defensive. It may take the enemy considerable time but, I reckon we-all know that, in the end, our side don't stand a chance against

Yankee numbers and resources. They'll surely ravage our country, so let's face facts and do what's sensible."

Stoically the old lady's faintly oblique eyes had hardened like those of a squaw facing a winter's march through hostile country.

Accordingly, before Rodney returned to the 11th Cavalry he and Bushrod one night quietly had filled four grain sacks with solid silver salvers, goblets, tableware, plates, platters, tureens, candelabra, anything of sterling. Even valuable items of fine Sheffield plate were sacked, and the lot loaded onto scrawny pack mules which carried them up the mountain behind Moluntha to a small cave discovered by chance in their youth while out deer hunting.

Upon their return they'd given Loretta and Grandma Ruthelma a minute description of the cache and landmarks; they had required both ladies several times to repeat, verbatim, the cache's exact location so there would be no necessity for drawing a possibly dangerous map.

Presumably, the family silver still reposed where it had been hidden, since no one had even been suspected of approaching the hiding place. All the same, Rodney asked, "Bush, have you ever checked the spot?"

The cripple shook his head. "No. In my condition I might have been too easily followed."

Loretta queried, moodily staring at laced, work-worn hands, "Wonder how much might all that plate fetch nowadays?"

"Lord only knows," Rodney grunted. "None of us are qualified to make an estimate. Incidentally, we'll wait as long as we can before making a move. With conditions being as they are in the South, it's certain there'll be a lot of plate offered on the market. It will probably go for a song when ready cash is so badly needed."

From under lowered brows Rod shot a glance at his brother. "Don't we hold mortgages on quite a few farms and some buildings in Bristol and Abingdon?"

Bushrod spread hands in a gesture indicative of helplessness. "Damned if I know. Some might be worth something — most probably not. Can't tell till we go through whatever papers we still have. Plenty have been lost or destroyed and, around here, we've been a sight too busy just trying to stay alive to worry over such matters. Loretta's collected everything she could find."

It came Loretta's turn for her shoulders to slump. She uttered a faint sigh. "I did what I could after those damned Yankees rode away, but there wasn't very much I could find in the way of records."

She looked hard at her brothers. "On the debit side, all we have left is a half-wrecked estate, a ruined lead mine, an interest in salt works of questionable value, weed-choked fields, and no breeding stock worthy of mention, so I needn't point out we've *got* to find cash right away."

The three sat in silence a long while, listening to the shrill, monotonous peeping of tree frogs and the plaint of a whippoorwill in the distance.

Rodney broke the silence. "Will you two please give me your considered opinion concerning Samuel Shepherd? So far as I can deduce he's clever, an expert bookkeeper and accountant — must be, since he served with the Paymaster Corps for so long.

"Question is, would he prove completely trustworthy in matters where personal gain might take precedence over the interests of others?"

Again, stillness lasted until Bushrod said, "I like him, for all I've only known him a week or so. I find Shepherd is well-mannered, apparently well-educated, and with important connections, if he's to be believed. I'd agree to trust him if he weren't half-Jewish. I've always heard one never can altogether depend on members of that race. They're always out for themselves."

"Ever have experience with Hebrews?" Loretta queried thoughtfully. "None of us ever have had dealings with other than those of our own sort."

"What say you, Rod?"

"There were very few of his persuasion among the fighting forces but I've heard plenty about Jewish shrewdness when matters stand to their advantage."

Loretta commented, "That's only hearsay, then. Has one ever done you, or anyone you know well, any wrong?"

"No."

"In that case I'd say let's suspend judgment, since the fact remains we must at once find someone to put our affairs in order."

Unexpectedly, Bushrod spoke. "Shepherd might do all right if he suspected he was being watched."

"By whom?" Loretta asked.

"What about the Forsythe girl? She's well-educated and, from what I've observed, she's pretty smart with figures."

Rod laughed, "Don't forget she's a Yankee; they're sharp, too."

Loretta slapped a mosquito from her cheek. "More hearsay. Personally I'd trust her, so I think Bush may have a point. Suppose she helps Shepherd and at the same time keeps an eye on him? Caroline can handle that part of our problem. They've become right friendly."

"Not a bad idea," Rod stated after momentary hesitation. "One thing is certain. From what I've seen of Margaret Forsythe under all sorts of conditions I'd say, Yankee or no Yankee, she's dependable as the day is long. What do you say, Bush?"

"I'll go along."

They relit their pipes. "Now that we've agreed on this, what *are* we going to do for ready cash? We need more men to get this place going, but how can we pay them?"

Rod said, " 'Aye, there's the rub,' as old Shakespeare puts it."

"Hardly a day goes by but some personable veteran hasn't stopped by begging only shelter and a few mouthfuls of food. I'd say that the scum mostly have traveled on west or have headed for Texas."

Rod nodded, "True enough. One man came in this afternoon, name of 'Watts,' steady-looking fellow. He claims to be a master carpenter and joiner and God knows we need one. I'd like to keep him here but we can't pay him and we've scarcely enough food to feed ourselves a few days longer." Slowly he pounded one hard fist against its mate, then sat straight, jaw set.

"Now listen, you two. Here's what I intend. Tomorrow I'll take the wagon and a few men and ride toward Grundy. On the way I'll stop in at 'Edgewood' and have a talk with Lewis Renfrow. If he can spare us some supplies and a little money I know he'll help to the best of his ability but, if he's changed, like so many others have, I'll have to offer him a small mortgage. In the meantime I don't see what we have to lose through sounding out Sam Shepherd."

Loretta said evenly, "As usual you're making sense, Rod." Without hesitation she gathered her skirts and stood up.

Bushrod chuckled, "Damned if I don't believe you've been thinking along this line for quite a while."

"I have, and I'm going right now to find him."

Before Rodney realized it Loretta was hurrying up to the house and soon returned with Samuel Shepherd's chunky figure trudging in her wake.

The Tilt brothers arose when the former paymaster drew near. What with his gray uniform and colorless skin and hair, Rodney thought he appeared almost ghostlike by this brilliant starlight.

Awkwardly, Rodney cleared his throat and more than ever suggested a throwback to his cavalier ancestors. Samuel Shepherd also appeared to gain in stature and dignity. "My brother and I have been discussing family affairs," Rodney informed.

In a strained voice Bushrod commenced, "Before we proceed any further, sir, we require that you raise your right hand and swear by the God we all worship that, whatever is said and decided here, you will forever keep it to yourself."

"Will you so swear?" Rodney queried softly.

The narrow-shouldered, somewhat plump figure stiffened a trifle. "If it will reassure you all," he glanced at Loretta, "I do so solemnly swear."

They formed an odd group; the straight-backed spare young woman in flowing dark skirts who stood nearly as tall as her rangy twin; the crippled veteran slightly bent through supporting himself on a cane he was forced to use; and the half-Jewish stranger within their gates.

"Please seat yourself, sir," Rodney said. "We must now face urgent and immediate problems."

Shepherd bowed slightly toward Loretta, "In honor of this occasion, d'you mind if I smoke one of my last seegars?"

Once the group had seated themselves Rodney repeated the situation at Moluntha as discussed before Shepherd's arrival.

Shepherd listened, eyes fixed on the sky, until Rodney had done.

Bushrod demanded brusquely, "Well, sir, in your opinion what can and should be done?"

Said the former paymaster, "If you could guess how much thought I've already devoted to Moluntha and its present condition you'd be astonished." He spoke with a faint English accent and without hesitation used erudite words which exactly expressed his thoughts.

"May I say that I feel confident that with patience, shrewdness and foresight, your property can be restored to gracious and profitable operation." Faded trefoils of silver braid on Sam's sleeves gleamed dully as he spread hands in a characteristic gesture.

"Speaking only from observation and knowing nothing about the previous financial situation of your estate, I would observe that your most immediate concern is to obtain ready, negotiable cash and credits necessary to commence rebuilding, to replace essential equipment and to pay and feed such laborers as will be needed." He arched heavy, silver-hued brows. "Am I correct?"

"You are," Bushrod grunted. "But even a dumblock could tell us that much. The question for a clever man like yourself is, where are we to find this ready cash you mention?"

Sam's gaze shifted to Loretta. "I believe I can help to answer that and at the same time demonstrate a measure of the gratitude I feel for your having protected and befriended me in my hour of need."

He tapped that slight bulge about his middle. "I have in here exactly one thousand, seven hundred and seventy-six dollars in United States Treasury notes." He smiled faintly, "Odd, isn't it, that this sum should coincide with the year in which the American Colonies declared Independence?"

By God! Real money was becoming available! A surge of surprised relief warmed Rodney's being, but all he said was, "Let us pray said date proves as fortunate for Moluntha as it did for America."

Bushrod added bitterly, "At least to begin with."

"I don't pretend such a paltry sum would help much toward restoring this property, but I'm offering it to you with heartfelt thanks for all you people have done for me."

Thoughtfully, Bushrod stroked his ragged yellow-brown beard. "And what, Mr. Shepherd, will be the rate of interest you expect?"

Rasping something unintelligible, Shepherd leaped to his feet. Loretta was astounded by the malevolence written across the former paymaster's normally composed features. He swung over to the cripple, spoke in icy accents. "Sir! This is an uncalled-for insult. Were circumstances different I'd slap your face!"

"— And you'd wish you'd never attempted such a thing. Aren't you part Jewish?"

Shepherd said coldly, "Yes and proud of it! I can only explain your words, Major Tilt, on the ground that you are not only poorly educated, but also an untraveled fellow of limited understanding."

Sharply Rodney said, "You are quite right, Mr. Shepherd. Bushrod, you've done yourself — all of us — and our friend small credit. Shame on you!"

Cheerfully, he could have wrung his brother's neck for jeopardizing a moment so critical for what he'd in mind.

Loretta sprang to her feet, trembling hands clenched. "Bushrod! Apologize immediately — else I'll never again speak to you."

Rodney noticed and was astonished at the vehemence of his sister.

The cripple swayed erect and offered his hand. "Sir, please forgive my ignorance and unwarranted rudeness. I can only say in explanation that my judgment perhaps has been warped by pain — it's never been worse than at this moment. Can you accept my sincere apology?"

Breathing hard, Shepherd delayed a long moment before gripping hands. "Of course, sir. I already have forgotten all about this *contretemps*. Suppose we return to practical considerations?"

During a brief instant Sam Shepherd debated but as quickly abstained from mention of the gold concealed near the path to the graveyard. While the stars crept along their orbits the four remained silent in the gazebo, absorbed in respective thoughts, calculations and emotions.

Finally Rodney invited, "Tell us, in your opinion, what is most likely to take place concerning the government and the restoration of law and order to the Southern States?"

Shepherd's shoulders rose in a shrug. "I doubt if even the Delphic Sibyl herself could find ready predictions about that. Oh, if *only* that villain, Booth, hadn't murdered Mr. Lincoln!" His pale gaze circled anxious faces about him and expressions only half-revealed by starlight. "I fear anything can happen during the next few months."

Loretta asked, "Will all Southerners be disenfranchised, or will temporary State governments run by Southerners be tolerated, or will our States be readmitted to full membership in the Union?"

"I fear nothing reasonable or lenient can be hoped for."

Bushrod sighed, bent forward, resting elbows on knees. "More likely the North will clamp down and enforce some form of military government."

Again the former paymaster nodded. "I fear your prediction will prove correct, especially since Radicals in both houses of the United States Congress are shrieking for vengeance on what they term 'the Rebellion.' Such politicians are growing in strength despite everything the new President, Mr. Andrew Johnson, can do to contain them.

"Why, Black Radicals like Thaddeus Stevens, Garrison and their sort, even before the war ended, were proposing to grant every Negro over the age of twenty-one the right to vote — even if the poor fellow can't write his own name, and wouldn't have the least notion about what he'd be voting for."

Somberly Rodney said, "We will never stand for that, and will fight again, even if we lose — which we will, of course."

A shiver rippled down Loretta's spine. "Such a move would prove disastrous to all concerned, North and South — not that I mean the — the blacks, I mean shouldn't, in due time, be granted the right to vote."

Down in the valley a fox commenced to bark, creating a tiny sharp sound amid the immense stillness of the night.

Again Rodney slowly beat one fist against the other. "Well, let's hope for the best, since we're all Americans and it's not in our nature to stand for injustice, once passions have cooled."

Loretta said, "All this talk about the future is getting us nowhere. Let's get down to cases."

Rodney smiled at his twin. "Right, so, as we'd say in the Army, let's consolidate our position here at Moluntha and establish supply lines as fast as possible."

Shepherd started to speak but Rodney held up a hand. "Bad as things look right now I don't think we yet need draw upon those funds you've so generously offered, my friend. Such monies, of course, would be repaid as soon as practicable."

"There's no hurry, Colonel. I only hope you'll permit me to linger here for a reasonable while — till I can get your affairs in order and make plans for my future. Oh —" He snapped his fingers. "I forgot to tell you that one of the men passing through mentioned that the post office at Gladesville will be reopened within the next few days. When it is, perhaps we won't feel we're acting in the dark."

Commented Loretta, "Yes. It's important in many ways that we get in touch with the outside world again. For instance, Meg Forsythe's very eager to post a letter to an uncle who lives somewhere up North. I'd like to write to Eliza Peabody."

"And I to Marc," Rodney said recalling their encounter at Appomattox. He wondered briefly how much Marc had been in earnest.

"Incidentally, Mr. Shepherd," Loretta was saying, "will you give us your frank opinion concerning Miss Forsythe?"

"She's not only an attractive young lady but undoubtedly well-educated, straightforward and clear-thinking. I feel confident she'll prove invaluable in assisting me make what order I can out of your affairs. She appears capable in a good many other directions."

Loretta commented curtly, "In other words we seem to have in her a — a paragon of efficiency?"

"Yes. Something like that. Have you heard whether or not the Wise County Courthouse was ransacked?"

Wearily, Bushrod shook his big head. "Not that we've heard of."

"Then we might come across valuable documents or duplicates thereof there."

Stiffly, Rodney heaved his wiry figure to its feet. All this business talk and the implications behind it was tiring as it was unfamiliar. If only a campaign was being discussed, he'd be feeling a lot less fatigue. "I think we've talked enough for now. Suppose we retire and think over what's been said. Incidentally, tomorrow I'll be taking along the wagon with an escort and heading for Lew Renfrow's place. Possibly he might be able to spare us necessities to tide us over for a time."

# 20

❖

# Uncertain Expedition

THE WEATHER on this mid-June morning appeared unable to make up its mind. Although sunlight sketched bright patches along the valley, gray clouds and skeins of lacy white mists hovered among foothills and mountain tops. Nearly all the inhabitants of Moluntha Garrison turned out to watch Jasper settle onto the driver's seat of the farm cart, a large and sturdy vehicle drawn by a pair of big-hoofed and heavy-boned cavalry mounts, which in the past probably had been broken to hauling or plowing. Their harness had been improvised out of so many odds and ends of rope and leather it promised to give out sooner than the animals.

Sitting their horses and wearing ragged country coats and no uniform beyond gray, yellow-striped breeches were Rimfire Hamrick, Peter Tyler and a likely-looking young fellow who'd recently appeared giving his name as Bill Stearnes, late of the 10th Alabama Volunteer Field Artillery. All were armed with revolvers and carried single-shot, breech-loading Sharps carbines slung across their backs but there were no sabers — such being purely wartime weapons.

Rodney Tilt was wearing patched brown riding breeches and a long-skirted gray gabardine jacket he'd bought in Cambridge, Massachusetts, way back in 1860. Oddly enough, both garments still fitted reasonably well.

In the wagon had been stowed a tent, a kettle and a few rations and some fodder — after all, Edgewood lay well over twenty miles distant and was accessible only over the roughest sort of country tracks. Not having been used for such a long time wind-felled trees and frost-loosened rocks must be blocking the route at a good many points.

A round-trip, Hannibal and Jasper reckoned, couldn't be accomplished in under five days at the very least.

Once the party started to form up, little Oliver piped, "Hurray for Uncle Rodney! Please bring back some toys. Mine are all busted."

Caroline called, "Hope you'll be pleased over how much we'll have got done before you get back. Give fond good wishes to the Renfrows and tell them to drop over soon as things settle down — we owe them a visit." She didn't mention that they'd last seen each other early '61.

While settling into his saddle Tyler glanced down at Meg, who'd just handed him a small case of shaving articles he'd overlooked. "We'll return fast as we can, don't doubt that. In the meantime don't take unnecessary chances. Remember, now that the weather has warmed this country it fairly swarms with rattlesnakes."

Serenely she peered up into the Texan's intense blue-black eyes and smiled. "Thank you, Peter. May the Lord watch over you."

At length Rodney tightened Resaca's reins — the stallion was acting spry considering the fact he'd enthusiastically served Avalon an hour ago.

Wistfully, veterans among the onlookers watched the wagon lurch into motion and outriders take position.

"B' Jesus," one growled, "wisht I was goin' along. Diggin' post holes ain't my idee of fun; I'm itchin' to feel the shape of a scabbard 'neath my knee and the drag of a carbine on my shoulders."

Bushrod astonished everybody, especially Caroline, by singing out in his old-time voice, "All right, boys, let's raise 'em a farewell shout!"

Hats were whipped off and swung as the high-pitched Rebel yell rang out three times.

Once the wagon had jolted and rumbled out of sight, Bushrod called for his horse. "Come along, boys, looks like it might rain and we need to finish the lower pasture's fencing."

Growling, the men commenced to collect tools, but Sergeant Knox hurried toward the stables. Gloriana, as he called the mare he'd found on the way back from the surrender, must be just about ready to drop her foal. He was about to summon a fellow supposedly knowledgeable about such matters when Meg intervened. "He's more needed elsewhere. I can help if need be."

Loretta started and stared. "If I weren't ladylike, I'd say, 'I'll be damned'!" She laughed, then followed Caroline toward the house.

Caroline queried, "Ever met anyone like Meg Forsythe? As a Yankee might say, 'In my book she's all wool and a yard wide.'"

Toward midday Meg sought the horse trough and there washed blood from her hands, thanking goodness that Philemon's mare had had normal delivery of a pretty little golden-bay foal.

"Good thing it turned out a filly," Knox had observed, using the back of a hand to wipe sweat from a deeply furrowed forehead.

"Why so?"

"Come a couple of years, she can get another thoroughbred fit to enter in the Tilt studbook."

"But Gloriana has no papers."

"True, but I reckon after all that's happened to records down here, folks ain't going to be over-fussy about a missing link on the dam's side, provided the sire's pedigree ain't been — er — interrupted."

"How are you going to name her?"

Knox rubbed reddish stubble covering his pointed jaw. "Why, ma'am, Lorena after that song we used to sing so often during the War. That is, if the Colonel agrees."

"But — but she's yours."

"No, ma'am, I figure I don't rightly *own* anything. The horse I rode here, Gloriana, and her foal, belong to Moluntha. You like the name?"

"Yes. It's pretty even if, in a way, it does perpetuate the — the War and all its grief. You expect to move on once this place is put together again?"

"Doubt it. Think I'll 'bide here, which is about the prettiest part of God's country I've ever laid eyes on. Maybe I'll catch some hard-workin' female woman who'd be fool enough to marry me and settle close by. I'd admire to watch the Tilt blood lines get back to where they once was. How 'bout you?"

"I, well, I've not yet made up my mind and probably won't till I hear from an uncle I have up North. I've written him, but the Lord alone knows whether I'll ever hear from him."

Knox drawled, "Heard say there's a post office opened in Gladesville. Soon's the Colonel gets back some of us will ride over and start yer letter on its way. Reckon there'll be quite a few others goin' out, too."

Before she quit the stable, where the long-legged foal lay still wet and weak, on a heap of dry rushes, she queried, "When can you tell whether Avalon really is in foal?"

The farrier sergeant deliberated, then squirted tobacco juice from between gapped, amber-hued teeth. "Can't really be sure for a few weeks — but I'm bettin' she is — my God, you should have seen Resaca go to work!" He chuckled. "Beg pardon, but that stud sure acted like he was aimin' to make up for lost time."

The concern Hannibal and Jasper had expressed about the state of the road over the foothills to Edgewood proved well-founded. Beyond doubt, no wheeled vehicle had followed its course in at least two years. Time and again the wagon had to be pulled up to wait until the escort, with axes, spades and crowbars, cleared a passage of sorts. As a result, two days passed before the party debouched upon a country road showing signs of recent usage.

As Rodney long had known, only a few widely scattered dwellings existed in this region; now they numbered even fewer. Some homes had been abandoned so long their roofs had fallen in, and the little fields around them were overgrown with tangles of underbrush, briars, and saplings. Only here and there along the road connecting Gladesville with Wise County Court House did cabins show smoke above their chimneys.

It was when the party reached Edgewood's handsome brick gate posts, each topped by a ball of white marble, that Rodney's hopes faltered, on noticing how high brambles had climbed up them, and that unfilled potholes pitted a long and winding driveway leading up to Lewis Renfrow's handsome but unpretentious home.

However, once the last rise barring view of the Renfrow home and outbuildings had been passed, noticeable changes became apparent. With rising relief Rodney noted that here fields and fences had been tended and that crops were flourishing so, to all intents and purposes, Edgewood could not have suffered too much.

Leaving Peter Tyler in charge of wagons and escort, Rodney cantered ahead until on nearing the main house he cupped hands and raised a fox-hunter's view-halloo, "Hark away! Yoicks! Yoicks!" so loudly that a pair of Negroes hoeing a vegetable garden turned and stared. He pulled Resaca up beside a granite mounting block and swung as lightly out of the saddle as he had in the past.

In the long-unpainted front doorway appeared Lewis Renfrow's spare figure, withered left arm still dangling uselessly. His craggy but freshly shaven squarish features lit while he ran down his front steps.

"Rod! By God, it can't be! Rod! Welcome back to Edgewood!"

After tethering Resaca they both climbed up the steps. Rodney smiled faintly. "And I'm just as delighted, Lew, but possibly you won't be so overjoyed when you hear what I have to tell you about Moluntha and why I've come to see you."

"Never mind that for the moment. Come on in. Cathie's out gathering eggs. Place may look a bit run-down but things aren't as bad as they seem. Purposely, I've left various appearances of neglect and disrepair in order to discourage would-be pillagers and give 'em a notion there's nothing left in Edgewood worth bothering about."

That Renfrow's reasoning had worked out well soon became apparent. Being situated nearly as remote from county roads as Moluntha, the

Renfrow property had escaped depredation save for a brief descent by a party of Mosby's Confederate partisans who'd driven off all the horses and other livestock they could find, but solemnly had paid for them with almost worthless Confederate banknotes. That Mosby's men hadn't been entirely successful, Lew Renfrow explained, was only because he'd received warning in time and so had been able to send to safety a few cows and choice horses. Since this raid had occurred nearly two years ago, some losses already had been made good.

Certainly, when they appeared at a run, Catherine Renfrow and her four tow-headed youngsters, though poorly dressed, did not appear at all underfed.

"You can order your men to bed down in the stables," Lewis grimaced. "They'll find *plenty* of empty stalls in there!"

Long since, Rodney had noticed that most of his neighbor's labor was black — he even recognized a few. Apparently, having been born on the property and well-treated, these people thus far had been disinclined to abandon humble security for the doubtful blessings of freedom. Jasper, especially, enjoyed noisy attention from old friends hungry for news.

At length the host gestured with his withered arm. "Come into the office, Rod, and let's talk."

"That's what I've come for, Lew, and not to match gamecocks for a main this time."

"I'm hard up for cash and I expect you are, too, but if it's food and supplies you need, as I suspect from that wagon you've brought along, possibly I can help a bit."

# 21

# The Ball Gown

ABOUT TWILIGHT of the fifth day since the expedition had departed, ex-corporal Peter Tyler appeared at Moluntha Garrison alone — whereupon those at home were aroused to a high pitch of anxiety. Had the expedition been bushwhacked? Had the wagon broken down, or had Edgewood been destroyed since last heard from?

Meg, Caroline and Loretta easily outdistanced Bushrod's halting gait in hurrying out into the stable yard.

Keeping his attention mainly on Meg, Tyler vigorously swung his hat about his head.

"Ease up, everyone! Nothing's gone wrong."

Loretta demanded sharply, "But why are you alone?"

"The Colonel sent me on ahead to tell you things are all right, but our wagon's so heavy-laden we'll need help to pull it across a stretch of Rickettson's bog."

Through force of habit the Texan stiffened to attention when ex-Major Bushrod Tilt limped up, calling, "When will the Colonel be reaching that boggy ground?"

"Not till sometime tomorrow, sir, probably late in the afternoon. Loaded as it is, the wagon is making terribly slow progress, even though Mr. Renfrow loaned the Colonel a spare horse."

"Heavily loaded, eh?" A huge smile broke through Bushrod's yellow beard. "That's capital!"

It warmed Tyler's heart to read relief written broad across so many faces of varying hues. Did Margaret Forsythe's greeting appear unusually cordial? Certainly a soft and unusual luster had appeared in those dark-rimmed hazel eyes.

Bushrod interrupted Tyler's conjectures. "What's he bringing?"

"Don't know for sure, sir. Colonel sent me off to reconnoiter the route just when they were loading, but I saw hardware, grain sacks, hams, bacon and flour waiting to be packed." Yipping shouts greeted this announcement.

For the first time in countless weeks a semblance of genuine jollity prevailed at supper — for all it was exasperating not to know just what the expedition might be fetching back, or how much.

Caroline said while commencing to collect dishes, "Bush, Loretta and you, too, Meg — let's prepare a surprise party. Let's get ourselves and things prettied best we're able, and give Rodney a treat."

Even Bushrod nodded. "Good idea. It's high time we forget sorrows and let this old house hear merriment again."

Momentarily, Bushrod meditated digging up a few pieces of silver to celebrate this faint rebirth of hope, but at once decided against the idea. Samuel Shepherd, who'd already retreated to work in an improvised office, mustn't even suspect its existence.

Early next morning Lydia and Pookie assisted the ladies, set about using rags and a liberal amount of the only polish available — elbow grease — to improve the appearance of patched and battered furniture. Wild blossoms and a few hardy survivors from the cutting garden were brought in and arranged to Caroline's taste.

In the late afternoon Bushrod's wife and Meg disappeared upstairs, leaving Loretta to continue mending what appeared to be a hopelessly torn lace tablecloth. After a bit, when she heard the young women upstairs giggling and talking like excited schoolgirls, she guessed they must be going through the contents of a cowhide trunk Shepherd and one of the men had lugged down from the garret that morning.

She sighed, wishing she'd had time to assemble a trousseau and get married before David Petty had dashed headlong off to war, never to return. He'd perished of typhoid fever at Fort Donelson.

Impulsively, Loretta put aside the tablecloth, then sought the living room, where Shepherd was attempting to replace or caulk broken panes with a kind of pitch gum recommended by Hannibal.

Donning a faint smile, Loretta observed, "You're doing fine, Mr. Shepherd, though I imagine you're a sight handier with a pen and ink. How is work on the records progressing?"

Shepherd grimaced, shook his snowy head. "I'm afraid there are many gaps among them and a lot of papers have become so torn and waterstained they're nearly illegible. However, Meg and I are making headway but it's only a beginning."

More giggles sounded above. Shepherd wiped plump hands on a turpentine-soaked rag, then raised pale brows. "What can the ladies be up to?"

Loretta sniffed. "I suspect my sister-in-law and Meg are trying to fix up something pretty to wear to a sort of gala dinner we're planning after the wagon comes in. All day we've been plotting a celebration, but I fear 'twill prove only a poor substitute for the kind of dinner parties we used to give."

Thanks to Bushrod's reinforcements the wagon, its contents heaped high under a tarpaulin, and with axles creaking through lack of grease, arrived next day shortly after noon, but from the Colonel's austere expression those at Moluntha guessed they'd better not expect too much.

That the return from Edgewood must have been arduous was inescapable. One of the wagon's back wheels was canting outward at such an odd angle it seemed ready to collapse at any moment, while the three horses pulling it held their heads low, and were lathered with sweat and mud. They looked really done in.

Cheers and Rebel yells went up when the cart, scattering hens and chicks and to frenzied barking of the hounds, Brandy and Flip, creaked to a stop in the stable yard. Bushrod supervised unloading the supplies, ordered them stored in the barn till they could be listed and suitably distributed.

To eager questionings Rodney said cheerfully, "Let's not go about this piecemeal. Presently, I'll give you-all a detailed account. However, first things first." Grinning, he pulled from his saddlebag a small stone bottle and took a brief pull before passing it to Bushrod.

"Been waiting for this moment ever since we left Edgewood."

"What is it?"

"A sample of Lew's best corn squeezings. 'Tis pretty raw, aged all of three months he claimed, but it's a damned sight better than branch water."

Shepherd in particular looked impatient. Apparently Rodney was too weary to notice bunches of blossoms and wild flowers effectively arranged in a miscellany of crocks and jars, and that the dining room's parquet floor, although far from glistening, had regained a measure of its mellow hues.

Once the inhabitants of Moluntha had congregated in the cardroom, Rodney described his dealings with Renfrow who had added, among other nonessentials, two jugs of kerosene!

Delightedly, Caroline clapped hands. "How wonderful! If you only knew how I hate these smelly tallow dips we've been using."

Dropping onto a chair with muddied legs outthrust, Rodney continued, "Also, Catherine's sent Loretta a bag of assorted flower seeds and a short bolt of gingham — all she could spare by way of cloth."

Loretta said thankfully, "God bless her, and us for having friends like these!"

Although Edgewood had barely been brushed by the war, Rodney went on, the Renfrows also stood in desperate need of ready cash to replace farming necessities of various sorts.

"Lew also told me that a good many estates 'round this part of the county, especially in the lowlands, have been abandoned more or less temporarily, and how desperately concerned everyone is about our immediate political future."

Margaret Forsythe queried, "Didn't you give Lew Renfrow any money for all these things?"

Intently, Shepherd's pale eyes sought and fixed themselves on Rodney's deep-set jet ones. He thought but didn't say, Rodney should have taken along some of the United States bills I offered.

"Why, yes," Rodney said shortly. "That was the only embarrassing thing about the whole business. Lew wanted me to take the supplies free of charge and replace them in due course. But, well, I learned how badly he needs a doctor and medicines for one of his children who's been poorly a long time, so, well, I *made* him take the money we took off the guerrillas, but he only agreed to accept it after he'd written out a mortgage for a section of prime timberland." Hitching back, he delved into a pocket of his riding breeches, then passed a rumpled sheet of paper over to the ex-paymaster. "Here, take a look at it. Is it in order?"

Sam winced at the wording but nodded. "It's crude, but I guess it would stand up in court."

"Well, we'll never find out if you're right."

Once the mortgage had been handed back, Rodney folded it into a loose square then, creating a brief, snarling sound, ripped it up. "This," he remarked casually, "is the way gentlemen around here solve such difficulties."

Cavernously, Rodney yawned. "Lord, I'm so tired I can feel my hair graying."

"Shouldn't wonder," Caroline smiled. "I'll bet you haven't enjoyed six hours' real sleep since you left Moluntha."

"Oh, I'll be all right once I wash and change my shirt."

Loretta said quietly, "No, Rod. What you need is a good supper and a full night's rest, for you'll be extra busy tomorrow. Besides we're going to get dressed up tonight, forget problems and enjoy the best dinner we can manage. I'll tell Jasper to lay out your best uniform."

In a guest room recently set aside for Margaret Forsythe's use as an improvement over her original accommodation, Meg smoothed the luxurious-feeling bodice of a ball gown of pale-blue satin, the bouffant skirts of which flared gracefully away from a waist so slim the wearer must never have had to wear a corset.

"How does it seem, Carrie? Do I look fit to frighten the Dutch or possibly to please them?"

Bushrod's wife arose, brow wrinkled, and tested the bodice's left sleeve. "I think the shoulder here looks a trifle full." She spoke with difficulty because of a few very precious pins held between her lips. After making quick adjustments she stepped back smiling, with blond head cocked critically to one side. "You look simply ravishing, my dear! Though probably I shouldn't say so, I doubt whether poor Louisa ever looked so well in that color, especially since she was brunette and had less of a bosom." She stepped back, and began rolling up a tape measure she'd been wearing slung about her neck. "Now tell me something; do you know how to make a formal curtsy?"

Meg laughed. "Not really. Up North, even society girls seldom are instructed in such matters. Please, will you teach me how to make one?"

Without effort, the young woman from New Orleans swept a fluid and very elegant court curtsy, then raised dingy gray skirts to indicate how the feet should be placed. "The main art lies in bending the knees evenly during the dip of your body, and then raising yourself and straightening up without apparent effort."

"Oh, I'll never learn," Meg cried after several attempts. "I'm awkward as a cow on ice."

"Well, never mind. To offer a really elegant curtsy requires years of practice. Besides, everybody will be so taken by your looks they'll not be critical. A good thing Louisa wore that ball gown only a few times. It would be impossible really to alter the cut or to remove spots or stains." Caroline glanced up, brows raised. "Why are you looking so thoughtful?"

"Oh, I know it's silly but, somehow, I feel, well, uneasy over wearing a dead woman's balldress. I'm not sure it's right. I'd feel differently about everyday garments — the use of such is necessary and practical under the circumstances — but a party dress!"

Caroline's large and liquid dark-blue eyes flashed. "You mustn't think that way. We're starved for a bit of loveliness, and a beautiful gown is a beautiful gown no matter what its history. I declare, you look especially winning in pale blue.

"Lord! What a change from when I first clapped eyes on you all unkempt and wearing a dirty Yankee uniform." Impulsively, she kissed Meg's cheek, then commenced to collect sewing articles. "Now, before you go down to dinner, be *sure* to fix your hair the way I showed you." She sniffed. "Isn't it awful not having toilet soap, lotions, proper combs or fresh ribbons?"

Meg said, "I only hope to please the gentlemen. I think your brother-in-law looks almost worn-out."

"Yes, Rod needs bucking up. It's strange, but have you noticed that, ever since Rodney's return to Moluntha, he's almost never mentioned his wife, for all he was deeply and truly in love with her?"

"Maybe he's locked that part of his life aside and has resolved to forget — if that's possible."

"Perhaps. Lord knows Rod's met with more than his share of griefs and responsibilities. Here, let me help you out of the gown; then I'll go out and try to find flowers suitable for a bouquet. When he was a young gay cavalier Rodney always noticed such trifles."

Caroline helped lift the heavy satin gown over her companion's head. "Oh, if only we had a little more to do with, but I do hope the dinner party goes well! Anyhow, Jasper has helped by cleaning and pressing the gentlemen's uniforms and by polishing buttons. I've even talked Bush into getting out his old dress tunic and pants." Caroline summoned a wry smile. "Believe it or not, we've had so little to eat they still fit Bush perfectly!"

Meg smiled brightly. "Don't you worry, dear, we'll make out and have a fine, large evening. Oh, I forgot to tell you, Carrie, Corporal Tyler has volunteered to act as butler for the occasion."

Caroline sobered a little. "Isn't Tyler the strange one? He says he knows how to set places and how to serve at table even if, as he said, he'll have to wear a flour sack for an apron." Caroline continued thoughtfully. "Wonder where a Texan ex-cavalryman ever learned the elegant deportment and speech he uses in the presence of ladies?"

Meg yearned to confide what she'd learned under the serape that rainy night, but remained silent. Hadn't Father always taught that a Forsythe's word, once given, was sacred?

Caroline completed collecting her meager supply of sewing materials. "By the bye, if you wish to post that letter you said you're writing, you'd best finish it. Rodney says he intends to lead a detail over to Gladesville post office tomorrow or the day after."

By fading light of late June Margaret Forsythe reread the letter she'd begun after many tribulations, and began to complete it.

28th June, 1865

My Dear Uncle Azael,

How I hope and pray this letter will reach you quickly or, at worst eventually. This is the first occasion I have made bold to write but I feel I must as a matter of family duty inform you that I am at present alone in the world. After undergoing many grim experiences I have become a "working guest" with a Southern family living near Abingdon in the Westernmost part of Virginia. Abingdon, or what remains of it, is the nearest town of any size. My address, should you condescend to write, as I fervently pray you will, is:

> Care of Colonel Rodney A. Tilt,
> Moluntha Garrison,
> (Near Gladesville,)
> Wise County,
> Virginia.

Please make careful note of this address, Dear Uncle; to me a reply means my sole hope for a decent future.

It is with infinite regret I recall having met you on but a single occasion and that long before this terrible Rebellion commenced.

She paused to dip her pen.

First off, have you received any word from my Mother or any of my family? I fear you have not because, whilst living in our last refuge among the mountains we were set upon by a band of ferocious outlaws who murdered both my brothers in cold blood then carried off Mother and Sister Agnes. I have no way of knowing where they are if they still live. Those villains were so brutal perhaps it would be better if they already have departed to rest in the bosom of Abraham.

Uncle Azael, being a lawyer, might be impressed by her choice of words. She continued:

Respected Uncle, I am writing this epistle to you for, as near as I know, you are my sole remaining close relative, therefore I fear, as your niece, I must trespass on your good nature in this fashion.

Although the Tilts are a proud old Southern family they differ greatly from residents of the so-called "Tidewater Counties" and are not arrogant or pretentious. They have taken me in, have been most kind, and generously they have shared what little remains to them by the way of food and clothing. It is almost as if I were one of their blood.

I strive to do all I can to "earn my salt," as we say at home, but I cannot in all conscience go on indefinitely accepting the Tilts' protection and hospitality.

Almost guiltily she glanced over to the ball gown gleaming on its wicker mannequin. It was so beautiful her heart quickened.

Colonel Rodney Ajax Tilt, the head of this family, is a fine, upstanding gentleman with a distinguished war record, but I fear the late conflict has ruined him and his family as well as most of his kin and friends.

She paused, used a rag to wipe a blob of ink from a rusty steel pen which most likely had been manufactured down East some twenty years earlier.

I assure you, Respected Sir, that despite many vicissitudes I have kept my
virtue and our family's honor intact.

If and when I see you, I will give you a strict and truthful account of all
that has happened since my Dear Papa was killed.

She wetted lips, tried to find the right words while switching about
the single sheet of fine notepaper given her by Loretta. It was precious
as fine gold nowadays, so, in the interests of economy, she commenced to
write vertically across previous lines. This might have led to complications
for the reader had not her script been so precise and delicate in quality.

From various sources I have ascertained that Colonel Tilt, so recently returned from the field, finds himself in grave financial difficulties from which it
seems doubtful he can extricate himself before much time passes. Therefore,
not wishing to remain a burden on his already straitened circumstances, dare
I request you to send me to Colonel Tilt's address a modest sum of money in
United States funds, sufficient to permit me to purchase railroad transportation
to the Northeast? Once there, I trust I soon will be able to support myself
through honest and possibly gainful employment. Here in the South there are
no such prospects. We have been informed that railroads and the telegraph
rapidly are being restored to normal.

Dear Uncle, will you please —

Her ink-stained fingers quivered —

lend me fifty dollars? I herewith solemnly promise on arrival in Portland to
give you immediately any unused money and will repay your loan as rapidly
as possible. Please understand and believe I am *not* requesting this loan as
charity. I beg you, sir, please to understand my position. I pray your address
has remained the same.

Kindly let me hear from you at your early convenience.

I am, respected Uncle,
Your affectionate and
dutiful Niece,
Margaret Denning Forsythe

P.S. Herewith I enclose what I believe to be the correct return postage. A
Mr. Samuel Shepherd, a gentleman also temporarily staying here, has kindly
advanced the necessary sum.

Still bent over the writing desk, Meg watched the twilight deepen, and
despite a lapse of many years attempted to visualize gaunt and long-
faced Uncle Azael. Did he yet wear that bushy, forked gray beard; did
he still enjoy a full head of hair as did most of the Forsythe family?

She sighed, then with meticulous care printed Uncle Azael's name
and address on an envelope of strong brown paper Shepherd had discovered somewhere. Of course it went ill with the delicate notepaper, but
what did that matter? On the back she completed the return address.
Because glue on the envelope's flap had become hardened through age,
she licked it many times before bearing down hard again and again.

Later, she'd see whether she couldn't come across a bit of sealing wax and then borrow a seal from someone. Somehow, a letter thus secured seemed of more importance than an ordinary missive.

Although water in a pool in a brook running almost parallel to the path leading up to the cemetery had been only slightly warmed by the hot late-June sun, Pedro de Cinquegrana y Gonzales stayed in just long enough to complete scrubbing his short but muscular bronze-hued frame with a chunk of harsh, homemade lye soap. This day was as near perfect as the poet — whose name he couldn't recall — had described.

Once the Texan had washed himself and his scant laundry to satisfaction he felt both unaccountably lighthearted and impatient to behold Margaret Forsythe clad in finery. As usual, his heart lifted at the thought of her calm manner and slender good looks, so, perhaps it was as well this water remained sufficiently chill to cool the Latin strain in his blood.

Wasn't it absurd he hadn't, as a born *hidalgo* been allowed to share the meager amenities of Moluntha Garrison? Yet he understood. Even if the Army of Northern Virginia had ceased to exist, certain military customs and observances would continue for an indefinite period. For example, men might not mingle socially with commissioned officers or their dependents.

How persistently thoughts of Margarita — privately, he'd always thought of her by the Spanish form of her name — entered his thoughts, creating a powerful and steadily mounting craving. Often, before he fell asleep, he'd picture himself as lord of a splendid *hacienda* with Margarita presiding as an ever-gracious and capable hostess. No indolent, unworldly and spoiled Mexican girl for Pedro de Cinquegrana y Gonzales! What he needed was a wife able to aid and further certain soaring ambitions. He needed Margarita's quick intelligence, education, practical and seemingly boundless energy.

He ducked his head beneath the surface and though his eyes stung like fury, soaped hair roached by ex-Sergeant Knox into some semblance of order.

Knox had drawled, "Damn' if this isn't like clipping a shavetail!"

"A 'shavetail'?"

"Old Army term for trimming a young mule's tail, which is why new second lieutenants are nicknamed thataway." All the same, Knox had borne down gently enough to leave sufficient locks to permit Tyler's combing them into an unruly part.

While drying himself with handfuls of dried fern the Texan absently watched iridescent soap bubbles go whirling downstream. He nodded to himself. Tonight, reckon I'll finally behold my love as befits her station and loveliness.

Bitterly he envied the long hours she spent working in company with that enigmatic white-haired and pale-skinned ex-paymaster. There, he was coming to think, was someone to look out for — unpredictable. Laboriously the pair of them would spend hours sorting and cataloguing piles of documents, yellowed and growing brittle with age. Surely, some must date back into the 1830s?

Pedro's chief consolation was that, apparently, the Colonel treated this Yankee girl with no greater courtesy or interest than he extended to any of the other ladies.

But of one thing Pedro de Cinquegrana y Gonzales felt certain; Margarita he must have, even if violence proved a last resort.

With care he pulled on a pair of pants of coarse white linen which, with certain other objects, including a bottle of Malaga wine at the moment chilling in the brook's icy water, he'd acquired at Edgewood more or less honestly. Wouldn't the Tilts be astounded when their make-believe butler poured *real wine!*

A pity he hadn't been able by hook or by crook to obtain a white shirt, only a cotton garment of faded blue. Fortunately, his boots had remained in fair condition, so could be polished after a fashion with wax from a comb found in a wild bee tree. Would Margarita pay any attention, no matter how slight, to these attempts to improve his appearance?

Pedro drew a deep breath and decided on making a cautious detour to that pile of stones in a sumac clump where the half-Jew had hidden his bag of gold coins. Exactly how much it contained he still didn't know — wouldn't do to examine too closely and possibly upset some delicate device of Shepherd's which might serve to alarm him.

For an experienced tracker like himself it had been no trick at all to trace Samuel Shepherd's progress toward the stone pile. Employing infinite care, he'd lifted a moss-covered triangular-shaped rock just enough to reveal a leather bag which on hefting he reckoned must contain sufficient gold to start himself and Margarita southward.

Good! The moneybag appeared to have been untouched. The ex-paymaster, Tyler was aware, nearly every week went to inspect his cache after dark. Always unobserved, he'd dogged Shepherd on several occasions, and carrying a well-cleaned revolver — just in case.

Through a deliberate effort Tyler switched his train of thought so, with his dripping bundle of washing, he started back to a newly reconstructed former slave cabin he shared with Knox and Hamrick. On nearing the estate's main house he heard Jasper tuning a battered banjo which, though lacking a string or so, remained capable of rendering some mighty lively tunes.

Loretta was pleasantly astonished by the quiet efficiency with which Peter Tyler, looking fresh and neat as never before, took over setting the dinner table.

To a discerning eye, what with its ragged edges and her unskillful mending in evidence at various points, the covering-cloth left much to be desired; still, she hoped no one would take too much heed since a brown earthenware beanpot holding a great clump of deep red roses graced the table's center and was flanked by a pair of handsome cut-glass kerosene lamps which, thanks to Lew Renfrow's generosity, at long last had been refilled.

As fast as she produced miscellaneous remnants of once-fine tableware, the ex-corporal distributed each piece to its proper position. Of course there was no silver to dine with — only ugly iron and pewter utensils with wooden handles, mostly of army origin. Luckily, an even half-dozen delicate wineglasses had survived. Tyler deftly put these in place — why he did so puzzled Loretta, but she didn't inquire.

The Texan moved efficiently about, smiling because he reckoned his bottle of Malaga would just about fill them even, although, to Lydia's curiosity, he'd held out a half-cup to flavor the ham.

Loretta made minor adjustments to the roses and unbent sufficiently to remark with unusual pleasantness, "I declare, Corporal"— privately convinced that the war might soon recommence, she continued to use military titles no matter how humble the rank —"at some time you must have seen a deal of high-class dining. You know exactly where everything should go."

"Thank you, ma'am. I *have* seen —" he almost said "attended"—"quite a few formal dinner parties." Tyler did not feel called upon to add that on such occasions it was he who had been waited upon.

For the first time Loretta noticed how finely featured was this short and wiry Texan with the red-brown complexion and wavy hair. Also she became aware that this pseudo-butler bore himself with a certain faint but clearly recognizable air of distinction. "— And what are we to have for our banquet?" she demanded, although aware that the Texan had spent much of the late afternoon helping Lydia and Pookie in the kitchen.

"Why, ma'am, we're going to offer one of Mr. Renfrow's best hams, the one sent especially for your enjoyment. Also, there'll be some early carrots and yams, corn muffins, and a delicacy known to Hannibal as 'fiddlehead greens,' or budding ferns. I've sampled some and found them really tasty."

"Yes, I know. We've been eating such for some time." Just before retiring to dress, Rodney's twin watched Tyler skillfully arrange fronds of sweet fern in a sunburst pattern about the beanpot of roses.

Teeth glinted whitely when he asked, "And how, ma'am, shall the guests be seated?"

"The Colonel, of course, will occupy the head of the table whilst I will preside at its far end. Mr. Shepherd will be on my right." She bit her lip an instant. "I think Miss Forsythe, as the only other guest, should sit at the Colonel's right; Major Tilt will be at my left and Mrs. Caroline Tilt at my Brother's left." To her surprise she heard herself inquire, "You approve this arrangement?"

Again the Texan's smile flashed. "Why, yes, ma'am. I don't think your decision could be improved on." Silently he added, If only *I* could be the one to sit beside Margarita, and *por Dios*, some day I shall! "And at what hour shall dinner be announced, ma'am?"

Loretta hesitated. "Why, around half-past eight or thereabouts. I expect the gentlemen will assemble somewhat earlier in the cardroom to take the customary sip of liquor. We ladies will join them in the —" she started to say "drawing room" but changed to "— living room."

"Very well, ma'am." He bowed just a little. "By your leave, I've arranged for music during dinner; to be played outdoors, of course."

"Music! What a splendid idea. Is it yours?"

"Thank you, ma'am. 'Twill only be better than nothing at all."

"But who — what?"

"Jasper will strum awhile, then a trio of my friends with fair to middling voices will sing a little. I presume you will not wish them to commence until after the main course has been served?"

Loretta debated, "I think it would be jolly if Jasper could play us in to dinner — with 'Dixie' for choice. The singing might commence toward the end of the meal." Her tanned cheeks deepened in color, she smiled widely. "How can I thank you, er, sir, for your help and thoughtfulness?"

"*No hay de que, señorita*," Tyler murmured, bowing slightly from the waist. "There is no necessity."

At precisely half-past seven Samuel Shepherd recombed collar-length, platinum-hued hair, then pursed full lips while giving a final and totally unnecessary rub to buttons glowing as they had not since the fall of Richmond. He hoped Loretta wouldn't heed the poorly mended tear in the skirt of his coatee, and certain stains which had persisted despite all efforts.

While winding a sash of white silk about his still rotund middle, he heard Bushrod limping below, then, almost immediately, Rodney's brisk tread.

In the cardroom, lit by a pair of those smoky tallow-dip candles so abominated by Caroline, the officers gathered, looking remarkably spruce despite campaign-worn uniforms. Bushrod, beard freshly trimmed, had stuck a yellow rosebud into a buttonhole and gravely had presented his companions with one each, saying, "We *will* be gay, dammit!" and while supporting himself on his cane actually smiled at Shepherd. "This must be a night to remember."

"Hear! Hear!" Shepherd cried, raising his glass of well-watered "corn squeezings." "Yes, gentlemen, *Nihil desperandum.* Let us take solemn oath not to delve into the past. After all, what we have suffered is done and can't be undone, so let us enjoy tonight and hope for brighter tomorrows!"

Rodney nodded while pretending to savor the raw drink. "Well spoken, sir. Beyond doubt you enjoy an ability with words worthy of a man with your background."

Smoothly he changed the subject. "Trust the ladies won't keep us waiting too long — this bourbon of Lew's seems about done for."

The men chatted and through transparent efforts recalled humorous anecdotes until the sound of light feet descending Moluntha's wide and winding staircase directed them into the dimly-lit living room.

When he beheld his wife Bushrod gaped, so effectively Caroline had dressed. and curled her pale yellow hair and even had trained a love-lock over one shoulder. She looked radiant, years younger and almighty seductive in that full-skirted pink evening gown.

Loretta in dark green grosgrain had disdained the use of curling tongs, but her hair had been neatly plaited and gathered into a bun, into which she had tucked an elaborate rosette fashioned of bright yellow ribbon — cavalry colors. That her gown undoubtedly was too full she didn't care about, as, raising a nosegay of yellow daisies, she dropped the gentlemen a stiff little curtsy.

Her gaze then shifted to Shepherd. "I wish it were possible for this company to indulge in a sip or two of sherry before dinner but, well, we're here to enjoy what's available, aren't we? Besides, I've an idea we may be in for a pleasant surprise at table, thanks to our volunteer butler who, to my surprise, asked for and has set out wineglasses. What he intends to fill them with remains secret."

Loretta raised a brow toward Caroline. "What in the world can be delaying Margaret? Usually she's punctual to the dot."

Caroline fluttered, "When I started downstairs she was putting the last touches to a bouquet she's contrived especially for this occasion." She treated Rodney to a fleeting smile which didn't escape Peter Tyler's notice. "But I'm sure she'll join us directly."

Margaret, however, was meeting trouble with more than her bouquet. When she tightened those drawstrings of aged silk which supported pantalettes beneath her ball gown she pulled too hard, whereupon, to her horror, both ribbons snapped, allowing the frilly and lavishly embroidered lawn garment to sag to the floor!

Frantically Meg gathered up her skirts and was horror-stricken to learn that both ties, which normally would have been crossed over her waist and then knotted into place, had parted halfway along their length! What to do! In a hurry she attempted to pin the fabric together, but always the rotted material gave way.

Mercy! She could hear voices from below growing increasingly impatient. The Colonel was a stickler for punctuality; she reached a decision which sent floods of color into her cheeks. She'd no choice but to appear below wearing nothing whatever beneath her gown! Of course, probably no one could ever guess at her shameful state, since her bouffant skirt and three petticoats were sufficiently full to betray her lack of intimate lingerie.

In a desperate hurry she smoothed the gown and subconsciously was titillated by the sensuous pressure of satin upon skin normally covered with cotton or wool cloth. Pausing only long enough to recapture a measure of composure, she picked up her bouquet and, trembling almost perceptibly, started for the staircase, eyes shining with an unusual luster.

Just before she reached the head of the staircase Loretta had suggested with a touch of asperity, "Rodney, shall we take our places? Margaret surely will appear soon, but there's no point in allowing Lew's fine ham to grow cold."

Without expression, Peter Tyler pulled back Loretta's armchair while she indicated the seating arrangements.

Rodney said, "Too bad, but let's sit down."

"Yes, she will be here very shortly," Caroline insisted.

Once the guests had been seated to the strains of "Dixie" Tyler brought in his Malaga, turned the big green bottle, poured so skillfully not a drop marked the tablecloth. He completed pouring amid expressions of surprised delight.

To everyone's astonishment Bushrod hiked himself erect, beard agleam in the lamplight and raised his glass in courtly fashion. "Ladies and gentlemen! May I first offer a toast to our lost Cause, which may not after all be lost. The South *will* and *must* rise again!"

Everyone stood, sipped; then Bushrod continued. "And now let us drink to the fair stranger fate has sent within our gates!" By accident he had timed his words exactly to coincide with Meg's appearance in the dining room's doorway.

Everyone remained standing, frozen by this apparition. Clad in Louisa's beautifully designed pale-blue ball gown, Margaret Forsythe, most effectively revealed by the lamps, appeared to have come direct from some celebrated modiste's atelier.

Two light-brown corkscrew curls framed the girl's strong but well-formed features and her hazel eyes shone like those of a night-hunting feline.

"Ladies and gentlemen, I beg pardon for my tardiness." Blushing even deeper, she executed the best curtsy she could manage, then, smiling radiantly, began, "Colonel Tilt, I hope you will find pleasure in my poor efforts to enter into the spirit of this occasion?"

Glass poised, Rodney Ajax Tilt stood transfixed, his inner being heaved about a heart that seemed to crumble. Narrowly, Peter Tyler watched the effect of Margaret's unintentionally dramatic entrance; also he noticed how the Master of Moluntha's wineglass commenced to shake, and that his strong, well-formed features had assumed the inflexibility of a death mask.

Brightly, Caroline raised her glass. "Come, one and all, let us drink to our lovely Yankee guest — would that there were more like her!"

Rodney remained still until, with an automatonlike motion he raised his glass, but, just before its rim touched his lips, the stem snapped. He said in a toneless voice, "How clumsy of me. Nevertheless, here's to you, Miss Forsythe."

Only Loretta, knowing how profoundly, if inarticulately, he'd adored his wife, could sense the anguish racking her twin. Never had Loretta's always lofty opinion soared to such heights as at this moment when, obedient to iron self-discipline, he drew himself erect, well-polished buttons on his tunic gleaming, and looked steadily down the table at Margaret Forsythe still clutching a bouquet of yellow roses. She advanced, hazel eyes huge and preternaturally bright, to occupy the chair at her host's right which Tyler smoothly pulled out.

Shepherd's amazement was profound. Could this lovely vision be the same down-to-earth young woman with whom he'd spent more time than anyone else at Moluntha?

Oh, Lord, thought Loretta. Why hadn't Carrie had sufficient sense to stop Margaret from carrying yellow roses, Louisa's favorite flowers!

Shortly following the toast, as Jasper's banjo continued to jangle outside, Tyler deftly substituted a small mustard container for the host's broken wineglass.

"I —" Meg hesitated, turned to Rodney, "I trust you aren't displeased with my appearance." Thank God he couldn't suspect those absent pantalettes! "Caroline advised me. I know she meant only for the best, so, if in some manner I have offended you please believe I am most contrite." Her voice softened. "Never would I knowingly say or do anything to offend you, sir."

"You have not offended me. You look almost too lovely to be real." He drew a deep, slow breath, then signaled Tyler to pass a platter of clove-studded ham, the fragrance of which noticeably had been enhanced by a cupful of Malaga.

Gripped in a bittersweet mood, Loretta surveyed the diners. All-too-many blue moons had passed since Moluntha's Sheraton dinner table thus had been graced.

Caroline seemed a replica of that dainty bride who had arrived here years ago, all gaiety and deceptively shallow of character. It was on Margaret Forsythe the young woman from New Orleans fixed her attention, noted how straight the Northern girl sat and how deftly she managed her ugly knife and fork.

Shepherd remained amazed over Rodney Tilt's self-control; also, he noted the silent encouragement being afforded by his twin. What a gracious and joyous place Moluntha must have been before the war. The ex-paymaster's lively imagination easily pictured a much longer table occupied by men dressed in the latest fashion and graced by magnificently gowned ladies. Then there must have been gleaming silver candelabra and tableware, fine place plates and rows of assorted wineglasses ranged before each guest — instead of a single goblet. What had become of them?

Hadn't he attended similar dinner parties in Baton Rouge and New Orleans! When his gaze encountered Loretta he felt immeasurably elated by her treating him to a slow little smile when she lifted her glass in his direction saying, "Here's to a swift mending of Mr. Shepherd's fortunes."

Toward the end of dinner Loretta surprised everyone by turning to Shepherd, "Since the music tonight was not all that it might have been, I — I wonder if possibly you would conclude this occasion by singing something gay in Ladino?"

Bushrod merged heavy brows, "And what, pray, is 'Ladino'?"

Briefly Shepherd hesitated but the appeal in Loretta's eyes was urgent so, briefly, he described the language and its origins. Why, oh why, had the Colonel's twin chosen this means of reminding the family about his Jewish blood?

Nevertheless he got to his feet and used a spoon to beat a rhythm on his wineglass. Presently he threw back his head and began to sing in a clear, rich baritone:

> Na-ni, na-ni que-re el hi-jo
> El hi-jo de la mad-re. Dicho se haga gran-de
> Ay, ay dur-mi-te mi alma,
> Que tu padra vie-ne, ne con muncha-ale-gria!

During the following two verses Shepherd took care not to allow his gaze to seek Loretta.

When he resumed his seat it was amid gentle applause.

Caroline burst out, "Oh, Lordy! That sounded perfectly wonderful even if I couldn't understand a word. You've really put the cap on an evening I reckon none of us here will ever forget!"

"Well, from the sublime to the ridiculous," Rodney said in a changed voice. "Would you like to hear the song about the darky preacher and the bear?"

Utter and pleased astonishment gripped Loretta and Caroline. What? Rodney about to sing? They both were aware he'd a more than passable baritone voice. Meg remained mute with astonishment.

"Of course, please, please!" cried Caroline. "This will really make this party memorable!"

As if shedding a constricting garment the Master of Moluntha smiled broadly and held his body less taut:

Oh, a preacher went out huntin' tho was on one Sunday's morn
His thoughts was about religion but he took his gun along.
He shot himself some very fine quail and one little measly hare
But on his way returnin' home he met a great big grizzly bear.
The 'coon got so excited he dropped his gun and skinned up a
persimmon tree.
The bear sat down upon the ground and the 'coon climbed out on
a limb
He cast his eyes to the Lord in the skies and this is what he said to
Him,
"Oh, Lawd, didn' you rescue Jonah from the belly of a whale
And then three Hebrews rescu'd from the fiery furnace so the Good
Book do declare,
But, Lawd, if you can't he'p me for goodness doan' you he'p that
bear!"

Jasper, standing outside the dining room windows, hardly could believe his hearing. Laws, how long since Cunnel Rod had raised his voice in song? Gingerly, his fingers arranged themselves on the banjo just in case —

"Oh, how good it was!" Caroline burst out amid clappings, the loudest of which came from Tyler and Shepherd.

Meg, with stars in her eyes begged, "Is there a second verse?"

Loretta said, choking slightly, "Of course, Rodney, do go on singing."

"Please," Bushrod said. "You lift weights from all of us."

Flushed, Rodney looked about, then shrugged in mock surrender. "All right, but on your heads be it."

Jasper readied his pick and played an accompaniment just as he had after a winning battle, when all the gentlemen felt fine.

Oh the 'coon stayed up in that tree I think was all night,
He said, "Oh Lawd, if you don't he'p the bear you'll see one awful
    fight.
Just about then the limb let go and the 'coon come a tumblin' down.
You ought to seen him get his razzor out befo' he hit the groun'
When he hit the dirt he cut a right an' lef', he put up a dirty game
    fight,
But the bear then grabbed him and sque-e-zed him a little too tight.
The 'coon then lost his razzor but the bear held on with a vim
So he raised eyes to Lawd in skies and once more said to Him,
"Oh Lawd, didn' you save Dan'l from the lion's den and then
Three Hebrews from the fiery furnace, so the Good Book do declare.
Oh Lawd, if you cain't he'p me for goodness doan' you he'p that
    bear!"

While striking a final chord on his instrument Jasper muttered softly, "Everythin's goin' be all right from now on, sho' nuff."

No one could warn him he was a better body servant than a prophet.

Jasper's last chord faded away amid wild applause raised by almost everyone at Moluntha.

# 22

## Letters Northward

ON THE DAY FOLLOWING the dinner party it seemed as if Nature all at once had decided to make up for three weeks of gloriously fair weather. A great storm vaulted the Cumberlands and adjacent mountain ranges with a velocity which at times approximated hurricane force. Cloudbursts of howling, wind-driven rain in no time at all converted mountain creeks and brooks into raging white torrents. Huge branches thrashed madly and tall trees crashed over in countless numbers. Wild animals sought any refuge they could find, however there was ample space in Moluntha Garrison's barn and stable to accommodate the estate's handful of domestic animals. Rain beating through boarded-up but glassless windows created puddles no amount of mopping could hope to cope with.

Since the projected expedition down to Gladesville was out of the question certain members of the household, once their indoor chores had been completed, seized this opportunity to compose long-deferred letters.

To Marcus Peabody, Rodney Tilt wrote:

> Moluntha Garrison
> 1st July, 1865
>
> My dear Friend Marc,
> So much has happened since we met on the field of Appomattox I will not even attempt to fill you in on all that has chanced. Suffice it to say that after surviving various unpleasant experiences I reached home with but a handful of my original Company.
> Alas, at present Moluntha little resembles the dwelling you remember. How-

ever, I am most thankful that sufficient of the estate remains to grant us shelter and give us incentive to attempt to make a fresh start. So many friends have refused to rebuild, have abandoned their property and are going abroad.

Upon my return I was vastly relieved to find here my brother, Bushrod, who was crippled in battle, his wife and their small son Oliver, also my twin sister Loretta whom I'm sure you must well remember from the old days. With the aid of a few former slaves who have remained faithful under very trying conditions they managed to make out after a fashion.

Rodney put down his pen and emptied a pail filled with rainwater leaking through a weak spot in the roof. After drying hands on the seat of his pants he resumed:

Last year the property briefly was occupied by Union cavalrymen who did considerable damage to the house and outbuildings and carried off all manner of loot, but they offered no harm to any of the occupants.

The four veterans from the Army of Northern Virginia I brought home and other paroled former soldiers have remained at Moluntha. Among them is an officer, a curious fellow by the name of Samuel Shepherd who held the rank of paymaster-lieutenant. Although half-Jewish, Mr. Shepherd does not look like a Hebrew and seems to possess none of those unsavory traits attributed to that people.

Also we have living with us one Margaret Denning Forsythe, a remarkable Yankee girl whose people, says she, settled generations ago, near Portland, Maine, but whose family were living near Nashville, Tennessee, when the war broke out.

Her father went with the Union and was killed at Shiloh so, as Unionists, her Mother and the rest of the family were forced to move from place to place until they were attacked by bushwhackers who murdered her little brothers and carried off her mother and sister. Nothing has been heard of them since.

While on my way home we came upon her on a mountain trail, lost, forlorn and starving. Miss Forsythe has a pleasing personality, is obviously wellborn, well-educated, capable and industrious. For all she is a Yankee, we Tilts by now have come to consider her almost as one of the family.

She has, I believe, an uncle by the name of Azeal Forsythe, a lawyer dwelling at Falmouth Foreside and practicing in nearby Portland, Maine. She has prepared a letter to this uncle advising him of her whereabouts, since he is her only close relative, and she wishes to return North. She will sorely be missed if she should depart — she is so cheerful and warmhearted.

Her letter, among a few others, will be posted with the first mail to leave Moluntha since the termination of hostilities. Only God knows whether it, or any of the others, ever will reach their destinations.

Thus far I have not found opportunity to inspect damage to the Ajax mine which your Father did so much to develop. As soon as I can determine what repairs will be needed at Wytheville, I will write, giving details.

Needless to say, my grief over the tragic death of Louisa and our baby last winter remains as a thorn in my heart but I strive to control evidences of my sorrow over their loss, as well as grief for my Mother, who recently was slain here during an attack by partisans.

I earnestly trust that you, your Father and all your family are well and that by this time you will have been discharged from the Service.

He paused to switch horizontal his small sheet of notepaper, then continued to write at right angles across what he'd already put down.

I would *greatly* appreciate it if you could send me a few newspapers now and then. Here, we are starved for news of the outside world, therefore it remains impossible for me to make even simple plans for the future. To do so, I must learn at least something of what is taking place within this unhappy Nation. All we hear are rumors, some wildly exaggerated for good or for evil; often many are contradictory. As yet there is no telegraph line to Gladesville, but one soon should reach Wise County Court House which, perhaps would be a better address for letters or telegrams rather than Gladesville which is but an unimportant village.

Again, let me thank you, Marc, for your generosity at Appomattox, and the willingness to aid me you expressed last spring; these have gone far toward sustaining my hopes for the future.

Loretta and Bushrod join in sending fond greetings and hope we may soon again share good times.

Please let me hear from you at your earliest convenience. As I have said, I will write, describing the state of the mine, without awaiting a reply to this letter.

Please present my respects to your Father, your good Wife and family.

> Your old Classmate,
> Rodney Tilt

At this same moment someone else was busy with pen and ink. Samuel Shepherd, having come across the terminal page of an agreement containing only a pair of lines or writing across its top, had scissored these off and had attached them to the balance of the document. Thus he'd obtained almost a whole unspoiled sheet to write on.

As usual Shepherd wrote smoothly, using that same gracefully flowing script which, at school, had won him prizes in penmanship, and commenced a letter to his Mother in Baton Rouge.

Carefully, the silver-headed ex-paymaster selected the right words to outline his adventures since he'd fled the blazing Confederate capital. Pausing, he bit his lip in concentration while weighing possibilities and probabilities before continuing:

For the first time in my life, dearest Mother, I find myself quite undecided about what course to take in the near future. Shall I return South where everything political, legal and financial must remain unstable for a long while, or shall I travel to the Northeast, where industry flourishes and the economy remains undamaged?

I can of course alter my name, which is quite well-known about Richmond and New Orleans, and make no further mention of my Hebrew blood, since in Yankeeland this is a dire handicap I no longer wish to tolerate, especially because I have been expelled from my Father's religion.

On the other hand, I feel sure that in the North any position of importance surely will be bestowed on returning Union soldiers.

He paused, listening to an especially wild gust drum against the windowpanes he'd so laboriously replaced.

A third course remains open. Believe it or not — my mercantile ancestors probably will turn over in their graves at this — I have conceived an ever-

growing affection not only for this beautifully wild countryside but also for
Loretta Tilt, who is handsome and is my host's twin sister.

Also, it seems probable that once the Tilt family's Ajax lead mine begins
producing, I could improve upon its management and financing and, through
employing patience and a certain amount of effrontery, develop said mine into
a highly profitable operation.

I am completely confident I can accomplish this, since at present and for
some time to come, lead will be at a premium throughout the South for purposes of reconstruction and replacement.

If only the currency problem can be resolved quickly, much could be accomplished toward mercantile recovery.

I believe I shall remain indefinitely here in Western Virginia where I am
paying my way through putting into some kind of order the terribly muddled
affairs of this once-fine estate. In this task I am being assisted by a young
Northern woman, namely one Margaret Forsythe, who is quick to learn, industrious, and able to cope with figures.

Please don't worry, dearest of mothers, your son is *not* destitute! I managed
to bring from Richmond a store of gold coins plus several hundred dollars in
U.S. greenbacks — which is the only currency of any value hereabouts. I
imagine that in Baton Rouge, having been captured so early in the war, order
of a sort must long since have been established by occupying troops.

I am not informing any of my Father's relatives in New Orleans as to my
whereabouts and request that you, also, remain silent for the time being. I may
correspond with them later, should business considerations make it advisable.

I pray that you have escaped the yellow fever, malaria and cholera which I
have heard have been raging along the lower Mississippi. Through not having
heard from you in so many months I am deeply concerned.

Shepherd reread his letter, then added:

If it is in any way possible, please send me some newspapers as soon as may
be, for here I am as if blinded and cut off from the rest of the world as if I
were dwelling in the heart of the Sahara Desert.

> Your ever dutiful and
> most loving son,
> Samuel

Settling back in his chair he fell to wondering what his mother, Lucy
Caldwell — once reigning belle of Baton Rouge society — would look
like when, as, and if he ever saw her again. Shrewd, arrogant and an
aristocrat to her fingertips, Mother probably would have impressed the
Federal conquerors and so might have saved from destruction some of the
family's property.

He'd debated dropping more than a hint about his attraction to Loretta
Tilt who seemed at times to reciprocate his interest in an inarticulate
fashion. He decided against bringing up the matter. Before Joseph Shepherd had died back in 1860 she must, through her marriage with a
Hebrew, have experienced many painful experiences; there seemed no
point in opening similar wounds.

Although the day following the big storm dawned gray and uncertain
Rodney set forth for Gladesville in company with Tyler and Hamrick and

carrying a packet of letters in a rainproof pouch improvised out of an old Union Army rubber sheet. All three riders were armed with well-oiled revolvers and carbines, and bestrode horses grown strong and sleek. Although this region reportedly at least, had become peaceful, one never could tell.

Whatever damage other hamlets and villages might have suffered, no perceptive change appeared in Gladesville. Riding and driving horses still drowsed at well-gnawed hitching rails, dogs ambled about aimlessly, and barefoot children played simple games. No one hurried. There were two noticeable differences — no plump people were to be seen, and women outnumbered ablebodied menfolk by a wide margin.

Deeply wrinkled and nearly toothless old Tom Dilworth, who'd been postmaster ever since Rodney could remember, grinned broadly, offered a gnarled hand when Rodney tramped into his general store *cum* post office.

"Welcome, suh! Welcome! Welcome! Plenty of folks 'round here will be glad to hear you're back safe and sound."

Among other information Rodney learned that only United States currency was acceptable, also that the telegraph line to Wise County Court House was in the process of being restored but to what extent old Tom had no idea.

He also learned that Union forces occupying this part of the State not only had established their headquarters at Bristol on the Tennessee border but were maintaining detachments at Abingdon, Saltville, Marion and Wytheville. Yes, Yankee patrols did occasionally ride through Gladesville but these were appearing less frequently as time went by.

Rodney produced a five-dollar greenback borrowed from Sam Shepherd after some hesitation.

"Here you are, suh." The postmaster placed a collection of stamps on the counter.

"Any newspapers, Tom?"

"Nossuh. The few I git are snapped up fast as they come in. Folks 'round here are nigh crazy trying to find out what's going to happen to us."

Tyler, who'd also entered the store, noted that trade must be starting to revive since various shelves did not stand quite bare, although the merchandise on exhibition was scant and of poor quality.

With care Rodney separated stamps for the ten letters he'd brought along and had started to affix them when, chancing to glance through a grimy window, he recognized the lanky figure of Major Matthew Ford, with whom he had served on several campaigns. The Fords, he knew, owned extensive farm and timber lands near Moccasin Ridge. Possibly Ford might possess information worth knowing?

He beckoned Tyler. "Finish stamping these. I've just seen someone I need to talk with."

He ran out into the sunlit street, yelling, "Matt! Matt Ford! Hold up a minute!"

The other spun about. "By God, if it ain't Rodney Tilt! How are you, you old rascal?" He hurried back, hands extended.

Peter Tyler continued unconcernedly to stamp letters until he noticed one bearing Margaret Forsythe's name and address written across its back flap.

To serve a couple of gaunt and sunbonneted women who'd entered carrying market baskets containing eggs for barter — cash transactions had been rare for many a blue moon — the postmaster moved languidly in their direction.

Yielding to impulse, Tyler pocketed the letter to Azael Forsythe before slipping the rest into the "out-going" slot. Shamefully anxious to read Meg's letter, he turned to Hamrick, who stood in earnest conversation with a personable young female and he called, "Should the Colonel come back and miss me, tell him I'm 'tending to urgent business in the public jakes."

Once in the ill-smelling two-holer he secured its wooden button-latch then, after seating himself, used his razor-sharp sheath knife neatly to slit the envelope's end just enough to permit withdrawal of the slim single sheet within; should anyone take notice of said slit they'd most likely set it down as the work of some censor.

When he'd finished reading Margaret's appeal, Peter Tyler fighting down a sharp sense of guilt, tore her missive into minute fragments. He'd not have Meg Forsythe leave Moluntha except with him, by God.

He found only a small measure of justification by recalling the ancient maxim: "All's fair in love and war."

# Part Three

# Wavering Hopes

# 23

# Various Measures

Although for over a fortnight messengers were sent riding down to Gladesville every other day, no mail addressed to Moluntha Garrison had arrived. Now that all reconstruction which could be accomplished without the expenditure of hard money had been completed, Tilt's attention was diverted to crop cultivation, to felling timber, and to clearing fields overgrown with brambles and other weeds.

For Margaret Forsythe a bright moment came when Knox informed her that Avalon unmistakably was in foal by Resaca, so, before this coming winter's snow melted, another long-legged thoroughbred should join Lorena in prancing about the home paddock.

Food crops, in Hannibal's opinion, looked uncommonly promising, probably because so many fields had remained fallow over nearly four years. Already, corn stood taller than the average man's head; turnips, beets, potatoes, yams and other root vegetables also appeared to be thriving beyond normal.

Through barter with various nearby families, the pigsty again was becoming so well populated that, if salt could be obtained — which seemed likely — there ought to be plenty of ham and bacon on hand before Christmas. On credit Bushrod somehow obtained a pair of milch cows much to little Oliver's benefit.

On ever more frequent occasions Rodney invited Margaret Forsythe to join him whenever he rode out to inspect some remote section of his property and, to the unspoken relief of Bushrod and Loretta, their brother after such excursions seemed to have lost much of that taut grimness of outlook and manner he'd acquired during the war. Nowadays he laughed more readily and even sang or cracked jokes on occasion.

Whenever they rode Meg again was forced to don the murdered Yankee youth's light-blue, yellow-striped breeches; she'd nothing else to wear. The very sight of them was depressing.

One warm and sunny afternoon, after dismounting to stretch legs and water horses, Rodney remarked unexpectedly, "I expect Sam Shepherd must resent my taking you from the office so often?"

"No call to worry," she assured. "We've accomplished about all we can with the records remaining in Moluntha, but there are so many serious gaps among deeds and titles something needs to be done. Bushrod and Sam believe some time ought to be spent in the Wise County Court House to discover what papers may still be on file."

Once more suggesting a curvacious youth, she settled onto a fallen tree trunk and Rodney seated himself quite close alongside. "Expect you're right. Don't understand about such things; never had much of a head for figures or business matters; always was more interested in the horse breeding. When we go to survey the Ajax mine and the King Salt Works I might find some records which might fill in the gaps you've mentioned. About the salt works I'm not too concerned; from all I'm told extracting salt from the saline springs around here isn't a complicated process, so soon we should realize a bit of money from that direction."

Gravely, she nodded and then looked intently into Rodney's small and very dark eyes. At the same time she summoned a faint smile. "Let's hope so; I know it's lack of ready cash which mostly bothers your peace of mind."

"True enough," Rodney admitted, "but I'm otherwise disturbed, by loneliness of, well, a particular nature, which subsides only when you're nearby." He scraped a smear of mud from his boots. "Forgive me, but I'm selfish enough to hope that when you hear from your Uncle you won't be over-eager to leave Moluntha. All unsuspecting you've done wonders toward making me feel life's worth living. When I learned of Louisa's death I felt as if most of me died with her."

Soberly, softly she said, "I'm so glad if I've helped even in a small way towards restoring you to your old self. I — I well, I'm tickled pink, as we say, or said, at home."

Swiftly she then diverted the trend of conversation. "Have you had any word yet from your friend Marc Peabody?"

"No, but perhaps Hamrick will fetch in some mail this evening."

Impulsively he took her sinewy, long-fingered hand and experienced inexplicable pleasure that she did not at once withdraw it. "I wonder,

Meg, whether you ever can sense the extent of my admiration for your courage in facing this harsh and uncertain world by yourself?"

"Why, why thank you, Rodney!" For him she muted the iridescence of this moment by adding, "— and your family, too. All of you have been so very generous and kind."

In stony silence he bent to pluck a stalk of sweet grass and chewed on it until she remarked, "I see wild strawberries yonder. Wouldn't you like some? I know I would."

While they were getting to their feet he said, "Forgive what may seem impertinence, but haven't I noticed that you and Peter Tyler spend considerable time together and appear to enjoy each other's company?"

"I will admit I've a certain fondness for Peter. Perhaps it's because he's looked after and helped me ever since the day Z Company found me. To me Peter Tyler is a mass of contradictions; a real mystery. Ever since I was a small girl I've enjoyed trying to solve riddles and puzzles."

"You aren't, er — more than just fond of him?"

Meg looked aside. "Why, Rodney, I really can't tell. Peter Tyler's courage, sense of honor and good manners appeal to me, yet, for some reason, I sense there's a dark and possibly dangerous side to his nature to be considered if I —" Breaking off, she stooped to gather strawberries she dropped into a wide-brimmed straw hat.

Beneath his wide, black mustache Rodney's narrow lips tightened. "Then you have taken more than a passing interest in him?"

"Yes. Peter has always been courteous, never dull company, and can tell the most exciting tales about his adventures in Mexico and down in Texas. One could listen to him for hours. Now hold out your hands and try these berries."

While licking scarlet stains from her fingers Meg said carefully, "I presume you are aware that your estate cannot continue to operate much longer without spending a substantial amount of cash? There are so many badly needed items which can't be improvised."

Absently Rodney nodded. "I know, but I can only learn the full extent of my problems until I've visited the Ajax mine." He accepted a handful of berries, ate them one by one while they sought their mounts.

Desperately, he fought down an urge to gather this girl, so desirable in so many ways, into his arms. Dear God! Hadn't they stayed empty far too long?

"Yes," said he throwing a leg over Resaca. "I know, somehow I *must* raise a considerable sum of money in a hurry. I'll consult my family straight away."

When they gathered reins and headed homeward, the sun seemed not to shine as bright as it had previously.

So, mused Rodney, I've been right about Tyler all along.

Samuel Shepherd felt flattered that he'd been invited to attend another private conclave of the family. Why? Various theories he'd formed were resolved when the group gathered at the gazebo which, it appeared, was their accustomed rendezvous for intimate conversations.

Rodney asked, "Loretta, what do you say?"

"I speak in favor. In fact, I've been wondering why it's taken you two brainy men so long to realize the obvious."

Bushrod said quietly, "Sam, we reckon the time has come to include you in a little secret of ours." He raised a brow in Rodney's direction who gave an almost imperceptible nod. Bushrod continued, giving Shepherd the details of the family's buried treasure.

Samuel Shepherd managed to look surprised, even though he'd long ago deduced what this "little secret" must be about. Hadn't he, off and on, heard Lydia complain about having no silver to polish? He also was aware that most affluent Southern families had been given to burying valuables whenever enemy forces came near.

Bushrod produced a list which accurately described the hoard in detail.

Loretta demanded, "Do you think it's possible to dispose of some of these pieces for ready money?"

"No telling what your silver might bring in these uncertain times. Personally, I've no knowledge on the subject." He shrugged, stared down the moonlit valley. "However, I do, or rather did, know certain dealers in Washington qualified to honestly appraise your property. They even might obtain you top prices."

"Why Washington?" Loretta wanted to know.

"That's the nearest market; the farther you travel the greater the reward. I'm sure you must know there's precious little ready cash to be found south of the Potomac."

Rodney drew a slow breath. "I'm convinced you appreciate the extent of the trust we're placing in you. This is a matter of critical importance to us all."

The ex-paymaster stood up, bowed. "Ma'am and sirs, please believe I feel deeply honored by such an expression of confidence."

Abruptly his manner changed. "To begin with, suppose we discuss the safest means of conveying your, er, possessions to their destination — but before I go any further, I think it wise to have some member of your family accompany me."

"Why?" Bushrod asked.

"To attest —" his mouth hardened momentarily, "that I'm not attempting to dispose of stolen property."

After a brief pause Bushrod said, "Loretta, reckon it's you who had better go with Sam. I still don't get about easily and Rod has too many other responsibilities here. Will you go?"

Said she promptly, "Why of course. I'd be delighted. How I yearn to see an undamaged city again and well-dressed, well-fed people!"

Two days later, inhabitants of Moluntha Garrison were mystified over watching a pair of small but very heavy trunks being loaded onto the farm wagon, and more so when Mr. Shepherd and Miss Loretta climbed onto the driver's seat beside Jasper. The Colonel and ex-Corporal Hamrick, it appeared, were to escort them down to Abingdon and the railroad. That both went heavily armed attracted nobody's attention.

# 24

---◄◉►---

# Train Number 35

FOR A WHILE Colonel Rodney Tilt feared they were going to miss the late afternoon eastward bound train out of Abingdon. A nearly worn-out wagon trace had snapped on a sharp rise and it had required Jasper and Hamrick what seemed like an exasperatingly long time to splice and render it serviceable once more. Nevertheless, around four o'clock, the little valley town's rooftops became visible at the foot of a long and very steep hill.

From what Rodney had ascertained in Gladesville it appeared that the Virginia & Tennessee Railroad's Number 35, a combined freight and passenger train, was supposed to run daily between Knoxville and Lynchburg. Usually it arrived in Abingdon around mid-afternoon to take on wood and water. Since no bells or whistlings had been heard and no smoke was rising above or near the depot, plus the fact that a crowd of people, carts and wagons still were lingering beside the right-of-way it appeared that Number 35 had yet to arrive.

Loretta's color shone unusually high and, despite weariness, her faintly oblique eyes sparkled. Merciful heavens! Come to think on it, she'd not really been away from Moluntha Garrison in almost three years. What a strange and exciting sensation to see so many people gathered in one place!

She recognized very few faces while the wagon came creaking up to the baggage platform — evidently rebuilt by Union engineers, its timber looked so fresh and sound.

While Shepherd and Loretta went to purchase tickets Rodney and ex-Corporal Hamrick dismounted and stood guard over the battered old trunks; Jasper watered his lathered and dusty team. Nobody seemed to pay much attention when Tilt, Hamrick and Jasper had to strain to transfer the trunks from the wagon which promptly was driven off to join others standing in shade cast by a huge sycamore.

Meantime, Rodney, having reached a decision during the trip, looked about until he found a Union sergeant and a detail of cavalrymen waiting by the depot's far end. Confident in civilian clothes, he sauntered over and engaged the noncom in conversation after noting that his troopers were carrying extra halters and bridles.

"Expecting some new animals, Sergeant?"

"Yessir. We're expecting a batch of remounts on old 35. She drops off a few horses here and there all along the line as needed, but Lord knows when she'll show up."

"Why?"

"Them railroad engineers of ours was so all-fired hurried rebuilding the line last spring we've been havin' considerable trouble with weak bridges, temporary culverts and the like. Reckon mebbe that's why this train's so blamed late. I dunno but —" In the distance sounded a faint series of whistles. "Reckon that's her at last."

Rodney smiled and produced one of Shepherd's precious five-dollar greenbacks. "My friend here," he indicated Hamrick, "and I aim to get to Wytheville soon's we can. Wonder if the officer in charge would object to carrying our horses —" he almost said "mounts" but collected himself in time "— that far?"

The Sergeant scratched a bristly lantern jaw. "Dunno, but I reckon 'twill be all right since we've orders to act as accommodatin' as we kin to you locals. All depends who's in charge."

Nobody seemed in much of a hurry even when the train puffed into sight, huge, bell-shaped smokestack spouting sparks. Hissing, wheezing, and oozing steam the locomotive clanked to a stop.

Passengers on the train appeared few so there was plenty of room in a pair of dingy-windowed, dark-red passenger coaches.

Once both trunks had been stowed among nondescript luggage in the baggage car, as usual, coupled directly behind the locomotive's tender, Shepherd approached Rodney. "Tell me, d'you think I should remain on guard over the trunks?"

Rodney hesitated. "Don't know but that that would risk drawing undue attention but you'd better be on hand when you change over to the Orange & Alexandria at Lynchburg. Should anybody question why they're so heavy just tell 'em it's clock-making machinery, too delicate to stand being crated."

Followed a brief interval during which the five dollars surreptitiously changed hands. The Sergeant in charge then rode up to tell the locomotive's engineer he'd have to pull forward his train far enough to bring a pair of horse cars opposite an animal unloading ramp.

"Right. I'll move this rattletrap forward soon's the reg'lar baggage gits stowed," promised the engineer, squirting tobacco juice from his cab.

Rodney encountered no trouble whatsoever with the bored and grimy-faced Second Lieutenant in charge of delivering remounts. Once eight animals had been towed down the ramp the Sergeant explained what Rodney wanted, adding, "They're all-right people, sir."

The Lieutenant nodded, then beckoned Rodney, "All right, bring your horses aboard." Fortunately Resaca and Hamrick's mount were too tired to protest, so entered a horse car without acting up.

Jasper looked mighty downcast until Tilt handed him three five-dollar notes. "These should see you through the night. Mind you rub the team down well and then have that weak front wheel axle fixed. You'd better buy a new trace and try to get the rest of the harness really mended."

"Yessuh. When will yo' be returnin' home, suh?"

"Inside of three or four days; I'm going to take a look at the Ajax mine. Tell Mr. Bushrod so far everything's gone all right and that I've decided to go on to Wytheville. Anything else?"

Jasper scratched his woolly pate. "Lydia say we needs white flour, salt and some pepper powerful bad, suh, and a new teakittle."

Rodney smiled down from the passenger coach's steps. "I'll do my best to accommodate her."

The trip to Wytheville attested the truth of what the Sergeant had said concerning this line's poor condition. On several occasions the train slowed where gangs of white-supervised black laborers were making various repairs along the right-of-way. Never had Loretta experienced such violent joltings, bumpings and swayings. Dusk had fallen long before Number 35 finally panted into Wytheville's shabby little depot.

# 25

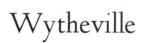

# Wytheville

ONCE THE TRAIN had clanked and clattered to a halt in Wytheville, Samuel Shepherd, appearing anything but smart in an oversized gray flannel suit tailored for the late Otho Tilt, took Rodney's hand between both of his at the same time murmuring, "Don't worry, we will return with a handsome sum, you can rely on that." Something in the ex-paymaster's very pale blue eyes seemed to carry conviction — at least Rodney hoped so.

While bussing Loretta's cheek with unusual intensity he said, "Good luck, my dear. If possible, send news of your negotiations by telegraph via Wise County Court House; also your probable date of return. I'll see that someone rides over there every other day."

"I'm entirely confident everything will go well," Loretta whispered. "Samuel counts on locating useful friends in Washington. Trust you'll find the Ajax isn't so badly wrecked as we've heard."

Once their horses had been unloaded along with a few Federal remounts, Rodney and Hamrick lingered beside the stock ramp until the red rear lamps of Number 35 vanished into the night. Both men, while swinging into their saddles, heard a church clock's bell strike nine booming notes.

"Hold the horses and wait here," Rodney instructed. "I'm going in for a talk with the stationmaster."

The fellow wearing a green celluloid eyeshade was tapping out a message on his telegraphic key. When he'd done he glanced up then, grinning widely, held out his hand. "Why, 'tis Mr. Tilt! Heard you was back but 'tis mighty fine to see you in the flesh."

"Yes, it's good to get back home."

The fellow made clucking noises. "You may think so now, but wait till you see the state the Ajax is in. Meantime, is there anything I can do for you? If so, just speak out. Us Rebs must stick together, these days especial."

It was somehow reassuring to recognize such respect in a civilian. "Why, yes, Phillips — that's your name isn't it?"

"Yep, and I'm proud you should remember it so long."

"Are any officials who lived here and worked at the Ajax still around?"

"Why, yes, sir. Your Dad's general manager, Dave Brownlow, came back from the fightin' several weeks back — unhurt. Then there's Dick Stafford, who was the chief engineer, and there's Dr. Trimble. On account of his rheumatics and 'cause he was needed here so bad, he stayed home throughout the war. He's the one who always cared for the Ajax's injured help. Remember him?"

"Only by name, I'm afraid."

The stationmaster raised furry brows. "Where at d'you aim to put up at this hour, sir? I axe only 'cause both hotels and all boardin' houses are jam-packed with folks waitin' for their homes to get fixed fit to live in again."

"Don't know, but possibly Mr. Brownlow might accommodate us."

"Likely he could; he's got a big house, but maybe you've forgot, sir, his place lies a mile or so out of town and it's gettin' late. Yankee patrollers might halt you."

"That's so." Rod, weary to the very marrow of his bones, groaned softly. Lord above! Would this day never end? Seemed hard to realize he'd quitted Moluntha only this morning. "Thanks, Phillips, we'll look about and find what we can."

He led Hamrick along a number of dark, unpaved streets toward the center of Wytheville. Now that Number 35 had departed they were nearly deserted. Lights glowed in only a few dwellings.

Rodney sighed. "Stationmaster said the town's full of people on account of so many returning residents, some have to double up with friends or relatives. We'll be damn' lucky if we can locate beds of any sort."

"Hell's pecker, suh, many's the time we've slept on bare ground. Just space in a hayloft and bait for the hosses would be dandy."

Once, they instinctively stiffened when a detail of blue-clad provost's guard approached, but paid no attention to this pair of travel-stained riders.

The only signs of activity encountered came from a small body of Union troops encamped in the public park; some were noisily gambling and others were drinking. They next approached a brilliantly lit saloon in which a commotion of some sort was taking place.

Rodney quickly identified it as the Pocohontas, a tavern of ill repute.

Hamrick observed, "Sounds like a rookus is goin' on. Wisht I could join in, it's been months since I've enjoyed a good free-for-all!"

"Forget it, Rimfire. You should have had your bellyful of fighting by now."

They were less than half a block short of the Pocohontas when the disturbance rose to a loud and drunken crescendo. The saloon's swinging doors burst open and out onto the dusty street surged a tangle of staggering, yelling and punching figures.

Rodney and Hamrick reined in to watch the brawl. Excitement of any description was more than welcome after the weary monotony endured at Moluntha Garrison.

Despite darkness the situation soon became clarified. At least half-a-dozen burly fellows were attacking a tall, broad-shouldered, and coatless individual who appeared to be defending himself with more than ordinary skill.

Arose shouts of, "Lemme take a poke at the goddam cardsharp." "Tramp him flat!" A blade flashed. "Hell, I want his cheatin' balls for breakfast!"

More patrons lurched from the saloon and lingered on a board sidewalk to enjoy the fracas. Although the tall man put up a fine fight his assailants were too many. When a hard punch to the jaw knocked him off balance someone dealt him a savage kick in the groin and he doubled over convulsively. More blows beat him flat onto the ground whereupon yelling, drunken attackers began kicking the fallen figure.

Tilt urged Resaca forward when yelling assailants continued to kick the prostrate figure. "Come along, Corporal, else they'll surely kill him."

All the while shouting at the top of their lungs, he and Hamrick spurred into the crowd. A big man made a snatch at Rodney's reins but reeled aside under a hard kick to his bearded chin.

Someone in front of the Pocohontas shouted, "Whoever you are, clear out! This goddam sharp's been cheatin'! Cleaned me out and plenty others! Bastard's gettin' no worse than his due."

Once Resaca and Hamrick's mount charged into them the struggling mob dispersed, yelling obscenities and vows of vengeance.

A big, bushy-haired fellow bellowed over his shoulder, "Neither of you is sheriff nor a law officer, so leave us be! We're only dealin' out justice!"

In a far-carrying, parade-ground voice Rodney yelled, "Maybe so, but we'll not let you murder this fellow without trial — no matter what he's done. By the looks of him you've pretty nearly accomplished your purpose; go get yourselves another drink."

Growling imprecations, the attackers straggled back to the Pocohontas. One of them sang out, "You two had better clear out of town quick else you'll pay dear for this come morning!"

Paying no heed, Rodney dismounted to discover whether the victim remained alive. Terribly beaten, and bleeding from half-a-dozen wounds, the unknown remained sprawled in the dust with pants' pockets turned inside out. A cursory examination indicated that a kick in the mouth not only had knocked out some teeth but had rendered this cruelly battered individual senseless.

Rimfire Hamrick's short body bent low over his cantle. "He still alive, suh?"

"Yes, but in bad shape. Get down and help sling him across your saddle. If I remember right, Dr. Trimble's house isn't far off."

Ignoring taunts and curses from the saloon's entrance, they heaved the unconscious figure, limp as any sack of grain, across Hamrick's horse, much as they'd carried off stricken comrades during the war. Followed by the dismounted Hamrick leading his horse, Rodney at a slow walk followed familiar, tree-lined and dusty streets till he recognized the white-painted latticed and pilastered porch of the doctor's residence.

Fervently he prayed Dr. Trimble might be at home and still awake. Insistent pounding on the front door presently brought the frail, bespectacled old physician, in his night shirt and shielding a candle with one hand, to the door.

"Good God! 'Tis Rodney Tilt! Somewhere I heard you had returned home. What's wrong?"

As briefly as possible because he could hear blood dripping steadily from behind, Rodney described what had happened. Without hesitation the doctor called over his shoulder to an open window on the second floor, "Bessie, Bessie! Get on your wrapper, chunk up the kitchen stove, then light the lamps in the consultation room. Rodney Tilt's just fetched in a gravely injured man."

Before long the unknown lay supine on a battered brown leather couch, breathing heavily. Blood from a cut on his left wrist commenced to drip onto a threadbare carpet.

"Who is he?" Dr. Trimble queried while adjusting steel-rimmed spectacles.

Rodney shook his dark head, "No idea at all. Only know he was getting beaten to death outside the Pocohontas — supposedly for cheating at cards. Probably he got no more than he deserved, but I couldn't stand by and see him murdered. Please see how badly he's hurt."

Following a cursory examination, nearly bald Dr. Trimble grunted, then peered over his glasses. "I'd say that, like the signed cat in the adage, he's better than he looks. For all he's been cut here and there and his wounds are bloody, they don't amount to much. What's more serious is that he's likely suffered some broken ribs and possibly a fracture of the jaw. Since his breathing is leveling out, he ought to come to before long. Here, help me get his fancy, frilled shirt and those sporting-house pants off him."

The doctor's wife appeared, her pepper-and-salt-colored hair plaited into a single, heavy braid which dangled down her back. Elizabeth Trimble appeared quite unperturbed; during the course of the war she must have attended dozens if not hundreds of equally bloodied and battered persons. She disappeared and promptly returned carrying a blanket and a mop. Meanwhile, from a drawer the doctor produced rolls of bandages, pledgets and sticking plaster, also a dark bottle which, he confided, contained a disinfectant of his own invention. "I've had luck with it."

At the end of half an hour the still-insensible unknown's knife wounds had been dressed, but his jaw was continuing to swell.

Dr. Trimble went over to rinse hands in a basin twice emptied but still containing pink-hued water. Said he, "Right now there's nothing more I can do. He looks sturdy, so I'll leave him alone and keep an eye on him."

Rodney queried, "Any room in your stable? The town's jam-packed."

"True, but we've a spare trundle bed for you. Your friend can bed down in the stable. There's hay in the loft so he shouldn't be uncomfortable."

Once Hamrick had led away the horses, Rodney lingered and dispassionately surveyed the tall figure with dark red hair, whose bronzed complexion was emphasized by a variety of white bandages. His long crooked nose and narrow, gaunt features suggested a bear's. Presently, the unknown drew a slow, deep breath and half-opened bloodshot, very bright-blue eyes.

"Sounds to me as if the patient is about to wake up," observed the doctor.

"Who are you?" Rodney bent low over the couch.

"Jim Manlove," the wounded man mumbled through swollen lips, "Gunner's Mate, C.S.S. *Alabama*. How'd — I —" But he then grew incoherent and fell silent.

Dr. Trimble shook a shiny, nearly hairless head and rearranged his spectacles. "This fellow still must be out of his senses. What would a sailor be doing this far inland?"

"Don't know and don't care." Rodney fetched a huge yawn. "Will you let him stay here till morning? I promise I'll take him off your hands then."

"Don't worry on that score."

"Many, many thanks to you and your good wife."

"Don't mention it. I've handled more serious cases at your dad's mine. Seen it yet?"

"No. We're riding out there tomorrow."

"You won't like what you'll find. By all accounts, those damn' Yankees were pretty thorough."

"I guess so from all I've heard. Tell me, did this fellow call himself 'Manlove' or am I mistaken?"

"No. That's what he said, 'Jim Manlove'— never heard such a name before. Incidentally, he's not unconscious now, only sleeping."

Mrs. Trimble tossed a well-worn quilt over the bandaged figure, then beckoned. "Come along, Mr. Tilt. You look nearly as dead-beat as your friend."

"Manlove's no friend and, if any part of what I heard outside the Pocohontas proves so, he's never going to be one."

"Well, come along and no nonsense. There's a trundle bed upstairs we keep for emergencies and unexpected guests."

# 26

# Ruins

NEXT MORNING Rodney turned out later than he'd intended, thanks to slumber of nearly complete exhaustion. He found Hamrick grooming the horses and cleaning bits by sloshing them in a horse trough.

Rodney said, yawning, "I understand a Mr. Stafford, who was chief engineer at the Ajax mine, lives only a couple of streets away. After breakfast I'll try to find him; he should give me a good idea of what needs to be done out there."

While they were finishing breakfast, Mr. Stafford came riding up to Dr. Trimble's house astride a bony gray gelding and inquired for Colonel Tilt. After they'd shaken hands the latter queried, "How did you know I was here?"

"Why, just after sunup Doc Trimble sent a message."

Stafford was small and wiry, his quick gestures reminded Rodney of a bird — a particularly apt analogy since the ex-chief engineer had a long, pointed nose.

"I'm mighty pleased to see you, Mr. Stafford. Since time is of the essence, I propose we ride out to the mine and make a survey right away. I want to see for myself what's left."

Stafford shook his head. "I fear you'll be aghast over what you'll find."

"Everyone seems to think so. However, I'm glad you're along and can give sound advice. As you probably have heard, I know hardly anything about the operating side of this mine."

He hesitated. "Is the Ajax really so badly damaged as everyone says?"

"You'll have to see the property to understand the extent of destruction."

The town was quiet and shadows still long when Rodney, Stafford, and Hamrick rode out of Wytheville parallel to a two-mile-long spur of narrow-gauge railroad running to the north and east. Birds flitted and sang among weeds and bushes which had grown to considerable height between crossties; rails were encrusted by a heavy coat of yellow-brown rust. The three rode in silence until they came upon a trestle, charred and otherwise so thoroughly wrecked Rodney at a glance could tell it would have to be entirely rebuilt.

"You'll recall that this is the first of two trestles," Stafford informed somberly as they jogged along. "The other, over Bland Creek, is longer and higher. The damn' Yankee raiders ruined that, too."

Rodney's already acute sense of desperation increased when, on reaching the high trestle crossing Bland Creek, he saw a huge gap near its center. Lord! What would *that* cost to replace?

The balance of the ride was accomplished in silence broken only by the clip-clopping of hoofs.

Said Stafford as they were rounding the last of several foothills leading up to the Clinch Mountains and presently would sight the shaft's head, "Brace yourself, Colonel."

Although before the war Rodney had visited the Ajax mine only infrequently, he perceived at once that only the tall brick chimney to the ore crusher and refinery remained standing, stark and lonely above piles of charred debris and broken machinery. However, the brick pumphouse seemed intact, as well as rough wooden barracks in which miners had lodged.

"The house seems all right, but what about the pumps themselves?" Rodney queried in a subdued voice.

"They were carried off," Stafford told him. "Yanks must have had use for them elsewhere, which means numbers three and five galleries are flooded and will stay so till new pumps are set to work."

The mine's two-story clapboard office building also had been set afire but, as Stafford pointed out, the fortuitous arrival of a rain squall had preserved a large part of the structure. All panes in its remaining windows had been shattered. Somehow, this trivial damage seemed to emphasize the pervading air of desolation.

Stafford then led the way to a shed which had sheltered a locomotive specially designed to serve the Ajax's narrow-gauge railroad. The rusting, shattered remains of the little engine still lay where the raiders had found it.

"How did they manage to wreck it so completely?" Rodney growled.

Stafford explained, "Probably they wired down her safety valve, then fired the boiler till it exploded."

It was infinitely disheartening to find a few flatcars still standing on a siding all but concealed by bushes and vines.

Even the entrance to the mine itself had been blown up; gaps remained large enough to permit one to clamber over a mass of rotting timbers and tumbled rock and so enter the main shaft.

"At a quick guess, Mr. Stafford, how much money d'you think will be required to restore the mine to working condition?"

"Can't even risk an estimate," stated the ex-chief engineer. "That's not my line of work. You'd better ask Mr. Brownlow 'bout that. I figure he can give you a rough idea of how much money's going to be needed."

"Give me a guess, anyhow."

"Well, at least a hundred and fifty thousand dollars, maybe more. What with the war just ended and everything, I don't yet know where to begin finding replacements."

$150,000 at the least! So staggering a sum tolled in Rod's mind like a funeral bell.

By the time they returned to Wytheville, the July sun was beating down with such unrelenting force that the horses needed watering and a brief rest before setting out for the former general manager's place on the edge of town.

From David Brownlow, a gaunt horse-faced individual, he ascertained Stafford's guess had been reasonably accurate.

"Yes, Colonel," Brownlow stated, tugging thoughtfully at a short gray beard. "I'll venture that at the least a hundred and fifty thousand might get the Ajax operating. Ever since I got home I've been writing trying to find out where we can find necessary machinery and other equipment if, and when, you can raise such a sum." He spread hands in a gesture indicative of hopelessness.

"Had any luck?"

"Not so far. Things being as they are, I've had only a few answers, mostly discouraging, but I'll keep on till I find a firm able to manufacture and deliver needed essentials." He grimaced. "Sorry, Colonel, but I fear I won't be able to arrive at a sound estimate in weeks, maybe months."

On his return about midday Rodney Tilt roused from that slough of despond into which he had sunk since riding away from Brownlow's office. God above! What could be done? One hundred and fifty thousand dollars seemed an utterly impossible sum. Certainly sale of the family's silver, even under the most profitable of terms, would fetch nowhere near the sum Stafford had mentioned.

Conversation with the engineer during the ride back to Dr. Trimble's confirmed what he'd already suspected; there wasn't even the ghost of a hope of negotiating a mortgage here, since no one could possibly foresee what direction the Union Government's fiscal policy would follow. Therefore he couldn't hope, locally, to negotiate a sizable mortgage on either the mine or on Moluntha Garrison, for that matter. A possibility that Marc Peabody might prove of some assistance cast the only ray of hope onto what appeared an otherwise hopeless situation.

Rodney's sense of despair increased when Stafford commented, "Everybody 'round here's on edge over what measures the new government will take toward collecting land taxes owed over these last four years. Only one thing is sure — our conquerors are damned well going to demand *and collect* their 'pound of flesh,' with interest. Were I you, Colonel, I'd go have a talk with Martin Dillworth. He was your Daddy's lawyer, and he's as knowledgeable about such matters as anyone 'round hereabouts. In case you don't know, he still keeps his office on Main Street. How much longer d'you expect to stay in Wytheville?"

"Another day anyhow, maybe longer," Rodney replied, as by an obvious effort he straightened in his saddle. "I'm going to try every possibility of finding sufficient credit to keep Moluntha going for a while. My father has a lot of friends hereabouts."

"Better say 'had.' Many of them were lost during the war, while the rest — even the well-to-do ones — are no better off financially than you, I'm afraid, so I can only wish you better luck than I fear you'll find."

On reaching the edge of town Stafford gathered his reins. "I'll turn off here. Look me up the minute you hear anything encouraging. Good luck, sir."

# 27

---

## James Manlove, C.S.N.

ARRIVING AT Doctor Trimble's pleasant tree-shaded home on this scorchingly hot and humid afternoon, Rodney was considerably surprised when Trimble, on letting him in, informed that Manlove had recovered sufficiently to move about and at present was resting upstairs. "That fellow must be constructed of steel, whalebone, and rawhide. I've seldom seen such vitality."

"But what about his broken bones?"

"Hasn't any. I discovered, on closer examination, his ribs were just badly bruised while his jaw was not broken, only partially dislocated. I reset it."

"Where is he?" Rodney asked incredulously.

"Elizabeth and I helped him upstairs after some rough-looking citizens heard he was here and came looking for him." Dr. Trimble smiled, stroked a sparse gray goatee. "They only went away when I swore by all that's holy the rascal was dying. Guess I must be a convincing liar, since they seemed satisfied and didn't try to force their way inside."

"How soon d'you think he might be able to ride?"

"Maybe tomorrow, maybe not. At best, he could travel only a short distance, tough as he is. Some of those knife cuts are fairly deep and he's lost three teeth besides. When he's fit, we'll wait till dark, load him into my buggy, then drive him out of town. If you think it's advisable, you might persuade Mr. Brownlow to take him in."

"Thank you, but I'll not impose on a friend till I find out more about this fellow."

Wearily, Rodney collapsed rather than sat onto a chair, bowed his head, and covered his face with both hands, until he felt the doctor's hand on his shoulder.

"I reckon matters at the mine must have been as bad as you'd heard?"

Rodney uncovered deeply tanned and haggard features. "Yes. Things there are even worse than I'd been led to expect."

Exerting obvious effort he arose. "Well, Doctor, before I call on Mr. Dillworth I think I'd better go upstairs and have a talk with that rascal."

He found the disheveled patient slumped on that same trundle bed he himself had occupied the previous night. Certainly, the man calling himself "Manlove" presented a pitiable figure, what with a hugely swollen jaw and liberally tattooed arms bandaged in several places. Old bluish burnt powder spots speckled his forehead.

Since he was clad only in an old dressing gown of the doctor's, more bandages secured about hairy and muscular thighs and legs were revealed.

At best Manlove could never have been deemed good-looking, since the blunt nose of his square-shaped face was canted to one side; no doubt the result of a brawl. His large right ear was thickened out of shape — "cauliflowered," as a boxer would describe it.

Manlove sat up, peered through a tangle of long and dark-red hair, then mumbled, "I'm sure all-fired grateful for what you did for me last night, Cunnel Tilt."

Rodney dropped into the depths of an armchair with a comfortably sagging cane bottom. "Damned if I yet know whether you were worth the trouble or not, but they surely would have finished you off if Hamrick and I hadn't mixed in." The Master of Moluntha's jet gaze fixed on the gambler's bright-blue but swollen and bloodshot eyes.

"Suppose you tell me about yourself. Incidentally, you'd better not try to lie."

Mumbling because of his swollen mouth, the wounded man straightened slightly, eyes intent on his dusty, sunburned questioner's expression.

"What is your real name?"

The other replied sharply, "Manlove, James Armstrong Manlove, and because of my family name many's the fight I've had — to set people straight about it."

A faint smile formed beneath Rodney's drooping black mustaches. "Shouldn't wonder. Now give me a straight answer and perhaps I'll help you some more. Were you cheating?"

"I — I'll try, sir. You see, Cunnel, I swear to God Almighty I *weren't* cheatin'. But I admit that, to keep afloat, I been gamblin' ever since the

Feds chased my battery out of Petersburg and the army got surrendered at a place called Appomattox."

Sharply, Rodney queried, "What battery were you with?"

"Why, 'twas Captain Tucker's Naval Battery of Gen'ral Ewell's Division. Joined up after we'd scuttled the little gunboat I was servin' in before those damn' big Union ironclads blocked the James. Since the surrender at Appomattox I been kind of wanderin' from one place to another. Always have been lucky at cards so, once I got rid of my uniform, or what was left of it, and had won some civilian duds, I took to gamblin', but mostly with Yankee garrison troops," he added hastily.

"You say you were serving in one of our gunboats? You're a sailor?"

"Yes, sir. Have been all along."

"How come you joined our navy?"

"Why, sir, I hail from Otway, North Carolina. When I was twelve my Pa he died and Ma remarried a mean son of a bitch so I run off to sea."

"Where is Otway?" Rodney instantly demanded.

"Why, 'tis just a little village lyin' to the south of Beaufort. Like I said, since I was a lad of twelve I been voyagin' all 'round the world and have seen a lot and done a lot — reckon that's why I don't talk much like a Southerner."

Rodney had noticed this, wondered whether this explanation wasn't a trifle too pat. "Suppose you tell me why they accused you of cheating?"

Slowly Manlove shook his bandaged head, at the same time gingerly easing his wounded left wrist. "Well, sir, I came to Wytheville followin' such an uncommon run of good poker hands in Christiansburg nobody'd play with me anymore, though no one ever accused me of doin' nothing wrong. When I came to the Pocohontas I lost plenty the first night but I came back so strong durin' the next two sessions that a fellow, name of Rigby, who, among others, had lost a bundle to me, no doubt figured on gettin' it back, so he slipped a marked deck of cards into my coat pocket once I'd hung it to the back of my chair. I still was winnin' when Rigby suddenly pulls a derringer out of his vest, levels it at me, and roars that I'd been cheatin' all along!"

Elbows on knees, Rodney leaned forward. "Were you playing with marked cards when he accused you?"

Manlove winced at the suggestion and violently shook his battered head. "Not that I knew of, but Rigby might have had marked cards of his own —" Manlove stiffened. . . . "By God! I remember now! Rigby called for a new deck just a few hands before he pulled that gun.

"After those bastards jumped me they searched my coat and found those damned pasteboards I spoke of. After that, sir, they stripped me of my money belt, turned my pockets inside out, and stole every cent I had before the tavern keeper and his bouncers broke in and 'llowed if they was about to slay me they'd have to do it outside. 'Twas just then, when I came so close to cashin' in my chips for keeps, you and yer friend interfered — for which you'll find me truly grateful and mebbe —" he batted discolored, swollen eyelids, "rewardin'."

Seldom had Rodney Tilt found himself in so complete a quandary. Certainly the man lying before him appeared as disreputable-looking as any he'd ever beheld. Yet somehow the ready ease with which Manlove spoke, unless he was a very practiced liar, seemed to convey just a shade of authenticity.

As if reading his mind, the navy man queried anxiously, "Are you believin' what I say, sir?"

"I'm not sure yet, continue. Tell me just how you, a sailor, came to be an artilleryman at the siege of Petersburg."

The hurt man almost stifled a groan. "I sure will, sir, if you'll kindly ask the sawbones below for a small swaller of liquor. I — I feel mighty weak and shaky."

Despite his better judgment Rodney went downstairs and returned carrying two tumblers of watered bourbon — he could use a drink himself.

After they'd sipped a moment Rodney directed, "All right, go ahead, but don't try to bend the truth even a little."

The bandaged man nodded solemnly. "I swear, sir, what I'm about to speak is God's own truth; if there's a Bible handy I'll take oath on it.

"I'm feelin' a mite dizzy. Mind if I settle back, for 'tis a long tale I've to tell." He then sank back to rest his powder-marked head on the ticking-covered bolster he'd been using when Rodney appeared.

Outbreak of the war, Manlove related, found him in New Orleans where, because he was a sailor of considerable experience, he'd at once enlisted in the Confederate Navy and promptly had been assigned for service as a petty officer aboard the C.S.S. *Sumter,* which was among the first far-ranging Rebel commerce destroyers to put to sea. After having evaded Federal blockade ships she had commenced a long and daring cruise, during which she'd taken, plundered, and sunk or burnt over a dozen Yankee merchantmen.

Toward the end of her cruise the *Sumter* had touched in England where, Manlove stated, he'd been recruited to serve as gunner's mate aboard a new sloop-of-war, the C.S.S. *Alabama,* which had just been completed but lay in a British yard unarmed because of neutrality laws; she was to receive her guns and munitions somewhere on the high seas. Manlove claimed he'd served aboard her throughout her long and destructive career — the details of which he omitted — until, in a spectacular duel with the U.S.S. *Kearsarge,* she was sent to the bottom the year before off the French port of Cherbourg.

Ignoring homely street noises drifting through windows opened against the stifling heat, Rodney listened intently, but even when sipping his drink his gaze never shifted from the speaker's battered visage, about which a halo of flies were buzzing, attracted no doubt by the smell of blood staining various bandages.

Rodney told the speaker, "So far, yours sounds a likely yarn. What happened after the *Alabama* sank?"

"My luck held long enough for me to get picked up by a small boat from the *Deerhound* — some English lord's yacht which had been standin' off-and-on to watch the fight. She put me ashore in Liverpool and 'twasn't long before I landed a berth aboard the *Annie Laurie,* a blockade runner built 'special for that trade. Everything went all right till, off Wilmington in my home state, a Federal gunboat chased the *Annie Laurie* ashore, then shelled the hell out of her till she burned up.

"Me and some few others managed to swim ashore. Then I went up to Wilmington where I bought shares in the *Saucy Minx,* a small privateer schooner fittin' out for a cruise about the Gulf of Mexico in hopes of pickin' off Yankee merchantmen."

The injured man must be feeling stronger since he sat up and spoke more distinctly while describing how the *Saucy Minx* had prized a pair of big brigs out of Tampico and bound for Boston. The privateer had looted both prizes, then had loaded all captives aboard one ship as a cartel before burning the other.

Fascinated, despite himself, Rodney felt inclined to believe that not even the most convincing of liars could so readily invent so complicated yet so plausible a tale.

Once Manlove had consumed the last drops of his drink he continued. "We'd scarce left the burning wreck and the cartel than a hurricane blew up almost 'thout warnin', and drove the *Minx* ashore on a tiny key — one of a cluster of uninhabited coral reefs.

"Well, sir, us survivors soon realized the *Minx* was stove in for keeps. We was still thankin' God four of us was still alive when, through the storm-wrack we sighted another vessel, a big steam brig flyin' the tatters of a French flag bein' driven onto another key not too far off. When she struck, her masts snapped and she was rolled clean over onto her beams' ends with great rollers pourin' over her. 'Twas a terrible sight." Manlove's voice grew louder with his recollection. "We watched a few of her people try to launch a boat but it overturned right away and they was drowned.

"Livin' on turtle eggs and coconuts for food and water, us fellers off the *Minx* took a couple of days to fashion a raft out of her wreckage stout enough to carry us over to what turned out to be a French steam packet named *Circe*. Like I said, she was lyin' half-buried in sand on her beams' ends and was one of the sorriest sights I ever laid eyes on. Anyhow, we climbed aboard the wreck but found nary a livin' soul anywheres."

Suspense rendered Rodney impatient. "Come to the point, man. What happened next?"

"Why, sir, it turned out from her papers — one of us could read French — she was carryin' pay for the Mexican emperor's French troops."

"You mean Emperor Maximilian's mercenaries?"

"Yes, sir." The speaker's color heightened in what could be seen of his features. "We scrambled about till, in the captain's quarters, we came across a small, iron-bound chest. Because it was padlocked and chained to a stanchion we figured likely it must contain somethin' of value; even thought it might be a pay chest."

"Was it?"

For the first time Manlove hesitated, then, as if having arrived at a decision, replied slowly, "Yes, sir. When we shot off the padlocks we saw it was brimmin' with big gold coins!"

"How many of your survivors witnessed this?"

"All four of us, sir."

Voices from Dr. Trimble's consultation room below could distinctly be heard in a brief ensuing silence.

"Well, what did you do?"

"Well, sir, we figured the best idee was to raft the chest ashore and bury it on a nearby key after we'd helped ourselves to a double handful apiece."

The injured man commenced to speak more rapidly. "Then we rafted ourselves to the Mexican mainland near to Cabo Rojo, and after fillin' our pockets with coins — I had my last one in the money belt they ripped off me at the Pocohontas — we buried the chest in a spot easy to recognize if you were in the know. Well, that same night we was attacked by natives who'd noticed the wrecks and was comin' to loot. They murdered two of us, but me and a feller named Pleasants got away in the dark and hid till daylight.

"Well, sir, to cut a long story short, me and Pleasants struggled up the coast, starvin' and half-dead of thirst, till we could steal a canoe and paddle offshore. Next day we was lucky enough to get sighted and picked up by a blockade runner which carried us through the Yankee blockade to Wilmington, North Carolina, which lies not too far from where I was born."

"You've lost track of Pleasants?"

"Yes, sir. As a Navy man I thought I'd best serve in a Confederate gunboat flotilla operatin' on the James River, but Pleasants 'llowed he was set on joinin' troops fightin' Sherman's advance. Before we parted we swore, if we was still alive, we'd meet at the Globe Hotel in Richmond come the first of next year and talk about recoverin' the pay chest."

"And where is the key on which the French ship got wrecked?"

Manlove's manner underwent perceptible alteration. "That, sir, I reckon is my ace in the hole which should make worthwhile your keepin' me alive. And I hope you will, sir. I owe you my life and I'd sure like to pay you back when the time comes."

# 28

# Disaster

Dawn was breaking late because a series of violent thunderstorms and heavy rainstorms had struck during the night. More seemed on the way, but ex-Paymaster Lieutenant Samuel Shepherd experienced a huge sense of relief since, at Lynchburg, both trunks had been trundled safely across a broad wooden platform dividing the Virginia & Tennessee line from the tracks of the Orange & Alexandria Railroad and loaded into Alexandria-bound Number 7's baggage car.

He waited unobtrusively in light rain until he watched the baggage man slide-to and lock the car's door. Then, aching with fatigue, he climbed steps leading into a passenger coach coupled immediately behind the baggage car.

He found Loretta Tilt, obviously worn-out, hunched over and munching halfheartedly on a soggy sandwich purchased in the station. Her normally bright and faintly slanting dark eyes looked dull and violet-shadowed but she made an effort to brighten up when Sam, after wiping moisture from white-stubbled features, dropped onto the seat at her side.

"Everything go all right?" she queried, brushing crumbs from the front of a dark-brown traveling cloak.

"Yes. I watched our trunks stowed in a corner and other baggage tossed on top." He sighed and, forcing a wan smile, accepted a limp sandwich filled with meat from some tough and very aged hen.

At long last the locomotive whistled valiantly, then chuffed and briefly spun its wheels on wet rails before gaining traction. Couplings clattered and steam smelling of oil billowed about while various brakemen uncranked brakes to their cars. Spouting fountains of sparks from its bell-shaped funnel, the wood-burning engine gradually gathered momentum until presently houses, then a gray landscape, commenced to slip by, veiled in rain. Passengers didn't bother to peer outside, only made themselves as comfortable as possible against the long ride ahead.

Having slept hardly at all the previous night, Loretta before long commenced to sag toward her companion and her head in a rusty-black, frilled poke bonnet drooped onto her breast. She roused a little when Shepherd made bold to slide an arm around her to steady her against the car's violent joltings.

"Thank you," she murmured over the somehow soothing rhythmic *click-clack* set up by wheels passing over joints between the rails.

"Now I feel the time has come to make a confession," she admitted. "I — I've — well, from the beginning I've thought highly of you. Now I feel my regard has grown into — into, well, something more tender."

His silver-hued head canted until it came to rest against her bonnet and shoved it askew as his arm tightened about her.

"D'you know, Lorrie — I've always called you that to myself — long ago I fell deeply and truly in love with you. I'd have spoken out — if only I weren't a half- "

Her grimy hand darted up to seal his lips. "Don't speak of that. I've thought it over time and again. Your blood and breeding count for nothing with me."

For a moment her eyes opened and peered into his, then she sighed and snuggled back into the support of his arm. "If you really want to marry me I-I'll be content to go wherever you decide."

"Content to leave Moluntha?"

"Moluntha belongs to Rodney, and, well, I think I've lived and suffered there too long. I've yet to see the great, wonderful world outside. Will you show it to me?"

"Oh, I will! I will!" He glanced about, realized their fellow passengers already were dozing or reading, so hungrily kissed her mouth and was astonished by the amazing warmth of her response.

"You can't imagine the plans I've made over and over again. You see, I've some gold coins I've never mentioned before, hidden near the graveyard at Moluntha — over five thousand dollars' worth. With that we could make a beginning in Savannah or maybe in New Orleans, where I've friends in the shipping business so, before long, I'm sure I can provide you with comfort if not luxury."

Loretta murmured after quickly kissing him, "All I need to know is that I love you and trust you, for better or for worse. I'm convinced you'll make a wonderfully kind and considerate husband." She pressed herself closer to him, relaxed. "You can be sure, Samuel, I will do my level best to please you in every way for as long as we both shall live."

"Amen, dearest, and now let's try to rest a bit. We can plan more sensibly later on."

Still another squall drummed against the windowpanes and a wild wind roared about the cars; sometimes it seemed as if rain struck with the force of waves.

A bearded man sitting across the aisle roused sufficiently to call over, "If this ain't the wust goddam tempest I *ever* heard tell of! Yep, we bin catchin' plenty of hard thunderstorms these past few days. Heard tell they've suffered some turrible cloudbursts up-country. They must —" He broke off because the locomotive started whistling hoarsely to drive a forlorn cow off the right-of-way.

Despite the tumult Loretta went to sleep, hand still nestled inside Shepherd's. Damp, smelly, and nearing complete exhaustion, Sam nevertheless reveled in such sublime happiness he couldn't drop off and, unseeingly, viewed a succession of straggling hamlets pass, their muddy streets quite deserted.

The country was growing hilly again, he noted, and must have been drenched over a considerable period. In small, red-hued little ponds water lay, and everywhere in hollows, clearings, and even on unplowed fields.

At length Samuel Shepherd finally succumbed to fatigue and dropped instantly into a deep sleep even as Number 7 commenced to descend a steep grade, so wasn't aware when the train commenced to gather speed, gradually at first, but then with increased momentum at a rate which set the engineer to whistling frantically for brakes.

Fast, faster, the swaying, madly jolting train sped down toward a deep ravine through which a raging torrent was rushing. Hurriedly constructed last spring by U.S. Army railroad engineers, the bridge, its foundations weakened or swept away, inclined slowly to the left and then collapsed. The locomotive and all its cars hurtled downward amid sickening shrieks of terror and a mad crackling of riven timbers to dissolve into a murderous tangle. Despite sluicing rain the splintered wreckage readily took fire.

A lengthy conversation in Mr. Martin Dillworth's office only served to emphasize the utter impossibility of raising funds locally. The lawyer steepled fingers beneath a short, pockmarked nose. "I'm terribly sorry, Colonel Tilt, but, much as I hate to admit it, that's the way things stand. Till the Radicals in Washington make up their minds what they're going to do with us, there'll be no credit or mortgage money available."

He shrugged, then bit off a chew of tobacco. "As it is, I'm right hard-pressed to pay my rent on this office."

"You've always done well for the Ajax property, Mr. Dillworth, so —" Rodney made a transparent effort to sound hopeful —"I'm confident you'll keep on doing your best. Please let me hear from you as soon as you hear anything about our back-tax situation. I'm extremely worried on that score."

"You should be," the lawyer agreed. "That's where Yankee administrators and the scalawags they'll put in office first will put the bite on us Southerns."

Shoulders drooping for once, Rodney stumped out into the street, hoping he'd be in time for a bite of lunch at the doctor's. While trudging through a shower, he dismissed the lawyer's discouraging discourse and reluctantly faced a different problem. What should he do about Manlove? Was that hard-bitten character's tale credible, even in part? Um. When, suddenly, he'd told the ex-gunner's mate to repeat various details of his tale Manlove hadn't slipped up once — had repeated his account without even minor contradictions regarding dates, places and names — so it seemed possible he *had* been telling the truth.

He was opening the doctor's picket gate when he spied Hamrick galloping through the downpour — he never went anywhere on foot unless forced to.

"Cunnel! Cunnel, suh!" The bow-legged little man flung himself off and ran up, hard-eyed, with rain dripping from his broad-brimmed hat. There was something in the ex-corporal's taut expression which seemed to drive an icicle into Rodney's heart.

"Bad news?"

"Yes, suh. The wust! Oh, mah God, I doan' know how to begin to tell you."

"Tell me what?"

"About that train — the one your sister and Mr. Shepherd changed over onto at Lynchburg —"

Rodney squared shoulders and straightened, as always in the face of evil news. "What about it?"

"Why, suh, the Orange & Alexandria's train Number 7 from Lynchburg to Alexandria got wrecked when it ran onto a washed-out bridge close by Charlottesville."

"You sure?"

"Yes, suh, I was in the station when the news came by telegraph. It sho' 'nough was the connection with the train Miss Loretta and Mr. Shepherd boarded here."

Sickened, Rodney forced himself to go on talking.

"How bad was this wreck?"

"Bad as could be. Seems like one passenger car after another followed the locomotive into a ravine and the wreckage took fire."

Rodney steadied himself on the gatepost, stonily demanded, "Any reports of survivors?"

"The telegraph feller 'llowed they was only a few who was ridin' the tail-end coach, but they was mashed up somethin' turrible. Oh, God, suh. I sho' hate like hell havin' to be the one to bring you such awful tidin's."

Realization that Samuel Shepherd and his twin undoubtedly must have occupied the coach next the baggage car and therefore had been closest to the locomotive proved soul-freezing.

Hamrick reached out when Rodney swayed. "Ain't there nuthin' I kin do?"

"Yes. Lend me your arm till I get inside then ask the doctor to fetch all the liquor he can spare."

Not till considerably later did the Master of Moluntha come to realize that the family silver also must have been lost, probably beyond recovery.

# 29

---

## Apprehensions Mount

AFTER A WEEK had passed and neither Rodney nor any message from him had arrived, apprehensions mounted at Moluntha Garrison. On a sweltering early August evening Bushrod and Caroline sat in the gazebo where at least an occasional faltering breeze might stir the hot and humid atmosphere. Mechanically, Bushrod fingered his scant, yellow-brown chin whiskers while staring out over the familiar valley where now many pastures had been fenced. Alas, they still contained very few animals. He glanced at his wife who sat bent over, knitting woolen suspenders for little Oliver.

"I simply can't understand why we haven't heard from Rod," Bushrod grumbled once again. "He's never before been unreliable. If something is detaining him in Wytheville or somewhere else, why in blazes hasn't he telegraphed or sent word somehow? It's not at all like him."

Caroline's sleek blond head inclined, "Not at all. That's what's so worrisome. Last night I dreamed something terrible had happened."

"Bosh! 'Twas only a dream."

"I truly hope so." She glanced upward, winged brows merged. "I presume that, like me, you are wondering why we've heard nothing from Loretta and Sam Shepherd. She promised me faithfully to telegraph the moment they reached Washington, and once again when the silver had been disposed of. Of course, it *would* take some time for Sam to sell off the, er, merchandise to best advantage."

Worn out through anxiety and a hard day's work, Bushrod sighed gustily. "Possibly Lettie's wire has been lost or gone astray, since by all accounts communications in these parts remain uncertain to say the least."

Although sunset was flooding the countryside with an unusually rich red-gold radiance, neither of those in the gazebo took notice.

"Well, at least our crops are doing well," Caroline said, in an effort to dispell an almost overpowering sense of depression. "All along the rains seem to have fallen at about the right intervals. Besides, the horses are growing sleek and fat as butter. Gloriana's colt appears promising. Avalon too, is coming along fine. Knox looks after her as he would a pregnant daughter."

"True, but we still don't have enough animals to sell." Bushrod considered his wife, wearing an expression she'd come to recognize and dread. Anxiety had etched deep lines across his round, deeply tanned countenance.

"God knows what will happen if Rod doesn't show up soon." He continued heavily. "When Lew Renfrow rode over the other day he fetched along some pretty bad news but I didn't speak of it at the time. No use worrying you when there was nothing we could do about it."

"What did Lew have to say?"

"Somehow, he'd got hold of a fairly new Washington newspaper which said the Government is about to demand immediate payment of back land and property taxes — plus interest. In that case God alone knows how Rod and I are going to pay what's sure to prove a mighty stiff sum."

Caroline persisted in optimism. "At least sale of the silver should cover that."

"Let's hope so."

"Isn't it strange that right now the Tilt fortunes are entirely dependent on Samuel Shepherd?"

"Loretta trusts him."

"Why shouldn't she? Anybody can see with half an eye he's taken her in — in more ways than one, I fear."

Hunched over, Bushrod slowly beat clenched fists against one another. Finally he straightened, then shifted his bad foot into a more comfortable position. "If *only* Rod would come back and read his letter from Marc Peabody. Maybe, through the law of averages, it might contain encouraging news."

Beyond the barn, reconstructed but still unpainted, Rod's stallion neighed at a mare in heat in an adjoining paddock.

"How much confidence do you put on Marc's promise to help?"

"I'll take Rodney's word on that. For all he's a Yankee, and a New Englander at that, Peabody's not a fair-weather friend. Think I ought to open it?" He queried hesitantly, it being one of the family's cardinal rules that, no matter what, private correspondence must be considered inviolate.

Caroline's needles flashed busily, red-silvered by the sunset. "Maybe in this case, Bush, you ought to open it. Possibly it contains something requiring immediate attention."

"I was going to wait till tomorrow for Rod to show up, and I'm *damned* if I can explain not hearing a peep out of him in so long."

Caroline said firmly, "I think you'd better read what Mr. Peabody has to say. I notice you've brought his letter along."

A trifle sheepishly, Bushrod reached into a pocket of the badly frayed white linen coat he'd slung to his chair. Frowning, he used a penknife to slit the envelope, muttering, "Carrie, this is the very first time in my life I've done such a thing. However, I agree that circumstances justify such a breach of ethics."

Caroline nodded quick approval and, following a childhood custom, for good luck crossed fingers on both hands. "Oh, Bush, how I pray that for once we'll read good news of some sort."

Because it was summer, light remained strong enough to read:

> 28th July 1865
> 107 Bridge Street
> Providence
> Rhode Island

Dear Classmate Rodney:

Please forgive this tardy response to yours of the first of July, but so many complications have arisen since my return home from the service. There was no delay in obtaining discharge since Congress, "to economize," is cutting down the armed forces — at a dangerous rate, or so it seems to me and other responsible citizens. Who knows for sure that if the Radicals are too vengeful, rebellion won't break out again — especially in the southwest where considerable bodies of irregulars are said to be still under arms?

I was indeed pleased to learn that matters at Moluntha were not quite as bad as you had anticipated when we talked at Appomattox. I am convinced that with your determination and intelligence and with the cooperation of your family and friends you will make out.

Now I must give you a piece of information which I fear will not prove encouraging.

Caroline's hopeful expression vanished. "Oh Lordy, here it comes!"

First off, I returned home only to learn that Father's partner recently absconded with nearly all of Peabody & Sons' company funds. So far, all efforts to trace the villain have proved futile, largely because it appears he at once took ship to England and the Continent.

In any case, for the time being we are hard-put to continue manufacturing textiles. However, since our company's credit standing always has ranked among the highest, and because our business friends — even competitors — are proving cooperative, we should have our company back to normal production inside the next few months. There's a great demand for textiles in the South, but how can the poor devils pay, with the chaotic financial conditions they are laboring under at present?

I would, were it possible for me, forward immediately a sizable sum but, alas, certain unsavory creditors, most of them shirkers and crooked contractors, are pressing me so hard at this moment I can only forward to you a thousand dollars which I trust will help tide you over for a while. Please, dear friend, believe that if I could send you more *I would!* And I will do so, should matters here improve unexpectedly, without an instant's hesitation. Unless I hear to the contrary, I presume you would like the sum mentioned above deposited in your bank at Wytheville? Just let me know when to forward the money.

Bushrod broke off, sighing, "A thousand won't go far toward covering even urgent expenses but —" he forced a grin —"still it's better than a kick in the rump with a frozen boot, as we used to say in the Service."

"What else does Mr. Peabody say?" Caroline prompted.

By way of encouragement, Rod, I believe it will be quite possible, once the economy has settled down a bit more, to form a stock company — say the Ajax Mining Corporation — and sell enough shares to restore the mine to production. Of course such a move would mean that the Tilt family no longer would control the mine in its entirety. Suppose we offer for sale shares amounting to a maximum of forty-five percent of the whole issue? We'll find no lack of investors for, even in Boston and New York, the mine is known for its richness and there is an enormous demand for lead everywhere.

Do let me hear from you promptly regarding the state of the mine and give me an estimate of the sum necessary for its restoration to production.

To obtain better light Bushrod shifted across the gazebo, assumed a surprised look. "Carrie, here's something Meg will be interested to hear about."

Regarding your mention of Miss Forsythe's uncle, upon receipt of your letter I at once wrote to that gentleman at the address given by her and, after a considerable delay, received information from Azael Forsythe's attorneys that he had died only recently. I am writing again soon to attempt to learn what disposition is being made of Azael Forsythe's estate, if any, and will suggest that they communicate with her at your address. Is this a good idea?

I am glad to say I found Eliza and our three young ones, two boys and now a girl, all very happy that the war is over. They are well and flourishing like the green bay tree of Holy Writ.

It goes without saying, dear classmate, I'm terribly anxious to hear how you are making out. Pray extend my respects to your brother and sister. It must be wonderful after all this time for your family to be united again despite those sad gaps in its ranks.

We, too, have suffered enormous losses in men — almost two for every one lost by your side. The streets seem filled with cripples and women wearing black.

I am experiencing varied and baffling readjustments in settling down and otherwise returning to civilian life.

As soon as is practicable, combining pleasure with business, I intend to come out and visit you and see the mine.

Ever your loyal friend and classmate,

Marc

Bushrod slumped back on his seat. "And that, my dear wife, is about that."

Caroline went over to place a hand on his shoulder, "Cheer up darling; Marc's news isn't as bad as it might be. If that thousand reaches Wytheville in time it might appease the tax collectors for a while."

Well-rounded bosoms rose in a sigh. "Poor Meg! She was building such high hopes on hearing from her uncle. I'll have to be extra tactful while letting her know what's happened."

One of Bushrod's eyebrows climbed. "I presume you've noticed Meg doesn't appear quite so anxious to quit Moluntha as before?"

"Of course. She keeps asking why Rod doesn't return and appears deeply concerned in her quiet, Yankee way."

Over the monotonous shrill peeping of tree frogs and a hum of insects, Bushrod said, "I've been meaning to speak of this, Carrie, and it may amount to nothing, but I'm not happy about the way Meg and that curious fellow, Tyler, spend so much time together. I wonder if we haven't made a mistake by accepting his tale that his widowed father is a Mexican general at present leading troops against Emperor Maximilian's forces, and by including him in our company as a social equal?"

Briefly Caroline ruminated. "Perhaps. But it has been good to have him to balance the table and liven up conversation, especially with Rod away. What a storyteller he is!"

"You like him, don't you?"

"Yes, in spite of his dark complexion and some of his foreign mannerisms. You've got to admit, dear, Peter Tyler always has conducted himself in a well-bred manner and is courteous to a degree. I've not found him forward in any way toward me or to Meg, for all he sometimes looks at her like — well, like a man seriously in love." Caroline continued, "There's nothing Tyler won't do for her, no matter how trivial or exacting." She tucked her lip between her teeth. "Still, I don't like those long rides they take together. I feel certain Rodney wouldn't approve. What I most fear is that Meg doesn't sense the depth of Tyler's devotion."

"Call it 'passion,' my dear, and you'll come nearer the mark." Bushrod went on, "And how do you think she feels toward him? Being a female, you should know whether she can cope with his temperament for, if he's telling the truth, he's part Latin, never forget that. Such can grow pretty intense when heated up."

"Wiseacres to the contrary, no woman can tell much how another woman really feels toward an appealing admirer." Caroline's manner changed and she went to pick up her knitting. "While we're on the subject, something important happened that night I was fool enough to let Meg wear Louisa's ball gown. I can't tell you exactly what it was, but

I'll never to my dying day forget Rod's expression when she appeared. Anyhow, he seems to have taken a new lease on life."

"Naturally he was taken aback — Meg looked so truly beautiful — better than she has before or since — but I think that's all there is to it, so far as I've noticed."

"Then you've not been observant. I've noticed her scanning the road to Abingdon but, should Tyler appear, she quickly seems to forget what she was looking for."

# 30

---

# Pedro de Cinquegrana y Gonzales

T HOUGHT PETER TYLER, not even the colonel's failure to return or even to communicate could account for solemn expressions and the air of constraint exhibited by Bushrod Tilt and his wife at the breakfast table. He felt especially sympathetic since he himself had spent a wretched, nearly sleepless night, arguing with himself, formulating plans of importance, only to change his mind again and again about which plan he'd better adopt.

How pleasing it was to be associated with well-bred people once more! His self-confidence had risen steadily ever since he'd been accorded the honor of joining them and soon had discovered that his efforts to enliven conversation at mealtimes were far from being unappreciated.

Glancing across the table at Meg, he noticed she was wearing a faint frown in place of her usual cheerful expression. Light, brownish shadows beneath her eyes argued that Margaret Forsythe also must have suffered poor repose. All in all this was scarcely a lively company.

While they ate, he and Bushrod briefly discussed the day's work; then, after Bushrod had clumped out, he caught the Forsythe girl's eye, said lightly but with a serious underlying quality, "If the weather proves agreeable suppose we ride over to Rushmore's Pool and have another go at those choosy brook trout? You're becoming quite proficient with a dry fly and need only a little more instruction to qualify as an expert."

Not long ago a pair of fine English fly rods which had belonged to the late Major Rushmore Tilt had been discovered, together with reels, a net, and a book of rather moth-eaten flies.

Meg deliberated, said uncertainly, "Why, I don't know. Suppose we talk about it after lunch?"

Successfully Tyler suppressed an inexplicable irritation over such unprecedented diffidence. Hell! If Rodney remained alive he *must* appear very shortly. Um. If certain moves he had in mind were to prove effective they'd stand a better chance of success if the Master of Moluntha weren't around.

Bowing, Tyler excused himself, at the same time wondering what news could have reached his host and wife to plunge them into such gloom.

As she and Caroline arose from the table, Meg characteristically brought matters to a head without delay, took Caroline's hand, brought her face-to-face. "My dear, a ninny can tell something bad has happened. Do you care to come up to my room and talk it over?"

The older woman's smooth, heart-shaped features contracted. "I expect you're right. Last night, Bush and I learned of certain things which seriously affect our future *and* yours. Yes. We'd better go have a little heart-to-heart."

As usual Margaret Forsythe's room was tidy. Since she'd been a small girl she'd always made her bed once she was dressed. Next she'd tidy her washstand and empty the chamberpot into the slop jar — then dispose of its contents in the privy before going to breakfast.

Caroline said, "What prompts you to want to talk?"

"I sensed something had gone very wrong the moment we sat down to eat. I'm sure Peter Tyler was aware, too."

In soft, troubled accents Caroline described Bushrod's hesitancy over opening Marc Peabody's letter.

Meg's hazel eyes widened. "You've said it contained something concerning me?"

"Yes, dear, I'm afraid so."

" 'Afraid'?"

"Yes. I fear this uncle you wrote to is dead. Apparently Mr. Azael Forsythe passed on shortly before Marc wrote to him on your behalf." She continued hurriedly, "There's no telling yet whether your uncle read your letter before his death. Oh, dear Meg, after all you've suffered I wish I didn't have to be the one to give you such disappointing news."

So, Uncle Azael was dead! Now she must be truly alone in the world, penniless, with only her good health and naturally buoyant disposition to help face the future. More than ever her sense of not belonging, of having no one to consult with or to be advised by, seemed crushing, almost intolerable. Only Peter Tyler remained undeniably devoted. He was like the shade of a rock in a weary land. Yet she really knew nothing about him save what he'd so long ago confided concerning his past. Was all this talk about a powerful father and glittering future sheer moonshine? No. Somehow, Peter always had sounded convincing.

Caroline put an arm about Meg, sitting rigid, white-knuckled hands clenched on her lap. "I'm sorry — so desperately sorry for you, dear. All you can do is to go on hoping, like us Tilts, that things must get better."

"Marc himself is having a difficult time since returning from the War." Again Caroline sounded diffident over having opened Rodney's mail. "Seems his father's partner ran off abroad taking along most of the firm's liquid assets. Poor Rodney! He was *so* hopeful of prompt and important help from that direction."

When Meg betrayed no reaction Caroline mechanically smoothed ash-blond hair and continued. "Marc did write, however, that he hopes, as soon as things settle down a bit, he'll be able to form a stock company and so raise sufficient money to get the Ajax producing once more."

"That's good," Meg said listlessly. "But can Mr. Peabody accomplish this in time to save Rodney from foreclosures and raise enough, right away, to pay taxes to keep Moluntha going?"

"You mean, can Marc send some ready cash in a hurry?"

"Yes. I doubt if there's a hundred dollars hard money available on this property."

"Are you sure?"

"Haven't Sam Shepherd and I worked on the books for weeks?"

When Caroline's eyes filled Meg roused, and ran to fling arms about her and kiss her cheek.

"Oh, dear, what shall we do? Everything seems so hopeless."

"We must —" Meg brightened momentarily —"stand together, Carrie. As you just said, eventually things must turn out right. Haven't you 'forgotten there'll be some real money available as soon as Sam and Loretta return from Washington?"

"Yes, I suppose so, but I don't like this not having heard from them since they left." Her chin quivered. "Didn't we suffer enough through the war years?" She heard Oliver racing around downstairs and hurriedly dried her tears. "I must see what he's up to. Meantime, why don't you go fishing with Peter Tyler? To get out of this house for a while will do you good, and Peter always is entertaining company."

Rushmore's Pool was situated on the far side of a steep ridge rising not far to the northwest of Moluntha Garrison. Although the distance wasn't great, the trail leading there was steep in several places and with often treacherous footing. This secluded spot had been a favorite refuge for Rodney's father who, during undergraduate years at Oxford, had acquired a passion for fly casting — a peculiar sport seldom shared by other Tilts.

While riding, Meg astonished herself by telling her wiry, dark-visaged companion much of the news mailed from the East. She felt free to do so, since Caroline hadn't sworn her to secrecy and the information was bound to come out pretty soon anyhow; therefore her talk really couldn't be considered betrayal of confidence — a fault deeply condemned under the Forsythe code of ethics.

Tyler commented while maneuvering cased fly rods beneath low-sweeping boughs, "I've been thinking about the news you've confided and am filled with admiration for the way you've faced what must be a crushing blow. My dear, I deem you a living monument to courage."

Meg turned a dusty, sweat-streaked face over one shoulder and managed a smile. "Thank you, Peter. That's the most encouraging compliment I've ever received." She actually chuckled. "I've been called many things but never before a 'monument.' Will you build me a pedestal?"

"A tall one, and I'll worship before it!"

"That presents a most exciting prospect," she called back after bending under a branch. "You certainly can compose picturesque compliments. I suppose that's the Latin in you. Well, let's hope the fish are hungry."

A faint grin spread over Tyler's high-cheekboned, copper-hued countenance when he pulled a small tin box from his saddle bag and held it up.

"In case the trout prove too choosy I've dug us some barnyard hackles."

" 'Barnyard hackles'?"

"Angleworms. They'd shock my English mother were she still alive. In her family's book, the use of worms for taking trout ain't considered sportin', y'know. However, they're generally productive if the noble trout proves really finicky."

Riding behind her, Peter struggled to ignore the burning desires beginning to surge through him. Those few occasions in Abingdon on which he'd been able to gratify such needs had only served to stimulate his cravings, for Meg.

Hunching forward in the saddle while his mount buck-jumped up the last rise, Tyler forced himself to calm, attempted to evaluate the situation resulting from that damn' Yankee's letter.

Um. Are matters worse, after all? Margarita remains more alone and robbed of hope than ever. Um. No matter how hard the Colonel tries he'll not be able to keep Moluntha going much longer, so she'll have to move on. Lucky he's been away this long. Whether or not Margarita realizes, she thinks a lot about him. For all she's probably not in love with him or he with her, I'd be a fool to gamble on that.

The graceful way her long-limbed body yielded to her mount's movements when they started downhill sent fresh heat coursing through him. *Seguro.* It would be wise to act promptly, yet at the same time, despite that bend sinister in his breeding, he still was the son of a *hidalgo*. Were his father still living it should not prove too difficult to trace Francisco de Cinquegrana y Gonzales. At last report he'd been among Benito Juarez's leading generals in that Zapotec Indian patriot's efforts to drive out of Mexico Austrian-born Emperor Maximilian and his mercenary troops — now including a well-trained force called the Foreign Legion.

Before long Rushmore's Pool lay below, its dark-green hurrying waters hemmed in by sweet-smelling ferns and stately spruces and pines. In silence they dismounted on a small, grassy meadow where on previous occasions they'd tied up their mounts and picnicked before he'd set about instructing her in the difficult sport of fly casting. Wasn't it fortunate that instruction of this sort often required him to encircle her with his arms so his face could occasionally brush her coarse, light-brown hair and unnoticed, kiss it.

Once they'd dismounted Meg eased her cinch, saying, "I'm a fraud, I fear."

"Why?"

"I don't know whether I feel much like fishing today. I took this excuse to get away from the house. Somehow, I feel lower than a snake's belly."

"I understand." Nodding pleasantly, Peter draped a folded saddle cloth across that fallen tree they usually occupied. Fishing today was about the last thing he had in mind. "Indeed I do."

She glanced sharply up, wide lips slightly parted. "What do you mean?"

He settled onto the log close beside. "You and I both now know that, barring miracles, there is no future at Moluntha for either of us. The Colonel has fought and is fighting a stubborn defense but, as a veteran, I know when the odds are too great and defeat becomes inevitable."

Flushing, she crushed a hungry mosquito, kept her gaze on the horses cropping on the little clearing's lush grasses, and made no effort at withdrawal when, gently, he took her hands between his calloused but finely formed ones. He smiled faintly, "Margarita — I hope you don't object, but in my private thoughts I always think of your name that way — please hear me out. I have guessed for some time that you feel more than a passing fondness for me. True?"

"Ever since that — that famous night beneath the serape I have increasingly come to admire your unswerving sense of honor, also your sensitivity toward people and difficult situations. Besides, I've noticed how much you've done in a quiet way toward putting Moluntha back on its feet, by your handling of the animals, especially."

Ivory-hued teeth flashed as he made a deprecatory gesture. " 'De nada,' as they say south of the Border. What I did was chiefly to remain near you." He edged closer until his knees brushed and remained in contact with her faded, yellow-striped blue riding breeches.

"I'm glad you stayed, Peter," she murmured, then raised clear hazel eyes to meet his.

"Why?"

"You must understand that I — well, I have thought much concerning the possibilities of the future — yours and mine."  ▪

Impulsively he kissed her hard brown hands several times. "You really have?"

"Yes, Peter, I have indeed. You see —"

He broke in and abruptly knelt before her. "*Por favor*, Margarita. Allow me to confess that for long I have adored you, have hungered for your love with every fiber of my body and soul. *Muy querida*, I want you for my wife, to be la Señora de Cinquegrana." He reached upward to clasp her face and poise his mouth just short of hers.

"Oh, my adored one, now I can tell you of the plans, the great schemes I have made for us; ones which will lead to high honors, to great possessions and toward establishing a famous family. No! These are not the ravings of a love-stricken idiot. All this *is* possible!"

His declaration was tremendously exciting but at the same time too confusing, too precipitate, so she drew back almost imperceptibly. "Peter, dear, Peter! Please hold on. I'm flattered, but I can't give you an answer right now."

"Oh, Margarita. Let your heart guide you. Why shouldn't we foreigners face life together? Neither of us belongs among these savage mountains. Think. Is there a future for either of us at Moluntha, decent and genteel though the Tilts are?"

When she tried to speak he pressed a finger across her lips. "My dearest, allow me to continue and to speak of practical considerations. For one thing, I've come to possess quite a few gold dollars — please don't ask where or how I acquired them — but they are sufficient to carry us away from here to Memphis and down river to New Orleans. Once there, we will marry and I will seek out my father. What glorious future awaits us! Believe me. I know it will be as I say."

"Oh, Peter! Peter!" She didn't realize she was gasping. "I'm s-so confused. What are you s-suggesting?"

"That we ride away from here as soon as possible. The gold, and what supplies we'll need to start with are already prepared. Remember this, *mi corazón*, we gain nothing by remaining at Moluntha.

"I feel in my heart that you do love me and I know I *must* have you!"

His arms closed about her so hard she would have cried out but his mouth was crushing too eagerly against hers. Hitherto unfamiliar yet delicious currents eddied through her, and the whole world seemed to spin crazily. During a dangerously long instant she responded but then, when his hands gently cupped her breasts, she pushed him away and got up.

"Don't!" she choked. "Peter, remember who and what you are, and who I am. Believe me, dear Peter, I do feel sorely tempted to do that which we mustn't, at least not now."

Shaking, he also stood up, intense dark eyes penetrating. "Margarita! If you swear you truly do love me I will continue to be patient. If not, I'm damned if I'll wait any longer, and to hell with the consequences!"

Somehow, she collected a measure of poise, disheveled and flushed though she was. "I can't answer you now, Peter, because — because I'm simply not yet sure of myself. I'll freely admit I'm extremely fond of you and cherish our, well, our special relationship."

He stepped back, staring intently. "Possibly you have thoughts concerning someone else?"

"Thoughts, perhaps, but nothing more," she admitted, nervously pushing aside a stray lock of hair. "Please, dear Peter, as a *hidalgo*, I beg you to grant me a little more time to weigh such an all-important question. You won't regret it; somehow I feel sure of that. Yes, it is quite possible I may decide to ride away with you. You're quite right, Moluntha doesn't offer a real future for either of us."

The ride homeward was accomplished in silence only broken by casual comments on the scenery, the ripening crops, and a likelihood that it might rain pretty soon; so many birds were acting restless and slate-hued clouds leisurely were starting to obscure the southern sky.

Once they'd climbed a rise from which Moluntha Garrison could be sighted, they simultaneously became aware that unusual activity was taking place below. People, white and black, were milling about, and a pair of lathered horses, heads hanging wearily, were being led toward the stables.

Both sensed that, at long last, Colonel Rodney Tilt had returned home.

# 31

# Reassessments

NEVER since the outbreak of the war had Colonel Rodney Ajax Tilt felt more hopeless, more dejected, more ineffectual. Good God, how could he give Bushrod and Caroline his appalling news? When his little party had started to breast the last rise in the road to Moluntha he'd sent Hamrick trotting ahead to alert the people. Lost on him was the beauty of his home's setting, the richness of crops grown tall and rapidly maturing, and the considerable reconstruction already effected.

To James Manlove, who was looking about in something like awe, Tilt said, "Some private conversation with my family is necessary so when we reach the house lead my horse 'round to the back and make yourself comfortable. Hamrick can show you where to go."

The broad-shouldered ex-gunner's mate raised a tattooed arm in a loose salute, "Aye, aye, sir." Then, wearing a serious expression on his battered features he said, "Anythin' I kin do to ease matters? I'd sure hate to stand in your boots right now."

"Thanks, Jim, not now." He dismounted and lowered his voice. "I'll send for you later and we'll talk again about that chest you mentioned."

When Caroline, pale hair flying, rushed to embrace him, and Bushrod limped out onto the driveway, he looked about for Margaret Forsythe, experiencing an inexplicable sense of disappointment. How often in the past hadn't Meg raised his flagging spirits when things went extra wrong?

One glance at her brother-in-law warned Caroline that stark tragedy of some description had struck, so deeply were grim new lines graven on Rodney's bold, weathered features.

"Oh, Rod! Rod! How we've worried over you," she cried and, tears running, flung arms about him and kissed him hard. "Thank God you're back!"

Bushrod gave his brother a bear hug such as they customarily exchanged following long separation. Bitterly Bushrod wished he could sob but, of course, such relief was out of the question.

Once the three of them gained the living room Bushrod unlocked the base of a Sheraton corner cupboard and produced a half-bottle of well-aged bourbon. "Don't tell us anything till you've had a big slug. I've never seen you look so damnably done-in, not even after you rode home from Appomattox."

Rodney was sipping when a clatter of horses' hoofs sounded outside. Sharply, he demanded, "Who's that?"

"Only Meg and Peter Tyler. They've been off fishing."

A sense of relief invaded Rodney. When Meg hadn't appeared to greet him he'd half-suspected she must have received welcome news from her uncle and so had departed eastward.

At once Tyler sensed that this was no time to be present so, fighting down consuming curiosity, he helped Meg alight, then, after returning the unused fishing rods to the hall closet, led their mounts toward a group talking excitedly before the stables.

Heart hammering, Margaret Forsythe, damp and dusty in her Union breeches, hurried indoors but a glance at the group in the living room checked a joyous outburst. Beyond doubt a major disaster of some description must have occurred. Nevertheless, summoning a bright smile she sped forward, both hands extended, "Oh, Rodney! Welcome! Welcome! How anxious we've all been over you."

He tossed off the last of his drink, then spread hands in a unique gesture of hopelessness. "When you have heard what's happened I reckon you-all will forgive my overlong silence; I felt I couldn't communicate until certain unpleasant facts had been proven beyond question or doubt."

Rodney's use of the word "all" didn't escape Meg's attention. Was he thus tacitly including her as one of the family? No. Common sense warned that probably at this moment he was too crushed, too exhausted to select precisely the right words.

Caroline said briskly, "Rod, I believe you'd best go and wash up. Meg will fetch you hot water. Meanwhile, I'll set some sort of food on the table. You look famished."

"I am. Haven't eaten since early morning. Thank you."

Head whirling, Meg dashed into the kitchen to fill a pitcher of hot water. Oh, Lord, what could have happened to make so strong a character for the first time appear utterly defeated?

Once the Master of Moluntha had consumed hot yams, some quickly warmed collard greens, and a few slices of cold ham, he wiped ragged mustaches, then heaved a sign which seemed to rise from his dusty boots' soles. "Well, that's better, but there's no use postponing what I have to tell you. Suppose we proceed to the cardroom? Brace yourselves for the worst."

Rodney Tilt saw Meg hesitate and take a backward step. "No, please come along, Margaret. My news affects you too."

The moment they'd seated themselves Rodney went over to rest an elbow on the handsomely carved walnut mantelpiece. "Reckon I'd better give you the worst first." He then described the death of his twin and Samuel Shepherd, and explained that as soon as he'd heard Hamrick's news he'd verified it by taking the first train to the scene of the wreck.

Despite horrors witnessed during the war he'd been utterly appalled on viewing the charred, indescribably tangled mass of wreckage heaped at a deep ravine's bottom. Curiously enough, he told his frozen-faced listeners, only the locomotive's bell-shaped stack had remained recognizable amid that ugly black-and-gray mound of ashes.

He then had devoted the next few days to ranging the neighboring country on the odd chance Loretta and Sam possibly might have been among a handful of survivors carried off to nearby farms or dwellings. But he'd heard or seen nothing concerning them.

His voice cracked, "And so we've lost still another member of the family. Oh God! What have we Tilts done to deserve so much sorrow?"

Following a brief pause Bushrod demanded in a toneless voice, "I presume you found no trace of — of the silver?"

"None. Undoubtedly it melted and ran off in driblets. I suppose traces of it might be found if one bothered to explore the creek's bottom."

During the recital Meg's gaze never shifted from the speaker's sunken and haunted black eyes. If only she could find something encouraging to say or to do, but the prevailing sense of tragedy seemed too profound to be penetrated, let alone dispersed.

A kerosene lamp was burning low by the time Bushrod had described the contents of Marc Peabody's letter.

"If this doesn't put the cream on the bottle. Oh, how perfect!" Peals of harsh, mirthless laughter, long and rising in pitch, escaped the Master of Moluntha and continued until Bushrod yelled, "For God's sake stop that! You sound as if you're going insane!"

Through a supreme effort Rodney controlled himself, sat in panting silence. "Thank you, Bush. I'll be all right now." He turned, "Sorry, Meg, that you too have met with grievous disappointment."

Said she evenly, " 'Tis small compared to yours but, like you, I guess I'm becoming hardened to receiving bad news."

Discussion of the mine's condition and the prevailing chaos in the financial world by common consent would be postponed. This was just as well since, as abruptly as if he'd been clubbed on the head, Rodney Tilt swayed, then collapsed onto the nearest armchair and plunged into the sleep of complete mental and physical exhaustion aptly described by Shakespeare as "Deaths' half-sister." A description of James Manlove and some of his extraordinary adventures also must wait.

No one in the cardroom suspected that, despite pretensions of always acting the *hidalgo*, Pedro de Cinquegrana y Gonzales hadn't been above crouching below a window opened to the summer's sultry heat and listening to what was said, although clouds of mosquitoes rendered this eavesdropping nearly intolerable. What most darkened Tyler's mind was that frequency with which, unintentionally perhaps, the Colonel addressed his account neither to his brother or his sister-in-law but toward Margarita, although the Yankee girl contributed little or nothing to the conversation.

Rodney Tilt's spirit commenced slowly to revive after Margaret Forsythe once again had recited the burial service before a wooden cross planted in the graveyard and bearing Loretta's name — for all that her remains never would rest beneath it. Peter Tyler found one result of the train wreck reassuring. Samuel Shepherd, just before departure, for some reason best known to himself, hadn't checked his hidden gold, so hadn't discovered that his hoard was missing.

It seemed that, since no one apparently was aware of the existence of the former paymaster's cache, there'd be no inquiry as to what might have become of it. Surely, even so modest a treasure should prove sufficient to finance the start of at least one of several schemes he'd been considering since he'd removed Shepherd's gold.

Surely Margarita must realize that, if Rodney Tilt had serious intentions in her direction, she was being courted by an incipient bankrupt. Were she half as smart as he deemed her and if she really wasn't in love with Tilt would she continue to play a losing game and live, at best, in genteel poverty for the rest of her days?

The matter of timing his moves now loomed all-important.

# 32

—◄◈►—

# Readjustments

ONCE THE MASTER of Moluntha had learned of Tyler's acceptance into the family group he, without hesitation, invited the Texan to stay on. But, sensitive to the new tragedies, Tyler knew better than to remain and announced pleasantly but firmly he reckoned he'd move his few effects over to a newly completed cabin at present occupied only by former Farrier Sergeant Knox. Instinctively, he foresaw it would be unbearable were Meg to betray evidence of increasing affection for her host.

Within himself he cringed at the prospect of not being near Margarita as frequently as before. It didn't escape his attention that although Bushrod and Caroline emphatically had urged him to continue in the main house, Meg's insistence that he remain appeared a trifle less than whole-hearted.

Rodney said, "I'll be sending Jim Manlove to join you and Knox." He added with a half-smile, "If you've a mind, you can form a noncom's club; even if Manlove is a sailor I'm sure you'll get along."

On the surface they did. The ex-Navy man in his clumsy way made every effort to prove useful and agreeable. Tyler remained reserved but tactful, while Philemon Knox frankly admitted he was pleased to be relieved of living alone in this rough-and-ready cabin still redolent of resin and freshly sawed lumber.

At first Manlove felt confused by the complex situation he'd encountered, so retreated into wariness until he could learn more about personalities involved. He'd never seen a property anything like this one; imagine a great, handsome estate whose wealth hadn't been founded on planting rice, sugar cane or cotton, but on the mining of lead, the boiling of salt and the breeding of fine horses.

Before long he noted that the handful of blacks living on this property differed in many ways from those generally abject, surly and unintelligent slaves he'd known and grown up with along the seaboard. Hannibal, Lydia and Jasper and even young Pookie all were alert and well-spoken; that these people possessed self-respect in varying degrees was due no doubt to some sort of education.

This also was true of three Negro former soldiers who, bewildered by new-found freedom and having no roots anywhere, had straggled into Moluntha to remain and work for the sake of board and lodging, since right off, Hannibal had warned these strays they could expect no pay money for the time being. Mebbe they'd get some cash later on, but not now. Nevertheless the trio, like some white veterans, were content to stay.

Tyler soon decided that Manlove and Knox were going to get on well; both were fond of gaming of various sorts. If Manlove at times seemed distant and moody, his companions couldn't know he was itching to get heading down to the Gulf of Mexico; for although Wilmer Pleasants had appeared straightforward and honest, wasn't there always a chance that, before the agreed time, his fellow survivor just might go searching for the pay chest on his own? Surely, it was plain common sense to get down to that cluster of keys off Cabo Rojo lying north of the fishing village of Pamiahua Mayor as fast as possible.

While squatting on a stump behind the stables he absently watched the sun climb over the mountains opposite and absently massaged freshly healed sores on tattooed arms. On occasion he still experienced dull aches and pains in those cuts and bruises suffered in Wytheville.

He felt perplexed by that bandy-legged, bronze-featured Texan calling himself "Peter Tyler." For all he'd been only a corporal during the war, there could be no doubt that Tyler was educated and well-bred, so he should have held a commission. Why hadn't he?

Tyler also had traveled extensively and spoke Spanish far better than he, his own knowledge of that language being confined to words and phrases useful aboard ships, in brothels or among waterfront dives. There was something in the Texan's devil-may-care attitude which appealed to him even if he did seem smarter than himself.

Once Manlove had moved in, Knox observed, while biting off a chew of tobacco which caused his lean cheeks to bulge like those of well-fed chipmunks, "B'God it's great to hear news fresh from the outside. We bin here so long we know what another feller is going to say before he even opens his mouth." He studied this big sailor's battered face and powerful shoulders with sudden misgivings. "Know anythin' 'bout hosses?"

"Only a little, 'bout as much as any boy raised on a farm. Me, I understand mules better, but just tell me what you want done and I'll do it, so long as I'm 'round here."

Tyler came, sat down and, using a sailor's palm and waxed thread commenced to splice a broken quarter-strap. Said he without looking up, "Jim, that sounds like you don't aim to linger at Moluntha overlong."

"No, and that's a fact," Manlove admitted. "Don't forget most sailors are born with itchin' feet."

Briefly, Tyler again tried to guess what reason had prompted Rodney Tilt to fetch this hard-bitten seafarer all the way from Wytheville, knowing he probably couldn't earn his salt. *Por Dios*, the Colonel *must* have some underlying reason, but the more he explored this riddle the more baffled he became until, arriving at no satisfactory explanation, he gave up, and while stitching the worn leather strap turned his thought toward Margarita.

From all he'd been able to observe, matters in Moluntha Garrison appeared to have reverted to the pattern prevailing before Rodney, his twin, and Sam Shepherd had departed.

A new light had been cast on the situation especially when Tilt, privately, had disclosed loss of the family's silver. Therefore, the Texan calculated, the Tilts' only source of income was confined to small dividends occasionally paid by the rebuilt King salt works in Saltville in which the family held a considerable interest.

Um. The thought therefore occurred that Rodney must have fetched Manlove home because of some as yet unrecognized factor. True, Manlove had described the scene outside the Pocohontas and his rescue by the Colonel, but this account wasn't really necessary, Hamrick having already told him and Knox all about it, as well as describing the Ajax mine's ruinous condition.

On the second evening of his occupancy of the N.C.O.'s cabin he was sitting on a rail enclosing the barn's stableyard when he noticed Rodney and Meg leave the house and start sauntering along that path which led down to the gazebo. His lips flattened on noticing how close together they were walking, engaged in some conversation which caused her to keep looking up at her companion. Only the fact that they weren't holding hands relieved mounting and consuming jealousy to a degree.

That afternoon he'd surreptitiously sought Shepherd's cache. To his discerning eye the ground around the hiding place remained undisturbed; therefore the risk he'd taken in removing the hoard to a hiding place of his own choosing had been unnecessary. Since no one else seemed to know about Shepherd's wealth no one would miss it.

How long would matters at Moluntha remain static? Again he speculated over Manlove's ill-concealed eagerness to move on. Why? *Why?*

WHY? Now, everything seemed to hinge upon Margarita's emotions toward the Master of Moluntha, that, and the new precariousness of Rodney Tilt's finances.

At the sound of footsteps he looked up, saw James Manlove returning from the pump lugging a bucket of water. "Heyo," he called. "What for are you sittin' there like a bump on a log?"

Tyler got down, summoned a grin. "I was just thinking about something in the past."

"And mebbe a little about the future?"

"Yep. I reckon that just might be so."

"How about a little game of poker tonight? Just to pass the time."

"I wouldn't mind but I haven't any money."

"Neither have any of us but we could play for marked red beans counting for dollars and cents; such could be redeemed for cash later on."

"Sure, let's play." Manlove set down his bucket.

"These damned silent hills and trees are crowdin' me in. Dunno why, but I need open spaces somethin' fierce. Besides, I crave for action of some sort."

Tyler inclined his narrow, dark head. "Yep, I reckon most of us veterans are growing fed up with this peaceful, humdrum life. We've lived with excitement too long, I expect."

Manlove's bright blue eyes narrowed a trifle. "What do you figger to do about that?"

"Like you, I feel ready to pull up stakes before long and move on toward action of some kind. Maybe down in Mexico."

The tip of Manlove's tongue appeared through a gap in his teeth. "Really want to move, eh? Somehow, I've got a idee there's someone 'round here who's, well, mighty interestin' to you."

Tyler chuckled. "Did you now? Well, friend, you're wrong on that score. Come on, let's find some fellows and have a game. Got any cards?"

The larger man nodded. "Yep. Came across a deck whilst I was in Wytheville. They ain't too worn or greasy." He eyed the Texan carefully. "You given to gamblin' much?"

"I guess so, but not necessarily with cards."

"Dice maybe?"

"No. Granted reasonable odds, I prefer gambling with life, sometimes against death."

Again the gazebo served as a backdrop for confidences and weighty decisions. Before taking familiar seats Tilt paused, moved close, gazing fixedly down into Meg's deeply tanned and upturned features. Thanks to a few days' comparative rest Meg thought his features by the afterglow seemed less haggard.

For some reason, before supper, Rodney had clipped his mustaches and had donned his least worn white linen coat. He even had tucked a rosebud into his lapel which prompted Meg to wish she too, had spruced up, but here she was clad in the same ill-fitting and work-stained garments she'd worn all day. She'd no notion that a peculiar radiance in her expression was causing him to take no notice of her untidiness.

Tilt queried in a gentle voice, "Can you guess why I — I've invited you to accompany me here?"

She flushed. "Why, to discuss business matters I presume; I know you've a hundred worries to plague you. Can't you possibly forget them for a little while?" To her surprise she took his hand. "Please Rodney, let me lend you whatever comfort and encouragement I can."

A smile, more genuine than he had worn in a very long time, spread about that old saber scar marking his left cheek. Soberly, almost coldly, he said, "Why, yes, dear Margaret, there *is* something you can do. Will you marry me?"

Heart pounding, she heard her voice as from a distance saying, "Yes, Rodney, I will." Eagerly she entered the strong encirclement of his arms. They kissed avidly and yet to Margaret's surprise without overwhelming passion.

Looking years younger, he said, "I didn't realize it at the moment, but that time I saw you in Louisa's gown I, well, I suddenly felt in the depths of my being that only you could mean as much to me as she once did; that I've something to live for."

"Oh-h. I'll do my best to make that hope come true!"

When they kissed again the gazebo seemed to sway on its foundations. Presently she murmured, "Oh, dear Rodney, if only I could find the right words to tell you how very much I love and admire you, not only for yourself but for all you stand for."

A strange, unromantic proposal this, Rodney suddenly realized — no kneeling, no passionate claspings, no fervent promises from either, but rather a controlled yet joyous recognition of the inevitable.

After a while, as they sat on a small settee with his arms clasped tight about her, he straightened a trifle, then spoke in his usual incisive manner. "As you already know, my dear, I stand on the verge of bankruptcy. However, there *is* a faint hope it can be avoided. You know of course about the contents of Marc Peabody's letter."

"Yes. Bushrod and Caroline showed it to me — only because I was concerned." She pressed closer. "Oh, Rodney, I hope you don't mind my reading your letter."

"Not at all. Under the circumstances you had every right to. I've already sent a telegram asking Marc to forward me that thousand dollars he mentioned as soon as possible. You see I *must* pay certain pressing bills and debts of honor."

"Honor?"

"Yes, my sweeting, by that I refer to money borrowed from fellow officers toward the end of the War. Our pay then arrived irregularly or not at all."

"I understand," she said, kissing him gently. "If *only* I could help out, but with Uncle Azael dead I fear that's impossible. Oh, dear, is there no end to your troubles?"

"Every storm must pass sooner or later — as Grandma Ruthelma used to say."

"What about Mr. Peabody's idea of forming a stock company? Wouldn't that give you working capital?"

"Yes, I suppose a company could be formed, but to organize such a project usually takes a lot of time and that's another thing I can't afford. I fear such help will arrive too late. I've heard a government revenue agent is setting up an office in Wytheville — along with a parcel of scalawags."

"I've heard that term 'scalawag' used quite often. What is its exact meaning?"

"My dearest, a scalawag is a Southerner who shirked duty in the armed forces, stayed at home or in Richmond and made plenty of money as sutlers, contractors, dealers in illegal cotton, and importers of blockage-run weapons and supplies which they sold to our government at an outrageous profit."

"We've plenty of rascals like that up North."

For the life of him Rodney still couldn't explain to himself why he'd yielded to his emotions so abruptly. Heretofore, he'd managed to control them, even under severe stresses. Possibly his headlong proposal had been prompted by realization that the only times he'd enjoyed any measure of serenity and peace of mind since he'd returned were when Margaret Forsythe was nearby.

As a rule she was not only cheerful and encouraging but practical as well. Besides that, she was damned attractive physically although probably she wasn't aware of it.

Somehow he felt convinced that beneath this Yankee girl's calm and logical exterior glowed ardent passions and urgent needs. Only God could understand how desperately he needed someone to love him and help him overcome a multitude of worries and responsibilities. Not that Bushrod and Caroline hadn't been, and still were, great help.

All the same, Moluntha wasn't really their home — not that he'd ever dream of hinting at their departure. There was plenty of room here, besides, for the time being, there wasn't any place for them to go.

Uncomfortably, he confessed, "I'm astonished at myself, darling. I fear I've spoken and acted like an ill-bred, unromantic boor. You deserve a far more romantic proposal, but somehow I *had* to learn how you felt." He shifted on the settee so that her head might rest more comfortably upon his shoulder.

Somewhere below, a lost calf bawling for its mother afforded an effective anticlimax to the iridescence of this moment.

"Will you pardon me, my dear, if I ask you to tell me something?"

"Of course. What do you want to know?"

"Haven't you and Peter Tyler been, well, more than a little attracted to one another?"

Typically, Meg attempted no evasion. "You're right. Recently he asked me to marry him." She didn't think it wise to say how recently.

"The hell you say!" Rodney burst out. "I'd no notion matters had progressed so far. How did you reply?"

"I told him I couldn't be sure exactly how I felt toward him so he'd have to wait for an answer."

"And then what?"

"He acted mightily put out but, like the gentleman he professes to be, he agreed to wait a few days."

Rodney raised a brow, asked carefully, "And how do you expect a hothead like Tyler is going to take our betrothal?"

Meg stirred comfortably in the muscular refuge of his arms and recalled that scene beside Rushmore's Pool. "I don't know why, darling, but I feel confident Peter will abide by his code. What do you think?"

"I imagine once the announcement is made he'll probably pack up and move on."

"Yes. He's scarcely the type to linger here eating his heart out."

"I suspect at the bottom he's on fire and not overscrupulous over how he gets what he wants — especially with women. Still, I'd hate to see him go. Tyler's been a good friend, a reliable worker and a fine trooper. Maybe he'll linger if I press him."

"Possibly, but he seemed so daft over me I'm not sure it would be sensible to keep him here."

It was fortunate that neither of them could foresee the Texan's reactions to their engagement.

Margaret Forsythe's lingering doubts about her betrothal ended when, hand in hand, they returned to find Bushrod and his wife about to retire upstairs and told them their news.

Caroline burst into delighted laughter, rushed over to hug and kiss the Northern girl. "Oh, *how* I've prayed this might happen!"

Bushrod was polite in offering hearty congratulations. But suppose Rod had offspring by this girl? Such would leave Bushrod with no chance of succession to Moluntha. All the same, Bushrod bear-hugged his brother, slapped his shoulders. "Damned if I ever thought I'd welcome a Yankee into our family, but I surely do this one!" As if to emphasize his presumed happiness he limped forward to kiss Meg's cheeks.

Caroline, eyes shining, warmly kissed her brother-in-law, then bubbled, "I know Margaret will give you all you need in the way of love, encouragement and devotion!"

Rodney draped an arm about his fiancée's shoulder, said gravely, "I'm entirely confident of that." His manner changed. "The only fly in the ointment is that we can't marry as soon as we want to."

Caroline's eyes flew wide open. Bushrod asked evenly, "Why must you wait?"

Said Colonel Rodney Tilt, "How can I expect Margaret to marry a fellow head over heels in debt and with a most uncertain future? Why, I couldn't support her even halfway decently."

Impatiently Meg broke in, "Please don't listen to him. I've already said I don't care a fig whether or not we'll be well off. I think by now you all know me well enough to believe that to me material wealth doesn't matter in the least." She smiled. "If Rodney has a fault it's that he's so bull-headed about certain things!"

Rodney laughed quietly. "Guilty, your Honor. It's simply I feel now isn't the right time for us to marry. Our country remains torn in all sorts of directions. Real peace and prosperity lie in the far distance I'm afraid. However, this I do promise — the minute I'm solvent we'll have such a wedding people will talk about it for years."

Bushrod nervously stroking chin whiskers said, "If I were you, Rod, I'd keep this betrothal a secret till you're ready to wed. You see it might stand in the way of —" he broke off.

"— Of his marrying some rich girl?" Caroline cried. "Shame on you, Bush! Such an idea shouldn't even have crossed your mind."

Eyes hard, Rodney drew himself up until he made Meg appear small by his side, though she wasn't. "Tomorrow morning we'll ring the old slave bell to call in all hands. Then I'll make the announcement."

# 33

---◦◦◦---

# "Corn Squeezings"

B Y THIS TIME the war had been over long enough for various lanky, hard-bitten veterans to return to previous occupations such as operating stills hidden high among the mountains. Although initially they encountered considerable difficulty in securing sufficient grain to revive their activities, moonshiners soon found themselves besieged by patrons clamoring for their product — for all that they could offer was raw, colorless and, as some said, tasted like water out of an old boot.

It wasn't long before Rimfire Hamrick rode home, red-eyed and unsteady and carrying a stone jug stoppered with a corncob. Its contents he sold to Peter Tyler who readily shared this treasure with Philemon Knox and Jim Manlove.

At about the same time the betrothal was taking place in the gazebo below, the three men in the N.C.O.'s cabin were beginning to "feel their oats" as Knox observed with owlish dignity while banging his tin cup on the plain board table they were sitting around.

Said Tyler, "Reckon we'd be pie-eyed already if this snake juice tasted a mite better."

Manlove passed the back of a tattooed hand over his battered, powder-burnt, blue-speckled forehead. "B'God I've tasted some powerful liquors in my time but I vum this stuff's fit to melt a frigate's anchor chain!"

Knox said, tilting more colorless liquid out the stone jug, "Iffen you'd lived in the mountings long as Rimfire and me, you'd say these corn squeezings ain't so bad. Tastes like it's been aged."

"Aged!" Tyler cried, making a face but keeping his attention on Manlove. "Are you out of your mind?"

"I'd bet this stuff is easy a month old." Knox nodded to himself. "Y' see, I use to do a bit of distillin', for myself mostly, afore I rode off to the war." He turned a gap-toothed grin on Hamrick. "Iffen you see the man who made this stuff tell him he should color his brew with burnt sugar, if he kin find any; besides improvin' the flavor some it lends his booze a healthier look."

Casually, Peter Tyler saw to it that his companions' tin cups were kept a-brim and watched their every expression while, with shameless embellishments, he recounted certain amorous wartime experiences in detail.

Presently, Manlove felt moved to song so, in a hoarse but not unmelodious baritone he bawled anchor songs and bawdy sea chanties.

Then, of all things, Philemon Knox raised what sounded much like a hymn. The melody at least was authentic, but its lyrics never would have graced a Sunday school banner. Following another round of moonshine, all three joined in singing "Lorena," "Darling Nellie Gray," and other sentimental songs popular with the Southern armies.

Although his eyes remained reasonably clear and steady Peter Tyler sang louder than the rest but appeared to become a trifle uncertain in his movements.

Having long since learned from Hamrick about his and the Colonel's rescue of Manlove, Tyler had become more than a little intrigued by this battered sailor. Pausing occasionally to swat at mosquitoes, he subtly directed conversation toward the latter part of this ex-gunner's mate's career. "C'mon, Jim, tell us more about yer doin's. Us soldiers never heard a damn' thing 'bout what our Navy did at sea."

Manlove, speech thickening, then described the loss of the C.S.S. *Alabama* and subsequent adventures aboard the blockade runner and the *Audacious Minx*, that small privateer schooner he claimed to have helped to fit out in Mobile.

Eyes grown heavy, Knox sighed deeply before sinking back to set up a fitful whiffling for which Tyler was grateful, since the ex-sergeant several times had interrupted the trend of Manlove's narrative.

"Yessir. I've sure played in muddy luck right from the start of this damn' war," Manlove growled. "Thought for sure I'd reached the end of my days when my schooner got caught in a hurricane not far below Tampico and got driven onto a key."

Tyler poured the raconteur another drink. "Then what happened?"

"The *Minx* broke up in jig time and we was still spewin' up seawater when we sighted a steam brig bein' driven ashore another key, just like us. Turned out to be a pay ship bringin' money for the Mexican Emperor's French troops."

"You actually watched this ship driven aground?"

"Yep."

"How'd you learn she was a pay ship?"

"Well, because —" Manlove suddenly surged to his feet, heavy jaw outthrust and tattooed fists clenched. "Say, mister. Ain't you askin' too damn' many questions? Just you mind your business and I'll 'tend to mine."

Apologetically, Tyler offered his hand. "Sorry. I didn't mean to pry. Let's shake and have 'nother slug of rotgut."

Still glowering and not altogether pacified, the ex-gunner's mate sat down. "Funny, all along I've liked the cut of your jib and was thinkin' mebbe you and I could become real good friends."

"Why not?"

"Well, we just might git along provided you quit pryin' into matters which ain't properly yer business. Anyhow, thanks for the booze; I ain't felt so fine in a 'coon's age. Wisht there was some hookers handy; I'm 'bout ready to bust my britches!"

Peter Tyler also was feeling fine but with no thanks to the raw liquor. Those words "pay ship" all at once had solved a number of questions such as why the Colonel had fetched a seafarer like James Manlove all the way back to Moluntha Garrison.

Peter Tyler was awakened shortly after dawn by rapping at the cabin's door so faint he barely heard it over Sergeant Knox's strident snores and Rimfire Hamrick's loud breathing. Still in his underwear, he opened the door and found Pookie waiting, fearful and big-eyed, with kinky hair secured by strips of rag into a half-dozen little topknots. Poised for flight, she held out a square of paper.

"Mistress Meg done tol' me 'liver this to you, suh." She then scampered away leaving Tyler in the grip of miserable presentiments.

Rubbing eyes reddened by tobacco smoke and alcohol, the Texan remained in the doorway to read a note written in Margaret Forsythe's careful Spencerian script.

2 a.m., 9th August, 1865

Dear Peter,

I find myself not sufficiently brave to inform you in person that I have reflected on your proposal with the greatest of care and thoughtful consideration of various problems!

A minié ball seemed to have exploded in Tyler's brain. To steady himself, he grabbed the door's frame before reading on:

I find that a long-standing attachment and deep admiration for Colonel Tilt, since his return has blossomed into sincere and deep-rooted love. Last evening he asked for my hand which I joyfully and without hesitation gave to him. Alas, we both are aware that some time must pass before we can be wedded.

A drop of blood caused a faint *splat!* on the board flooring. Tyler stared, unaware he'd bitten his nether lip so hard.

Relying on your keen sense of honor I feel confident you will accept my decision without rancor and that you, Rodney and I will always remain true friends.

An announcement of our betrothal will be made at midday from the front doorsteps. Should you choose to be absent I will be saddened but will understand.

Sincerely,
Margaret Forsythe

Tyler dressed and strode out into the cool, early morning sunshine with thoughts tumbling about his mind like a litter of tussling puppies. Seating himself on a stump behind the spring house, Pedro de Cinquegrana y Gonzales tested, then discarded, several lines of action.

Only on one point did he find any consolation: no date for the wedding had been set. What with Tilt's precarious financial situation, he, himself, should find time to execute certain moves he'd decided on. One fact remained indelibly stamped in his mind; Margarita eventually must become his wife or, failing that, his mistress.

The tenth day of August commenced much as usual, so Rodney was working in his office when, around ten of the morning, Thomas Larkin, unofficial foreman over the half-dozen Confederate veterans who'd lingered at Moluntha for the sake of board and lodging knocked, then entered, clutching a frayed straw hat before him. He clicked heels and stood to attention.

"Permission to speak, suh?"

"Of course. What's on your mind, Larkin?"

"Suh, I hesitate to intrude but, well, last night me and some of the other fellers got to jawin'."

Rodney relaxed in the high-backed armchair behind his desk. "What do you want to talk about?"

Larkin's eyes wavered, then his gaze dropped. "Sorry, suh, but some of us figger we jest can't make out no longer 'thout touchin' a little pay money for tobacco, liquor and suchlike. Well, suh, some of the younger fellers said they was about set to go down to the flat country and seek jobs payin' hard money."

For some time Rodney had been anticipating and dreading this moment, but kept his features composed, although beneath the desk his fists clenched themselves. "Of course, I understand your position and I wish to God I could pay you-all your due but, as matters stand, I honestly can't expect to touch any cash-money in the near future."

He shrugged and looked Larkin full in his heavily bearded face. "I expected to be able to pay you-all your back wages as soon as my sister and Mr. Shepherd returned from Washington." He grimaced, "But of course you've heard of Miss Tilt's and Mr. Shepherd's death and the loss of the silver they were going to sell. As it is, I'll be eternally grateful for your help and confidence in me during these hard times. If any of you choose to stay on you've my word the instant I receive real money you will be paid in full."

Larkin shifted his weight from one foot to the other and licked bearded lips. "Laws, Cunnel, we-all know you bin sufferin' a heap of woes but —"

Rodney raised a slender, sunburned hand. "I've not the least right to ask any of you to stay here any longer but can't you persuade your fellows to stay till — say, after the crops are in, 'round the first of September? By then I'm sure I can raise enough money on the harvest to pay you."

"Well, suh, reckon that's reasonable enough fo' me but I cain't speak for the rest exceptin' Jim Davis and maybe Ted Grimes; we all served in the same battery and they think the world of you. Is there anythin' more, suh?"

"No, Larkin. I'm sorry but, barring some miracle, that's the situation."

When the door had closed Rodney stared fixedly at a portrait of his grandfather done by Charles Willson Peale. Old Brian Tilt's painted gray-blue eyes seemed to remain focused relentlessly upon him. They seemed to say, "In our time, your great-grandfather and I met and overcame no end of hard times. We expect you to do the same, else you're not a true Tilt."

Once the old slave bell had stopped clanging, Rodney took Margaret by the hand and, flanked by Bushrod and Caroline, advanced on the front stoop and briefly announced his intention of marrying Margaret Forsythe.

To her utter astonishment Meg noticed Peter Tyler standing right in the center of the front row of onlookers. On the Texan's rugged copper-brown features she could read no trace of emotion of any description. His expression remained as impassive as that of any cigar-store Indian.

Once Rodney had finished, cheers led by Knox and Hamrick were raised before the drab little gathering dispersed and went back to work.

When Peter Tyler learned that more than half of the white veterans were getting ready to move on, he sensed the moment had come to hazard everything on a gamble he'd been considering ever since Manlove had dropped that significant expression "pay ship."

Alone, he rode up to Rushmore's Pool, where it seemed easier to think clearly and to work out details. He didn't bother to set up the fly rod he'd fetched along. He thought and thought until it became clear that the key to this situation depended on the judicious use of Samuel Shepherd's gold.

For one thing, everyone knew Rodney Tilt must lay hands on real money right away to keep Moluntha going. And there was second reason. Surely, the Colonel must find funds to finance an expedition he and Jim Manlove almost certainly intended to make.

On returning to the main house Tyler sought Rodney Tilt and wrung his hand with convincing earnestness. "I've come, sir, to wish you and Miss Forsythe my most sincere hopes for your enduring happiness together."

When Rodney's hand gripped Tyler's the latter experienced a sense of grim satisfaction. As for the Master of Moluntha, he felt relieved, for somehow he'd felt that some day Tyler might cause trouble, being the fiery-tempered individual he'd proved to be on occasion. Also, he was surprised by the Texan's affable manner at this particular moment. Possibly he wasn't really in love, but had only been flirting?

He returned his attention to the present while Tyler was saying, "It's been a pleasure, sir, to know Jim Manlove. He's the greatest spinner of yarns I've met in years. In fact he's kept Knox and me awake nights describing adventures, particularly that time his little privateer, the *Audacious* something got caught in a hurricane and wrecked in the Gulf of Mexico."

On his chair Rodney Tilt stiffened imperceptibly. Great God! Had that fool Manlove been blabbing? Probably he had; the ex-gunner's mate had been smelling of liquor lately, and in private he had stated how anxious he was to get started on a journey down to the key he'd mentioned to forestall any efforts by Pleasants to jump the gun. Sharply, he queried, "Did Manlove say anything about, well, a pay chest?"

"Not in so many words, sir, but he made it plain that for some reason he's in a big hurry to get down to the Gulf again so I've figured there must be something of value involved."

"What are you leading up to?" Tilt demanded, jet eyes fixing the Texan like bayonet points.

Without waiting to be asked Tyler seated himself, smiling a little; by now he was sure he'd appraised the situation correctly.

Yes, by God! Jim Manlove must be in a hurry to get back to where the pay ship's treasure lies. Possibly he was fearful someone might beat him to it. Also, Tyler had heard that, because the Colonel had saved Manlove's life, some sort of an agreement must have been arrived at between them. Where he held a priceless advantage lay in the fact that, lacking ready money, neither Tilt nor Manlove could hope to reach the hiding place in the near future. Paying no attention to a swarm of bluebottle flies buzzing about his head, he drew a deep breath and took a neck-or-nothing plunge.

"Colonel, sir, I've really come here to make a proposition which I hope will appeal to you. It so happens I'm in possession of quite a few gold pieces which I can produce any moment I've need of them."

"For God's sake, where did you —"

Tyler's calloused brown hand shot up and his smile vanished. "Hold hard, sir! Neither you nor anyone else ever must ask how or where I came by that gold. Suffice it to say that it's mine and you can have enough of it to relieve you of present difficulties for a while."

For a long moment Rodney said nothing, racked his brains to explain how this increasingly curious individual might have acquired what sounded like a small fortune and why, at this particular moment, he should make such an offer? Said he carefully, "Thank you, but to offer so considerable a sum there must be a string attached."

Tyler said promptly, "No, sir. All I ask is that you let me go with you and Manlove on your expedition to the Gulf. As you know, I'm uncommon handy with a gun and, better yet, I speak fluent Spanish and understand the natives' ways. They're a savage lot, most of them."

"I'll think it over. How much could you — er, lend me? Of course I'll repay you the moment I'm able, and with interest."

"Would three thousand solve your most pressing obligations?"

Miserably aware that, before doing business of this sort, he must consult Manlove and insist on learning how Peter Tyler had come into possession of such wealth, Rodney hesitated. If he insisted, he'd pass up his only chance of keeping Moluntha; also, he'd otherwise be unable to finance an expedition to Cabo Rojo.

Tilt forced a broad smile. "Very well, if Manlove agrees on your coming along, I'll accept your most generous offer, condition and all."

He then offered his hand and at the same time wondered how Meg would take to the notion of his departing again so soon and for an indefinite length of time.

# 34

---◆---

# News from the Northeast

FOR ONCE the mail brought encouraging news in the form of a letter from Marc Peabody, who wrote to tell Rodney he'd forwarded the promised draft for a thousand dollars to the Ajax mine's bank in Wytheville. He then went on to state he was taking preliminary steps toward formation of an Ajax Mining Company and would take further action as quickly as he received legal authority to act on behalf of Rodney Tilt and other interested parties.

Peabody also predicted that the sale of shares in this enterprise probably would require considerable time and effort, since much fluid capital in the Northeast was being invested in railroad building in the Midwest and toward the Pacific, as well as extending already established local lines. Also, he pointed out, many factories and mines in the North were being enlarged or modernized. Apparently, many possible buyers preferred to risk their money somewhere where they could conveniently watch how their investment was being spent. Marc added that he'd encountered considerable opposition toward investing funds anywhere in the South but remained hopeful all the same.

Rodney informed the assembled family, which now included Margaret Forsythe. "That's all very well but, because of this," he held up an official-appearing document which had arrived in the same mail, "more immediate steps must be taken."

"What is that you've got?" Bushrod demanded.

"A notice that inside of three months all back land taxes must be paid plus an additional amount falling due in 1865. Failing payment, the property in question would be condemned and offered for sale."

In a taut voice Meg asked, "How much does the Government demand?"

Frowning, Rodney shuffled papers. "Near as I can make out our indebtedness amounts to something like nine thousand dollars."

Silence invaded the room. Not that everyone present hadn't been expecting bad news from the Court House — but $9,000!

"So much for that!" Rodney picked up Marc's letter, then glanced at his fiancée. "Marc also writes that he's heard from your Uncle's lawyer in Portland. He reports that Mr. Forsythe's will is to be probated before long. Unfortunately, the lawyer hadn't made mention of any provisions in regard to the will in question."

Forcing a smile, he looked at Meg. "Well, at least the lawyer is at work. Let's hope your late Uncle has remembered you."

Slowly Meg shook her head. "That's scarcely likely since, as I've told you, I only met Uncle Azael on but one occasion."

"Well, let's hope for the best. Suppose we all go about our duties and digest this information and we'll talk again later."

Once he was alone Rodney settled back on his chair, fingers laced behind head, and for a good while stared unseeingly at the ceiling's fly-speckled plaster. Rousing, he sent for Manlove. He appeared before long, sweaty and sunburned from work in the estate's sawpit where fresh planks were being cut to replace another burned-down cabin.

"Take a seat, Jim," Rodney directed. "Think the time's ripe for us to talk about a certain secret we've been thinking about."

Using a hooked forefinger, Manlove scraped sweat from his forehead, flicked it onto the floor. "Well, sir, I'm right glad to hear you say so, on account I've been losin' a heap o' sleep lately worryin' whether Pleasants is wasting no time gettin' back to the *Circe*'s pay chest."

"For certain reasons I'm just as anxious as you to get going right away, *if* you'll agree to certain provisions."

Manlove raised a brow. " 'Provisions'? Meanin' what?"

"Well, Peter Tyler approached me the other day and confided he's got a fair amount of gold hidden nearby."

Instantly, Manlove demanded, "Where'd he get it?"

"He won't say. I didn't persist for obvious reasons."

"How much has he got?"

"I don't know the exact amount but he swears 'tis sufficient to advance enough funds to pay pressing bills and also to buy and provision a vessel fit to carry us down to Mexico."

Manlove's battered and already red features turned redder yet. "Mexico! Now how in hell did that damn' sly Texan find out about our secret?"

Leaning over his desk, Rodney spoke sharply but in low tones. "Apparently Tyler got you drunk one night and you blabbed something about the wreck of a pay ship."

The ex-gunner's mate caused small report in clapping hand to forehead. He groaned. "Oh, my God. Now I remember. 'Twas last Thursday night we'd a drinkin' bout on liquor Tyler'd bought — the underhanded son of a bitch!"

"You didn't tell him where it was or how much money was involved?"

"Hell, no!"

"You've never confided that to me, either, except that the wreck lies somewhere near Cabo Rojo."

"Then how did Tyler catch on?"

"I suspect he must have been puzzled about why I'd fetch a sailor up into these mountains. Probably he got suspicious and figured you must know about something mighty important."

"Christ! That's it!" Manlove burst out. "What else did that foxy bastard say?"

"He's offered to foot the cost of an expedition down south provided he's cut in on the deal."

Manlove growled, small and bright-blue eyes narrowing, "How did you answer that?"

For a long moment Rodney kept the other in suspense.

"I said the money, if any, might be split six ways; three for yourself, two for me and one for him, plus a refund for whatever he spends getting us to Cabo Rojo. Does that strike you as fair?"

Manlove got up, sought the nearest window, and stood with unseeing eyes watching a load of firewood being driven around to the kitchen. Manlove worked hard to assay various values. On the surface seems like the Colonel's notion is a fair shake. Of course, he'd be payin' Tyler's money out of *his* share but that's his business. All the same, the Colonel might come out of this all right. Yep, It'll be a long while before he gets home again and accidents *could* happen anytime along the way.

He returned to face the desk. "Well, sir. Can't say as I fancy the idee of lettin' a third party sit in on our game." He shifted a cud of tobacco to the other cheek. "Howsumever, since we can't otherwise get down to Cabo Rojo I reckon we may as well deal him in."

Tilt rubbed his chin, made a small rasping sound, then said with deliberation, "Don't see how we can avoid it and that's a pity; Tyler's too smart to suit me. He'll have to be watched from start to finish, but without his suspecting we don't altogether trust him. Very well, now that's settled, from what port do you figure we ought to sail?"

"New Orleens," came the prompt reply. "There'll be plenty of ex-Navy men driftin' round the levees — hard-nosed fellers who may prove trustworthy — up to a point."

"How many men do you expect we'll need?"

"That depends on the size and rig of the craft you buy."

"What's your notion?"

"I'd say a lugger or a small schooner which could easy be handled by five or six men. We don't want too big a craft — only one stout enough to mount a swivel gun. Them's real dangerous waters we'll be cruisin', sir, 'specially with that war still draggin' on in Mexico."

"Very well, we'll sail well-armed. What else?"

"Our craft must have plenty of foot but needin' only a moderate draft. God alone knows how many uncharted sandbanks and reefs we'll come acrost; too many, anyhow, to risk sailin' a deep-draft vessel."

"It will be up to you to find a boat that five men can handle."

"Why five?"

"A matter of odds," came Rodney's crisp reply. "With five aboard there'd be the three of us against two outsiders. Goes without saying you'll be very choosy about picking candidates and I'll pass on them before they're enrolled."

"You mean 'signed on.'" Manlove chuckled. "What's the first step?"

"Find Tyler and fetch him here. We'd better seal our compact now, then concoct a cover story."

"When do we shove off, sir?"

"Come two days' time."

For some time Rodney had been toying with the fabrication that this expedition was going to make an attempt to smuggle munitions to insurgents fighting Emperor Maximilian's Army. Decidedly, there was a ring of plausibility to this idea. Everywhere it was rumored Benito Juarez's backers were ready and able to pay high prices for serviceable weapons and ammunition of any description.

Soon Manlove returned with the Texan, who seemed excited under his cool, well-controlled bearing. Once they'd tramped in, Tyler firmly closed the office door, then sought one window after another opened to the summer's heat and peered outside — well aware of how much could be learned through discreet eavesdropping.

Tilt invited the others to be seated then, perhaps needlessly, pointed out that this was a huge gamble since there was no certainty the pay chest had remained where Manlove and the others had buried it nor was there any indication of the actual value of its contents.

The Texan jerked a nod. "Sure it's a gamble, but one I'm ready to make. I can't stand this dull place any longer."

"Me too," Manlove grunted. "Always have craved action and plenty of it."

Tyler queried, eyes intent on a map Rodney was unfolding across his desk, "What route do we follow to reach New Orleans?"

Using a forefinger Tilt indicated the route. "We'll take the railroad from Abingdon to Knoxville and Memphis, then we'll find a steamer that'll carry us down the Mississippi; must be plenty of them by this time."

"That should be the quickest way," Tyler agreed, "and the likeliest place to do our business. New Orleans is a busy port so we oughten to attract undue attention. Now let me get this straight once and for all. *If* we find this specie, Jim Manlove is to get three parts of it, you, Colonel, will get two parts and I will receive one part. Correct?"

"Yes. Are you sure you're satisfied?"

"Yes. I'm ready for anything to get away from here."

"Well then, partners, let's shake hands."

They were on their way to the door when Tilt called, "Just a moment. To keep our understanding in order I will prepare in triplicate a draft of our agreement which all of us will sign. Oh, one more thing. Our departure will require some sort of an explanation so, just before we leave, we'll suggest we're departing on a gunrunning expedition to Mexico; no more than that. But we must wait till the last minute before dropping hints or every ex-soldier on this place will be clamoring to join us."

Tyler looked his admiration. "Colonel, that's a smart subterfuge. You can rely on Jim and me to hold back till the last minute."

Manlove said deliberately, "You're right there, Pete, but before we go any further the Cunnel and me want to lay eyes on that money you've bin talkin' about."

Unconcernedly, the Texan nodded. "Don't blame you a bit. In your shoes I'd want to be sure of that, too. I'll bring the gold here first thing tomorrow morning." Acidly he added, "If you like, feel free to count it."

Tilt smiled like a friendly wolf. "No need. Your word is good — with me, at least."

However, Manlove, gambler-like, insisted on a showdown inspection, so after dark Tyler slipped away to seek that rocky little den in which he'd concealed Shepherd's property. On reaching into the cache he almost got struck by a dormant rattlesnake. Perspiring furiously all at once, the Texan backed away. By God, here was a near-run thing! Imagine getting killed at a time like this by a pesky snake! Using a broken bough he prodded the reptile into the open, then clubbed it to death. Then, even while the snake still was writhing, he pulled out the stout leather pouch he'd fondled so often and again reveled over its weight.

# 35

## Vale! Vale!

Members of the family of course well understood the true objective of this expedition and also recognized the necessity for a subterfuge or cover story. They agreed to admit, if questioned persistently enough and then only after oath of secrecy, that the Master of Moluntha, Manlove, and Tyler were about to depart on a gunrunning expedition to Mexico. It went without saying that some ex-soldiers begged piteously to be allowed to go along but without exception courteously were refused.

Caroline Tilt took the news of the impending departure with stoic calm; too often she'd bidden loved ones farewell and had watched them ride off; then worry and wait, worry and wait until it became evident that some of them never would come home.

Now that Manlove and Tilt had actually inspected Tyler's gold and even had counted it, it seemed a turning point had been reached. They figured the hoard amounted to around $5,500, mostly in English, Spanish and French specie. American gold coins were very few. Very shortly after Fort Sumter had been fired upon gold and silver coins all at once had vanished from circulation.

On the afternoon before the departure Bushrod said to Rodney's surprise, "Why don't we invite Tyler to a farewell dinner? After all, since he's going with you he might as well understand how much this family trusts him."

"Besides," Caroline added quickly, "he'll make good company on this serious occasion."

Thanks to a bottle of passable sherry obtained by the Texan from some mysterious source, a strained atmosphere pervading the dining room gradually became dissipated and no reference to the forthcoming expedition was made.

Throughout the meal Rodney's gaze seldom shifted from the face of his outwardly composed fiancée, now occupying the hostess's chair opposite, once graced by Louisa.

Surprisingly, Bushrod appeared to be extra cheerful. Could it be that, subconsciously, the cripple was growing aware that should disaster overtake this adventure Moluntha would become his property? Meg pondered such a possibility but couldn't make up her mind so dismissed the thought as unworthy of him and of her.

Presently Peter Tyler arose, "made his manners," and then departed, explaining he'd a few things to get together and that he also had to arrange with ex-Sergeant Knox for returning the departing men's mounts from Abingdon.

Caroline, sensing that Rod and Meg must be yearning to be by themselves, remarked, "The moon is full tonight, so why don't you two visit the gazebo and view the valley? It's especially beautiful at such a time."

When gently her foot touched her husband's under the table, Bushrod sipped the last of his wine, thrust his napkin into its ring, then arose smiling almost paternally. "Come along, Carrie. Reckon we'll have a busy day tomorrow and I'm a bit weary. Suppose we retire?"

Once good nights had been exchanged Rodney, still aglow with Tyler's wine, led his bride-to-be down Moluntha's freshly scrubbed steps, all silvered by the moon, then paused and faced her, saying in undertones, "I didn't want to ask at dinner, but I presume Bush already has told you I've given him above two thousand dollars hard money to stand off creditors while I'm away?"

Intently Meg studied his bold features. "Yes, he did, darling, but he didn't touch on one important matter."

"And what might that be, my pet?"

"How did you come by so large a sum?"

"I borrowed it from Peter Tyler."

"But where did *he* get it?"

"That's a matter he absolutely refuses to discuss so I didn't insist; didn't want to spoil what looks like my only chance of avoiding bankruptcy. Perhaps it's wrong not to know but I'm sure you understand I've really no choice in this matter."

"Of course," she said quietly, then lifted her lips for a quick kiss. "Oh, Rod, I'd feel so blissfully happy if it weren't for this dreadful separation."

When they followed the path to the gazebo a number of recollections flooded Meg's mind. She remembered Tyler's mentioning during that unforgettable proposal that he'd an important sum of money put away but hadn't explained how he'd come by it. Warmed by the wine, the beauty of the night and Rod's nearness, she abruptly dismissed the subject.

Oh, Lord. How could she stand his being away on this admittedly risky adventure and for an undetermined length of time? All-too-familiar pangs of agonizing anxiety and uncertainty returned to harass her, just as they had before Z Company found her on the trail, ages ago it seemed. It wasn't right that, now the war was over, matters should conspire to take away this man she'd come to love beyond expression. This was like giving a trusting child some yearned-for gift only to have it snatched away — for how long? Convulsively, she hugged his arm, tingled at the strength of it.

Rodney, thinking along similar lines, slipped an arm about her waist, was infinitely stimulated by its warm softness. Just short of the gazebo he halted, swept her into his arms. Nearly forgotten emotions, dormant since Louisa's death, flooded him like waters released from an ice jam suddenly broken. Avidly, he crushed lips against the moist and writhing sweetness of her mouth, became aware of her body's entire length surging against him. Dazed with joy, he conducted her into the gazebo and to a rattan settee they'd occupied on other occasions. "My own sweet darling, if *only* I could begin to tell you how deeply I adore the very ground you tread, how much I *need* you!"

She flung arms about his neck, crushing her breasts against him, then, head swimming, gasped, "— And I need you, too, dearest — I crave your love in — in so many ways."

They blended almost convulsively and all the world beyond the settee grew distant and unreal. Realization of how soon they must part, perhaps forever, burst like a mortar shell in Rodney's brain, and as they writhed in mounting ecstasies a naturally ardent nature asserted itself. His palm slipped downward over the fabric covering the magical softness of her thigh, but on reaching her skirt's hem hesitated. Far from repelling, she surged upward to meet him. "Oh, yes, darling, oh, yes, yes!"

In a rapturous mood but again in command of themselves, they much later sought Moluntha Garrison. On the way neither made mention of the bliss they'd shared. Only one shadow darkened Rodney's contentment. During their lovemaking Meg had uttered no moans or cries of pain as evidence that her maidenhead had been penetrated. He said nothing, only took refuge in an often-heard explanation that females given to riding spirited horses sometimes suffered a rupture of the hymen. Best let it go at that.

Meg, having listened on occasion to whispered descriptions of pangs suffered by a bride on her wedding night, also wondered. Certainly she'd experienced nothing in the least unpleasant; could there be anything wrong with her? Then another disconcerting thought struck. Could she have gotten in the family way? Fear became forgotten as, arm-in-arm, they neared Moluntha, aware only of almost unsupportable joyousness.

Light rain started falling next morning. Ever-romantic Caroline thought it was as if Moluntha Garrison and all the countryside were weeping over these impending departures. Poor Meg! How valiantly she was striving to conceal poignant misery; even usually ebullient little Oliver seemed subdued at the prospect of Uncle Rodney's going away. No more rides together.

Following a hearty farewell breakfast the party's mounts were led around to a front door that still showed bullet holes. Once saddlebags and blanket rolls had been strapped in place, Resaca's glossy black neck arched. He reared and pranced about, pretty much as he used to in the good old days. To a lesser degree, ex-Sergeant Knox's undoubtedly thoroughbred mare Gloriana imitated the stallion's curvettings.

In Caroline's opinion Rodney's manner was altogether composed, but on the grim side. Peter Tyler's expression remained unemotional as it had been while listening to the announcement of the engagement. The Texan made his way over to Meg, looked her full in the face, then, clasping her hands gently between his, said evenly, "Please wish me good luck, Margarita, till I return to you, as surely I shall." Then he turned stiffly away and stood to horse like the veteran cavalryman he was.

Consciously she sensed enigmatic meanings behind the Texan's formal and well-restrained farewell.

Caroline, while kissing her brother-in-law, whispered, "So glad you're taking Peter Tyler along; he's artful and has been in love with Meg for too long a time!"

Manlove, who'd probably had a drink or two, was the only noisy member of the departing group. The ugly ex-gunner's mate acted almost child-like, shouting and waving elaborate farewells and showing boundless pleasure over being off toward the sea at last.

Caroline glanced at Meg waiting for a final embrace. The Northern girl's naturally red lips looked pale, so flat had they been drawn against her teeth; although her eyes were swimming she did not weep.

Once the engaged couple had exchanged a final hug and kiss — already they'd said all there was to say — Rodney straightened his revolver's belt, then mounted Resaca whose reins were held by Bushrod who, blinking, cried, "God go with you and bring you home safe and sound!"

As loudly as if he were commanding a battalion Colonel Rodney Tilt shouted, "Prepare to mount! Mount!"

Hamrick, Larkin and Jasper, detailed to lead the adventurers' mounts back from Abingdon, in unison swung into their saddles; only Jim Manlove was awkward.

"Forward, ho!"

Amid cheers the little party moved out.

# Part Four

# The Expedition

# 36

---◦◉◦---

# The Schooner *Queen of Hearts*

O<small>N THE THIRD DAY</small> after James Manlove had navigated the small and once luxuriously appointed schooner out of the Southwest Pass — one of the Mississippi's many outlets — it lay becalmed and helpless on an oily sea. Land was nowhere visible, only sea-weed, occasional bits of driftwood and smudges of smoke beyond the horizon.

Rodney Tilt lay on a straw pallet in the shade of the mainsail, sweating hard and staring up at the slack canvas above, which, to reduce visibility, had been dyed with walnut juice by its recent owners, who nevertheless had been caught red-handed by the United States Revenue Service and convicted of smuggling. Even with the war at an end a large number of former U.S. Navy gunboats continued to patrol principal exits from the mighty river's delta.

Rodney laced fingers under head, once more reviewed events of the past fortnight, and decided no one could truthfully pretend that Lady Luck hadn't accompanied the expedition thus far.

The trip from Abingdon and Memphis and on down to New Orleans had been accomplished without a single untoward incident. Also, James Manlove had been lucky in so quickly locating this swift, black-painted craft of around three hundred tons' displacement. Registered as the *Esmeralda* of Algiers, Louisiana, she'd been offered for sale by a United States marshal who only wanted to get rid of her and seemingly didn't give a thin damn how much or how little this condemned craft fetched.

In high good spirits Manlove had returned from Algiers across the river. "Minute I clapped eyes on that little beauty I knew there weren't no point goin' on lookin'. Yes, sir, me and Pete Tyler scarce couldn't believe our ears when the auctioneer knocked her down to us, rigging and all, for nineteen hundred bucks, hard money."

To be sure, the *Queen of Hearts*, as Manlove, ever the inveterate gambler, had rechristened her without inviting opinions, could have done with a fresh coat of black paint and she needed sundry minor replacements in her rigging's running gear, but such would have to wait — time was of the essence.

The ex-gunner's mate had insisted, "We can do without such repairs; 'taint as if we're headin' for Europe, around the Horn, or even down to South America. Besides, by now the hurricane season's over and we likely won't meet up with much hard weather. I'll bet you anything you want to risk the *Queen of Hearts* is near ideal for our purpose; we're damn' lucky to have found her so quick and bought her so cheap."

Rodney had agreed. Lying so low in the water and designed so narrow in the beam and with a clipper bow, this speedy former yacht with her brown-dyed sails *should* prove difficult to spy at long range.

While Manlove was procuring necessary papers, Rodney and the Texan occupied themselves by haggling for eight cases of somewhat rusty, but otherwise sound, Confederate rifle-muskets, plus several thousand rounds of ammunition. As Peter Tyler pointed out it might prove wise to have on board tangible evidence of the schooner's announced mission, a blatant attempt at gunrunning. Fortunately, authorities at the Customs House had turned a blind eye. Wasn't the Government in Washington at present assembling veteran forces with the avowed intention of crushing the forces of Emperor Maximilian and his sponsor, Napoleon III, for flagrant violation of the Monroe Doctrine?

Rodney Tilt quietly made a further investment by purchasing a quartet of Spencer carbines, which, if Blakeslee magazines were employed, could be fired seven times without reloading; he therefore also obtained a dozen Blakeslee magazines and a moderate supply of brass cartridges to fit in them. Such weapons being scarce and much in demand, the carbines hadn't been easy to find so he'd had to pay a stiff price for the notably efficient weapons. Still, he'd felt they were well worth it in view of the fact that the *Queen of Hearts* would be manned by only five men and she'd be cruising along an admittedly dangerous coast.

Neither Manlove nor Tyler had caviled over the price paid and readily agreed that these stubby-barreled 52-caliber carbines should be kept apart from the rest of the contraband and secured in a locker in the former yacht's main cabin. Without comment the Master of Moluntha took possession of said locker's only key.

"I've never handled pieces like these," he'd admitted, "but I soon can learn to and will instruct you. Everybody I've met swears these Spencers are dead accurate up to two thousand yards and won't jam when heated up, like some other repeaters."

Among other supplies, Tyler and Manlove procured staples such as yams, rice, cornmeal, molasses and a couple of small barrels of ship's biscuit — hard as iron and about as palatable. For meat they bought salt pork, bacon, hams and, as special treat, a case of U.S. Army Commissary tinned beef. They got the last cheap because, during their travels, some of the tins had got badly bent out of shape. One, in fact had had its seal broken and stank to high heaven so was rejected. The chandler had laughed, saying, "Here's a sound one. Don't pay to monkey around with tainted meat, no matter how cheap it comes. Feller I knew was kind of hard up so he et some and was planted six feet under next day. Since ye're such good customers I'll toss in some canned butter, free, for good measure."

Once the provisions arrived and were stowed everyone felt the cruise indeed was about ready to start, but that matter of the fellow who'd died from food poisoning set Rodney to thinking. When he broached the matter of medical supplies, Tyler agreed. "I was just thinking the same thing. Whilst I was with the Fifth Texas I got a small wound and spent some time in a field hospital. While there I did orderly duty and got considerably interested in medicine." He nodded to himself, "Yep. Might become a doctor some day; most patients I 'tended seemed to think so, too."

"Then you'll see to selecting medical supplies? Nothing fancy, just adequate."

The Texan beamed. "Sure thing. I learned a deal about philters, purges, healing ointments and such, and can use surgical instruments near as neat as a regular doctor."

The run down the Mississippi from New Orleans had not been notable save when the *Queen of Hearts* had passed various wrecks of partially submerged gunboats. They also had sighted the already overgrown ruins of Forts St. Philip and Jackson, bombarded and later seized by Admiral Farragut 'way back in '62.

Propping himself on an elbow, Rodney turned a badly sunburned face toward the bow on which were two recruits selected by Manlove and passed upon by Tyler and himself. Lackadaisically, they were greasing and otherwise cleaning a number of small arms, mostly single-shot English Enfield rifle-muskets and a variety of revolvers manufactured abroad for the Confederacy.

His gaze at first lingered on that rangy, black-bearded Cajun who'd called himself Antoine Bilotte. Manlove had been particularly anxious to sign on this sharp-eyed native of New Orleans because he knew more than a smattering about navigation, also because he'd proved a claim he knew the Mexican Coast from Brownsville all the way down to Vera Cruz and beyond like the back of his broad, leather-hued hands.

"How'd he prove that?" Rodney had asked, thoughtfully fingering his jaw.

"Why, 'though I'd covered various place-names on our chart, Bilotte spotted most of 'em with hardly any mistake. Should anything happen to me, Tony ought to be able to sail you back to New Orleans or Barataria Bay 'thout much trouble. It's my guess Bilotte's done more than a little privateerin' in his time and maybe a bit of piracy if the right opportunity came along. Besides, Tony can talk and even read French, which might come in handy sometime soon."

The other new hand was a half-Indian Mexican who gave his name as "George Duck." This hatchet-faced individual was quite short, wiry, bandy-legged, and agile as a startled lynx. Around thirty years of age, he spoke slowly and seemed a bit simpleminded. On the other hand, he'd been to sea a lot and, better yet, understood several coastal Indian dialects. Furthermore, this *mestizo* proved to be just as handy, or maybe handier with a knife than Peter Tyler. Grinning, he'd once claimed he could emasculate a wasp on the wing. It proved instructive while sailing down the Mississippi to watch the pair flick blades and hardly ever miss a little target they'd set up abaft the foremast.

At the moment ex-Corporal Peter Tyler remained below despite the main cabin's sweltering heat, studying and mentally photographing a fairly up-to-date U.S. Navy chart of that stretch of Mexican coast they were about to visit. It was significant, Tyler noticed, that Jim Manlove had neither marked nor so much as described the *Queen of Hearts'* destination, beyond that their goal was called "Seven Palms Island," which he reasoned must lie among any one of the dozens of clusters of keys fringing the coast like a series of miniature barrier reefs. Sensibly, he couldn't fault Manlove for such caution. He'd have been an utter fool to speak out.

When asked where he intended to offer the firearms for sale, the schooner's tattooed skipper had grinned, exposing gaps left by teeth knocked out in front of the Pocohontas, as he'd drawled, "Well, now, I don't know right now, but I'll decide in plenty of time. Maybe we'll offer our hardware in Tampico el Alto, or Tecoluta or maybe even in Tuxpan." He glanced at Tilt, still scarlet from sunburn. "I'm hopin', sir, you won't haggle overmuch over prices. The sooner we get to where we're bent the better I'll be pleased!"

Tilt dozed until Manlove called sharply, "Better 'rouse up and look alive, sir. There's a snatch of wind headin' this way, which is good because a vessel has just showed tops'ls on the horizon. Better pray yonder slant of wind reaches us before that craft comes sufficient close to take a really good look at us." Manlove glanced up to a faded Stars and Stripes hanging limp from the *Queen of Hearts'* main gaff. "That rag just might serve to fool him. If that craft yonder is a Yankee bulldog her commander just might figger, considerin' our size, we ain't worth alterin' course for."

The *mestizo*, George Duck, also had noticed those distant topsails and came padding aft on splayed and calloused bare feet. A gold hoop swinging from his left earlobe winked brightly. "Cappen, you see ship to east?"

Manlove grunted, "Yep, 'bout three minutes ago."

Everyone breathed easier when a strong puff overtook the *Queen of Hearts* and stirred her lifeless brown canvas. Reluctantly her fore and main booms stirred, creaked, and slowly started to swing out to starboard. Soon the little black schooner answered her helm and commenced to move smoothly along to the disappointment of several large, pale-gray sharks circling the becalmed vessel. Now they commenced to swim along a parallel course, just as they had since the Mississippi's delta had been lost to sight. Their triangular dorsal fins effortlessly sliced through the surface only a scant distance off either beam.

Presently Manlove lowered an ancient, brassbound spyglass. "Can't yet make out whether she's got steam as well as sails — there's no smoke showing so she probably is only a sailer. Yep. She's a fair-sized brig and sailin' a northerly course. Anyhow, I don't figger we've real cause to worry for maybe another half hour. Don't think she'll spy us 'less she's got some hawk-eyed bastard in her crow's nest."

Uneasy silence descended over the once well-holystoned teak deck. Tyler, fingers tapping restlessly against his sheath knife's scuffed leather scabbard, looked especially uneasy. By God, it was a new and most unpleasant experience this, to find himself so completely dependent on the judgment of another. Judging by the Colonel's grim expression, he reckoned Tilt must be feeling pretty much like himself, otherwise why should he start again cleaning the revolver he'd fetched home from Appomattox for all his Webley shone as speckless as ever?

Without interest, the Texan then surveyed a pretty little white-and-black tern perched and drowsing comfortably on the weed-strung back of a huge and somnolent green turtle of which there were many around. George Duck cleverly had snared one and hauled it aboard so, come evening, the *Queen of Hearts* complement should feast on turtle stew.

At the end of half an hour it became evident that that distant vessel at last must have sighted the black-hulled schooner and was changing course in her direction.

Manlove rasped, "Damn that brother-buggerin' sister-seducin' son of a bitch! Take the tiller, sir, and keep her steady as she goes whilst I see to trimmin' the sails. If this breeze don't pick up she'll have us under her guns long before dark!"

Very soon the former yacht was stepping smartly along under billowing sails trimmed to best advantage by Manlove and the Cajun called Bilotte. "She's a sailin' cruiser all right, with no steam, so God send this wind sharpens, else she'll close in and order us hove-to. Wish to Almighty Jesus our papers and manifest looked more convincin'.."

Disconcertingly soon it became evident that the pursuing vessel indeed was a sail sloop-of-war and a fast one, for during the afternoon she gained with disconcerting rapidity until, as the sun dipped low over the ever-roughening Gulf, she was near enough to permit Manlove to study her in detail and discover that she mounted a heavy swivel cannon amidships.

Dodging bursts of spray now flying high over the bows Tony Bilotte made his way aft.

"Mon Capitaine," he called, "eese there *no* way to lighten thees craft? That damn' brig soon weel come een range."

Manlove turned to Tilt, grim and silent beside him on the stern locker behind the wheel. "He'll start firin' rangin' shots any minute, so if we don't lighten this vessel pretty damn' fast 'twon't take him long to order us to heave-to or get sunk."

Tilt, dark hair streaming, snapped, "Isn't there anything we can do?"

The other glanced over the shoulder of a soiled and sweat-sodden red flannel shirt. "He's coming up fast so, damn it, we've no choice but to lighten ship."

"How?"

"Barrin' our anchors we can't jettison anythin' heavy enough to make much difference save maybe —" he pointed to the stack of arms chests lashed down and secured beneath a tarpaulin amidships — this former yacht having no cargo hold.

"They heavy, much heavy," Bilotte anxiously pointed out. For very good reasons he wasn't in the least eager to be taken and carried back to New Orleans.

Manlove turned to Tilt. "Don't know how ye'll fancy this idee but, if we're to stand any chance of outrunning yonder bulldog, we'll have to dump them guns fastest as we can though I sure hate to lose the money they cost."

"We've no choice. They'll have to go." Tilt started forward, swaying to the motion and shouting for axes and hatchets to be broken out. Followed by Bilotte he lurched toward where George Duck sat crouched in the lee of the stacked arms chests. Axes were snatched from their racks and all three men worked in so desperate a hurry that soon all eight ponderous chests laboriously had been shoved over the rail to raise brief sheets of spray.

That the sacrifice, much as it infuriated Tilt, Tyler and James Manlove, had been worthwhile quickly became evident — especially after one of the schooner's two heavy bow anchors had been cut away. The sleek ex-yacht now fairly raced along. Panting, they steadied themselves against the shrouds and watched the expanse of whitecapped seas separating the vessels widen perceptibly.

All at once the brig came about, Union flag snapping smartly. When her broadside became presented, a cloud of gray-white smoke appeared, went whirling off to leeward; then a sparkling pillar of spray briefly was raised by a roundshot falling nearly a hundred yards astern of the fugitive. When the brig fired a second shot everyone aboard the *Queen of Hearts* grinned; this time the projectile raised a spout even further astern than the first.

The brig ceased firing. Apparently her commanding officer had concluded there was little to be gained through wasting ammunition on so small and elusive a target.

By sundown only the brig's topgallants remained visible on the horizon. George Duck seemed especially happy. Said he in Spanish-accented English, "Me most glad!"

"Shouldn't wonder," Bilotte remarked while biting off a chew of tobacco. "Weren't you tried for piracy not long ago?"

The other's narrow dark head bobbed. "Sure. Me condemned hang, but me escape. No want more U.S. Navy."

Amen to that, thought Manlove, recalling the *Alabama*'s memorable duel with the *Kearsarge* — that, and the sad fate of those Rebel gunboats on the James below Richmond.

"I expect we ought to be pleased but —" Tyler's gaze rested on that empty space and crumpled tarpaulin abaft the foremast. "Damnation! And I was so sure we'd turn a pretty penny on that hardware."

"Better to lose money than get our necks stretched," Tilt commented drily. "Hanging's so damned permanent."

Manlove turned to George Duck. "Go below, fire up the galley stove, and cook us a mess of turtle meat."

Once sail had been shortened for the night and the crew filled up on turtle meat stewed with crumbled hardtack and cornmeal, pipes were lit and Tilt went aft and drooped onto the stern locker to join the Texan who, with uncommon ability, had learned how to steer.

Manlove also appeared and stood steadying himself against a backstay. After drawing a deep puff Tilt beckoned his companions closer lest he be forced to speak louder. "I reckon the three of us have been wondering, now that we've jettisoned the cargo, what we're going to tell the new men."

Tyler nodded. "To be sure. We must find some reasonable excuse for continuing our voyage."

Manlove's battered features briefly were illuminated when he drew hard on his pipe. "Well, like you, Colonel, I been thinkin' on that. Maybe our likeliest tack is to tell 'em I've remembered 'bout the wreck of a French supply ship which likely would have been freightin' in arms for the Emperor's troops."

"Yes, but why wouldn't such a vessel have been ransacked long ago?" Tyler queried.

"She got drove aground in mighty lonely waters."

"How far offshore would this wreck lie?" Tilt demanded.

"Oh, mebbe two — three miles off the mainland."

Manlove appeared to reach an important decision. He bent lower before continuing, "Might as well tell you we'll be headin' for one of a bunch of keys lyin' off Cabo Rojo. 'Twas on one of 'em, lyin' not too far from the place where that French ship got drove ashore, we buried the pay chest."

"You're *sure* you can find the right one?" Tyler asked softly.

"Sure as I kin touch the tip of my nose," growled the ex-gunner's mate. "Spot I've in mind has seven coconut palms growin' on it — or had, a year and a half ago — to make it easier I call it Seven Palms Island though 'tain't really more than a key bigger than the rest."

"Meantime it's up to you, Jim, to convince Bilotte and the halfbreed why we're keepin' on. You could make the explanation stick better than either the Colonel or me," said Tyler.

Manlove paused in turning away. "Oh, one thing more. Tomorrow morning we'd better fly Confederate colors. In these waters coastal craft are less likely to bother us; most local folks have heard that all along the South always has favored Juarez and his backers 'gainst Maximilian."

"Think we're likely to meet more Yankee cruisers?" Tyler queried.

Manlove shrugged, "You can't never be sure about such a thing. For example, who in hell'd figger on our meetin' a Yankee bulldog 'way out near the middle of the Gulf?"

Tilt broke in, "It's the kind of thing we'll have to watch out for. Since we're in this up to our necks we've *got* to trust one another all the way. Or, as Ben Franklin once put it, 'We must all hang together, else we'll hang separately.'"

"What are you drivin' at, sir?" Manlove demanded.

"Suppose something unexpected happens to you, and it could on a venture like ours. That would leave Tyler and me out in the cold not knowing *which* particular key to search for."

Swaying to his feet the ex-gunner's mate hesitated a long moment. "Yep. Reckon ye're right, sir. Ye're entitled to know bein' as how you've spent so much money and risked yer lives to get us this far. Tell you what. Come morning I'll mark Seven Palms Island on the chart."

Manlove hoped he sounded convincing. He'd foreseen this showdown coming, had decided it would be prudent not to indicate that the pay chest had been buried on another key close by Seven Palms Island in case, — well, just in case.

# 37

---◆---

# Seven Palms Island

THE BLUISH-WHITE TOPS of a mountain range showing well beyond the bleached and desolate appearing coast of Mexico lifted above the horizon two days later, shortly after the first all-but-exhausted land birds had commenced to perch in the rigging or fall helpless onto the deck. Driftwood, some with leaves still green upon it, and ever larger expanses of bright-yellow Sargasso weed billowed under clear, emerald-blue waves. Before long, strings of ragged-brown pelicans commenced to flap by, low over the water, grotesque creatures which in Tilt's opinion suggested some cathedral's gargoyles.

While taking his trick at the wheel, Tilt shifted his attention from the set of canvas to notice Tyler lying, apparently asleep, in the shade of the mainsail. Manlove was standing in the bows engaged in earnest conversation with the new hands. Abruptly, a disconcerting possibility presented itself. What was there to prevent Manlove from luring George Duck and the Cajun into a plot from which he and they might benefit hugely? Um. Come to think on it, all three were seafarers hard as nails, and with no more conscience than so many pimps.

After a while he called Tyler to rouse up and come aft. When he mentioned the conversation still going on forward, the Texan's ivory-hued teeth shone in a mirthless smile, "Believe it or not, I wasn't asleep and have been thinking along similar lines. Stands to reason we'd better stay damned watchful although I don't believe anything's likely to happen right away, probably not till we sight Cabo Rojo."

He glanced upward at a small hitherto carefully concealed Stars and

Bars, now proudly streaming from the main gaff. "Doesn't it do your soul good to see the dear old flag flying once more?"

"Wish to God we'd been able to keep it that way," came the bitter reply.

By midafternoon Manlove took the helm and without comment shifted to a course running more parallel to the coastline, but sailed the *Queen of Hearts* a good four miles offshore; now and then the flash of a sail had been glimpsed running between the schooner and the coast.

"The first port we'll sight," Manlove announced toward sundown, "should be Tampico el Alto, if my navigation ain't too far off."

Tilt asked, "How far to the south lies Cabo Rojo?"

"Not too far; ought to raise several groups of little keys before sundown but the one we're interested in won't be sighted till sometime early tomorrow."

Once a pair of fairly high conical hills hove into sight Manlove promptly altered course, steered even farther out to sea.

Tilt said nothing, only raised a quizzical brow.

"There are some fishin' villages near the foot of them there hills and some damn' ugly customers, Picaroons, or pirates if you prefer, hang out over there, as I've good reason to know."

Thinking back to that session in Dr. Trimble's stuffy little guest room Tilt recalled the ex-gunner's mate's mention of a murderous attack by natives which had left only Pleasants and himself alive.

Peter Tyler came aft and, intently scanning the coast, demanded sharply, "Why this change of course? Are we going to Seven Palms or not?"

"We are," Manlove replied, blinking in sunlight reflected off the water. "But I don't aim to approach that group of keys by daylight; I figger to approach 'em after nightfall."

"Why?"

"If just one fisherman, which we probably won't see, sights us, he'll be off to tell his mates. That's why I'll approach the Seven Palms group from the Gulf side and after dark so we can't be sighted. From now on there'll be no cookin' done during daylight hours. Smoke risin' from where we're going to anchor might prove a dead giveaway."

Peter Tyler did not feel particularly convinced that the new hands wholeheartedly had accepted the ex-gunner's mate's confident expectations of discovering munitions aboard a ship wrecked over a year earlier.

The Cajun especially seemed sullen and George Duck wore an uneasy expression on his flat, stupid-appearing, bronze-hued countenance.

Toward sundown Manlove altered course again. Then, posting Bilotte at the wheel, he led his partners below and brought out and smoothed a graying water- and grease-marked chart.

"Come twilight," he announced almost casually, "we ought to sight what's left of the French ship."

"Just where did the *Circe* go down?" Tilt tugged his dark mustaches, grown sadly ragged of late.

"Here." Manlove planted a calloused forefinger on one of several tiny keys. At once both Tyler and Tilt perceived that Seven Palms Island lay nearly three quarters of a mile distant from the wreck and that, on a direct line between the island and the *Circe*, lay two largish keys. Tilt's suspicions mounted. Why on earth would a handful of exhausted, starving men carry a weighty treasure chest all the way over to Seven Palms? It just didn't make sense. Why would they struggle past those intervening keys? Therefore it came as no surprise that, shortly after a particularly glorious sunset, the schooner, sailing under reduced canvas, neared an almost invisible key on which a few planks and ship's ribs rose stark and black above the sand. Hundreds of wheeling and screaming seabirds were coming in to roost on or near the wreckage.

"That the *Circe?*" Tyler wanted to know.

"Yep. All that's left of her. There was more last I was here."

As darkness deepened, lights began to glow at widely scattered points along the dark and distant shore, and brush fires flamed and flared with increasing clarity.

"Tell us the truth," Tilt stated rather than asked. "I think what we've come here for isn't on Seven Palms Island."

"True enough. But how did you figure that out?"

Tyler seemed quite composed while drawling, "The Colonel and I figured men in the condition you said you and your fellow privateers were in, wouldn't have rafted the chest all the way over to Seven Palms."

"You've figgered right. What we want is on the larger of them two little keys lyin' betwixt the French wreck and Seven Palms."

The Texan stared, asked deliberately, "Why did you lie to us?"

"Only as a precaution. No point in givin' away the true site till the time's ripe — which is now. We're now about to hide this vessel in a cove on the Gulf side of Seven Palms. And another thing, we'll only work when local craft ain't likely to sight us."

Darkness had descended by the time the silhouette of a palm-crowned island loomed close ahead, revealed only by radiant starlight and phosphorescent waves breaking along the shore. Manlove at once ordered canvas reduced with exception of the foresail; by slackening its sheets the vessel crept only cautiously along toward a narrow gap between two high and pallid sandbars.

An aura of excitement seized the schooner's crew. It had required sight of the *Circe*'s scant remains to convince the new hands that all was not as it should have been. When, smoothly, the **Queen of Hearts** had slipped into a small lagoon ringed in by sand dunes and coral rocks, the foresail was struck and the vessel slowed to a stop below coconut trees whose feathery tops appeared to be about on a level with the tips of the schooner's topmasts.

Only after the anchor had sped downward, trailing a tail of yellow-green phosphorescence, did George Duck clump below to kindle the galley's stove. What little wind there'd been died out completely.

To Rodney Tilt it seemed somehow incredible they actually had arrived so close to the goal. The Master of Moluntha stood, feet spread apart and arms folded, thinking of how much Meg would have enjoyed this, the loveliest sight he'd ever laid eyes on.

How might matters stand at home? If only he could communicate and reassure her of his abiding love and if — if there *had* been consequences from their final night together, well then, his devotion would only grow the greater. Yes. Surely she'd help Bushrod with business matters, give sound advice. Otherwise, he was feeling far from easy; there were too many "ifs" "ands" and "buts" about the present situation.

Standing there in the starlight he listened to conversations taking place forward. That, and the rattle of George Duck at work in the galley returned him to the present. Quite subconsciously his palm sought the familiar grip of the heavy Webley revolver dragging at its belt. He'd noticed that, since the schooner had anchored, both Tyler and Manlove had armed themselves.

After bolting a plate of turtle stew Rodney Tilt excused himself to go on deck and seek his favorite seat on the stern locker's stained and shapeless canvas-covered cushions. From here he was able to view most of the schooner's deck. The monotonous rumble of rollers lazily breaking over coral rocks lining the shore beyond the inlet should have proved soothing — but it didn't.

Presently Manlove strolled up and, puffing on a rank-smelling pipe, settled beside Tilt.

At length the ex-gunner's mate expelled a huge puff of smoke. "Well, what do you make of Seven Palms?"

" 'Tis a very beautiful spot but I count eight trees," Tilt replied pleasantly, "if you include that little half-grown one to the left."

"Didn't figger that one amounted to much," came the equable explanation.

After rising to look carefully about, Manlove reseated himself closer by and lowered his voice. "Now mind you, I've got no foolproof reason to suspect anybody but I think, sir, you and me had better renew our oaths to stick together no matter which way the cat jumps."

"Why d'you bring this matter up? Speak out."

"Well, to tell the truth I don't fancy the way that Texan looks at you sometimes — besides, he's too smart for his own good. Don't like men smarter than me. Besides —"

"— Besides what?"

"For a fact Pete's mad for the Forsythe girl. Knox told me that whilst you were away durin' the train wreck they was moonin' at each other all the time and was alone together a lot."

"Really? Don't you realize that once a gentleman gives his word it's binding?" Tilt got to his feet, said icily, "You seem to have forgotten that Miss Forsythe and I are to be married."

Manlove took a backward step, raised a hand as if to ward off a blow. "Sorry, sir. Please forget what I've said —" Silently he added, "If you can."

Well, anyhow he'd put the Cunnel on his guard no matter what he might be thinking.

In an altered tone Tilt spoke, "When do we start hunting?"

"I figure to set out about an hour before dawn. We'll leave the schooner here, take the gig and row to where —" his voice thickened, "I hope to God we find the cash. To make it easier, suppose we name that key Pay Chest Key?"

"Very well, but I hope you don't intend leaving this boat —" Tilt persisted in clinging to landsmen's terms —"with nobody aboard?"

"Hell, no! I aim to leave George Duck behind. Now, sir, you and me will take turns standin' watch. Suppose you go catch some rest. There'll be plenty to do come morning."

# 38

---

# Pay Chest Key

WHEN THE FIRST faint glow of light showed on the east horizon the gig was hoisted out and shovels and picks were stowed along its bottom, together with a crowbar and a small block-and-tackle because, as Manlove swore, the *Circe*'s chest was all-fired heavy. Each of the four men lowering himself into the small boat carried slung over his shoulder a Spencer repeating carbine.

Once the ex-man-of-war's man had slipped his tiller into place, Tyler, Bilotte and Tilt gripped oars and at Manlove's command commenced to row out of the cove. Only the gentle breaking of waves and the dull *thunk-thunk, thunk-thunk* of oars against thole pins broke the early morning's stillness.

While clouds of sea birds screeched, wheeled and dove about it the gig crawled toward a low, sandy key distinguished by an outcrop of coral rock shaped something like a clenched fist rising from its center. To all except Manlove this key seemed utterly undistinguishable from hundreds of others. Devoid of vegetation and rising no more than twenty feet at its highest point, Pay Chest Key's sandy surface couldn't have covered over three hundred yards in length by half that distance in width. To everyone it appeared obvious that a severe storm or a hurricane easily could sweep clean over this whole low-lying islet.

To James Manlove's indescribable and profanely audible relief it appeared that nothing of that nature had occurred since he'd left this key over a year and a half earlier.

Excitement commenced to tingle Tilt's fingertips once Manlove steered toward a gently shelving beach of dazzling white coral sand showing at various points the herringbone-shaped spoor of turtles come ashore to lay eggs during the night.

When Manlove ordered, "Easy all!" the rowers held dripping oars horizontal and peered over their shoulders while their craft grated softly onto the beach.

"Ship oars!" snapped the ex-gunner's mate in a strained voice.

To the gig's crew, tense as they were, it seemed little effort was required to heave her above the high-tide mark.

"Leave your carbines here," Tilt ordered. "Take digging tools."

Peter Tyler found his nerves keyed up as seldom before. Quickly he shifted the heavy-bladed sheath knife behind him.

Once the group had shouldered digging tools Manlove, feet slipping in the soft sand, led upward toward the fist-shaped knob.

It was reassuring to note how unhesitatingly the ex-gunner's mate proceeded.

If today was going to be as hot as Manlove anticipated he decided to work till midday, if necessary, then order the diggers to rest in the shade of the overturned gig until the worst of the midday heat was over. Too often he'd seen men keel over through prolonged exertions under a tropical sun.

Fighting down a fierce surge of excitement Rodney Ajax Tilt plowed up the highest dune alongside Manlove who, shouldering the crowbar, had commenced to pick a route among wind and sea-eroded outcrops of Aeolian sandstone toward that fistlike pinnacle — easily the highest point on this otherwise unremarkable key.

The others plowed along in their wake, scarlet-faced and already panting under spades and other equipment.

Halfway to the summit the ex-gunner's mate paused long enough to dash sweat from his forehead. "Reckon now you can understand what a job us castaways had to haul a heavy chest up so high."

"Why'd you do that?"

"Didn't dare leave it where even a extra high tide maybe could uncover it."

Tilt queried, "Does this place appear to have been seaswept?"

"Maybe, lower down, but this here high ground don't look like it's been struck much."

Tilt felt his heart commence to thud like the accelerating beat of a tom-tom. Turning, he realized that Tyler must be experiencing somewhat similar sensations. Oh Lord, he breathed, help me save Moluntha! Let the chest be here.

Gripping his spade in both hands, Manlove strode toward a half-buried slab of sandstone roughly pentagonal in shape. "If Pleasants ain't beat me to the draw or iffen a storm ain't moved this stone, the chest's somewhere close by."

By now the sun was well up, but hadn't yet begun to cast shattering, blinding rays.

Manlove drew a very deep breath, then expelled it, hissing through broken teeth. "What the hell are we waitin' for? Start diggin'!"

Manlove straddled the five-sided slab of sandstone, took a bearing on the pinnacle, then moved three paces to the right and halted, surveying the taut, unshaven and bronzed faces about him. "Reckon none of us are reg'lar churchgoers but let's everybody pray we strike pay dirt!"

Floundering amid a maelstrom of mixed emotions, Tilt set foot to his spade. The others did the same. Sand and small stones flew until a sizable pit had been dug.

"Say," panted Tyler, "just how far down is this damn' chest?"

" 'Round four or five feet," Manlove stated, blowing sweat from the tip of his blunted nose.

Tilt asked, "So why haven't we struck anything? This hole already is easily six feet deep."

Manlove ripped obscenities. "Damned if I know. Maybe the stone somehow or other got moved. Two of you dig slanting off to the left; me and the Colonel will dig right-diagonal from this hole."

Rodney Tilt bit his lip while making the sand fly. Suddenly he remained as frozen in midmotion as if struck by a bullet. His spade's tip had encountered a substance different from easily crumbled bits of coral rock. For the moment he said nothing, only shoveled furiously until a piece of smooth, faintly rusted iron became visible.

Tyler, working alongside, gasped, "God above!"

Manlove and Bilotte came running. Manlove raised a mighty yell. Now, b'God, now he might repay an indebtedness incurred up in Wytheville, Virginia — always provided something unexpected didn't interfere.

Shouting like lunatics, all four men made the sand fly until a stout iron chest lay exposed with a pair of heavy iron padlocks, obviously smashed by bullets, still dangling from their staples. The chest was handsomely built and bound by four bands of wrought iron, and showed a *fleur de lis* engraved on its top.

James Manlove flailed arms about like a madman; burbled, "You thought I was lyin' but there it is! By the livin' God, *there it is!*"

Tyler, however, said, "By the look of it *I* think it's been tampered with."

"Hell, no! Them padlocks are just the way we left 'em."

Sweat pouring down his face, the ex-gunner's mate unhooked the useless padlocks and with some difficulty raised the ponderous lid. A united shout arose. The sun, in nearing its zenith, cast full radiance onto the chest's gleaming, maddening contents.

Reactions varied. The Cajun began dancing about, tossing arms in a fantastic carmagnole all the while yelling something in New Orleans patois. Manlove and Tyler joined in, beating one another on the back. As for Rodney Tilt, he remained motionless, only grinned hugely while surveying the glittering hoard. What wouldn't this mean to Meg, to Moluntha and to all who dwelled there! A sobering thought stifled an impulse to shout for joy. Once this treasure was divided, would his share suffice to avoid the necessity of forming a stock company to restore the Ajax?

Tyler knelt, plunged naked arms up to their elbows into the glittering mass then, laughing wildly, several times allowed coins to slip and tinkle through his fingers.

Manlove selected out a louis d'or, held it up between stubby thumb and forefinger. "Damn' if this ain't the spit of the one I was robbed of back in Wytheville." He treated Rodney to a wide grin, "Ain't you glad you believed me? Yes, sir, 'tis Easy Street for all of us from now on!"

Bilotte, crouching beside the chest, washed leathery, black-bearded features with coins, kissed some of them. All at once Tilt, aware of tension, of a changed atmosphere, was the first to recover equanimity. Shading his eyes, he peered at that distant bluish coastline, then grabbed Manlove's arm and pointed to maybe a half-dozen triangular sails running well offshore.

"Hell!" snapped the ex-gunner's mate. "I don't like the look of them piraguas sailin' about, but 'less they've got a glass, which I doubt, most likely they ain't sighted us. Still —" abruptly he broke off. "Look at Seven Palms! Damn it t'hell, look!"

Everyone could see a slender column of gray-white smoke climbing leisurely into the sky's brazen blueness to form a noticeable cloudlet.

"Blast that idiot, Duck!" snarled Tyler. "What in hell is he up to? Maybe that damned half-breed's trying to signal."

Bilotte said, "May he hongry and ees cooking somethings."

"If he is I'll have his balls roasted for supper, by God!"

To everyone's astonished relief, that betraying pillar of smoke abruptly vanished. Tilt hurriedly estimated that the fumes could not have been visible for over five or six minutes — ten at the outside. He said as much, but all the same gnawing doubts persisted.

"Get a move on," Manlove snapped. "Sooner we get back to the island the better."

Rodney noticed the Cajun surreptitiously stuffing coins into his pants' pockets.

"Stop that!" When the fellow hesitated, Tilt's revolver appeared as if by magic. "Put that gold back where it came from!"

Cursing beneath his breath, the Louisianian sullenly returned the coins to the massive strongbox.

Manlove attempted to snap shut the battered padlocks but, failing, passed their shackle arms through ponderous staples securing the hasps. Then all four men, two at each end, grasped wrought-iron handles and heaved, but the chest proved so heavy it had to be heaved out of the pit by use of that block-and-tackle Manlove had anchored to a coral head.

Once more doubts assailed Rodney Tilt. How could a handful of ship-wrecked sailors possibly have manhandled this chest up from the beach? Certainly they must have been more numerous than Manlove had indicated. Further conjecture on the subject was ended by Manlove who, panting fearful profanities, was pointing eastward. "See them clouds?" he wheezed.

"They don't look like much," Tyler commented.

"No storm looks like much at the start," growled the ex-gunner's mate. "They may amount to nothin' but time's a-wastin'; let's get crackin'!"

It was all they could do to ease the pay chest onto the gig's bottom boards without causing damage but they managed it, trembling with exertion.

Although the gig's people kept casting anxious glances over their shoulders at Seven Palms Island, no more smoke was visible. However with amazing speed those clouds to eastward increased, darkened and came boiling over the dark-blue horizon. Once the gig had been shoved off and dripping-wet rowers had dropped onto seats, they made oar shafts bow under the power of their strokes. Manlove cast anxious backward glances. Had low-lying Pay Chest Key completely concealed the gig?

Bilotte panted, "Hey, *Capitaine*, looks like them sails ees come about to run along coast."

"Think they've sighted us?" Tyler gasped.

"Maybe not," snapped the ex-gunner's mate. "Mebbe they're only fish-ermen headin' home afore the storm strikes."

# 39

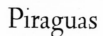

# Piraguas

U NDER A FITFUL and uneasy breeze the sea was commencing to stir
when the gig rounded up under the *Queen of Hearts'* counter and
her crew shipped oars. The frightened, narrow face of George Duck
appeared above the rail but he deftly caught the bight of the painter
cast up by Bilotte.

"What the hell was that fire?" roared Manlove. "'Less you've got one
damn' good excuse I'll skin you alive!"

"Pliz, Cap'n," the *mestizo* bubbled, gesturing wildly. "Me — smoke
while make spun yarn. Coal from pipe fall in yarn, it blaze up. Me put
out fire." He snapped his fingers, "Quick, quick."

"But not quick enough, you bloody idiot!" rasped Tilt. "You may damn'
well have given us away."

The matter ended for the time being after Manlove dealt the offender
a few violent cuffs. A steady increase of wind and the sight of huge
dark clouds rushing up prompted such a frantic burst of energy little
time was required to hook onto the gig's davit falls and to hoist her and
her precious cargo inboard.

To the end of his days Rodney Tilt never ceased to marvel over the
speed with which this tropical storm developed. By the time the gig had
been hoisted in and stops had been jerked from the fore and mainsails,
fitful blasts were rattling palm fronds overhanging this little lagoon. The
sun paled to a sickly yellow before disappearing altogether; the Gulf's
water turned a dull lead color streaked with foam.

"Stand by to heave anchor!" Manlove shouted.

Everyone had caught up capstan bars and were getting set to walk in the anchor when the *Queen of Hearts'* master abruptly ordered them to ease off.

"What the hell's the matter?" Tyler snapped.

"Ask Bilotte or even that fool, George Duck. Any sailor can see what the situation is!"

"Tell me *what* is wrong," demanded Tilt.

The schooner was lying in a small but deep lagoon the only entrance to which was narrow, passing as it did between two sandbars.

"We can't sail out through the inlet in the teeth of this wind. It's blowing square into the entrance so I daren't attempt tackin' out through that damn' narrow inlet," Manlove shouted. "I wouldn't try. We'll ride out this gale right here."

While the wind steadily increased, the sky grew darker and darker and, with almost miraculous speed, huge waves commenced to roar and shatter themselves against the shoreline. The warm air smelled damp and sour. Rain commenced to lash the deck with increasing fury. Everything movable on deck was secured and battened down once the iron-bound chest had been swayed down the main cabin's companionway.

Tyler yelled through cupped hands, "Goin' — be — hurricane?"

"No tellin'. 'Tis well past reg'lar season for 'em. All the same we're in for one hell of a blow." He stared at that charred section of deck from which rain was scouring away evidences of George Duck's carelessness.

"Then we got to linger here?" Tyler demanded grimly.

"Can't nowise tack out through that inlet till the weather lets up."

Ignoring gusts of salty spindrift drumming against his face, Tyler shouted, "Then we have to stay anchored overnight. What if —"

"What if 'what'?" Tilt demanded.

"If that damned smoke *was* noticed," the Texan shrugged, "shouldn't wonder but we'd have visitors soon's this gale lets up."

Manlove finished securing the mainsail, then went forward to make sure chafing gear on the anchor line was in place. "Well, friends, I figger we'll be stormbound till daybreak at the least. If this ain't a hurricane she ought to blow herself out durin' the night. We ought to keep safe enough in here."

"In that case," said the Texan easing a wide belt sagging under the weight of his long knife and revolver, "we'll have plenty of time to go below and find out how and where we stand by the way of plunder."

"What's better to do? — after we've readied all small arms." Lord, how Rodney itched to estimate his share. Would it prove sufficient?

Rain was spattering like spent birdshot on the single deadlight when without comment Manlove slid open the cabin's hatch and climbed on deck to be half-blinded by a particularly vicious squall. Now and then vivid flashes of lightning momentarily revealed the scene in startling clarity. This he took as a good sign since, in his experience, thunder and lightning seldom accompanied a genuine hurricane.

To Manlove's relief, when he peered into the forecastle he saw Bilotte and George Duck stretched out on their bunks and apparently sleeping. Only then did he return aft, reassured by the former yacht's steady swaying to her anchor, which appeared to be holding fast — why this was so, he'd discover later on.

By the light of a large whale oil lantern, smoking yellow-red and swinging to the schooner's restless yawing he was annoyed to note that his partners already had removed the broken padlocks, had raised the pay chest's lid, and in awed silence were surveying the glitter of its contents.

"Now that you're back, Manlove," Tilt said crisply, "suppose you and Tyler start stacking coins according to the country of origin. I'll list their number and value, whenever possible."

Pulses racing, they set to work. Despite all storm noises everyone could hear the rich clinking of coins being sorted and stacked.

Soon a long table with collapsible leaves fixed in the cabin's middle nearly was covered by little or tall piles of specie. The profiles of many long-dead monarchs and queens seemed to smile up at the sweat-bathed men. As soon as Rodney had enumerated each stack it was dropped into a row of empty cartridge boxes ranged on the deck beside the tally table. If all went well, small canvas bags would be sewn to accommodate the various shares.

"So far," Rodney announced, "looks like we've realized around a hundred thousand dollars' worth and there's still a third to be counted."

Presently, Tyler, hand groping deep into the pile for another fistful of those cold but gloriously warm-looking coins, stiffened abruptly. "Hey! What the hell is this?" There was that in his voice which caused his companions to stoop and join in peering into the coffer.

The all-too-familiar icy fingers of anxiety seemed to claw at Rodney's heart.

"Look, look!"

Tyler shoved aside the last layers of sovereigns, escudos, reales, louis d'ors and some pieces not readily recognizable and exposed a length of dull, silver-gray metal. Frantically, Manlove clawed aside specie until it became unmistakable that some cheating paymaster had lined the chest's bottom with a double row of leaden ingots.

Rodney turned away, once more tasting the bitter venom of defeat.

Till they ran out of breath, Tyler and Manlove, purple-faced, raved, ranted and vented sulphurous curses quite unaware that, despite driving rain and screaming wind, Bilotte and the *mestizo* were peeping through the deadlight. Tilt, glancing upward, glimpsed them. The instant they realized they'd been seen they vanished but Tilt, for reasons of his own, said nothing as his partners lifted out and flung aside a dozen-odd leaden pigs. All he said was, "This could have been worse; we've still so much treasure our shares ought to prove to be — let's say worthwhile."

Tyler quickly agreed but looked thoughtful. "What d'you say? Shall we resort these coins now, and try to arrive at a more accurate total value? Nothing better to do for the time being, is there?"

Still purple in the face, Manlove grunted, "Sure wish I could lay hands on that Frog son of a bitch who substituted those!" He kicked aside a pig of lead. "All right, let's go!"

Eyes once more shining, the partners set to work and arranged coins in neat ranks on the cabin table, and were so absorbed with handling this ever-magical metal they scarcely noticed the storm raging outside.

At the end of an hour all three were in agreement that this treasure certainly couldn't bring at a conservative estimate less than $150,000, United States currency. For a moment Tilt wondered how Maximilian's French troops had reacted on going unpaid, reflecting that the Foreign Legion especially were reputedly hard and brutal. At least the paymaster hadn't survived to enjoy the fruits of his trickery — if Manlove had been right about there being no survivors from the French brig.

Once the coins had been recounted and replaced in the coffer Tilt, recalling those faces at the deadlight said, "Don't know how you all feel, but I think we'd avoid possible trouble if, right away, we promise the new hands generous shares."

Manlove threw back his head to deliberate and in so doing sighted faces again peering down into the cabin. Said he, winking, "Well, now, I'd say a thousand dollars apiece ought to keep 'em in booze and fancy girls for a long while, provided they don't get their throats cut somewhere along the way."

"A thousand each! You can't be serious!" Tyler burst out, but then remembered Manlove's wink and upward glance. "I — well, I'd say that's about right." No need to complicate an already tricky situation.

Tilt nodded. "Very well. When shall we pay off and make final distribution of shares?"

Without hesitation Manlove said, "Day before I expect to raise the Louisiana Coast."

After Tilt had darted an upward glance and had seen the deadlight clear he said evenly, "One thing's sure, we'd better go armed at all times and from now on one of us three will have to stay awake and keep an eye out. Oh, and one more thing. As of now, I intend keeping carbines and other weapons, aside from our sidearms, locked in the arms closet!"

Sometime after midnight the gale faltered and then commenced to die out almost as abruptly as it had risen, so when dawn broke, the sky was clear and only moderate seas continued to thunder along the shores of Seven Palms Island.

As soon as it grew light enough Manlove ordered the Stars and Bars raised and caused canvas to be readied for instant hoisting. Then he and the rest manned capstan bars and commenced to heave in the cable. At first the dripping brown cable shortened readily enough but then, despite the crews' frantic heavings, it began to come in slower and slower until it stopped with the ship's hawsehole directly above the invisible anchor. No matter how hard they struggled and strained it proved impossible to heave in another foot of anchor line.

Snarled Manlove, for once appearing unsure of himself, "Damn' hook must be fouled good and proper." He turned on George Duck. "You're a good swimmer. Dive and find out what the hell's gone wrong down there."

"Sí, Capitán," the *mestizo* nodded. "But me need more light."

Minutes dragged until the eastern sky turned pearly-pink and last stars gradually paled and disappeared. Presently the *mestizo* slipped out of ragged pants — all he usually wore — and dove smoothly. Craning necks over the rail, they watched the dark, slight figure progress downward through emerald-blue water until it became lost to sight. When George Duck surfaced at the end of nearly two minutes, gasping and spitting, he swam on his back calling, "Anchor — caught bad 'tween two ledges."

"Can't anything be done about it?" Tilt demanded, anxiety written broad across sun-darkened features.

Tyler anticipated Manlove's reply. "Yes. We've no choice but to cut the cable and clear out of this damn' place fast as we can. I —"

"Stow yer gab!" snapped Manlove. "That there's the last anchor we carry. God knows we may need one bad sometime 'fore we next make port."

Presently the diver's naked red-brown figure clambered up a rope lowered from amidships.

Manlove demanded shortly, "How bad is that anchor fouled?"

"Catched 'tween two beeg coral rocks."

"How do they lie? This is very important."

"Face toward sea, Cap'n," panted the dripping, black-haired figure.

"Then if the ship is worked inshore it might pull free?"

"Sí, Capitán, ees possible."

Promptly the gig was lowered with the intention of towing the schooner toward the lagoon's western beach and in the distant mainland's direction.

Seized by sudden apprehensions, Tilt said, "Before we start towing, suppose I climb the rigging and see what's what?"

"Hell no!" Manlove snapped. "You'd likely fall and break yer goddam neck. Bilotte, you swarm aloft!"

With simian agility the Cajun at once clambered to the maintop and immediately was shaken by two most unpleasant realizations. First, the *Queen of Hearts*' mastheads, by several feet, showed above the tops of tallest palms in the grove, so, from the time the *Queen of Hearts* had anchored, she must have been visible to anyone using a telescope. But what shook Bilotte far worse was the fact that, not much more than a mile distant, three large piraguas crowded with men were sailing straight toward Seven Palms Island. It stood to reason they were benefiting from one of those offshore breezes which in these latitudes blew almost every morning.

"Capitaine! Capitaine!" the Cajun yelled down. "Piraguas coming!"

"How far off?"

"Mebbe one — two mile off."

"How many?"

"Three beeg wans."

"Come below, quick, quick!"

During a highly checkered career James Manlove had occupied many a tight corner, but this sure beat the rest to hell and back. "Gotta clear our o' here in a big hurry. T'hell with the anchor. Man the gig! Colonel, you and Tyler had best break out the artillery!"

Grabbing an axe from a rack under the bulwarks he ran forward and with three powerful whacks severed the four-inch anchor cable. Next, the ex-gunner's mate seized a spare halyard, coiled and dangling from a cleat at the foremast's foot, swiftly knotted it about the capstan, then threw the balance of the line overboard to be caught by Bilotte who with the others was running out the gig's oars.

"Pull for the outlet whilst I man the helm. If it'll do any good, pray God the offshore breeze reaches us right pert!"

Though all hands pulled till their back muscles crackled, the bow-sprit only grudgingly commenced to swing in a slow semicircle till the schooner's overlong bow pointed toward that all-too-narrow entrance. Waves from last night's storm still were pouring through it but carrying nothing like the force they'd had previously. Despite all efforts it soon became painfully apparent that it would prove impossible to tow the former yacht out into the Gulf's wide waters.

With a sureness commanding Rodney Tilt's respect, Manlove arrived at a decision and recalled the gig. Her panting, sweat-bathed crew scrambled aboard and raced about hoisting sails and setting jibs, only to discover that the rusty-brown canvas only fluttered as if unable to make up its mind from what direction it might be filled.

Once Tilt and the Texan appeared lugging the first of several armfuls of carbines and rifle muskets and ammunition, Manlove swarmed aloft to be appalled by realization that all three low-lying craft were sailing only about a quarter of a mile off and were about to round Seven Palms Island's northern tip. No doubt remained that unless an offshore breeze blew soon and hard, he and the rest of the schooner's company were in for the fight of their lives.

# 40

## The Repeaters

ONCE AN OFFSHORE breeze finally did arrive, it blew only fitfully. Manlove therefore posted the *mestizo* at the foremast-head with orders to report picaroons' movements. No sooner had George Duck arrived at his station than he shouted in a shrill voice, "Piraguas very close north — sail fast around reefs."

"Since we've got to fight, it's your deal now!" Manlove growled. Tilt assumed command. Ever since the picaroons first had been sighted he and Tyler had been busy loading the four Spencer 52-caliber repeating carbines and the few single-shot Enfield musket-rifles which hadn't been jettisoned. They laid out the rifle-muskets along the main cabin's top, but only after they'd charged all spare Blakeslee magazines for the repeaters.

Metallic cartridges for the Enfields were heaped in calabash bowls ready for quick reloading. He and Tyler then shoved six cartridges into each of the cylindrical Blakeslee magazines which could be inserted through an aperture in each Spencer's butt plate. An additional cartridge then was inserted into the chamber so, to all intents and purposes, each heavy, American-made carbine could be made to fire seven times before reloading.

Sweating heavily, Tilt, his now-heavy black mustache seeming to bristle, yelled at Manlove, "We going to get through the inlet?"

"Reckon so," came the surprisingly calm reply, "but not in time to outrun them damn' pirates."

Long since Tilt had instructed Manlove and Tyler how to handle the

Spencers. Bilotte had proved especially quick to learn how to manipulate the trigger-guard ejector.

Seabirds began screaming louder than usual while wheeling and circling excitedly above the *Queen of Hearts'* topmasts. It seemed they'd sighted the three piraguas lowering brown, triangular lateen sails as they bore down on Seven Palms Island. The birds might have been wondering why so many men were crammed into each slender craft fashioned of hollowed logs. Each was steadied by an outrigger, such canoes being far too tender on the wind and in rough seas to risk dispensing with such.

Closer inspection by the birds would have disclosed the crews below to be of mixed origins. Some were small but muscular pure-bred Indians, others, powerful *mestizos* and mulattoes. Quite a few coal-black Negroes were among them, but only two picaroons might have passed for white men. A few were wearing ragged blue, yellow or green shirts or striped red-and-white jerseys.

The weapons they brandished consisted mostly of ancient smooth-bore muskets, but the attackers also possessed a few modern single-shot rifled weapons plus a number of brass flintlock blunderbusses which, though nearly a century old, at short range still could deliver devastating blasts of pistol balls, scrap metal and even stones through bell-shaped muzzles.

The feeble wind again faltered, then died out shortly after the schooner, towing her gig, with agonizing deliberation was tacked through the entrance to that peaceful-appearing little lagoon and toward inevitable interception by the piraguas.

Feeling more sure of himself now that this had developed into a purely military operation, Colonel Rodney Tilt dispatched Tyler and his Spencer to defend the bows along with George Duck armed with an Enfield. Before they departed he directed, "Don't open fire till they come into about a hundred yards' range. I've been told these Spencers are dead accurate over three times that distance. When you open fire, try to snipe the helmsman or whoever seems to be giving orders. Try not to shoot too fast — our Spencer ammunition is kind of short. Don't forget, our only chance lies in stopping 'em before they can board."

He then posted Manlove in the waist. Handing him an extra pair of magazines he said, "You've now got nineteen shots to use. Keep firing on the nearest canoe no matter which side it's coming from."

The heft of his heavy carbine momentarily lent a measure of reassurance but once the leading piragua struck her triangular brown sail and got out paddles Tilt was dismayed to make out how many men had crowded into those long, low-lying canoes.

Keeping out of range, the piraguas ran past the almost motionless schooner bobbing helplessly on waves still rolling in from the eastward and waited to windward effectively blocking the *Queen of Hearts'* escape route.

A babble of voices came floating over water once more turned a sparkling deep-blue. What appeared to have been a conference ended when one of the largest canoes was paddled off to the right with the apparent intention of attacking the becalmed schooner's starboard side. The other two veered to the left, certainly to circle about and assail the quarry's port beam.

Familiar and not unpleasurable pre-battle reactions seized Rodney Tilt when the biggest piragua came paddling in and the sparkle of steel showed among huddled men. Shouldering his Spencer, he told Bilotte, "We'll open fire in a minute. Try to kill that big nigger in the red shirt — he seems to be in command."

The Cajun grunted, took careful aim at the leading canoe surging steadily nearer, paddles raising brief diamantine spurts of spray.

Colonel Tilt selected for his target a tall and thin yellow-faced fellow handling the piragua's steering paddle. Settling the Spencer's iron-heeled stock firmly against his shoulder, the Master of Moluntha drew a deep breath and half-expelled it before his right hand contracted evenly about the lock till the weapon belched smoke and kicked like a ticklish thoroughbred under a currycomb. A billow of grayish bitter-smelling fumes briefly obscured his vision but before it dispersed he'd worked the trigger-guard lever and smoothly ejected the spent cartridge case. Lord, what a *wonderful* weapon! If only the 11th Virginia had been equipped with some of these.

Next he sighted on a bushy-haired picaroon brandishing a cutlass in the bows. Reasoning that should he miss his primary target his bullet wouldn't be wasted among that concentration of pirates howling and preparing to shoot, he fired again. The attackers, stung by casualties, opened fire, caused dull, booming reports characteristic of muzzle-loaders and knocked splinters from the rail a few feet to Tilt's left. The rest of the balls drew splashes well short of the *Queen of Hearts*. Bilotte was shooting steadily but carefully so Tilt kept his attention on the steadily advancing piragua. His third shot provoked furious shouts and a ragged volley in return. This time several more bullets went *thunk!* into the bulwarks or hissed harmlessly by. Realization that thus far his shipmates were obeying instructions to fire slowly came as an encouragement, although paddles kept flashing and spaces of open, weed-flecked water lessened with dismaying speed.

In the bows Manlove furiously was cursing this continued lack of wind — that, and the fact that precious moments were being lost. Bitter-smelling black powder smoke obscured the enemy and cleared away only reluctantly.

"Other side!" He heard the *mestizo* shrill over a mounting crackle of musketry. A familiar savage exhilaration so shook the ex-gunner's mate he missed the steersman, a dark-faced picaroon wearing wide straw hat decked with a bedraggled green ostrich plume. All the same, his Spencer's heavy bullet knocked overboard a man leveling a long-barreled musket. Damn' thing shoots high and to the right, he cautioned himself as the ejected brass cartridge case tinkled onto the deck.

"Tyler!" he shouted toward the bows. "Switch your fire to those bastards closing in from starboard!"

The Texan's reply was lost amid a volley of shots but he at once fired twice into the nearest piragua; and a pair of clumsy-looking paddles ceased to flash and went drifting away. Howls and a spasmodic flurry of arms and legs further slowed the log canoe's advance.

George Duck fired his single-shot Enfield at the second craft closing in on port beam. He must have shot high since through coils of smoke he saw no results. Cursing, he snatched up one of the spare musket-rifles lying ready on the cabin's top and this time sent a big Indian splashing overboard.

Not until they had arrived some fifty yards short of the nearly motionless schooner did the pirates quit paddling in order to increase their rate of fire. Nonetheless, Tilt was relieved by the distinctive *boom!* of several muskets, obviously muzzle-loaders which would require considerable time to reload. In quick succession Tilt shot two more mahogany-faced picaroons.

That the attackers were being disorganized by the schooner's extraordinarily rapid rate of fire was obvious, yet the biggest piragua — the one attacking from the left — continued to bear down on the *Queen of Hearts'* bow. It was then that Bilotte got carried away and commenced shooting without taking time to select targets. Tilt saw him grab a reserve magazine, shove it into his carbine's butt plate and blaze away without sighting.

With a veteran's deliberation the Master of Moluntha meanwhile shot two half-naked individuals who appeared to be issuing orders. Of his Spencer's original seven shots he now had expended five; he wondered whether anyone else was counting shots.

By now several picaroons either had fallen or had been knocked overboard. These struggled, screaming, until sharks closed in with miraculous rapidity to silence them.

Peering through clouds of tear-starting smoke Peter Tyler in the bows realized the attackers now had come close enough to permit his glimpsing, while reloading his Spencer, a shifting pattern of varicolored faces, all open mouths and glaring eyes. Two men wearing faded red bandanas about their heads dropped paddles and caught up long-barreled muskets.

When they fired the Texan recognized the familiar buzz caused by bullets hissing past his head: one pierced the jib; the other lodged in the fore-mast. This piragua now lost headway until it lay dead in the water, its crew scrambling futilely about or lying flat on the bottom.

Bilotte and Tilt then fixed attention on the second canoe, still bearing in on the port beam, and delivered so effective a fusillade that it also lost headway.

The deep, bellowing report of a blunderbuss warned Rodney in time to shelter beneath the bulwarks just before a deadly charge smacked along and over the rail. Yammering outcries grew louder but the reports of firearms slackened so he risked rising long enough to throw his sights on a towering Mexican brandishing a cutlass and yelling for his fellows to resume paddling. Once the big man, hit, staggered, then splashed over-board between the canoe and its outrigger, the piragua's occupants again ceased paddling, but some diehards among them opened fire with heavy revolvers.

Manlove, firing from amidships, hit more men in the largest piragua. When arms and legs thrashed wildly, the ex-gunner's mate without hesita-tion dropped his hot carbine, and by grabbing up a single-shot musket-rifle fired for a third time in almost as many seconds. Once the smoke lifted somewhat it was apparent that the second piragua's crew had had enough. Their craft sluggishly was backing off toward its companion on which Tilt and Bilotte were continuing to fire.

"*Grand nom de Dieu!* Got their bellies full, now —"

The Cajun got no further. A stray pistol bullet hit him squarely between bushy brows and knocked him down to lie squirming slowly among spent cartridge cases strewing the former yacht's teak decking.

Again a blunderbuss boomed, sent most of its charge rattling along the schooner's side. One bullet, however, flew high enough to clear the rail and graze ribs along Rodney Tilt's right side. As when hit before, he experienced no immediate pain so continued swiftly to reload, for through drifting smoke strata he glimpsed predatory faces, black, mahogany-brown and pale yellow. Ignoring the warmth of blood starting to run down his leg, he used his Spencer to cut down, first of all, the only white picaroon he'd recognized, but then smoke obscured everything except for the fact that Antoine Bilotte was lying supine with a bluish-red hole showing in the center of his bronze-hued forehead.

James Manlove was first to notice a movement in the gunsmoke as if a puff of air had stirred and was thinning it. An instant later he glimpsed picaroon ramrods flashing and emptied his carbine so rapidly its barrel scorched to the touch.

Although those piraguas which had attacked along the starboard side had started to backwater, the largest craft still lay some twenty yards off and whoever now commanded her appeared determined to close in and board.

As for the Master of Moluntha, he was entirely too occupied with maintaining a steady rate of fire to notice that the *Queen of Hearts'* canvas was filling, that she'd come alive and was commencing to move.

Manlove bellowed, "Wind's up! Keep on shootin', everybody!" He came bounding aft, hurdled Bilotte's corpse, and spun the wheel. The *Queen of Hearts* rapidly gathered speed.

The picaroons howled disappointment and quickened their fire, but so obsolete were most of their weapons, they could only rage and fire a few shots, quite ineffective except for one slug which drew a long gash across Peter Tyler's left forearm and sent his blood splashing onto the littered deck.

Within the space of a few minutes the *Queen of Hearts* picked up more speed, pointed her long bowsprit toward the open Gulf and fled, with her tattered Stars and Bars streaming defiance.

# 41

---

## Into the Gulf

G RADUALLY MOUNTAIN RANGES along the coast lowered, to sketch a long and hazy, faint-blue line along the horizon. No sails showed in pursuit, thanks to a steady breeze out of the southwest, and the *Queen of Hearts*, Stars and Bars still snapping, made remarkably good time despite Manlove's fears that incrustations of barnacles and a recent growth of bright green weeds on her bottom and sides might slow her down.

For a time the survivors were too exhausted to do more than trim the sails to best advantage, then, despite the torrid and energy-sapping sunshine, to hoist in that gig which the former yacht still was towing.

Among other tasks Antoine Bilotte's blank and staring black eyes had to be closed and his body otherwise prepared for burial. Next, bloodstains were mopped from the deck and bullet-severed lines replaced. No one remarked on the astonishing number of holes punched through the schooner's dark-brown canvas. Quantities of expended brass cartridge cases, glinting under the blazing sun, were swept into the scuppers.

"We'll give the Cajun a decent burial as soon as possible," announced Rodney Tilt, increasingly conscious of pain in that bullet graze along his ribs. He said nothing, nor, for that matter, did Peter Tyler, who'd twisted a rag about the shallow, scarlet furrow dug across his left forearm. Said he, "Don't know whether Bilotte had any religion or not, but he was a first-rate shot; ought to send him off in style of sorts."

"Aye, sir, that we will, 'though I think it's wasted effort. The Devil already must have claimed his soul.", Manlove then went forward and returned lugging a tattered topsail. He beckoned George Duck. "Help wrap him up and lash him right. No use takin' time to sew him in proper-like; poor bastard won't note the difference."

Tilt turned to Tyler. "Suppose Duck fetches up a tot of rum along with the medicine chest; then let's see what can be done about our wounds."

The Texan nodded and smiled. "Should be a cinch. Neither of us is badly hurt."

"How can you tell?"

"I used to patch up comrades in the old Fifth Texas."

"Then you've had experience?"

"Sure 'nough. I caught what the Doc called 'intermittent fever' during the Valley Campaign, so spent nigh on six weeks in a so-called field hospital. Soon's I got better I began to take notice of how the doctors went about their business." He offered a battered tin cup of rum and water. "Take a slug, then let's see how bad your wound really is."

"As you can see, it's only a heavy graze along my ribs." Grimacing, Rodney stripped off his grimy red shirt exposing a stretch of torn flesh some five inches in length. By now it was bleeding only slowly although his once-white duck trouser's leg was splotched like a butcher's apron.

Once the *mestizo* had fetched the chest, Tyler opened it to disclose a case of surgical instruments, bottles and vials containing variously colored liquids; also, there was a pair of small circular tins, the gaudy pink labels on which proclaimed that their contents were a sure-cure called Cherokee Indian Balm.

"What's that?" Tilt queried.

The Texan chuckled. "Don't rightly know what's in it, but, smeared on a bandage or pledget, that stuff sure is soothing on an open wound. I was lucky to find some along with this." He held up a bone saw. "Lucky there's no call to use this."

As Tyler was opening a packet of dressings, lint and bandages and arranging them along the cabin's top, Tilt remarked, "One good thing about my family is that we all heal readily. How about you?"

"Oh, we're tough stock, too." The Texan then exposed the red and already encrusting gash across his brown and sinewy forearm. As in Tilt's case, the ball had passed without touching a bone.

"Think I ought to take a stitch or two along your side?"

"Don't think so; like yours, my wound is fairly shallow and, as I've observed, more often than not stitching often does more harm than good on minor wounds."

Typical of contemporary medical procedures Tyler made no effort to scrub his hands, only washed them in a bucket of seawater, then filled a sponge saying, "Next to pissing on it, there's nothing better than salt water for a raw wound. Besides," he added, "pissing does little good once such a wound is over an hour old — or so I've heard sawbones say."

That the Texan must have had some experience, plus innate skill, became evident by the unhesitant, almost expert fashion, in which he prepared to work.

"Hold on. I'll fix you up first," Rodney announced. "I, too, have made plenty of dressings in the field. Lend me that pig-sticker of yours." Using its point he scraped loose a lump of Cherokee ointment, then smeared it thickly on a compress of white linen which with a gentle sureness he applied to the crimson wound. Then, not awkwardly at all, he secured it in place with a roll of bandage bound tight, but not too tight.

"Damned if that ointment really don't do something. My gash feels better already," Tyler commented. "I can tell you've done this sort of thing before."

"Most anybody who's spent near four years campaigning could do the same, maybe better."

Tyler said, "I'd better get busy before this damn' hurt of mine starts to stiffen up. On account your wound is where 'tis, reckon I'll have to try using sticking plaster to hold the compress in place, 'cause your breathing would loosen bandages wound 'round your body in no time but, all the same, I'll risk a few turns about your chest; maybe they won't slip."

Tyler just had completed his task when George Duck padded up on blunt bare feet and reported uneasily, "Dead man ready, sar."

According to custom James Manlove brought the black schooner into the wind, then lashed the wheel; quickly she lost headway. "Anybody able to say a few fittin' words afore he goes overside? How about you, sir?"

Into Rodney Tilt's memory, with painful clarity, flooded memories of that scene enacted nearly a year ago in the little cemetery above Moluntha. Ever so clearly into his mind's eye flashed a vision of Margaret Forsythe standing, head bent, in a black opera cloak, yellow-striped blue breeches and a black chip hat, reciting the burial service over the raw black earth of his Mother's grave. Margaret. How could she have been faring? How her handsome features would light up if and when he came home — solvent. Had she become —?

Tyler shrugged. "Damned if I know much about praying. How 'bout you, Jim?"

Manlove shook his shaggy head. "Guess me and religion never have been on speakin' terms, you might say."

Tilt glanced down at the canvas-shrouded and tightly bound corpse. "I'll try to say a few words but first, haven't we forgotten something?"

Manlove followed his upward glance, "Yep, I'll halfmast our colors and stow them away. 'Twill soon be time to show the Stars and Stripes again."

"No more hiding our flag. I've a better idea. Since Bilotte once fought for the South, or so he said, we'll wrap the flag around him."

While the Stars and Bars was being lowered for the last time all three veterans stood to attention, swaying in unison as the yacht, having lost way, commenced to roll sharply in the trough of the seas.

Once the flag had been draped, Tilt bent his head and said in tired, toneless accents, "Dear Lord, we don't know what sins this man may have committed but, all the same, we beg of You, in Your infinite compassion, to receive his soul with mercy and grant him eternal rest. Amen."

Once Rodney had recited the Lord's Prayer, Manlove and the *mestizo* slipped Antoine Bilotte's body over the rail.

Relaxing, the Texan said a shade too loudly, "Well, boys, now that that's that, I reckon we all could do with a drink. God knows I could."

Manlove nodded, "Reckon I could, too. Duck, go fetch up the jug of Barbados."

The Texan's thoughts however were far from concentrating on alcohol; now that the Cajun wouldn't be claiming his thousand dollars the remaining shares would be slightly enlarged. Um. What a damned pity Bilotte instead of Tilt should have stopped that picaroon bullet. How neatly it would have solved a problem growing more difficult with each passing day. After swallowing a big gulp of rum, neat, he asked, "How long before we should make a landfall?"

Manlove tilted his head way back to drain the last drop in his tin cup and wiped his bristle-framed mouth on the back of a tattooed hand. "Inside of five or six days, provided we don't get becalmed."

A sharp twinge in his wounded arm, now supported in a crude sling, served to remind Tyler how lucky he'd been his wound hadn't proved more serious. *Wound!* The word struck a vivid spark in his imagination.

Even since the *Queen of Hearts* had left Seven Palms Island astern, the weather had remained ideal — which was fortunate since it was proving difficult to navigate with two of her scanty crew partially disabled.

Manlove took it to be a favorable omen that, for a while, schools of porpoises played gracefully alongside, and often, silver-blue flying fish skittered away from either bow to vanish into lazy, dark-blue rollers with the speed of a conjurer's trick.

One evening Manlove observed, "I'm gettin' almighty tired of fish, beans and salt pork. What say tonight we sample that bully beef you bought back in New Orleans?"

A broad grin widened over the Texan's bronze-hued visage. "Sure. Why not? But, by God, I never thought I'd live to see the day I'd eat bully beef by choice."

"Where's it stowed?" Tilt wanted to know. "Haven't seen it about."

Manlove said, "I know. Wait, I'll fetch a couple of cans." He reappeared carrying not two but three cans. At once both Tilt and the Texan wrinkled noses at a faint, foul odor which had begun to waft about the cockpit.

Manlove pointed to a dented dark blue can. "Sweet violets! The seal on that one must ha' been broke. Well, we can use it for fish bait I expect, or maybe to poison a shark." After shoving the spoiled tin aside he carried the remaining two forward to the galley.

A moment later Tilt arose, saying he'd urgent need to visit the officers' head, and, leaving the Texan at the helm, disappeared below, favoring his wounded side against the *Queen of Hearts'* steady but violent motions.

Returning on deck he found his companions smoking on the stern locker. Manlove was saying, "Them other cans are all right. What have you done with the spoiled one?"

"Heaved it overboard," the Texan stated. "Most fish won't bite on spoiled meat and that damn' thing stank like an old battlefield. I'd just as lief forget what one smells like."

On the fourth day out of the lagoon, sails began to be sighted in the distance and the smoke of several steamers drew dark streaks along the horizon.

Tilt braced himself to suggest hoisting the Stars and Stripes but Manlove shook his blunt, powder-marked head. "No point showin' that damn' rag till somebody comes close enough to recognize it. Besides, it's badly weathered and ready to fall to pieces; better save it for later on."

"That makes sense," Tyler agreed then added, "time for sick call." So saying he disappeared, to return presently with a roll of bandages, plasters, dressings, and a tin of Cherokee Balm.

From behind the helm Manlove squinted at Tilt's exposed side. When Tyler removed the old dressing it was malodorous, stained yellow with varying shades of red. Considerable pus also was in evidence.

Manlove commented, "Damn' if that wound looks any better. Wonder why?"

"Likely the ball drove bits of fabric from his shirt into the wound," Tyler suggested. "Still, they ought to slough out any time now." He thrust out an arm bared because his sleeve had been rolled up and the dressing removed. "See? Mine's coming along fine. I tell you this ointment can work wonders. Be patient, Rod, and try not to worry."

Next day, after determining the schooner's position, Manlove looked pleased. "B'God, I've seldom seen such a long spell of favorin' weather!"

"Then we're doing well?" Tyler queried.

"Hell, yes! Keep on like this, we ought to raise Louisiana tomorrow evenin' or thereabouts."

A relieved sigh escaped Rodney. The sooner he got to a real doctor the better. His gash obstinately had refused to close, was swollen, and was turning an angry purple-red. Right now it was throbbing and more painful than ever.

During the late afternoon when Manlove had completed shifting onto a new tack, he treated the Texan to a searching look. "What were you doin' in the fore crosstrees so early this morning?"

Airily, Tyler explained, "Why nothing. Wanted to find out whether anything resembling a gunboat might have heaved into sight during the night. From now on reckon we'd best keep a sharp lookout."

"— And that's God's own truth," agreed the ex-gunner's mate. "We'll be sighting more and more vessels." Manlove then forgot the incident.

Peter Tyler did not. Three days back, when only the *mestizo* was on deck, he'd carried a small, flat vial filled with putrid bully beef aloft to prevent its obnoxious odor from being noticed. The original can he'd covertly dropped overboard.

Absently watching flying fish dart away, the Texan fell to ruminating. Too bad the powdered salt he'd carefully worked into Tilt's compresses somehow hadn't caused a more serious infection. Who could have foreseen that blood poisoning wouldn't have set in long before now? However, this being the case, nothing remained now but to take a final step in his scheme. Adding to a rising sense of uneasiness came recollections of a conversation he'd had yesterday with the ex-gunner's mate who'd growled, "Can't figure why that hurt of the Cunnel's is gettin' so angry lookin' and swellin' so much."

Frowning, Tyler had said, "Yes, I'm sure worried over that. After all we've been through together I'd sure hate to see blood poisoning set in before he can see a doctor. It works fast and kills quickly." Steadily, he'd looked into his companion's small, bright-blue eyes. "Suppose anything fatal should happen to our friend, which God forbid; what course should we take?"

Following a considerable pause Manlove had answered slowly, "Well, first off we'd have to drop him over the side like Bilotte. 'Twould raise questions if he got buried ashore."

"Of course," the Texan had nodded, then softly added, "Wouldn't that mean you and I would own equal shares?" Through a supreme effort he'd kept his gaze steady and his voice even, but all the same he'd quivered internally. Had he been too direct? To his vast relief the ex-gunner's mate only had said, "Reckon that's about what would happen. Yep, you and I would share-and-share alike after holdin' out the *mestizo*'s pay, but right now swear you'll do your very best to cure the Cunnel. I think the world of him — in all kinds of weather he's proved a true friend."

"Of course. I feel the same way. Since Appomattox Rodney and I have been through a lot together; why we've even courted the same girl."

James Manlove had got to his feet and stretched, drawling, "All I say is, there's no call to cross bridges afore we come to 'em. I reckon the Cunnel, bein' tough as hickory, will pull through all right."

# 42

---❖---

# Bully Beef

DURING THE LATE AFTERNOON a succession of silver-gray rain squalls commenced to race over the sea, driving all hands below saving the helmsman, George Duck, who, wearing stained and patched yellow oilskins, steadied the wheel.

Pedro de Cinquegrana y Gonzales crouched in his stuffy little cabin aware that he could procrastinate no longer, so, from the medicine chest, took out a fresh tin of Cherokee Indian Balm. Although the ship was pitching and rolling violently under yet another squall, he carefully scraped the tin's amber-hued contents into a small wooden bowl. Perspiration sketched a sheen across his forehead when he brought out that vial he'd kept in the crosstrees and, using the tip of his heavy-bladed skinning knife, stirred a lump of evil-smelling matter into the balm until the salve appeared thoroughly and evenly blended, and didn't give off too much of an unpleasant smell.

Bracing himself against the motion, with infinite patience he refilled the tin taking care to leave an indentation just deep enough to lend an impression it had been used before.

Sardonically, the image of a ferocious Indian brave printed on the pale-pink label seemed to glare upwards. Despite himself, the Texan began to feel sick. It was wicked enough to shoot a man down without warning, but wasn't it far worse to cause his death by poison — no matter how quickly the venom took effect — the very idea went dead against his grain and all traditions he'd been brought up to respect. But this inner revolt faded when a radiant vision of Margarita, lovely, utterly desirable Margarita, loomed large, larger, until it eclipsed all other considerations.

Because rain was beating repeated tattoos along the schooner's deck, the daily change of dressings would have to take place below, a task normally performed shortly before George Duck would beat a dishpan to warn that supper was about ready.

Gingerly, Peter Tyler tested his arm. Although the wound sometimes itched like fury it had healed so well he'd regained complete use of that limb. Moreover his left hand didn't tremble a bit when, unhurriedly, he laid out the usual supplies. He deliberated dressing his own wound first but decided not to: it just might arouse suspicion if tonight, for the first time, he appeared with his wound already dressed.

A particularly violent squall struck the *Queen of Hearts*, caused her to list sharply to port and sent medical supplies onto the cabin's deck; soberly, he retrieved these before stretching out on his bunk to wait for this particular blast to pass and fell to wondering just how the ex-gunner's mate might have reacted to his hint about a fresh division of the pay chest's contents.

This same moment James Manlove, C.S.N., also reached a decision. Rain glancing off his oilskins, he turned the wheel over to George Duck, then made his way below to discover the Master of Moluntha slumped, eyes half-closed, on the cabin's green leather sofa. When Manlove appeared he sat up, blinking.

"With this kind of weather d'you still figure we'll sight land sometime tomorrow?"

Manlove shed his waterproof, hung it to a peg. "Yep. This ain't really bad weather, nothin' but short squalls. The glass is holdin' steady, even rising' a bit." He pulled out a quid of tobacco. Bothered by missing teeth he worried free a chew before saying, "Don't you fret, Cunnel, come a few days we'll be livin' high off the hog and rompin' fancy-free 'round New Orleens."

Tilt shrugged, felt pains like red-hot skewers lance his side. Why wouldn't this damned thing heal up? Every time he'd been hurt up till now, he'd not suffered the least trouble.

After lighting a pipe he leaned forward and lowered his voice. "Think it's going to be difficult to get our, er, property safe to a bank?"

"Shouldn't be too difficult. I know Barataria Bay pretty well. There's an inlet to a bayou that reaches up to within about two miles of the town. Provided we act coony enough, likely 'twon't prove hard to freight our winnin's up to town by dugout canoe and oxcart. But I wisht Bilotte was still alive. He'd have come in extra handy once we get ashore."

"Happy to hear we're going to land soon. Feel I've a touch of fever.

What I need is a real doctor. I guess Tyler's doing the best he can but I just can't understand why my wound's not scabbed over before now."

The ex-gunner's mate came to settle on the couch beside Tilt. Despite rushing noises of wind and waves he spoke softly, "Cunnel, you may not realize it yet, but the dangers we've already met mayn't prove a patch on what may happen ashore."

"Meaning?"

"We'll be dealin' with all sorts of rough and tricky rascals. Not for nothin' has Barataria Bay been a prime hangout for pirates and the like for nigh on two hundred years. On that account —" he paused, "you'd better carry this."

Delving into his waistband, Manlove produced a very small, single-barreled and snub-nosed cap-and-ball pistol. The whole weapon wasn't five inches long. Immediately Tilt recognized it as a lavishly ornamented Deringer.

"Figger likely this might come in handy some time or other — maybe sooner 'n we think. She's ready for use, loaded and carries a 31-caliber ball — I'll give you some spares later. Believe you me, Cunnel, when you shoot somebody at short range with this little beauty, he'll *stay* shot — for keeps."

Questioningly, Tilt stared briefly into the other's battered features but said nothing.

"Yep, when I was a gamblin' man I used to tote one of these wherever I went. Seemed sensible."

In rising appreciation Tilt raised and sighted the Deringer — its cool, smooth, faintly oily surface came as a fine, familiar sensation.

"Why didn't you use one at the Pocohontas?"

Scowling, Manlove shifted the chew about his hair-framed mouth. "Like a careless fool I left it in my room 'cause I'd run clean out of powder — lost my flask somewhere. Yessir, this here's the finest piece of hardware of this sort you'll handle in a 'coon's age!"

"Thanks Jim, but don't imagine I'll need this till we get ashore."

"Maybe," Manlove snapped. "Just you do what I say. Stow that gun in your bellyband right now."

Before obeying, Tilt examined the pistol more carefully — found it a beautiful little weapon. Easily it could be concealed beneath an average man's hand.

"Time I was gettin' back on deck. That blasted halfbreed can't hold a course worth a fart in a gale of wind; besides, I heard our sawbones's door open just now."

Scarcely had he donned his oilskins and clambered up the companion-way, butting into a blast of wind and rain, than Peter Tyler appeared carrying a tray of medical supplies. Said he quietly, solicitously, "Well, Rod, how are you making out?"

"Not at all well. I feel weak and a bit feverish; my side feels like it's on fire."

After setting down his tray Tyler seated himself in a revolving chair bolted to the deck beyond the main cabin's table, the fiddles of which had been raised against the motion. Tyler's deft brown fingers laid out tins, bandages and compresses as usual, then directed, "Shed your shirt and let's get to work."

But for the fact that the cabin had been battened down and therefore was nearly airless Tilt might not have noticed the faintest hint of a rancid odor apparent once the lid of a new-looking tin of Cherokee Indian Balm had been removed.

By weak light beating through the deadlight overhead, Rodney peered at the oily, yellow-brown salve. Did it appear a trifle darker than before, or was it only poor light and a touch of fever responsible for this impression?

A sensation very like that which usually gripped him just before a decisive cavalry charge became evident. While unbuttoning a faded red-and-black checkered shirt he watched his companion employ a blunt table knife to spread ointment thickly over one of the pledgets. Meanwhile Rodney noted the presence of a second can of balm lying already opened among other medicines, then heard himself say in a hard, flat voice, "You've been very good all along about dressing my wound first; this time we'll do yours to begin with. After all, this will be pretty near the last time I'll have opportunity to express gratitude for your consideration." He kept his gaze fixed on the other's sharp, dark features beyond the table. Had sudden tenseness stiffened them?

With an easy laugh Tyler started to pick up the compress he'd just smeared, "Really, Rod, this is no time for a grandstand gesture. Come around and let me remove the old dressing. Phew! It really smells 'gamey.'"

"I'm not making a gesture, I'm merely attempting to express gratitude for your unselfish thoughtfulness." Gradually gathering himself, Rodney Tilt seized the brown-smeared pledget and said quietly, "Pull up your sleeve and I'll replace your dressing."

The Texan's dirty blue cotton sleeve paused over the table. Still smiling, he extended a hand. "Give it to me."

"No. This time I insist you be cared for first."

He made as if to hitch up his trousers in front, but kept his hand poised over his belt's buckle.

"— And *I* insist on using this compress on you. Come on, I'll take off the old dressing right now!"

With the speed of an expert boxer Tyler leaped to his feet. His hand darted behind him to close over the handle of that long knife he customarily wore belted above his buttocks.

The instant he glimpsed the blade's gleam Rodney pulled out, then cocked and leveled the Deringer. "Steady, damn' you!"

As the Texan sprang, Rodney Tilt shot Pedro de Cinquegrana y Gonzales through the center of his chest, filled the cabin with a deafening report and blinding smoke. Under the heavy bullet's impact, Peter Tyler was knocked reeling backward. The long knife in his hand described a wide and futile semicircle before his knees gave way. Eyes rolling white, he toppled over; streams of blood, gushing from between his lips, splashed the deck and, under the ship's rolling, started to trace erratic courses over the deck.

Through billowing smoke, Tilt, swaying like a drunken man, heard Manlove yell down the companionway before appearing with a big Navy Colt cocked and ready. "Reckon I weren't so far wrong 'bout that Deringer bein' useful." He eased down the Colt's hammer then, oilskins streaming, sprang to stand over the slowly writhing figure.

Stomach churning, Tilt steadied himself against the table before bending to join Manlove over the sprawled, softly gurgling form and realized his shot had struck Tyler just above the sternum. Nevertheless the Texan still was alive so he grabbed up a tangle of compresses and bandages, attempted to stanch the hemorrhage.

"No use, *amigo*. I — fool — you — always fine shot —" The Texan's eyelids drooped momentarily; when he reopened them his gaze was blank, unfocused.

Twice, three times, the Texan spewed up quantities of blood but managed to gurgle, "*Por — amor — Dios —* my share to Margarita — promise?"

"You can depend on it."

"Margarita — I — too much —"

A great gush of bright arterial blood drowned out whatever else ex-Corporal Peter Tyler wanted to say.

# 43

---◄◉►---

# Shape of Things to Come

ONCE SHE HEARD ex-Corporal Rimfire Hamrick's yipping Rebel yell come ringing up from snow-dusted slopes below Moluntha Garrison, Margaret Forsythe knew the veteran had returned from his twice-weekly trip to fetch mail from Gladesville. Hurriedly she closed the ledger she'd been occupied with, jabbed a new steel pen into a cracked tumbler filled with number eight birdshot and ran for the front door to be immediately joined by Caroline and little red-cheeked, tousle-haired Oliver.

"My, I'm glad to hear that yell," Caroline cried, breath billowing in the frosty air.

"Rimfire don't holler like that," Oliver announced, "'less he's bringin' home mail. Ain't that so, Miss Meg?"

"Yes, and I'm *that* glad. Rimfire hasn't yelled very much lately."

Clasping shawls about them after urging the wriggling youngster into a well-worn overcoat, Caroline and Margaret hurried out into the winter sunshine which at this time of year, especially in the mountains, as a rule was more cheering than warming.

Caroline cast a glance at Meg when Oliver went whooping and pelting down the driveway to meet the veteran — one of his very best friends, as he'd proudly confided on more than one occasion.

By her sides unmittened fingers clenched into fists, and her lips contracted themselves into a thin, ruler-straight line.

While trotting Resaca up the driveway, Hamrick waved. Then, at pre-

cisely the right moment, he bent to sweep Oliver up and onto the pommel
before him. The feat was smoothly accomplished — they'd had plenty of
practice.

Standing in the chill sunlight and feeling the cold creeping up her legs,
Meg prayed silently because an unaccountable premonition warned that
a communication of deep significance lay in the worn C.S.A. haversack
Hamrick customarily used for a mail pouch. "Dear Lord, this time let
there be some word from him! Thou knowest he's been gone too long a
time. Please, please let there be some message from him."

"Fine afternoon, ladies," called Hamrick, once he'd eased Oliver onto
the driveway's snowy gravel. "Roads are froze up real dry and since there
ain't too many drifts I've made good time."

Caroline burst out, "Oh, for heaven's sake, Hamrick, haven't you
brought any letters?"

"Like usual, ma'am," he replied through a haze of frosty breath, "there
ain't much. Only a few old copies of the *Richmond Examiner* and oh,
yes, there's a letter for Miss Margaret from Newport up in Rhode Island."

Newport! Both women's hopeful expressions crumpled. Why, oh why
hadn't this letter been postmarked New Orleans, Memphis, Cincinnati,
or some other city along Rodney's possible route homeward?

As usual on such occasions the Northern girl had drawn herself up, was
standing straight and slim and vainly attempting to conceal overwhelming
anticipation and anxiety.

"It's for you, ma'am," Looping Resaca's reins over his arm, the
ex-corporal delved into his haversack, then passed over a crisp-looking
envelope. The moment she saw the address Meg recognized Marcus
Peabody's firm, strongly slanting hand.

Caroline burst out, "Oh, dear, let's hope this letter is encouraging. As I
recall, his last was scarcely heartening."

Meg nodded, numbly bit her lips and thought, if *only* this missive had
come from Rodney! Not knowing where he was, or what could have happened to him, was becoming unbearable.

Impulsively, Caroline flung an arm about her future sister-in-law as
through the snow they started back to the house.

Why? *Why?* Oh, WHY, hadn't Rod communicated? Perhaps he'd been
taken prisoner. Perhaps he was —— she couldn't even think the word.
Aloud, she said, "Let's go read this in the office. Too bad Bushrod's ridden
over to the east twenty."

Both held their breath when Meg broke a seal of bright red wax, then
with a brief, precise movement slit the envelope. Hands shaking, she
then unfolded and flattened a pair of notepaper sheets upon the paper
and account books strewn on the desk before her.

"Come closer, Carrie, and let's see what this is about." Bushrod's wife obeyed, peered intently over her companion's shoulder. Their silvery breaths mingled, for although either glass or oiled paper now sealed all windows, Moluntha remained very chilly indoors, although this winter was not as cold as last year's by any means. They read:

> 107 Bridge Street
> Providence
> Rhode Island
> November 7th, 1866

My dear Miss Forsythe,
     Since this letter (which please show to Mr. Bushrod Tilt and his wife) contains both good and bad news I will give you the good news first.
     Yesterday I conferred with Mr. Pocock, the lawyer who, as you may recall, has been administering your late Uncle Azael Forsythe's estate. I am especially pleased, in view of all your troubles, to inform you that, under the terms of his will, your Uncle has bequeathed —

Both young women tensed before reading on,

— Has bequeathed to you, as his only surviving relative, his entire estate which amounts to something in the vicinity of fifty-seven thousand dollars.

"Fifty-seven thousand! Oh, Lawsy! It *couldn't* be that much!" gasped Caroline, then ecstatically hugged Meg and eyes aglow, pecked her cheek. "Oh, I'm so *very, very* happy for you! Don't you realize that you've become an *heiress?!*"

The sheet of paper between Meg's fingers quivered. *Fifty-seven thousand dollars!* She simply couldn't believe her eyesight, felt herself alternately turning hot and cold.

"Oh, thank you, good Lord, thank you," she whispered. "From the bottom of my heart and being, I render thanks." She read on:

> Once the Will has been probated, your inheritance will be forwarded to whatever bank or place you may designate. Incidentally, Mr. Pocock does not feel that anyone will contest the Will. Apparently in his later years Mr. Forsythe became very much of a recluse.
>     May I tender my heartfelt congratulations to you, Miss Forsythe, for all I have never had the pleasure of meeting you but, knowing that you are affianced to my great good friend Rodney, I can only imagine what this bequest must mean to the both of you.
>     If you desire to, you may send your instructions regarding this matter in my care, or, if you prefer to deal directly with the administrator, here is his address:
>
> Jeffrey C. Pocock, Esq,
> 11½ Woodford Street,
> Portland,
> Maine

"Oh, darling!" Again Caroline's arms went about her companion. "How wonderful, how truly happy I am for you and for Rodney. There can be no telling what this bequest will mean to both of you."

Characteristically, the Northern girl was first to regain her poise. "As Father used to say, 'never count your chickens 'till they're hatched.' But you're right — so right! This *will* make a world of difference to us — to us all."

Caroline giggled, affected a hillbilly accent. "Shucks, Miz Margaret, doan you realize Bush an' me ain't nothin' but po' relations now?'"

"Oh, you sweet darling idiot! My inheritance, which may be delayed in being paid because the Will, according to Mr. Peabody, hasn't yet been probated, will be made over to Rodney the day he comes home."

Although fears continued to gnaw like rats at the back of Meg's mind, she resumed reading:

> I am happy to report that conditions seem to be improving in the mercantile way. We are informed that quite a few banks and businesses have reopened in certain Southern States for, as you may have heard, the Congress recently has recognized Loyal Governments in Arkansas, Louisiana, Tennessee and also in *Virginia*, thank God!
>
> Appointed provisional military governments, for the time being, will be responsible for enforcing law and order in the seven other seceded States.

Both readers noticed that Peabody had started to write "Rebel States" but then had scratched out both words, replacing them with "seceded States."

> At present we hear much talk about radicals establishing a "Freedmen's Bureau" the operations of which sober Unionists fear may cause all kinds of trouble through the South. I feel sure I wrote to you some time ago that President Johnson has granted amnesty to all former Confederate citizens willing to swear allegiances to the United States. There are, however, several exempted classes, among them holders of taxable property worth twenty-seven thousand dollars or more. These must petition for individual pardons. By way of encouragement I hasten to add that, thus far at least, the government has been extremely liberal about issuing such individual pardons.
>
> You may wonder why I dally thus before turning to the second and unhappy main point of this letter. Despite thorough and persistent efforts I have been unable to market more than sixty thousand dollars' worth of shares in the Ajax Mining Company. However, I feel confident that when conditions in the South settle down a bit more, I will encounter no difficulty in securing in full the amount required to re-establish the mine.

Caroline broke in, her joyous mood evaporating, "So that's what Mr. Peabody meant by 'bad news,' but he can't know how bad it is with Rodney still away and your inheritance not likely to be delivered soon. Then there's that damn' scalawag Georgian sitting down there in Wytheville and dunning for immediate payment of taxes and he means what he says. Last week he foreclosed on two properties but now," she heaved a sigh of relief, "with your bequest we may be spared such a disaster."

"Of course, provided I receive it in time."
They read on:

I am seriously grievously disturbed over neither of us having heard from Rodney. However, I hope and pray that by this time you will have received information of some sort concerning your intended. I gathered from your latest letter that, last Autumn, he had departed on a filibustering expedition down into Mexico. We heard that things are turbulent down there so, dear Miss Forsythe, we can only pray and live in hopes for the best. When Rodney does communicate I know you will immediately inform him how anxious I am to hear about the success of his expedition.

We are suffering a severe winter here so two of the children are down with bad colds.

Eliza is well and extends her greetings to you and to the Tilts.

As soon as I have news you may rely upon it I will forward it immediately. How I pray your intended reaches you before this letter.

Faithfully yours,
Marcus Peabody

# 44

────◆────

# Expedition's End

J UST A WEEK from the day ex-Corporal Rimfire Hamrick had fetched
in that never-to-be-forgotten letter from the East, Major Bushrod
appeared in his office stamping feet to rid boots of a light snow which
had fallen during the night. Mercifully, thus far the early winter had
proved comparatively mild, accompanied by unusually light snowfalls
but he brought in with him an aura of very cold air. Margaret Forsythe's
gaze followed him when he sought the office's fireplace on which Jasper
recently had dropped more sticks of firewood.

"Phew!" Swinging his arms he grunted, "As we soldiers used to say,
this is no weather to leave brass monkeys out-of-doors!"

Meg didn't understand what he meant, but all the same treated him to
a wide smile. If only she'd had news from Rod she'd have been the most
contented young woman in all Western Virginia. "Did Hamrick ride
down to Abingdon this morning?"

"No. Hamrick's caught a chill so Knox went in his stead. Don't know
how much snow fell in the lowlands last night so I scarcely know when to
expect him back, which is too bad. Like the rest of us, you must be on
tenterhooks." He combed tangled dark-brown hair and beard with his
fingers once he'd dropped mittens Caroline had knitted onto a chair.
"Can't imagine why I should feel this way in my bones, Meg, but sure as
I stand here, I'm convinced we are going to hear something from or about
Rodney very shortly."

That Bushrod Tilt's premonition had been more than well-founded became attested by the fact that, long before he normally would have returned, ex-Sergeant Knox appeared spurring his tall mare, Gloriana, so hard her fore hoofs sent spurts of snow flying aside like spray from under a hard-driven clipper ship's bows.

Bushrod beckoned. "Come here. Do you see how hard Knox is riding? By God, it's a wonder he hasn't killed that animal or broken her wind!"

Pausing barely long enough to pull on a heavy cloak, Meg ran after her intended brother-in-law now opening the front door and roaring, "Carrie! Carrie! Come down here quick! Something's happened!"

It seemed as if eternities elapsed before Knox pulled up before the front steps. When he flung himself out of the saddle, his mare's sides were heaving, her nostrils flaring, and neck lathered despite the cold weather. Knox was gasping as if about to collapse.

One look at the ex-sergeant's long-jawed and ill-shaven face started Meg's heart to leaping like a spawning salmon negotiating a high falls.

"Sir, sir!" panted the ex-sergeant. "News, good news!" He waved a slip of yellow paper.

"For God's sake, man, what is it?"

"Why, sir, this telegram is for Miss Meg. The Cunnel's done sent it from Cincinnati. It was delayed some 'cause the line got downed by a ice storm a couple of days ago."

Hannibal, Lydia and Pookie came pelting from the back of the sturdy old house and Jasper was running in from the stables, well in front of those veterans who'd lingered at Moluntha.

Oliver meanwhile jumped up and down, shrieking delight although he didn't in the least comprehend what all this excitement was about.

"Here," Bushrod said brusquely, and passed over the telegram. Caroline pressed hands against cheeks, her face in an agony of suspense.

The hand-printed words stood out boldly:

AM IN CINCINNATI SAFE AND WELL. WILL TAKE TRAIN TO ABINGDON DAY AFTER TOMORROW. EXPEDITION HUGE SUCCESS. MUCH LOVE TO ALL ESPECIALLY YOU.

                                                      RODNEY

Margaret Forsythe stood a long instant as though stunned, then dropped onto her knees on snowy front steps, bent her head and said softly but distinctly, "Oh, Heavenly Father, I — *we all* thank You beyond the power of words. Amen."